Cloak of the
Two Winds
Jack Massa

Triskelion Books

Published by
Triskelion Books
www.triskelionbooks.com

This is a work of fiction. All of the characters, organizations, and events portrayed in this novel are either products of the author's imagination or are used fictitiously. Any similarity to actual sorcerers, pirates, or witches, is purely coincidental.

Cloak of the Two Winds
Copyright © 2016, 2020 by Jack Massa

ISBN 978-0-9976461-0-8

Print Edition published June 2016

For Arthur and Kathryn Hinds,
and all of their ship's crew.
"In such company as this, I do not fear injury,
and I would see a wonder."

Part One

In the
South Polar Sea

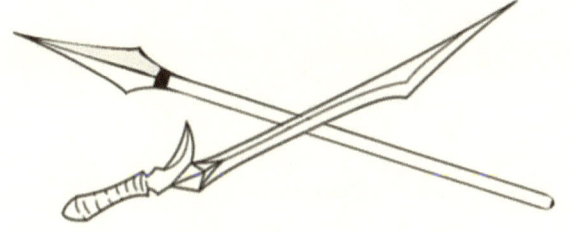

One

The freezewind had blown in the morning, changing the sea to ice. Under an overcast sky the ice stretched in all directions, gleaming with a light of its own—a pearly light born of witchery. So all the seas had gleamed for an age on the world of Glimnodd.

Two of the Iruks had climbed from the hunting boat and were skating around on the ice. Two others could be seen onboard the open, forty-foot craft, at the helm and atop the mast. The Iruks wore garments of deerskin and fur, with leather harnesses and hooded capes. Curved hunting swords and long knives hung at their sides. The skaters moved on ivory blades cunningly strapped to their sea boots.

Leaning on the massive bone tiller, the one called Lonn glanced at the two skaters from time to time. Otherwise his squinting gaze stayed fixed on the north, where a low dark ridge marked the Cape of Dekyll, the only visible land in all the bright emptiness of ice and sky. The Iruks had been lying off the cape for two days now, waiting. They had sailed to this spot because Lonn had dreamed that a merchant ship would pass this way, unarmed and laden with treasure.

"I don't believe that ship is coming," Karrol declared. The taller and brawnier of the skaters, she had glided up alongside the stern and stopped, looking pointedly at Lonn.

"I still believe it will," Lonn said. "Didn't the freezewind blow this morning? Haven't I said all along that in my dream we captured this galleon on ice?"

"Yes," Karrol said, "the freezewind blew this morning. And because we were lying at anchor the boat got frozen in, and it took us half the day to chop free. The freezewind often blows this time of year. That is why Tathian merchants don't sail in this season. Their galleons are slow and too easily caught in the ice."

Lonn made no answer but continued staring toward the Cape of Dekyll. He was starting to regret convincing the others to follow his dream.

But the dream had seemed *so vivid*, the opportunity so rare and vast. The Iruk people believed in dreams, especially ones that came during a hunt. And as leader of the *klarn*, the hunting band, if Lonn had not argued forcefully to follow such a dream ... Well, what kind of a leader would he be?

"This is senseless," Karrol said. "One day we are hunting yulugg with twenty other boats, chasing a good-sized herd. Then Lonn happens to dream of a ship. Now we lie off an empty point of land, alone, and nothing happens. I'd rather Lonn had dreamed of yulugg."

"Perhaps Lonn will dream of yulugg," Eben called from the masthead, "when the season comes for hunting ships."

Karrol snorted, and out on the ice Draven chuckled. Lonn clenched his jaw and glared at the north. He was beginning to wish he *had* dreamed of yulugg.

There were six in Lonn's klarn, three women and three men, all of them young, none older than twenty, though all were full-fledged warriors. At the start of the season they had taken a sacred oath, to sail and hunt and fight together, share warmth, food, and shelter. A klarn might last for many years, or it might be ritually dissolved at the end of any hunt. The way things were going, Lonn thought gloomily, he'd be lucky if this crew lasted the season—a sorry outlook indeed for his first voyage as a klarn leader.

Karrol hoisted herself over the rail and sat down heavily in the stern. "I think we should go back to the hunt. I'm going to call a meeting."

"We've had a meeting on this already," Lonn said.

"Yes." Karrol was unstrapping her skate blades. "We agreed to come here and wait for the ship. So we've waited two days, and the ship hasn't shown. I say it's time to reconsider."

Laying the skates aside, she rose in a graceful movement and stalked toward the forward end of the boat.

Sliding by on the ice, Draven threw out his arms in a shrug, then let them drop, slapping his sides as he showed Lonn an amused smile. Draven never seemed to lose his sense of humor.

Lonn shook his head. Pointlessly, he glanced at the windbringer, a four-foot fern-like creature that stood near him in a bucket of seawater. The windbringer looked back at Lonn through its single green eye. Though capable of understanding and making human speech, windbringers seldom had much to say to people.

Karrol stopped in front of the mast and lifted the flap of a low tent of white and gray hides. "Brinda, Glyssa. Wake up! Eben, come down from there."

"I can hear you plainly from here," Eben answered. "And one of us should keep lookout, in case Lonn's dream comes true."

Brinda and Glyssa had kept the late watch until sunrise, then worked all morning to help chop the boat free of the ice. Still, they scrambled from the tent immediately, tightening loose garments. Their hoods were back, revealing typical Iruk faces—tawny complexions, high cheekbones, slitted eyes accustomed to squinting.

Brinda, lean and muscular, was Karrol's older sister. "Why did you wake us?" she demanded, looking around sleepily.

"I want to have a meeting," Karrol said. "To decide if we should stay here or go back and hunt yulugg."

"You could have waited till we'd finished sleeping," said Glyssa with irritation. She was smaller, delicate for an Iruk woman.

"We've wasted enough time here already," Karrol said.

"We can hunt yulugg any time," Glyssa said.

"You can sleep any time," Karrol answered.

"*Not* if you keep waking us up!" Glyssa said.

"Your argument just became pointless," Eben called from above. "The ship of Lonn's dream is rounding the cape from the east."

His heart leaping, Lonn caught sight of the vessel, a dark speck emerging from the distant hazes. "Just as I dreamed," he cried. "And we're the only boat here to claim it!"

"That's no galleon," Eben shouted. "Too small, and the rigging is different."

"Whatever it is will sail right past us if we don't get moving," Glyssa called, pulling on her boots.

"Right. Jump to it!" Lonn yelled. "Karrol, Draven, loose the moorings. The rest of you lay on the ice sail."

The crewmates leapt to obey. However much they might argue over plans and decisions, a boat could have only one skipper. In the heat of a chase or a battle, it was Lonn who gave the orders.

The hunting boat was called a *dojuk*, made of wood, bone and hide, with one short mast and lateen rigging. Twin outriggers gave it stability in the water, while their bronzed bottoms served as runners on ice. By necessity, all seagoing craft on Glimnodd could sail both frozen and unfrozen waters. But the sleek, lightweight dojuk was especially swift and agile on either surface.

Draven and Karrol were out on the ice, prying loose the spikes that anchored the boat. They tossed the lines to Lonn who stowed them onboard, then returned to his place at the helm. Meantime Brinda, Glyssa, and Eben hoisted the long yard and made fast the halyard, then unfurled the stiff sail—made of hide stitched with sinew. They secured the sheets, then climbed overboard and placed themselves along the hull and the outrigger planks. Together with Karrol and Draven, they pushed the dojuk, their ridged boots giving them footing on the ice.

As the boat slid forward Lonn leaned over and spoke to the windbringer. "A fast one now to start us, Azzible. And tonight we'll be the richest klarn in all the Iruk Isles!"

"I will wish for it," Azzible replied in his quiet, reedy voice.

Windbringers were unique among the plant-creatures of Glimnodd in that they were fully sentient beings. They were unusual among fully sentient beings in that they could summon gusts of wind by wishing for them. In the wild, this faculty kept them free of certain insect parasites. Among humans, the ability endeared them to mariners of all nations. Most sailing vessels carried at least one windbringer, or *bostull* as they were also called.

Azzible closed his one eye and entered a state of trance. His wishing luck was good, for in a moment a gust appeared, stretching the dojuk's sail. The mast tilted, leather lines creaking. The dojuk spurted forward and in its motion came alive to Lonn. He braced his feet apart and steadied the helm, wrapping both strong arms around the tiller and clutching it to his side.

Whooping with excitement, his mates scrambled to keep up with the iceboat and jump onboard. Karrol and Brinda hauled themselves over the bulwarks. The others climbed onto the outriggers, then perilously clambered over the narrow planks back to the hull.

The wind-made ice was slick but uneven. The dojuk bumped and rattled as it gathered speed. The rush of air increased to a roar. Lonn shouted above it, ordering his crew. He gave Karrol and Draven, the strongest with himself, charge of the sheets, the steering lines. They stood at either rail, four paces in front of the tiller. Brinda and Glyssa passed out quivers containing steel-barbed, ivory spears, then took their places amidships. With a quiver slung over his shoulder, Eben climbed the ratlines to the masthead.

Lonn sailed on a long northeasterly tack, aiming to intercept the merchant ship after it rounded the cape. As the vessel drew closer, he could make out details—an oddly squared hull, two masts, and elaborate fore-and-aft rigging.

A Larthangan coaster: Lonn had seen the type before, but rarely.

"Not Tathian at all!" Eben yelled from aloft. "Larthangan."

This fact did not trouble Lonn. Larthang was even more remote and fabulous than the Tathian Islands. Besides, the ship's exotic, painted appearance rang true to his dream. The coaster was broad of beam and roughly twice as long as the dojuk. It was moving fast, but Lonn knew it must be clumsy on the ice. He marked the ship's course and shifted his rudder slightly, leaving the coaster wide space in which to turn.

South of the cape the Larthangan came about, booms swinging, two of the four runners heeling off the ice. By now those on board must have spotted the dojuk's sail. But given the northerly wind, they had no choice but to beat west, on a course closing with the Iruks. The coaster came off its turn with speed, and Lonn could see they were laying on more sail—hoping no doubt to outrun the dojuk.

The two vessels approached at a right angle, and Lonn held his course until the coaster had almost run past them. Then he swept the tiller to one side and yelled the command to come about. The Iruks jumped to it, casting off lines and hauling in others. As the dojuk turned the long yard spun round the mast, altering its tilt, then snapped into place as wind caught sail. Slowed momentarily, the iceboat gathered speed on its new tack.

Both craft raced westward now, leaving the Cape of Dekyll astern. The speedier dojuk steadily made up distance, and soon Lonn could count the sailors scurrying about on decks and rigging. He spied the helmsman atop the rear deck, shouting orders through a megaphone and glancing over his shoulder at the hunting boat. No armored men were visible on board, just as Lonn had dreamed.

"Ready your spears," Lonn shouted to his mates. He moved the tiller to veer in close.

"Steady," Karrol advised. "Not too near."

Annoyed by her caviling, Lonn edged the dojuk even closer.

They were running even with the Larthangan now, in easy spear range. The Iruks waved their weapons, whooping and roaring. Lonn called out in Low Tathian, the common trading tongue, ordering the ship to turn upwind and surrender, promising no harm to the crew.

Suddenly the coaster swerved, right in front of the Iruks.

"Look out!" Karrol yelled.

With no room to copy the turn, Lonn jerked his tiller the other way. The dojuk hiked high off the ice, outrigger and yardarm just missing the coaster's stern as they soared past.

Nearly thrown from the masthead, Eben regained his balance, swore and flung a spear at the fleeing ship.

"I said you were too close," Karrol screamed.

"Trim sail!" Lonn answered.

Slowed by the sail's position the dojuk came off the hike, jolting violently as outrigger struck ice. The Iruks readjusted their lines and in moments they were back on course, gliding in pursuit of the racing two-master.

This time Lonn steered to windward of their quarry, and told his mates to throw their spears as soon as they came within range.

Once more the Iruk boat outstripped the coaster, approaching this time on its starboard side. Lonn left more room than before, and when the Larthangan came about the dojuk matched the turn with ease.

They sailed now on a northeasterly tack, and for the third time the dojuk pulled even. The Iruks yelled and cast their spears—streaks of ivory arcing through the gray sky.

One sailor was struck, dangled a moment, then lowered himself from the rigging with a spear stuck in his side. The other crewmen aloft hesitated, then abandoned their exposed positions. On deck, most of the sailors cowered below the rails. A few picked up spears and threw them back, but their casts fell short or else missed wide, behind the dojuk.

"No warriors on board," Lonn shouted. "I dreamed it so!"

The Larthangan helmsman tried to veer away, but the dojuk now moved like the coaster's shadow. Unrelenting, the Iruks threw more spears, and Lonn thought that at least one more of the crewmen had been hit. The others on deck shouted in panic and gestured frantically at the helmsman.

"Turn upwind and save all your lives," Lonn called to them.

The helmsman hesitated, then answered through his megaphone. "Cease your attack! We surrender."

He turned his prow into the wind and ordered his men to trim sail. The crewmen moved quickly, but their efficiency was gone. They eyed the dojuk fearfully as they worked. The booms came about haltingly, and the coaster slowed with a violent flapping of sails.

Lonn roared with the exultant shouts of his mates as he pointed the dojuk upwind. In the past, he had taken part in the capture of several large ships, on both water and ice. But for a single klarn to net a vessel of the coaster's size—that was an almost unheard-of feat of piracy.

The dojuk had raced ahead of the two-master, but being lighter it slowed more quickly against the wind. The two vessels glided close together as their speed dwindled. Then the coaster dropped its ice-brakes—heavy serrated blades—and ground to a halt with a tremendous screech.

The Iruks lowered their sail, then leapt overboard. They dragged the dojuk to a stop and fixed one set of stakes and lines. Eben remained atop the mast, spear in hand, watching the nearby decks of the coaster. Lonn and the rest of his band took their weapons and charged across the shining ice. They climbed aboard using an accommodation ladder, which the Larthangans, on Eben's command, had hastily lowered over the side.

Stepping onto the wide main deck, Lonn counted eighteen men in the crew. Two of them lay on the deck, groaning in pain from wounds in the side and shoulder, while crewmates hovered over them. The helmsman stood alone at the edge of the quarterdeck, observing the pirates with a grim expression.

The Iruks used their spears to herd the unresisting crewmen to an aft corner of the deck. The Larthangans were short and scrawny, warmly but raggedly dressed. Their light-skinned, bearded faces, reddened by cold and exertion, showed a mixture of fear and frustrated rage.

"Your lives are safe," Lonn assured them. "Just don't make trouble."

Karrol and Brinda took charge of the crew. Eben came aboard, and he and Draven went below to search. Lonn and Glyssa climbed the ornate stairs to the rear deck. Scowling, the helmsman stepped aside to give them way.

Near the iron tiller mechanism, five windbringers stood in their buckets, five impassive green eyes fixed on the Iruks. No—it seemed to Lonn that one of the bostulls looked intent, strangely concerned.

"I am Troneck." The helmsman was a brawny man, with a weathered seaman's face and flecks of gray in his hair and drooping mustache. "I am captain and owner of this ship, the *Plover*. We are honest traders, seeking only to make our way back to Larthang in peace."

"I am Lonn of the Isle of Ilga. We are Iruks, and we take a part of the cargo that passes this way whenever we can. What are you carrying, captain?"

"Not much," Troneck answered. "Nothing worth spearing my crewmen."

"You should have stopped on our first warning," Glyssa said. "We are fighters, you are not. We don't like harming defenseless sailors, but you left us no choice."

"What are you carrying?" Lonn repeated.

"Some silks and lamp-oil from Nyssan. A few kegs of brandy. Also one passenger. If not for her insistence, we'd not be sailing home alone, with our holds half empty, and surely not on this forsaken course."

"Who is this passenger who gives orders on your ship?" Glyssa asked.

"A deepshaper, a witch of Larthang. But that's not the only reason we do her bidding. She saved our lives in Tallyba the Terrible. She delivered us out of the chains of the Archimage of the East. But to ensure our obedience once we were free, she required each man to give her a hair from his head. Now she holds those hairs woven in a magic design. If we disobey her, she may destroy the hairs, and our very breathing will cease. So much, at least, she has told us. If I were you, I would leave this ship before the witch takes hairs from you, or does something worse."

Glyssa frowned at this, but Lonn laughed scornfully.

"You cannot frighten us with stories," he said. "Where is this witch? We would see her for ourselves."

"Her cabin is below us."

Troneck pointed to one of two embellished hatches on the quarterdeck, with translucent covers designed to serve as skylights for the chambers below. Lonn and Glyssa drew their swords and crept toward the hatch.

"She must not be disturbed," cried the faint, sibilant voice of a windbringer.

Lonn started and pointed his blade at this bostull who, unlike the others, stood in a fine pail of carved ivory. "What is this windbringer?"

"A friend of the witch," Troneck said. "He came aboard with her luggage."

"She lies in *deep trance*," the windbringer said. "I implore you, leave her in peace."

"We won't harm her," Glyssa said.

"But you must not—"

The hatch at Lonn's feet was sliding open. He leaped back, sword raised to strike. But it was Draven's head and shoulders that rose into view.

"Lonn, Glyssa," he grinned. "You must see this."

Lonn lay down on the deck and lowered his head through the hatchway. Draven stood on a low table in the middle of a spacious cabin. The cabin was lit by numerous tiny lamps. And there were sparks of colored glass, prisms suspended about the cabin on lengths of thread. The air held a perfumed fragrance, smoky and sweet. An eerie feeling wafted up from the chamber, an aura of power both thrilling and frightening to Lonn.

"Let me look." Glyssa stretched to peer over his shoulder.

Lonn put his sword in his teeth and swung down into the cabin. He landed nimbly on the table, which Draven had vacated, then hopped to the floor.

Standing beside him, Draven pointed past sheer silk tapestries and peculiar dangling objects, to a broad bunk at the rear of the cabin. There, in daylight filtered through stained glass windows, lay a pale-haired woman garbed in blue silk and white fur.

"Is she awake?" Glyssa called from above.

"No," Lonn said. "Watch the quarterdeck. Find out what you can from the windbringer."

"Is this like the treasure you dreamed?" Draven asked, scrutinizing one of the prisms.

"I don't know." There had been gold and gemstones in the dream, not these tapestries and strange hanging baubles with their mirrors and feathers.

"What about the lady?" Draven asked.

"She's a witch of Larthang," Lonn answered. "Has she stirred?"

"Not once," Draven whispered, as they stepped noiselessly toward the bunk. "Not when I forced the door, not even when I touched my sword point to her nose. I'm not sure we could wake her if we wanted to."

"She lies in a trance," Lonn affirmed.

Pale and slender, the witch seemed hardly to be breathing. A fillet set with moonstones confined her blond hair, and rings of beaten silver adorned her long, slim fingers. Her hands held a silken cloak, of silver and black, clutched tightly under her chin.

"Pretty, in a frail sort of way," Draven remarked.

Lonn grunted. He felt vaguely menaced by the witch, even in her seemingly helpless condition.

Glyssa dropped down through the hatchway. She crouched on the table and gazed about, eyes brightening, then jumped to the floor and moved next to Lonn.

"Who's watching the quarterdeck?" Lonn demanded.

"Karrol. And Eben is helping Brinda guard the crew." Her voice grew solemn as she indicated the witch. "The windbringer says it would be very hard to wake her. He also claims her powers are enormous. And the captain insists she can control the Two Winds, that the freezewind blew before them all the way across the ocean."

"Hah! He takes us for ignorant savages," Lonn said.

"She doesn't look so mighty to me," Draven agreed.

"I'm not sure," Glyssa said. "Do we really want one of her kind for an enemy?"

"Hers is the only treasure on board," Draven answered. "Unless Eben found something?"

Glyssa shook her head. "Only some oil and a few bolts of silk."

"Then we must rob this witch." Draven looked at Lonn. "Right?"

Lonn twisted his mouth, uncertain. In his dream there had been no witch, and no need for such a dire decision. But to back down now would mean that chasing the dream had been for nothing. He would lose face with the klarn, be mocked by the whole village when the story was told. (And Karrol would make sure the story was told.) Surely this girlish witch could not really pose such a threat.

Lonn set his jaw and nodded.

Seeing this, Glyssa lifted her shoulders in a fatalistic gesture. Draven gave a short laugh and stepped to the bedside. His hand moved toward the witch's throat.

"Careful," Glyssa whispered.

Lonn raised his sword, heart pounding. Draven put his hand on the black and silver cloak and deftly yanked it away.

The witch cried out—a sharp withering sound. Glyssa stiffened, and Lonn steadied his sword arm from shaking. The witch's long fingers writhed in the air. She moaned, like one pained by the loss of something precious, then again lay still.

"I'm almost sorry for her," Draven said, his voice subdued.

He tossed the cloak to Lonn who held it up, a heavy garment with a strange, slippery texture. One of the full sleeves was black with an intricate design embroidered in silver threads. The other sleeve exactly mirrored the design, but with silver and black reversed.

"What's keeping you?" Eben's voice sounded from the corridor outside. "Brinda and Karrol are getting restless."

He swung open the door and strode in, then paused as he looked about the chamber. "Now here's some loot worth taking."

"It's the treasure I dreamed of," Lonn affirmed, thinking: *It must be.* "You three start packing it up. I'll keep an eye on the witch."

Draven sheathed his sword and started blowing out the lamps. He and Glyssa cleared the tables, collecting lamps, vials and small books, and dumping them into a large basket and an open, half-empty chest. Eben yanked down the tapestries, first testing the weave of each with his fingers. The prisms and dangling things were pulled down, strung together and stowed away.

While her cabin was being looted the witch of Larthang breathed fretfully in her trance. She stirred once, shifting her position and groaning. The Iruks quickened their efforts, and soon Draven and Glyssa were carrying the last of the booty away. Lonn followed them, backing out of the cabin, the sword still level in his grasp.

Eben put some of the crewmen to work transferring the witch's treasure, along with a few kegs of oil and brandy, across the ice to the dojuk. On the main deck, Brinda stood watching the other Larthangans—including the two wounded men and an old man and a boy Lonn had not seen before.

"Where did the old one and the child come from?" Lonn asked her.

"Eben ferreted them out. They were hiding below. One is the ship's cook, the other a cabin boy. It didn't look to me that your dream treasure amounted to much, Lonn. A basket and two small chests that can't be very heavy."

"They are witch's things, magical," Lonn insisted. "They will fetch a high price."

"That's not what I hear from this windbringer," Karrol shouted from the quarterdeck.

Mumbling an oath, Lonn scrambled up the steps to the rear deck, followed closely by Glyssa and Draven. Karrol and Captain Troneck stood beside the windbringer who had spoken earlier.

"His name is Kizier," Glyssa said.

Lonn bent over and squinted into the round green eye. "Is this witch friend of yours not wealthy?"

"What you steal will not bring you wealth," he answered. "They are mostly ritual objects made by Amlina herself. They are supremely important, but only to her."

"Then we shall give her a chance to ransom them," Lonn said. "Nine days hence, we will be in Fleevanport. Can you find Fleevanport, captain?"

"It is on the charts."

"Good. You can ask for us at the Sea Lion Hostelry."

"And tell the witch to bring plenty of gold," Draven added.

"And no tricks," Karrol said. "We are no fools, and our weapons and our tempers both are quick."

"Amlina will not ransom her possessions with gold," Kizier said. "But with trouble, more than you can guess."

Lonn grinned. "We are not afraid of girl-child witches. Nor of bostulls, no matter how cleverly they talk. We are Iruks, known to be fearless!"

"Ignorance prevents your being afraid." The windbringer made a sighing sound. "Take my warning: there are terrible powers involved here, powers that can sweep over you as a wave does a grain of sand."

"Let's take the windbringer with us," Draven suggested. "His yammering amuses, and he may know something of use."

The other Iruks agreed. A second windbringer was always an asset to a dojuk, especially in the changeful seasons.

"Tell the witch he can be ransomed with the rest," Lonn told Troneck. "And tell her that if she doesn't show up in Fleevanport after three days we'll sell to the highest bidder. I'm sure we'll get a nicer price than this bostull claims."

"You can't imagine what ruin you are tempting," Kizier cried, as Lonn and Draven lifted his bucket.

"You'll do the windbringer no harm," Troneck warned, "if you have any fear of reckoning with Amlina. She is fond of him."

"We have no fear of reckoning with her," Lonn answered. "And we don't harm windbringers."

"We will treat you well," Glyssa assured Kizier. "Don't be afraid."

Lonn smiled at that, thinking how tender-hearted Glyssa was, for a pirate.

When the dojuk was fully loaded and everyone back on the Larthangan ship, Lonn opened one of the remaining kegs of brandy. The Iruks filled stout ivory cups for themselves and offered the rest to Troneck and his crew. When the Larthangans refused to drink with them, the Iruks poured the rest out on the ice, a libation to the spirits of wind and sea.

Then the Iruks climbed over the side and returned to their hunting boat. They pried loose the mooring stakes and raised the stiff sail. Lonn put Kizier in the stern and introduced him to Azzible. He asked that both windbringers help them start the boat.

The Iruks swung the bow around, pointing it off wind, and began to push. The breeze picked up, whether or not with Kizier's help, Lonn could not know. But soon the dojuk was rushing along and the Iruks racing to keep up and hold on. One by one they scrambled on board, panting and joking excitedly.

Glimnodd's orange sun burned dimly in the northwest as the dojuk sped on, over ice that in the morning had been water.

Two

Lonn kept the wind at his back and let the dojuk run before it. His mates moved about the hull, lashing down the new cargo. Brinda climbed the mast to keep lookout, a wool scarf shielding all but her eyes from the fierce chill.

"Where are we bound?" Glyssa called above the wind.

"Home to Ilga, I think," Lonn answered. "We'll stash these kegs and lay in for a few days, then take the witch's things to Fleevanport."

He looked around at his klarnmates, who nodded or shrugged their assent.

Crouched in the stern, Eben said, "Better run southwest awhile first, Lonn. We don't want to meet up with our hunting fleet now."

Lonn had the same thought. The fleet, which they quit three days ago, was made up of boats from Ilga and nearby islands. These neighbors would be curious about their loot, and jealous. Since they had all started the hunt together, the other klarns had the right, under Iruk law, to demand a share. If refused they could take it all, and Lonn's klarn would be outnumbered twenty to one.

Lonn shifted the wind to his right shoulder and told his mates to bring in the sail.

While Karrol and Eben handled the sheets, Draven and Glyssa secured the last of the oil kegs up near the mast. From a cache in the hull, they brought out a wineskin and filled it from one of the brandy kegs. Then they took bed furs from inside the tent and carried them aft. Together with Karrol and Eben they sat huddled at Lonn's feet, keeping him and each other warm, but ready to jump up should they need to maneuver the boat. The two windbringers stood with eyes shut. Both had gone into trance to conserve body heat.

The Iruks passed around the wineskin and speculated on the value of the witch's treasure. It lay before them, lashed to the deck, sea chests rattling softly, loose ends of fabric fluttering madly in the wind.

Eben doubted the booty would trade for much in Fleevanport. Slim and sharp-witted, Eben tended to a grim and skeptical turn of mind.

Draven, on the other hand, insisted he was wrong. This venture, Draven felt sure, would bring then all great fortune. Lonn gave a half-smile at this, but held his peace. Draven was his kinsman, his closest friend since boyhood. Draven's carefree optimism was as constant as his courage and loyalty—all of these qualities great comforts to Lonn in his position as leader.

"Let's stop at sunset," Glyssa said, "and take a good look at the witch's horde."

The others readily agreed. The enchanted sealight made night sailing easy enough, but it would be cold this night, and there was no great hurry in reaching Ilga.

The dojuk glided on through the waning afternoon. After a time Draven started to chant in his deep clear voice, and the others joined him.

Old winds, blow for us
Wide seas flow for us
Give us your fishes
Give us your treasures
We Iruks sing to you

Away to starboard, Lonn spotted a column of steam rising. A fire turtle had melted its way to the surface for air. Another time the Iruks might swing aside and hunt the great reptile—though it was a monster and its breath white flame.

But this day the klarn had their catch, and Lonn held the easy course. With his mates snuggled at his feet, sharing warmth, he felt peaceful and content. After a time he let his hand drop to stroke the fur on Glyssa's hood, his fingertips straying to touch her cheek. She smiled up at him and squeezed his hand.

Sweet Glyssa, with her keen mind and gentle spirit. All of the klarn loved her. She had captured Lonn's heart; that was certain. When the day came that she was ready to lay down her spear and become a wife, Lonn dreamed she would choose him for her husband. Of course, he knew only too well that Draven also favored her. And whether Glyssa would choose one of them or someone else entirely ... well, those were worries for another day.

* * * * *

The sky had cleared to a bluish white. A small red moon, Rog, floated high in the north. In the northwest, the polar sun was sinking toward the edge of the world, tinting the seaglow orange. Lonn swung the boat in a broad turn, pointing the prow upwind. As the dojuk skidded to a halt the Iruks reefed their sail, then climbed overboard to fix the stakes and mooring lines.

Karrol and Eben broke out stores of dried fish wrapped in edible kiia leaves, and fetched a water skin to go with the brandy. Lonn brought more furs from the sleeping tent and laid them out before the helm. Brinda had climbed down from the masthead, and she helped Draven and Glyssa carry the fire bowl back to the stern. They filled the bowl with milky yulugg oil and lit it with a flint and fibers.

The crewmates sat knee to knee over the fire bowl and took their supper. All around them the light of day faded with the last glow of the orange sun. But even as the sky darkened the witchlight of the sea-ice seemed to brighten—a ghostly, blue-green luminescence.

When the Iruks had eaten their fill, they began to examine the witch's things. They untied the knots securing the load and opened the basket and the larger of the two chests. Lonn and Glyssa picked through the tapestries, murmuring about the unknown symbols embroidered on the silk. Brinda and Draven pulled out the prisms and hanging things and spun them on their threads. Eben leafed through one of the tiny books, frowning over the printed glyphs. The Iruks had come across books before but didn't exactly comprehend their function.

Karrol rummaged through the sea chest, carelessly draping garments over the edges. She lifted the black and silver cloak the witch had been holding in her trance and studied it a moment.

"Please be careful," Kizier cried out. "Please do not tamper with Amlina's things."

Lonn hadn't noticed that the bostull had come awake.

"We won't hurt anything," Draven said.

"You might, unwittingly. Or they might do you harm."

The Iruks paused, looked at one another, then hastily set down what they were holding.

"You mean these things are cursed?" Eben demanded.

"I mean that Amlina has put spells on some things, to guard them."

"But we've handled these things already," Lonn pointed out.

"Not everything," Glyssa said. "We haven't opened that smaller chest."

They all hesitated for a moment. Then Karrol drew her knife.

"This is foolish," she said. "How can we guess at the worth of the loot if we don't even look it over?"

She stuck her knife in the thin padlock of the smaller chest and began to twist it.

"Please," Kizier said. "You are making a mistake."

"Quiet," Karrol growled.

She pried at the lock while the others watched, their mouths drawn taut. The metal padlock stretched, then broke. Karrol removed it and raised the lid.

"There." She shoved the knife back into her scabbard. "I'm still alive."

The Iruks, chuckling, leaned closer to examine the contents of the chest. Karrol tossed aside candles and spools of thread, then lifted up a silver box with intricate filigree work.

"A jewel box," she said, lifting the hinged lid.

It looked to Lonn that a pink mist sprayed into Karrol's face. She took a loud gasp of air and then sneezed, dropping the box back into the chest. Immediately she sneezed again, doubling over at the waist.

"I warned you," Kizier intoned.

Karrol sneezed a third time and uttered a curse on the windbringer's roots. Her klarnmates gathered around her in concern.

"What happened?" Lonn demanded as Karrol sneezed again, more violently than before.

"A cantrip," the windbringer answered, "a minor design laid on to discourage petty thieves. The sneezing will last a day or two, I suppose. You are lucky it was nothing worse."

Karrol stood, both hands covering her nose, and continued to swear with tearful intensity between sneezes. Draven and Brinda stood patting her shoulders.

"We'll force no more locks," Glyssa declared, shutting the lid on the small chest. "These things we've already unpacked, let Kizier tell us about them."

"Yes," Eben said. "What are these books for?"

The bostull's flexible stalk rotated so his eye could look at Eben. "Mostly they are treatises on witchery, containing designs and cantrips, as well as maxims and theoretical discourses."

"But how does the witch use them?" Eben said, holding open one of the books.

"She reads them, of course. The words, in their patterns, help to focus the power of her mind."

"But how does this *thing* hold words?" Eben demanded with angry frustration.

The bostull's eye grew rounder, and he made a noise like a sigh.

"What is this for?" Glyssa asked, holding up one of the feathered ornaments.

"It is called a desmet. It too is used to enhance the mind's force. By its placement in relation to other hanging trinkets it helps to concentrate thought energy, whether for knowing or shaping."

"What do you mean by knowing and shaping?" Eben asked, and Karrol punctuated the question with a sneeze.

"I mean the two basic arts of witchery," Kizier answered. "These ideas are commonplace in most of the human realms, but obviously not here. You who dwell farthest south in the world truly are as children compared to the peoples of the Three Nations."

"Yes, so we've heard before, from the Tathians," Lonn grumbled. "But explain your meaning. What are these two magic arts?"

"In Larthang they are called *wei-shen* and *wei-xang*, deepseeing and deepshaping. For both depend on the practitioner's ability to merge with the Deepmind."

"And what exactly is the Deepmind?" Eben said.

"Ah, my honorable barbarians. When you have answered *that* question you have done with all wisdom. For the Deepmind is indefinable and inexplicable. It is the very urge of creation, the unfathomable principle that makes and moves all things. The sages of Larthang call it the *Ogo*—the 'drift.' But all these words can only suggest, never encompass its nature. Truly the Deepmind is beyond understanding."

"And how does the witch merge with what is beyond understanding?" Lonn demanded, baffled and annoyed by these mental gyrations.

"By deepening her own mind, by turning inward. In so doing one may learn to perceive the patterns of the Ogo beyond the limits of ordinary senses. This is the way of deepseeing. And, with more application, one may learn to participate in the forming of the Ogo's manifestations. This is the way of deepshaping, by which small cantrips are fashioned and mighty ensorcellments woven."

"We have shamans among the Iruk," Draven said, "Wise ones who speak with spirits to learn things, and can enlist their aid in forging charms. The two arts you describe sound much the same."

"No doubt your wise ones practice rudimentary forms of magic," Kizier answered. "But the arts of the Larthang have been refined by thousands of years of practice, proven, and recorded in writing."

"These trinkets we've taken from the witch," Lonn said. "They help her in these arts? Truly, they must be valuable then."

"Not in any way you might think," the windbringer replied. "The trinkets were mostly made by Amlina herself, useful only to her, or perhaps to another with her knowledge and skill. In a remote colony such as Fleevanport, they're not likely to attract much of a price."

"We should never have stolen them," Karrol moaned, woefully massaging her sinuses.

Draven clapped her on the back. "Don't despair, mate. I still trust Lonn's dream over the word of this bostull—who is a friend of the lady we robbed, after all. Let's take the hoard on to Fleevanport and see what price it brings."

"Draven is right," Lonn asserted. "Let's drink another round to toast our prospects."

"But only one," Glyssa said. "This drink of Nyssan is potent."

Lonn laughed and went to refill the wineskin. His mates packed up the witch's possessions, Glyssa putting things away with care while the others just tossed them into the basket and chest.

After they'd shut the lids and lashed them down, the Iruks guzzled the sweet brandy, emptying the wineskin in a single round. Then the crew prepared for bed. They made the tent larger, adding skins and rope supports until it covered most of the area between mast and prow. The chore progressed none too smoothly, the crewmembers' hands and brains befuddled with all the drinking, but at last it was done.

Karrol, still sniffing and sneezing, volunteered to keep lookout, saying she could not sleep anyway. She wrapped a bed-fur over her shoulders and climbed to the masthead.

The others carried their furs into the tent and spread them out. They removed their capes, harnesses, and boots and put their weapons aside, then lay down close together to share warmth.

But Lonn had trouble sleeping. The brandy was even stronger than he had reckoned. It made his head swim and his belly seethe. And Karrol's loud sneezing and swearing overhead kept startling him awake. The snatches of sleep he did get were troubled by weird dreams.

First, he saw his mates back on board the Larthangan ship, inside the witch's cabin. But this time when Draven snatched her cloak away the witch sat up. Her face was hard and white like bone, and her eyes were mirrors. Lonn stared into one of those mirrors and saw himself and Eben and Draven, but they were older; with long beards and silken robes, holding strange colored lanterns.

Later, Lonn dreamed of the dojuk hurtling over ice, chased by the other boats of the hunting fleet. Lonn kept yelling orders to his mates, but each of them worked to a different purpose, as though they couldn't hear or understand him. The dojuk careened wildly about, out of control and almost tipping over. Then the craft righted itself and started racing faster and faster, heading straight for a pressure ridge on the ice. Lonn yanked frantically at the tiller, but the boat would not respond, and the wall of ice reared closer and closer ...

Lonn awoke shivering, his skin covered in sweat. He pulled on his boots with shaking hands, grabbed his cape and crawled from the tent.

Above him, Karrol had bound herself to the masthead. She seemed half-asleep, breathing in long broken snorts and sneezing them out again. She took no notice of Lonn.

The night was cold, bright with the vivid iceglow and with multitudes of stars. Speedy, red-faced Rog hung low in the northwest and Grizna, the huge peach-colored moon, had risen in the northeast, a bloated half-circle. Polar auroras glimmered and pulsed to the south, a series of white arches shrinking away to the horizon.

Lonn walked aft and sat down beneath the tiller. Wrapped in his cape, hugging his knees, he pondered the evil dreams. The witch's mirror-eyes came back to him. What did the image mean? And the dojuk racing out of control—clearly a warning, but of what?

Nothing in the dreams made sense, and Lonn soon lost hope of interpreting them.

He had always been prone to powerful dreams. As a child it had even been suggested that he might be gifted as a *dreamseer*, might eventually train to become a shaman. But, though a sensitive child, in his heart he longed to be a hunter, to have his own boat and sail it fleetly over ice and sea. So he had learned to contain his deeper feelings, control them with the cold determination of a warrior.

Still, when dreams as strong as the one of the treasure ship came, he felt compelled to believe in them. And when dreams like the ones tonight arose, he felt baffled and frightened.

Head aching, he stared into the dazzling chaos of the sky. To the Iruks, the world was chaos—beautiful but terrifying. A warrior shielded himself from the terror by clinging to courage and action, to ritual and song, and most of all to the power of the klarn, the group soul that gave strength and protection.

But what if those were not enough? What if Lonn's stubborn insistence that they steal from the witch had exposed his mates to dangers they could not imagine?

Lonn gazed into the bright heavens, numbed by a fierce sense of foreboding. He pondered again, as he often did, if the others had chosen wisely in making him leader. True, he was best at piloting the boat, and as fierce a hunter as any. But being the leader required other skills, in which he felt himself sorely lacking—the ability to balance everyone's feelings and views, wisdom, diplomacy. Glyssa might have been a better choice, with her quick mind and easy nature, her gift for being liked. Or even Brinda, who though quiet and self-contained, never seemed ruffled and always acted with good sense.

But everyone had decided Lonn was the best choice, had assured him he would learn. Tonight, more than ever, he was doubting the wisdom of their choice.

Something moved forward on the boat, and Lonn jerked his head to look. But it was only Eben and Glyssa emerging from the tent. They knelt fastening on their capes and pulling up the hoods. They spotted Lonn in the stern and came toward him.

"Are you all right?" Glyssa asked.

He nodded. "Drank too much. Couldn't sleep."

"Same with us," Eben said.

"I heard you moaning," Glyssa remarked, leaning over close to Lonn. "Bad dreams?"

"Nothing worth telling."

"Are you sure?" Glyssa asked, looking anxious.

"They were vague and stupid dreams," Lonn grumbled, not daring to show weakness. "I hardly remember them now."

Glyssa frowned, unsatisfied, but did not press him further.

"Brinda and Draven are the only ones sleeping well tonight," Eben said. "We decided to come and have words with the windbringer."

Glyssa crouched beside Kizier and ran her gloved hand over the shiny base, where the brain was. The green eye above it flicked open, fully alert, for bostulls never slept and were easily roused from trance.

"We've been thinking of what you told us about the magic of Larthang," Glyssa said. "We would like to hear more."

"Indeed? What would you like to know?"

"The Tathians say that the witchery of Larthang is the oldest and strongest in the world," Eben said. "How did they come to possess such wisdom?"

"That is a vast question," Kizier replied. "To answer it thoroughly one would need to recount almost the whole history of Glimnodd."

"You may do so," Glyssa answered. "We will listen."

The windbringer shook a little, as though with laughter. "I will give you a shortened version then."

Lonn moved closer to better hear the windbringer's words. He put an arm over Glyssa's shoulder, and the three Iruks huddled close together.

Kizier recounted how the first deepshapers were witches of Larthang, who developed their arts more than seven thousand years ago, at a time when humans were the only sentient species in the world. By their witchery, he said, they made Larthang the greatest of nations, and lorded it over all of the world for centuries.

But these ancient ones were careless, ignorant of the effects their powers could have. Eventually, the world began to show strain from their immense meddling in the Deepmind. The weather grew colder. Snowstorms blew for months on end. New islands reared up while others vanished forever into the sea. It was even recorded that one of Glimnodd's moons flew off into the void, leaving only the two now known.

And nonhuman sentient species began to appear. Among these were the *torms*, winged people spawned by birds; the *myro*, sprite-like beings born of dolphins; and the bostulls, known to humans as windbringers. All of these sentient races had some ability to penetrate the Deepmind, but none that could match human deepshapers. That was until another kind of creature appeared in the sea—the *serds*, a kind of intelligent fish. These were few in number but great in their mental powers, and they lived for many times a human lifespan. The serds used deepshaping to make themselves able to breathe the air, then came out of the sea and enslaved the human world. They reigned over Glimnodd for many centuries, a time that came to be called the Age of the World's Madness. During that age, humans and other races were subject to the serds' cruelties and abominations.

But finally, the reckless deepshaping of the serds brought about their downfall. The scales of the Deepmind tipped back, and a new race of humans came into being. These also were people of Larthang, but their powers in the Deepmind were greater than those of their ancestors, whom the serds had defeated, and far greater than the suppressed powers of their immediate forbears, whom the serds had kept as servants and pets. Led by the Witch King Tuan Tuo, this new generation rebelled against the serds, slaying many and driving the rest back into the sea. A few serds, descendants of those survivors, are thought to dwell still at the dark bottoms of the ocean.

"The Dynasty of Tuan Tuo reigns still in Larthang," Kizier explained. "One hundred and fifty-three Tuans have held an unbroken line of succession for more than 29 centuries. Over all those generations, the arts of the Deepmind have been studied and refined by countless practitioners. But the greatest of these was unquestionably Eglemarde, the Archimage under the Fifteenth Tuan."

"The Weaver of the Winds," Glyssa said. "We have heard her name. Some Tathians worship her as a goddess."

"Indeed, and with fair reason," Kizier said. "For it was Eglemarde who recognized that the centuries of disruption, and the reign of the serds, had been brought about by too much witchery. She perceived that more cataclysms would inevitably come unless some balance could be achieved. So, by a monumental feat of magic called the First Great Ensorcellment, Eglemarde bent the course of the Ogo. From that time onward, excessive shaping forces have spilled out of the Deepmind and into the sea. Thus the surface of the seas came to glow night and day with witchlight.

"But this design alone proved insufficient, for the Deepmind was still reacting to the enormous stresses caused by the serds. So Eglemarde wove a Second Great Ensorcellment. She altered the workings of air and sea so that, at the times of greatest stress—which tend to correspond with times of changing weather—the magic winds would blow over the sea, venting the excess forces by changing the water to ice or the ice to water. The Two Winds she called Icemaker and Thawbringer, though they are now known as Glazer and Aubergale to the folk of Tath."

"It is over two thousand years since the Two Winds first blew on the sea," Eben said. "This we were told by a wandering scholar in Fleevanport."

"Two thousand, one hundred and twelve years," Kizier replied. "Thus it is recorded in Minhang the Beautiful, the Larthangan capital from whence the great design was cast. I see that you Iruks are more that is supposed in the Three Nations. You are ignorant, it is true, but not simple-minded. You have a thirst for knowledge and wisdom."

"You are no common windbringer either," Glyssa observed. "Your kind is deemed wise, but not with human wisdom. Our windbringer Azzible seldom speaks to us at all, except about calling the winds, or the warming and tending he gets."

"Indeed. An interest in human affairs is rare among bostulls. I am ... an eccentric in this regard."

Lonn thought he sensed concealment in Kizier's pause, as though the bostull had started to say something else.

Kizier resumed, "I hope you will consider seriously what I've told you, that you may recognize what powers can be unleashed from the Deepmind, and how dangerous it is to meddle with such things."

Glyssa and Eben appeared to ponder the windbringer's words. They eyed Lonn solemnly.

"We're not meddling," Lonn answered. "We're exchanging items for ransom. Our trade is piracy, not witchery."

"You are carelessly handling objects of great power," Kizier said. "All things that partake of the Deepmind may be fraught with hidden perils and unforeseen consequences. You would be wise to turn around and take Amlina's things back to her."

His warnings fanned the fears that Lonn had been struggling to suppress. But Lonn reacted with defiance. "Don't think you can scare us, little one-eye. We are Iruks, known to be fearless. We have won this loot fairly, and we are taking it to Fleevanport."

"You might not make it that far," Kizier replied. "By tonight or tomorrow, Amlina will have wakened and learned what has happened. She will order the captain to follow you."

Lonn watched a shadow of fear cross Glyssa's face. "The witch doesn't know where we're bound," he insisted.

"Your boat contains her possessions. She'll have no trouble following their emanations."

Glyssa winced, and now Eben too was frowning.

Lonn stretched, forcing a yawn. "Don't let this bostull worry you. His stories contradict. He says the witch's things are objects of great power, but that their worth in money is nothing. Then he warns that the witch will find us, but first he tells us to turn around and find her. Enough of his prattle. I'm going back to bed."

Glyssa rose and walked beside him. "I don't know, Lonn. This whole venture makes me uneasy."

Lonn put an arm protectively around her waist and kissed her on the forehead. "Don't worry, mate. We've got a lookout set. Hey, Karrol! You're awake up there, aren't you?"

Her bulky form shifted on the masthead. "Yes, I'm awake," she grunted—and sneezed.

Three

The dojuk raced before the fair wind over glassy wind-smoothed ice. A day and night's running brought them near the Iruk Isles.

But the next morning the weather changed. The wind blew strong and raw from the south, pushing wadded blue clouds across the sky. Lonn sailed close-hauled all morning, passing reefs and islands off to larboard—pieces of the Iruk Archipelago's outer crescent. In the middle of the afternoon, they raised Ilga.

A shimmering gray wall loomed over the island to windward, a snow squall blown across the frozen sea from the South Pole. They would need to land quickly to beat the storm.

Ilga was low and rugged. The white of snow and rime dominated the landscape, except where short conifers grew in clusters or dark lichens clung to wind-blasted rock. As they neared the island, domed lodge houses came into view, widely spaced along the beaches, clustered together in the village farther inland. The houses were made of yulugg hide stretched over the giant ribs of that sea beast, each with two or more domes linked by low tunnels.

Lonn sailed along the north shore of the island until spotting his klarn's own house, built on a low rise overlooking the sea. Then he angled in toward the beach, pointing the dojuk as close to the wind as it would sail. Normally with the shore to windward he would have approached in a series of short tacks, gradually slowing the boat. But with the squall compelling haste, Lonn held his course and let the dojuk gain momentum. Speed would be needed in the last thirty yards, to clear the three- and four-foot breakers solidified by the freezewind.

When the tack brought the boat in line with the lodge house, Lonn yelled for his mates to hold on, then swung the bow straight upwind. The sail luffed, flapping noisily overhead, and at once the dojuk slowed. It leapt the first breaker and crashed down, climbed over the second and slid into the trough, then smashed into the crystal-thin ice of the final frozen wave and shuddered to a halt just a few yards from shore.

"Good landing, Lonn," Glyssa cried as she and Eben moved to lower the sail.

"I'm surprised we're still in one piece," Karrol grunted. Her sneezing had finally subsided that morning, but with her nose and throat raw, her mood remained sour.

Lonn raised the rudder off the ice and locked it in position, then climbed over the side to help his mates. Heaving all together they pushed and dragged the dojuk onto the beach.

While the others tied the sail and lashed down the yard, Draven and Brinda climbed the snow-covered slope to the lodge house. They unlaced the entry flap on the larger dome and entered, emerging a few moments later dragging a broad sledge—the shell of a fire turtle fixed with bone runners. By the time they had pulled the sledge to the dojuk, the sailing gear had all been stowed and mooring spikes driven into the frozen ground. The wind was blowing harder.

Lonn glanced over his shoulder at the coming storm. "We might have time for only one trip. Let's take the witch's things and the windbringers."

"And one keg of brandy," Draven amended.

The mates worked quickly, handing the cargo over the side and stacking it neatly on the sledge. Eben and Karrol took ice axes and filled a large tub with glassy shards chopped from the frozen wave— sea-ice for the windbringers. Lonn helped carry the tub to the sledge.

They started up the beach, Lonn, Glyssa, Eben, and Draven on the lead ropes, Karrol and Brinda pushing from behind. The wind howled in their faces, stinging cold.

They had hauled the sledge a third of the way to their house when Lonn stopped abruptly. A fur-cloaked figure was marching toward them from the direction of the village, carrying an ivory spear. Lonn glimpsed a furrowed face inside the hood, a hooked nose and familiar, biting eyes.

"Greetings to you, honored Belach." Lonn shouted above the wind. The klarnmates bowed ceremoniously to the village shaman.

Belach stopped in front of them and thrust his spear into the frozen ground. "Greetings to you, Lonn, son of Orla, and to the hunters of your klarn." Then he waited, calmly blocking their way despite the oncoming storm.

Normally, with a boat landing unexpectedly on the island, a watch party would have come from the village to investigate. But with the squall coming on, Belach had no doubt been asked to come alone. Everyone knew shamans were impervious to the cold.

Lonn said to him: "Honored Belach, may I invite you to share the warmth of our lodge house, so that we may have words away from the wind?"

Belach showed a faint smile. "That is hospitable of you, Lonn. May I then assist in hauling your sled?"

Lonn and his mates muttered their thanks. The old shaman snatched his spear from the ground and tossed it onto the sledge. He took a lead place on one of the hauling lines and started up the hill with a ferocious burst of energy. The klarnmates struggled to keep up.

Shortly they reached the lodge house and dragged the sledge inside. The dome was twenty paces across, with walls of hide that bowed and shook now in the wind. Across from the main entrance, a low tunnel gave access to the smaller dome used for sleeping.

Karrol and Brinda closed the door flap and tied the laces. Draven and Eben knelt to make a fire in the circular stone hearth at the center of the dome. The lodge house had come to the klarn from

Glyssa's family, so it was her role to act as host. She took a water skin from the sled, poured a cup, and offered it to Belach.

"Share water and warmth with us, honored guest."

Belach drained the cup and smacked his lips. "My thanks to you, Glyssa, daughter of Sorcha." He turned to Lonn. "The villagers will wish to know why your klarn has returned alone. Where are the other boats you hunted with?"

Lonn felt all eyes turn on him. When he hesitated, Draven cheerfully supplied the answer.

"We left the fleet to go raiding. Lonn had a dream, and it led us to a Larthangan ship. We captured it and got treasure, which we mean now to ransom or sell in Fleevanport."

Lonn rolled his eyes, wishing briefly that Draven had been more discreet. But perhaps it was for the best after all.

Belach was frowning, scrutinizing the sledge in the dim light of the new fire. "That is the treasure?"

Lonn nodded. Everyone had stopped now and was watching the shaman. Belach stepped to the sledge and picked up his spear. He used it to lift a fur here and there, to poke at one of the witch's chests. Lonn noticed that Kizier was gazing intently at the shaman from his place at the back of the sledge.

Belach started to make loud, clicking noises with his tongue. He wheeled suddenly, waving the spear in the air. Then he froze and touched a finger contemplatively to his lips.

"There is power here. And danger."

Lonn's heart was pounding in his chest.

"What do you see, honored Belach?" Glyssa asked quietly.

Belach's eyes grew large and lost focus. His mouth started clacking again. Then he shuddered and sucked in a loud breath. He raised his finger and pointed it slowly around the chamber. "Much power. Strong winds. You are like terns, blown off course by the storm. Long voyage. Far away."

Lonn glanced around at his mates. They stood in the shuddering firelight, enthralled by the shaman's words and the power of his vision.

"What should we do?" Glyssa murmured.

Belach blinked. "Don't know. Powers are from far away—far from Iruk seas ... Klarn must decide ... All of you must hold fast to the klarn." He nodded, as though satisfied with that advice. Then he shook himself. "I will go back to the village now."

He began to turn away, then stopped and touched his spear-point to Lonn's chest. "If you gain goods in Fleevanport from this treasure, you must share a fair portion with the village. Remember."

Like many of the younger Iruks, Lonn and his mates were apt to linger when they traded in the Tathian settlements, enjoying themselves till their money ran out. Hence the shaman's stern reminder.

"Of course," Lonn answered. "We understand."

The shaman smiled at the others, then stepped toward the entrance. Lonn and Glyssa hastened to untie the flap for him. Belach stopped a moment and placed a hand on Glyssa's shoulder, then bent his head and marched out into the storm.

"I want to have a meeting," Glyssa announced, as she bent to re-tie the cords. "We need to talk about this."

"I agree," Karrol said. "The sooner the better."

Lonn sighed, but made no protest. Any klarn member had the right to call a meeting. And after hearing the shaman's words, it would be well if everyone spoke their piece.

"Let's bathe and eat first," Draven said.

"Yes," Eben agreed. "Whatever we decide, we're not going anywhere till this storm ends."

Lonn glanced at the others, who nodded their assent. "All right," he said, picking up a spear. "Then let us put the klarn to rest."

The Iruks each took a spear from the sled and followed Lonn to the doorway. Glyssa went to a cache in the far wall and brought out a ceremonial cup, made from the skull of one of her ancestors, fitted with gold. She filled the cup with water, then brought a spear and lined up beside the others.

Glyssa sipped from the cup, then poured out a little water for the klarn soul. She thrust her spear into the ground and said, "For now the hunt is over. Let the klarn be at rest."

She passed the cup to Karrol, who repeated her words and actions. Each of the mates did likewise, Lonn last of all, so that the klarn soul went out of their bodies and into the spears, which stood as a barrier to guard the entrance of the house.

The ritual ended, Lonn experienced a familiar weariness in his bones. But the peace and contentment that usually followed the closing of a hunt were missing. Instead, he felt unease at remembering Belach's warnings, and a nagging apprehension over what the meeting would decide.

* * * * *

The mates set to work unpacking the sledge and making the lodge house ready. They placed the witch's things against the wall, near the crawl-tunnel that led to the smaller dome. Lonn and Brinda carried the windbringers and the tub of sea-ice to the hearth. Draven and Glyssa lit fires under two massive cauldrons, filled with ice, that stood along the wall. Karrol laid an iron grill over the hearth. Eben opened a cache in the floor where meat was stored in the permafrost. He brought out strips of lamnocc meat and laid them on the grill. Karrol lit two Tathian lanterns, made of bronze and glass, for extra warmth and illumination.

Lonn started to open the brandy keg but Glyssa said they should drink tea instead. She didn't want the meeting swayed by the recklessness of strong drink. Brinda and Karrol seconded her on this, so Lonn filled a kettle with water and set it over the fire to boil.

The mates removed their harnesses and boots and warmed their feet on the hearthstones. Kizier and Azzible gazed contently at the fire, the ice in their pails melting away. The red meat thawed on the grill, fat dripping down and hissing in the flames. Presently the kettle rattled. The Iruks brewed black Tathian tea in ivory mugs. As soon as the meat was cooked they picked it off the grill with their knives and started eating.

By the time they had finished the meal, the ice in the cauldrons had melted and the water warmed. The Iruks took turns filling two wooden tubs and bathing. Soaking in hot water was a luxury hunters enjoyed whenever possible. But this night Lonn felt too preoccupied to fully relax.

After their baths the mates dressed in warm indoor robes, fur hats, and slippers. They sat in a circle beside the hearth, knee to knee. They kept silence for a long time, listening to the wind and the soft sputtering of the flames. Finally, Glyssa stood. As she had called the meeting, it was her place to begin.

"I have a bad feeling about robbing the witch," she said. "I've had it from the start. Everyone laughs it off, but it keeps coming back."

"I've not been laughing," Karrol muttered. "I was against following Lonn's dream from the beginning."

"True," Glyssa replied. "Not everyone has laughed ... What troubles me is, we don't know what we've taken on. We don't know what this witch can do. If we believe Kizier and that Larthangan skipper, then she's very strong. And that 'minor spell' that Karrol took in the face: that was real enough. Lonn had bad dreams the night after we stole the treasure. And now Belach has warned us of danger. I have a feeling that something is hunting us. I think it must be the witch."

"Let her come if she can find us," Draven said. "We're keeping a lookout, and sleeping with our weapons close."

"Sure," Glyssa said. "But that might not be enough. I want us to reconsider what to do with the loot. That's why I called the meeting."

"What would you have us do with it?" Eben asked.

"I'm not sure. But we don't have to take it to Fleevanport. We could go and barter it at another harbor. Or we could run it out on the ice and dump it. I don't know. I want to hear from the rest of you now."

As she took her seat, Lonn glanced uneasily around the circle. Glyssa's words had stirred up his own uncertainty. Yet backing down from their current course felt impossible.

Karrol rose to speak. "You all know how I feel about this venture. I've thought it a waste of time from the start. And I'm the one who's suffered from it. I want nothing more to do with this witch's hoard. I'd just as soon take it out on the ice and leave it there. That's my opinion."

She sat down heavily, and Draven jumped up.

"Mates, I feel we are worrying far too much. I took a close look at the witch in her trance, and she didn't appear so powerful to me. Even if she *can* track us across the open sea, as the windbringer claimed, I am not afraid to face her, either here or in Fleevanport. As for Belach, it's true that he sensed danger, but also great power. He did not predict disaster for us, only a long voyage far from our familiar seas. If that comes true, is it so bad? Why did we leave the other boats and go pirating on our own, if not to find some excitement and adventure? So I say we cast away our fears and sail to Fleevanport as planned. That is my opinion."

When Draven sat down, the Iruks looked from one to another. Lonn sensed that now was the moment to speak. Grunting, he climbed to his feet.

"I have respect for Glyssa's intuition," he said. "But in this matter, I must agree with Draven. I may have had bad dreams the night after we looted the ship, but if so they were vague and confusing, and I don't recall them now. I still remember the first dream, in which this treasure brought us wealth. It was a strong, promising dream. We've often talked about wanting more than the life we have now, a richer life such as the Tathians enjoy, with more comforts, less worry about running out of food in the winters. That's why our people took to pirating in the first place. I think this treasure might be our chance for such a life. So I say we stick to our plan. That is my opinion."

He sat down and looked around at the others, trying to judge if his appeal had swayed them. After some moments of silence, Eben stood.

"There is something to be said for both sides," he remarked. "We might have been rash in stealing from this witch when we don't know the extent of her powers. But that is over and done with. So then, supposing the witch finds us? If we're trying to dump her things, or return them, or take them elsewhere but Fleevanport, she'll realize we changed our plans from fear of her, and she'll have that much more advantage. It seems our best choice now is to stick to the course we've started on, and to face the witch boldly when we meet her. That is my opinion."

After Eben sat down, Brinda climbed slowly to her feet. She was Karrol's sister, yet their temperaments could not have been more different. Stoical and quiet, Brinda always weighed decisions at length and was often the last to speak in a meeting.

"It is a reckless venture we're on, mates," she began. "But we knew that from the start. I also put great store in your feelings, Glyssa. But as things stand, more recklessness seems called for. Eben gives me good reasons and besides, we're not likely to sell the loot for much outside of Fleevanport. So let's sail to Fleevanport and see what happens. That is my opinion"

Lonn nodded his approval as Brinda sat down. "Four of the klarn agree," he told Glyssa and Karrol. "Will you two also be guided by us?"

The question was a point of ritual. The dissenters could ask for a vote, but this obviously would not change the decision.

"We may as well," Karrol said. "It's plain you won't see things our way."

Glyssa looked uneasy but nodded her agreement. "I suppose you're right. At this point, going on with it is probably best. Still, if we had it to do over ..."

"But we don't," Draven laughed.

The Iruks put their hands together in pile. "We will sail to Fleevanport and sell our booty there," Lonn intoned. "This is the decision of the klarn."

"Agreed," they all said, and separated their hands.

"Now let's have some drink and toast to our luck in Fleevanport," Draven said.

The Iruks filled their tea mugs with the purple brandy of Nyssan and drank, leaning on furs piled in front of the fire. Lonn felt the pleasant warmth of the liquor seep into his blood, dulling his apprehensions. Soon he was light-headed and sleepy.

Glyssa stared somberly into the fire and drank almost nothing. When the others spoke of going off to bed, she volunteered to keep the first watch.

"One of us can stay with you," Brinda offered.

Glyssa shook her head. "I'll be fine. I'll have Kizier to keep me company."

The mates climbed to their feet. One by one, they embraced Glyssa.

"Keep a spear close," Eben told her. "And shout out if there's *anything* strange."

"I will."

Lonn hugged Glyssa and kissed her on the lips. "When your watch is over wake me," he whispered. "We can lie together."

Glyssa smiled and tugged the hat over his eyes. "Go to sleep," she said.

Carrying their swords and cups and the half-empty keg of brandy, Lonn and the others crept through the low tunnel to the inner dome. They lit a fire in the oil stove, and piled bed-furs on the sleeping platforms.

Soon the dome was warm, though the squall blew outside with untiring fury. Listening to the storm, Lonn felt a twinge of apprehension, and wondered if he should not go and stand watch with Glyssa. But it was only the wind, he told himself, and soon he drifted off to sleep.

* * * * *

Left alone in the outer chamber, Glyssa put on her leggings and boots, then went to check the entry flap of the dome. Satisfied the knots were secure, she returned to the fireplace.

The ice in the bostulls' pails had all melted, so Glyssa emptied them at a place where no furs carpeted the sandy floor. She refilled the pails with seawater from the wooden tub. Green-leafed creatures, the bostulls mostly nourished themselves with light and air. But they needed fresh seawater every few days to stay healthy. Azzible breathed happily as the warmed water swelled his roots. Kizier whispered his thanks, then questioned Glyssa in Low Tathian.

"If I may ask, I am curious about the old man you met outside and then welcomed into your house. I sensed power in him."

"Yes." Glyssa placed the kettle back on the fire. "He is a wise one. He sensed danger in the witch's things. That is why we held a meeting."

"Ah. I observed your formal discussion. I wished I knew your language so I could have understood what you were saying."

Staring dully at the fire, Glyssa shook her head. "Nothing came of it. We decided to sail on to Fleevanport as planned."

"That is regrettable," Kizier sighed.

Glyssa lifted a shoulder and let it drop.

"You are a curious people," Kizier remarked, "if I may say so without impertinence. Among Tathians and Larthangans, you are known as bloodthirsty savages, with no trace of gentleness or mercy ..."

Glyssa smiled wanly. "Such a reputation is useful for pirates."

"So," Kizier said. "But you are also said to be untutored primitives, barely touched by civilization. Yet I've not found you so. I've been greatly surprised at how well you speak Low Tathian, for instance. This would not only permit you to communicate with many people of the Three Nations, but it gives you a grasp of civilized modes of thought."

"My mates and I speak it better than some," Glyssa said. "When we trade at Fleevanport or one of the other Tathian colonies, we stay as long as our money holds out. We drink the mead, listen to the minstrel songs and the discourses of wandering scholars. We admire the Tathians and seek to learn their ways. Many young Iruks do likewise, but not all."

Glyssa had risen and was pouring more oil into the fireplace. "Of our klarn, only Karrol has a strong distrust of the Tathians. And even she has a taste for their mead."

Kizier stared thoughtfully into the brightening fire. "The traditional ways of your people are almost unknown in the Three Nations. This group you call the *klarn*, for instance. It seems to be more than just the crew of your boat. You share the same house as well?"

Glyssa sat down again, hugging her knees. "Yes, a klarn shares all things in common. This lodge house came from my mother's family. It was built by my uncle and his kinsmen. The boat came from Lonn and Draven's family."

"They are brothers?"

"*Cousins*, I think the Tathians would say. They share the same grandmother."

"Ah. So the klarn becomes a sort of second family?"

"Oh, it is much more than that. The klarn has its own spirit, which we all contribute to, and draw from. Iruks believe that all creatures have something to protect them and make them strong. Yulugg have their size, volrooms their tusks, fire turtles their shells and flame, lamnoccs their great herds. The Skeddans and other folk of these parts have animal totems. We Iruks have the klarn."

"Remarkable. And is the number always six—three women and three men?"

Glyssa poured water from the kettle into her tea cup. "Sometime five, sometimes as many as eight. Even more, if there are fledgling hunters in the group."

"And the fact that women and men sail together ... How can I ask this delicately? Do you ... What are your customs for mating?"

Glyssa frowned at the bostull a moment, then laughed. "Oh, no. There is no ... coupling when a hunt is on. That is forbidden. All of that energy is given to the klarn, do you see? But once a hunt is over and the klarn is put to rest, then we are free to choose lovers, within or outside of the group."

"I see. And what happens if a woman comes to be with child?"

"That seldom happens to hunters. But when it does, the woman must lay down her spear, until the child is born and weaned. After that, she may choose to raise the child, or leave it with the village women and take up her spear again."

"The village women?"

"Yes. Some women do not become hunters. They live in the village with the old ones and children. They raise the children and do other kinds of work. They also are free to sleep with men of their choosing, or with other women."

"Indeed?" Kizier sounded amazed. "I must say, your customs around mating and childrearing seem ... unstructured."

"Not really. Children always belong to the mothers. Sometimes the fathers help raise them, but more often it is the mother's brothers and male kinsmen. Among the Tathians, women and children always belong to a man. They think our customs strange; we think their ways silly."

"So," Kizier said. "And is there no possessiveness or jealousy?"

Glyssa shrugged. "Sometimes two warriors will fight over a woman, but rarely. More often the woman chooses the one she desires. Tomorrow, when the weather clears, we will take some of the oil and brandy to the village, and give it to our mothers. My mother, and Draven's, and Brinda and Karrol's are all still alive. While there, the men will probably find a girl who invites them to sleep with her. Or perhaps I will invite Lonn or Draven to sleep with me. I have love for them both. Draven brings me much laughter and joy. Lonn is more solemn, but his heart is deep and full of feeling."

"And do they also sleep with Brinda and Karrol?"

"No. Brinda keeps mostly to herself. Karrol is lusty, but she prefers women to men. Anyway, she would not sleep with one of her klarn. She believes it unwise."

"Most remarkable," Kizier said. "I know of other cultures with women warriors of course but, to my knowledge, your Iruk customs are unique."

"We need many hunters to feed our people," Glyssa said, thoughtfully swirling the tea cup. "Of course, some women are better suited to hunting than others. Karrol and Brinda for instance are very tough and strong. I am less so. Someday I expect I will become a wife, perhaps to Draven or Lonn. I think they both would like to have me." She smiled fondly at the thought. "But that is for later. For now, I enjoy the thrill of hunting, and sharing warmth with all of my klarnmates, and that is good, while I am young."

"I do not believe any traveler from the Three Nations has recorded the ways of your people. I only wish I had a scribe with me, to write it all down."

Glyssa looked at him, puzzled. "Why would you want that?"

As Kizier started to answer, the voice of the wind grew louder. It rose to a high-pitched scream, and Glyssa heard a sharp, ripping sound.

She jumped, snatched up a spear and faced the entrance. The door flap was split apart. A gust of snow blew in past the waving pieces—and something else, a wheeling thing of yellow light.

Glyssa stared, fascinated as the spinning light swooped toward her on the roaring wind. Amid the light, she saw bulging eyes and tiny teeth working up and down. She tried to cry out, but something choked the sound in her throat.

"Glyssa! Run!" Kizier shouted at the top of his meager voice.

Before she could turn away the wheel of light touched her forehead and sank within. Glyssa had an odd sensation of waking up to find herself there, numb and staring. The spear slipped from her fingers and dropped to the floor.

"Glyssa, come back to us," Kizier cried. "Glyssa!"

But Glyssa had turned and was walking. Her body moved without her volition. Another will had taken control, that of the bulging eyes and tiny bright teeth.

A devil has taken me, Glyssa thought.

She could feel the devil's nature, old and evil, full of knowledge, empty of pity. Inwardly she trembled, yet saw her step was purposeful and steady. She wanted to call out, to scream so her mates would come. But her lips would not move nor her throat make a sound.

She walked to where the witch's treasure lay and opened the large sea chest.

"Glyssa. Glyssa! Help her!" Both windbringers now were calling.

Glyssa swung her head toward them, and a force bolted out of her brain. A wall of yellow light flashed across the dome to the two windbringers, shocking them into rigid quiet. Now both stood still in their buckets, eyes and mouths shut.

Glyssa's attention returned to the sea chest. She lifted the witch's black and silver cloak and put it on.

As her body turned from the wall she strained wildly with her mind and succeeded in thrusting the devil away. A storm of yellow sparks flashed before her face, and she glimpsed the devil's eyes and teeth again. Then long claws seemed to slither down into her heart. Glyssa cringed at the pain, nearly blacking out.

She was only half-conscious as she moved across the dome. She parted the ivory spears where the klarn spirit lay at rest and stepped through the torn door flap. The shocking cold of the snow squall wakened her. But the claws twisted in her chest, quelling with agony her first impulse to resist. The devil was growing stronger, more perfect in its control.

Terrified, Glyssa watched herself bound and leap down the slope toward the dojuk and the glistening sea-ice. She cut the mooring lines with her knife. Then she put her shoulder to the bow and turned the boat, pointing it out to sea. This normally required the strength of three or four, yet Glyssa accomplished it. Perhaps she was dreaming; she hoped it was so.

She climbed on board, loosed the heavy kegs and rolled them over the side. Her knife cut the knots securing the sail, and then she bent her back and raised the yard. As the sail climbed the mast it bowed with the furious wind, pushing the dojuk a bit on the snow.

When Glyssa had secured the halyard and the sheets she stood beside the tiller, bracing her back against the stern. Prompted by the devil's will, she raised both arms and pointed at the sail.

The sleeves of the witch's cloak glimmered with some unguessable power. Glyssa's arms shuddered as a great wind roared into being. The wind filled the sail, and the dojuk lurched under her feet. The wind shattered the frozen waves near shore as it pushed the dojuk, tilting madly, out to sea.

Four

When Lonn woke the wind was quiet. The stove was cold and above it, where the chimney pipe jutted through the ceiling of the small dome, daylight shone in a blue crescent.

Karrol was standing between the two bed platforms, wrapping a bed fur over her shoulders. "Glyssa never called us to take her place." She picked up her sword and headed for the crawl-tunnel.

"She probably talked all night with the windbringer," Draven said. Still he rose, took his own sword, and followed Karrol, not bothering with a fur.

Lonn stared at the ceiling, trying to recall if he had dreamed. All he could remember was a disturbing sense of confusion and worry.

Then Karrol and Draven were shouting in alarm, saying that Glyssa was gone, that the dojuk had been stolen.

Lonn, Eben, and Brinda clambered out of bed and grabbed their weapons. As they hurried through the low tunnel Lonn could hear Karrol outside, screaming Glyssa's name.

Draven knelt by the hearth, trying to rouse the windbringers from trance. The witch's treasure, and all else in the chamber, seemed untouched—except for the door flap, which was split down the middle. Lonn ran to the entrance and looked outside.

Sunlight reflected blindingly on the new snowfall. Shading his eyes and squinting, Lonn spotted Karrol halfway down the slope, wading bare-legged through the knee-high drifts. She was still shouting Glyssa's name. Farther down, where the dojuk had been moored, six or seven rounded lumps lay partly covered by snow—the kegs of oil and brandy, abandoned. Beyond that—Lonn stretched his neck and stared in bewilderment—it appeared the dojuk had left a track, a shallow trench running out to sea.

"It looks like the snow was cleared, midway through the storm, to let the dojuk sail," Eben said. "Perhaps this witch really does command the winds."

Lonn crossed the dome on wobbly legs, Eben a step behind. Brinda had poured fresh oil in the hearth and was trying to strike a spark. Draven still knelt with the windbringers, a hand in either pail, churning furiously to get the slush off the roots.

"Azzible! Kizier! Azzible!" he yelled. "I've never known bostulls so hard to rouse."

Brinda got the fire started, flames sputtering across the oil. Suddenly Kizier opened his eye. Round and startled, it swept over the Iruks and past them across the dome.

"What happened?" Lonn asked. "Where's Glyssa?"

"Did the witch take her?" Eben demanded.

"No, not Amlina ... Some other." In a soft, quavering voice Kizier told them all he had seen and sensed last night: the ripping of the entry flap, the wheel of light spinning across the chamber and entering Glyssa, seizing control of her, making her a *thrall*, an instrument of its will.

"We tried to call you, Azzible and I both. But the one who'd taken Glyssa smote us, driving us into deep trance. I do not know who it was. A powerful deepshaper, that is certain."

By now Azzible had also come out of trance. Lonn and Draven questioned him, but he only confirmed what Kizier had already said.

"It makes no sense!" Eben exclaimed. "Why take Glyssa and our boat and leave everything else?"

"Your boat is missing also," Kizier murmured, gazing past them toward the chests and basket belonging to the witch. "I think I know the answer, though I pray that I am wrong. Have you verified that *all* of Amlina's possessions are still here?"

The mates looked at one another. "No," Lonn said.

The bostull's stalk nodded, a peculiarly human gesture. "I suspect you'll find the black and silver cloak is gone. It alone of all her things is worth such effort."

Brinda and Draven went to search for the cloak.

"Why is it worth so much effort?" Lonn demanded.

Kizier paused, watching as Draven and Brinda rifled through the witch's possessions.

"Why is it worth so much effort?" Lonn shouted impatiently.

"The cloak is not here," Brinda announced.

"Just so," Kizier muttered sadly. "The worst has happened, so you may as well know the truth. That cloak is the Cloak of the Two Winds, one of the great treasures of Larthang. It was fashioned by Eglemarde herself on the day she wove the Two Winds into the pattern of the world. Its threads contain the binding energy of that ensorcellment. The Cloak has the power to summon the witch winds."

"Then that would explain the trench," Eben said. "And how the dojuk could be sailed through a squall."

Karrol stomped into the lodge house, brushing snow from her bare legs. She staggered to the rear of the dome and started collecting her garments.

"There was only one set of tracks and they led straight to the dojuk," she panted. "Glyssa must have been bewitched ... Why are you all standing around?"

It took a moment before Lonn answered. "We're trying to figure out what happened. And what to do about it."

Karrol slid on her trousers. "What happened is Glyssa was taken! What we must do is go after her. She'll be easy enough to follow. The dojuk left a track wider than the outriggers, and all of it has frozen hard."

"How can we follow without a boat?" Eben demanded.

"On skates," Karrol said. "We'll have to go on skates."

"Ridiculous," Draven said. "We'd never catch the dojuk on skates. We're already hours behind."

"All the more reason to hurry!" Karrol flung a shirt at him. "Get dressed."

Draven caught the shirt and held it, looking dumbly at the others.

"Whatever we decide, we'll need to be dressed," Brinda said, and went to put on her clothes.

"We're going on skates," Karrol insisted.

"That's crazy." Lonn still stood by the fire. "We'll all freeze, or drown when the meltwind blows."

"What other choice do we have?" Karrol yelled. "Abandon Glyssa? Is that what you want?"

"Of course not. But there has to be another way."

"What?" Karrol shouted, tugging on a boot. "What other way, Lonn?"

The mates all looked at him, the klarn leader, hoping he had an answer. Lonn felt a terrible gulf open inside of him. He shook his head. "I don't know."

"No. You don't!" Karrol cried. "Your crazy dream brought us this trouble, but no guidance to help us out of it. Did you have other dreams that warned this might happen? Well, if you did, you forgot about them!"

Lonn clenched his fists, suppressing a flash of rage. He wanted to strike Karrol, so hurt was he by what she'd said. Yet her words were true, and he could hardly blame her, in her grief, for speaking them.

Scanning the faces of his mates, Lonn saw the same grief reflected on each. Their klarn was broken, and with it their spirit and confidence. For a mate to be killed in a hunt or battle would be bad enough. But those were known hazards, and the ghost of the lost mate would still travel with the klarn. But for a mate to be lost, torn away by some unknown fate—and for that one to be Glyssa, beloved by all of them—this was a pain beyond bearing. There was only one remedy: the klarn must be made whole again, whatever the risks.

"Karrol is right," he said. "We'll have to go on skates." He went to gather his clothing. After a moment, Draven and Eben followed.

"The dojuk may not have gone far," Brinda said as they dressed. "There's a chance we can catch it on skates."

"I think we should search the island first," Draven suggested. "There might be a dojuk laid in that we could borrow. Or steal."

But they all knew this was unlikely. It was yulugg season and any serviceable boat would likely be at sea.

"There's no time," Karrol answered, placing her knife and sword in their scabbards. "Every moment we waste lessens our chance of finding Glyssa."

The mates exchanged looks of painful uncertainty.

"It might be worth searching the island first," Lonn allowed.

"Fine." Karrol picked up a quiver of spears and turned her back on them. "You do what you like. I'm going now."

"Wait!" Eben shouted as Karrol stalked across the dome. "We have to act together. Karrol—you're breaking the klarn!"

"It's broken already. I'm trying to make it whole." Karrol pushed through the torn entry flap and was gone.

Eben jumped up, enraged, but Brinda, fully dressed now, grabbed him around the waist. "Wait. I'll go with her, Eben. The rest of you can search the island first, then come after us."

"We should stay together," Eben declared, still struggling to pull free.

"That's impossible now," Brinda said. "Karrol won't wait. Besides, if we split up we can both cover the island and start after the dojuk at once."

"She's right," Draven laid a hand on Eben's shoulder. "It's better to do both."

Eben ceased struggling and stared at the floor, defeated.

"We'll do what Brinda suggests," Lonn said. "But first we must raise the klarn spirit. There's only four of us, but that's better than nothing."

"No time," Brinda was picking up her weapons. "Karrol will be out of sight by the time we finish. You three raise the spirit and send it to the rest of us—to Glyssa too."

She fastened on her cape and headed for the entrance. "Karrol, wait for me," she called as she ran outside.

* * * * *

When she was gone, Lonn, Draven, and Eben stared at each other, stunned. The chaos and terror of what had happened settled on them now, and for a moment they were overwhelmed, paralyzed.

Finally, Lonn shook himself. "We must hurry."

They finished dressing. Lonn went to fetch the ceremonial cup. The men lined up at the door flap and hastily performed the rite, pouring libations and calling the klarn spirit to wake and come into them. Each of them picked up two spears, and Eben added words to send the spirit also to Brinda, Karrol, and Glyssa.

They armed themselves with swords and knives, and each took a quiver that held three spears. Though the journey might be long they took no food, only small water flasks tucked in their shirts. The furs and weapons encumbered them already, but they dared not leave those behind.

"With luck we'll return in a day or two," Draven said to the bostulls. "If not, someone will come by and find you. You'll be looked after, so don't worry."

"I wish you good fortune," Kizier said.

"We'll need it," Lonn muttered.

The Iruks tramped outside, into the brilliance of sunlight and snow. Karrol and Brinda had already skated out to sea. Lonn peered for a moment before spotting them, tiny specks receding in the glimmering distance.

Eben volunteered to go inland, to apprise the village elders of what had happened and to ask them to take the windbringers if his klarn did not return. He bid his mates good hunting and marched over the rise toward the center of the isle. Lonn and Draven stepped and skidded down the slope to where the dojuk had been moored.

The witchlight made the sea ice gleam even more brightly than the snow-covered land. Lonn and Draven sat at the edge of the trench and took the skates from their belts. The double blades of ivory fit snugly against the soles of their boots, but Lonn's fingers were stiff, their movements inept. He was still fumbling with the straps when Draven stood, muttered his farewell and skated off. He would circle the island to the east, leaving Lonn the western leg.

Alone in the huge silence, Lonn fought down a rising surge of futility and despair. He swore and tugged at the leather straps and finally got them tied. He rose clumsily and started off, skating inside the trench. The vapory sealight hovered about his ankles. Momentarily, the effortless gliding made him feel a little better.

The snow that fell during the squall had been transformed by the glowing enchantment of the sea into hard, skateable ice. This change took time, the radiant power seeping up, melting and then refreezing the snowfall. The trench could only have been formed by an interruption of this change, the layer of new snow cleared away so the dojuk could ride the solid ice beneath.

How strong a wind would be needed to move so much snow? Lonn shook his head. How could he and his mates hope to fight an enemy with such power?

A hundred yards from shore he stopped and turned. Ilga was a white hump rising from the pale blue luminescence of the sea-ice. Here and there dark details could be discerned, a wall of rock too steep for the snow to cling to, the two brown domes of the lodge house, only partly covered in white. Farther inland, columns of gray smoke drifted up from the chimneys of the village.

Skating east, Draven had already circled out of sight. Lonn stepped from the trench and started west.

The orange sun was past the top of the sky when Lonn and Draven skated back to the shore in front of the lodge house. They had met on the far side of the island, then circled back together. Eben stood on the beach waiting for them.

"No boats," Lonn told him. "We follow Karrol and Brinda on skates."

"And hope for the best," Draven added.

As soon as Eben had his skates on they headed out to sea. The trench ran straight and level, the smooth ice within perfect for skating. The Iruks lengthened their strides. Bent low, they swung their arms, gaining speed with every stroke. A gust of wind blew up behind them, moaning in their ears.

After a while, Lonn glanced back and saw that Ilga was gone, lost in the shimmering blue-white veil that hung upon the world. There were other islands off to his right, but none could be made out in the brilliance. It was like a dream, he thought, this mad flight on skates out to sea, in an icy trench that could not have been made by nature, with the same maddening vista everywhere. It was much like the weird, incomprehensible dreams that haunted him sometimes.

His empty belly rumbled with hunger. His legs in their fur leggings were drenched in sweat. He wished he could discard the heavy cape at least, but he knew he would need it later, in the freezing night.

The cold breeze remained steady in the south. This at least was fortunate. So long as a southerly blew there was little chance of a meltwind.

The mates kept skating, pushing the measured strides into their legs. In Second Winter, when ice was constant and there was often little wind for sailing, the Iruks were accustomed to skating long hauls from island to island, or making a circuit of many days on their skates, seeking the breathing holes of the sea lion herds. Lonn, Draven, and Eben were in such a long-distance rhythm now. They kept up the pace without faltering as the faint sun wheeled down through the afternoon sky.

The track was growing more shallow. The farther north the dojuk had traveled, the less snow there'd been to clear away. By sundown, the trench had risen almost to the level of the surrounding ice.

There was still no sign of Karrol and Brinda.

Daylight faded and the fiery constellations appeared overhead. Weak from hunger, thighs and backs straining, the Iruks pushed on. Their strides were ragged now, and slower. Only iron determination kept their exhausted legs moving.

Then Lonn's skate hit a nick in the ice and he fell sprawling. He slid a distance on his belly before his mates could pick him up. He tasted blood in his mouth and spit it out.

"Easy," Draven said.

But Lonn yanked free and skated off again. "I'm all right."

"There's no track anymore," Draven said, pulling even.

"We're keeping the same direction," Lonn answered. "We have to keep going."

"I know."

But the ache in Lonn's legs was growing sharper, and he wondered how long he could fight it. Karrol and Brinda came this far, he told himself, and farther. Still, it seemed hopeless. Even if they found Glyssa now they'd have no strength to help her.

A while later Eben skidded to a halt, doubled over and clutching his belly. Lonn and Draven stopped and skated back to him.

"Keep going," Eben said. "I'll catch up with you."

Lonn glanced at Draven, who shook his head despondently.

They had pushed themselves all day, putting only a few swallows of water in their stomachs. Eben's wiry frame carried less muscle than the others', but it would not be long before they too went down with cramps. Besides, if they left Eben here alone there was little doubt but he would freeze.

"Get moving!" Eben cried angrily.

"No," Lonn knelt and embraced him. "What's left of the klarn must stay together. We'll go on in the morning."

"It may be too late in the morning." Eben tried to rise, then fell back wincing.

"It may be too late already," Lonn said. "We won't leave you."

Draven bent over and wrapped an arm around each of their shoulders. Eben shook with weeping. "Please go," he said. "I don't want my weakness to cost us losing Glyssa."

"No. It's my fault," Lonn answered. "My dreaming started it all."

"Stop it!" Draven shouted. "I could blame myself too. When Glyssa tried to warn us, I was the one who laughed at her. And Lonn, we all agreed to follow your dream and sail to Dekyll. We could have refused. We all did what we thought was best at the time. What is the good of blaming ourselves now? None of us can go farther, Eben."

Tears of remorse filled Lonn's eyes. "Our klarn is broken, Draven."

"No," Draven hugged him. "We'll go on tomorrow. We'll find our mates."

The three Iruks huddled close, murmuring consolations to one another. At Draven's suggestion, Eben took out two spears and beat them together. They chanted to the spirits of the wind and the ice, begging them to keep the meltwind away and to protect their absent klarnmates.

Afterward, they lay down close together, sharing the warmth of their capes, and soon fell asleep.

* * * * *

Lonn's first awareness was of dread, creeping through his belly, unattached to any thought. Next, he felt numbing cold against his back. He tried to move and discovered massive, aching stiffness in every joint and muscle. And he remembered.

Lonn opened his eyes, pulled the fur away from his face. It was daylight, the sun low in the east. With a groan, he unwrapped himself from the capes and struggled to his feet. Draven and Eben rose slowly beside him.

Lonn scanned the bright panorama of ice and sky and detected no movement anywhere. Then he realized the source of his dread. A warm breeze blew on his face—from the north. The weather had changed.

"If the wind picks up now we're finished," Eben muttered.

"What should we do?" Draven asked feebly.

"We could turn back," Eben said. "Try and make it to land. Bru Isle can't be too many leagues southeast of here. If we turn back, we'll likely be giving up our mates. If we go on, we'll probably be giving up ourselves too."

"We have to go on," Lonn said, searching their eyes for affirmation.

Both of them gave it, nodding soberly.

They drank a little water, then picked up their capes and quivers. Lonn hoisted the quiver on his back, grimacing at the pain.

"A sail!" Eben pointed to the south.

Lonn peered into the shining distance. A glint of motion caught his eye—a speck, barely visible. "Should we make for it?" he asked.

"Of course." Draven was skating already, calling back to his mates. "If they're friendly they'll take us on board. If not, we'll make them wish they'd been friendly."

Lonn and Eben started after him, forcing movement from their deadened legs.

As the craft drew closer Lonn could see it was no dojuk, but a large vessel. It was sailing toward them, beating against the northerly breeze. Then the craft came about, fore-and-aft rig turning sideways to the Iruks.

Lonn's belly cringed with a new dread.

It was the Larthangan, the witch's ship.

Five

The Iruks skidded to a stop on the shining ice. The witch's vessel, still a half-mile downwind, was sailing from the same direction as they had skated.

"She's come from Ilga," Draven surmised. "She found our lodge house and got the story from the windbringer. Now she's hunting her cloak."

"Or else she never found Ilga, and she's still hunting the pirates who robbed her," Eben said. "Either way, we won't get a friendly greeting."

Lonn grunted. "If it's a choice between her displeasure and a meltwind ..."

Draven and Eben shrugged their agreement. They set off toward the ship.

A few hundred yards away the coaster changed tacks, aiming slightly to the Iruks' left as it angled into the wind. As the vessel drew closer, Lonn could hear the scrape of its iron runners on the ice. The three mates waved their arms and shouted.

In response the coaster veered, pointing upwind to slow— pointing now straight at the Iruks. They had to shuffle aside as the ship hurtled down on them, a tilting, ungainly behemoth.

A gray-clad figure hailed the Iruks from the high foredeck. By the slim shape and blowing gold hair Lonn recognized the witch of Larthang. She called to them through a megaphone.

"Come aboard if you can. We've slowed for you, but we'll not be stopping."

The bow rushed past the skaters as the witch shouted to them. Encumbered and weary as they were, the Iruks dashed for the ship.

The first runner slid by as they approached. Lonn and his mates just had time to stop, get their timing and pounce on the second runner.

Then they were crouching on the two-foot-wide runner top, streaming along in the rushing wind, the ice flashing inches below. Holding a precarious balance, they sat down and unstrapped their skate-blades, then tied them to their belts.

The coaster was cutting off-wind again, increasing speed. The Iruks inched their way along the runner top to a curved iron beam, one of two that connected runner to hull. When the coaster sailed on soft water these beams were drawn up into the belly of the ship, the runners fitting snugly midway up the hull. Lonn was familiar with similar equipment on Tathian ships, though he didn't understand the exact details of the mechanism. At present he was just grateful that the beams were fashioned with rungs, to serve as curved ladders. He and his mates climbed up the beam one behind the next, watching out for each other as best they could. The ice was a dizzying blur below their hands and feet. Once the ship hit a bump and Eben nearly fell. He was saved by grabbing Lonn's ankle above him, and by Draven who steadied him from below.

Lonn first, and then the others, reached the narrow ledge halfway up the ship's side. A short length of ladder, of stout rope with wooden rungs, had been dropped for them. The Iruks clambered up the ladder and heaved themselves over the rail, spilling onto the deck where they lay panting and exhausted.

The girl-like witch, Captain Troneck, and a number of sailors had assembled on the deck to confront the Iruks. Lonn looked up at them for some moments, before achingly climbing to his feet. His mates rose beside him.

The men of Larthang, lean and cold-looking in their wool coats and hats, regarded the Iruks with open hostility. They had armed themselves with ice-axes, knives, and belaying pins.

The witch stood before them, in a long coat of gray fur, her hands folded in the wide sleeves. She was taller than Lonn had thought, fully his own height or better. Her sea-blue eyes stared into his eyes and seemed to pierce through to his brain.

"I am Amlina, a deepshaper of Larthang," she said. "This ship is under my hire and command."

"I am Lonn," his voice grated. "This is Eben, Draven. We are Iruks of ..."

"You are three of the pirates who robbed me. I know this already, as I know that the Cloak of the Two Winds was stolen from you in turn—along with your iceboat and one of your crew."

"If you know who we are," Eben said, "why have you taken us on board?"

"Why do you suppose?" Amlina retorted. "To imprison you in glass beads to wear around my neck? To turn you into fish and watch you drown in the air? Don't worry. I haven't the time or inclination for such amusements. No. Kizier the windbringer convinced me to take you on board. For some reason, he believes there is worth in you Iruks, and that you might bring me good luck, though so far you've brought me only evil."

"And you accept his opinion." Draven smiled winningly.

"I consider it remotely possible he is correct."

"He is wise, this windbringer," Lonn said, grasping at the opportunity. "You seek your treasure, we seek our mates. There's no reason we shouldn't join forces now and help each other."

"Oh, indeed?" Amlina said. "I can help you by letting you stay on board, thus preventing your imminent drowning. How can you help me?"

"As fighters," Draven answered readily. "Your ship plainly needs protection. It would never have fallen prey to one hunting boat if you'd had a few warriors aboard."

"Besides," Eben said, "we know the seas and islands of this region, and you do not."

"I doubt the Cloak of the Two Winds will be in this region for long," Amlina replied. "Your other point, however, has some merit. I was forced to leave Nyssan without acquiring suitable bodyguards. Not that you are exactly suitable."

"We are Iruks," Lonn threw back his shoulders. "None are better with spear or sword."

"That may be so," Amlina said. "Still, I must decide for myself whether to take you into my service. This evening I will put the question to the Deepmind. You will have my decision in the morning. Meantime, you'll be given food and water. But to assure that you'll cause no trouble, I must take your weapons and chain you to the mainmast."

"No." Lonn and Eben gripped their sword hilts.

"There's no need to chain us."' Draven held up his hands. "We won't harm anyone."

"It must be done," Amlina insisted. "You've harmed two men of this crew already. The others understandably disfavor having you on board. I won't have their safety threatened, nor their efficiency impaired because they're worried about having their throats cut."

At a gesture from the witch the Larthangans started forward. In a blur of motion, the Iruks drew their swords. The crewmen halted.

"We've never been chained in our lives," Lonn declared. "We'll not have it now."

"You cannot fight me," Amlina said quietly. "Put down your weapons."

"Never."

"Put down your weapons."

Her voice, still soft, reverberated with a tone of irresistible command. Her eyes seemed to grow larger, until they filled Lonn's vision and burned inside his skull. Against his will, the sword drooped, then slipped from his fingers. Three swords rang dully as they struck the deck.

"Bring them," Amlina said.

Dazed by her witchery, the Iruks hardly resisted as the crewmen grabbed them. Their arms were pinned back, their knives and spears taken. Lonn tried to twist free, but his deadened arms were held fast. With Troneck supervising, the prisoners were half-marched, half-dragged to the mainmast.

Amlina was fixing a ring of chain shoulder high on the mast, with numerous tether chains attached. Lonn's weak struggles ceased for a moment, stilled by amazement.

The chain was gold and extremely fine—jeweler's chain. The tethers ended not in iron manacles but in delicate bracelets of gold filigree.

Then Lonn's amazement passed, replaced by panic. He gave a roar of defiance, kicked one of the sailors and almost tore loose.

"*Be still!*" Amlina ordered.

A new wave of numbness surged over Lonn's body. His hands were jerked up and the witch snapped the bracelets onto his wrists.

Lonn's arms hung limply in their fetters. He sank to his knees when the crewmen no longer held him up. The witch had moved on to lock the bracelets on Draven, then Eben.

The Iruks were chained facing the mast, but with enough tether so they could turn around, or sit on the deck if they chose.

By the time the witch stepped back to observe her work, Lonn had struggled to his feet again. The numbness was gone, burned away by a brightening rage. Staring at the tether chain, he began to tremble. A growl started low in his throat and grew to an ear-piercing howl. Distantly, he heard Eben and Draven also howling.

The Larthangans and even the witch shrank back as the Iruks thrashed in their bonds, straining to tear free. Having never been chained before, they reacted with savage ferocity.

"You cannot break those chains, however flimsy they appear," Amlina said. "Captain Troneck, tell them how the chains came to be on board."

"They belonged to the Archimage of the East, that's how. She had the whole crew fettered in that rig and another like it. Twelve of us pulling together could not even bend a single link. They are witch-chains. They work on the mind."

But the Iruks showed no sign that they had heard. Draven had his back to the mast, pulling the tether over his shoulder. Jumping about in frenzy, Eben flailed and yanked on his tether. Lonn set one foot against the mast and pulled with all the strength of his arms and back.

The chains began to glow with yellow witchlight.

"Leave them," Amlina told the crew. "They'll realize soon enough that their struggles are futile."

Slowly, on the witch's promptings, the Larthangans dispersed. Amlina was the last to go, following the captain aft to the quarterdeck.

Tugged and twisted, the witch-chains glimmered with greater intensity, but the metal showed no signs of stretching. Gradually the Iruks' mad howling dwindled to curses and grunts of effort, then to tired groans. One by one they sank to the deck, gasping and thoroughly exhausted, their wrists raw and bloodied.

The sailors stationed on the main deck watched the prisoners covertly, with stern looks of satisfaction or contempt. After a while, Draven shouted to one of these.

"The witch promised us food and water. Where is it?"

The rations were brought some time later, small pieces of hard biscuit and a half cup of water for each man.

"Surely you can do better," Draven complained. "Does the witch mean to starve us too?"

"You're lucky to have this," was the surly reply. "We've got little enough for ourselves."

* * * * *

Past mid-morning a call came down from the lookout—another skater had been spotted. The Iruks stood on their toes to see, but their view of the ice ahead was blocked by the raised foredeck and by two ships' boats, which hung forward on either rail. Their anxiously shouted questions elicited the assurance that it was indeed only one skater.

Not until the coaster slowed in the wind and the skater climbed aboard did they learn it was Brinda. Amlina and a party of Larthangans met her at the rail. They took her weapons and marched her to the mainmast, where they chained her beside the others. Brinda looked cold and miserable. She dropped to the deck as soon as the chains were in place.

The three men huddled to shield her from the wind. Draven took out his water flask and put it to her lips. Brinda drank all the water left within.

"Where's Karrol?" Lonn asked.

"I don't know. Ahead of me." Brinda gazed at each of them, her expression bleak but grateful. "I'm glad to see you, mates."

"We're glad to see you." Draven grasped her hand.

"How did you and Karrol get separated?" Eben asked.

"I couldn't keep up with her. We skated together all day and most of the night, without seeing anything of Glyssa or the boat. My legs started to give out. I called for Karrol to stop, but she wouldn't." Brinda sniffed, "She wouldn't stop for me, as if her grief had driven her mad. I kept on as best I could alone. Then the wind changed and I got frightened and turned around."

"Don't worry," Draven said. "We'll find Karrol."

"If the meltwind doesn't drown her first," Brinda answered, shaking her head. She barely had the strength to eat and drink the meager rations the cabin boy brought her. When she finished, she lay with her head in Lonn's lap and was soon asleep.

The *Plover* continued beating north, making good headway against the steady, warming breeze. Lonn sat with his back to the mainmast, keeping still so Brinda could rest. He stared vacantly about, scanning the coaster's complex rigging, the flamboyant ornaments on doors and hatches, the quarterdeck, where the stout

Captain Troneck manned the helm behind the cluster of windbringers. The witch had apparently gone below to her cabin.

Draven and Eben stood in their chains, restlessly circling the mast, stretching their backs to look for Karrol. Eben muttered a chant to the wind spirits, pleading that the thaw be forestalled, that Karrol's life be spared. The orange sun hung bright in the north, implacably heating the day.

When the wind gusted, sparks of silver erupted in the air, harbingers of the meltwind. Lonn winced and Eben swore furiously under his breath. Brinda sat up and looked around.

Amlina came out on deck and stood gazing over the rail on the port side.

A shout came down from the crow's nest—another skater off the port bow. Lonn and his mates were on their feet at once, straining to see.

"There!" Eben pointed with a fettered hand.

Just aft of where the ship's boat hung from its davits, Lonn spotted Karrol—a tiny figure approaching out of the immense brightness.

The Iruks cheered aloud, but next instant their voices went dumb. Behind the skater a silvery light was rising, brighter than the gleaming ice or the sunlit sky—the fluttering, baleful face of the meltwind.

"Oh, no," Brinda moaned.

"She will make it," Draven declared. "If there was ever a skater too stubborn to be caught by the wind, it is Karrol."

But Eben, staring, shook his head.

Now Lonn could see Karrol's arms flailing furiously as she skated. He squinted, trying to judge how much lead she had on the glittering front where the ice was changing to water.

She might have a chance, he thought, a small one.

Then the coaster swerved, blocking their sight of Karrol. The mainsail and boom swung creaking overhead as the vessel changed tacks, aiming close to the wind to intercept the skater.

Amlina had come forward on the tilted main deck.

"We'll do what we can to save her." She spoke in answer to the Iruks' stricken looks.

Lonn stared down at the chains binding him. If free, he might have a chance to help save Karrol. Suddenly it was unendurable to be helpless. A growl started in his throat again and grew louder as his lips parted, his teeth still clenched. He began whipping his tether up and down in a frenzy.

"Lonn?" Draven said.

"The chains work on our minds," he answered. "Are our minds not our own? Help me!"

Lonn braced his foot against the mast and yanked harder, ignoring the protest of his torn wrists.

His fury proved contagious. First Eben, then Draven and Brinda started tugging at their chains in the same tempo. The ring on the mast ignited with yellow light. Pulled taut again and again, the tethers threw off ruby sparks. Even amid his rage, Lonn was aware of the wave of silver radiance that loomed higher and higher as the meltwind neared the coaster's bow.

Hearing the excitement, many of the crewmen had come out on deck. They hovered at the rails, watching the skater's race for life, some making wagers on the outcome.

Flashes of silver light popped and fizzed in the air as the towering curtain of the sea change approached. It was almost upon the ship when a groan went up from the Larthangans. Lonn knew that Karrol had been caught.

Howling in torment, Lonn put both feet on the mast and arched his back. He heard a link snap and then he fell backward, his head and shoulders slamming on the deck.

Next moment, the meltwind engulfed the ship. There was a whir, like a song note, piercing to his bones, a stifling unbreathable warmth in the air, and the dazzling silver light everywhere.

Still on his back, Lonn slid forward as the deck plunged, the *Plover* running off the vanishing ice and crashing into the water. The deck lurched up again as the light and warmth and song note blew past. Cold spray glittered in the air as the ship's hull splashed through foaming waves.

Lonn bounded to his feet, unsnapping the gold bracelets—which, came off easily now—and flinging them away. The main ring of chain had broken on the mast and the other Iruks were also free.

The mates separated and ran to either rail. They shoved the Larthangans aside and looked for Karrol. Lonn spotted her off the starboard side, her arms wildly beating the bright water.

"Hang on, mate!" he yelled. "We'll get you."

At Amlina's orders, the sailors had gotten life buoys ready—hoops of cork covered in canvas and attached to ropes. One of these had already been thrown, but the cast had fallen short. Lonn darted back along the bulwark and grabbed a second buoy from the man holding it. He leaned far over the rail and flung the life buoy with all his strength.

The hoop hit the water beyond Karrol and off-line, but Lonn had wisely thrown it to her right, so the coaster's drift would pull the lifeline within her reach. In a moment Karrol caught the rope, a few yards from the floating buoy. She pulled her head well out of the water then and took a great gasp of air.

Lonn's mates were beside him, whooping with joy, Brinda pounding him on the back. Draven and Eben took hold of the lifeline and began hauling it in.

The Larthangans were falling back, muttering among themselves, confused and worried now that the Iruks had somehow gotten free.

Karrol had wrapped both arms around the lifeline and was straining to hook her leg over it as well. By the weakness of her efforts, Lonn could tell she was in no shape to climb onboard the ship. So he and Draven grabbed a rope ladder that lay nearby and tossed it over the side. They scrambled down the ladder to the ledge, then started down the arcing beam to the aft runner.

The silver wall of the meltwind receded in the south. Prow in the wind, the coaster had slowed to a drift in the still-turbulent sea. Lonn had almost reached the runner when a high wave dashed over the beam. He lost his grip and plunged into the frigid water.

For a moment he kicked in wild fright. Then his hand found the steel runner and he pulled his head to the surface. Coughing, he dragged himself onto the runner-top, which rode a foot deep. By now Draven had reached the runner, and he helped Lonn to sit upright.

The two mates straddled the runner, waist-deep in the glittering sea. They edged their way aft to where Karrol had been dragged by the lifeline and was feebly trying to get a leg up. Lonn grasped her harness and Draven her arm and together they hoisted her until she sat between them on the runner.

Brinda and Eben called down encouragement from the main deck. Lonn saw the witch standing behind them at the rail. He took the knife from Karrol's belt, cut the line from the lifebuoy, tossed the buoy up on deck. He tied the rope to Karrol's harness, knotting it securely, then slipped her knife into his belt.

Almost unconscious, Karrol was hauled up the coaster's side and helped over the rail. Lonn and Draven, moving with care, climbed back on board the way they had come down. They were halfway up the rope ladder when the hoisting machinery clattered into motion. The ship's runners rose on their beams until they rested firmly against the hull. The *Plover* was already turning off-wind, tacking to the east.

It occurred to Lonn that the witch might have ordered these maneuvers to occupy the crew, so that she could confront the now-freed Iruks alone. Amlina watched with hands in sleeves as Lonn and Draven dragged themselves over the railing.

Karrol lay on the deck, panting, Brinda supporting her head and upper body. The ivory skates were still attached to her boots, though her cape and quiver had been lost in the sea.

Grinning, Eben hugged Lonn and Draven in turn.

"Bravely done," Amlina added her own congratulations. "Come below with me now, and I'll see you have blankets and a stove to dry your clothes."

Lonn snatched the knife from his belt and pointed it close to the witch's face. "Don't think to trick us. We'll not be chained again."

He had to admire the witch: her placid expression never faltered. "I don't intend to chain you again. Obviously it would do no good, since you can break the witch-chains. Come, you can't stay out here in those wet garments."

"We don't trust you," Lonn said.

"And I don't trust you." Amlina shrugged. "But what choice do you have? You might kill me with that dagger—and several of the crew besides. But the others would catch you up and throw you into the sea."

Lonn clutched the knife-handle, glancing about at the sailors who watched from their various stations.

"Come below," Amlina said. "You can distrust me just as easily there, and you'll be out of the wind."

She stepped back, then turned and started across the main deck. Lonn lowered the knife, scowling.

"This witch is crafty," Eben muttered. "She backs down when we have the advantage. When she has it, she slaps us in chains."

Draven and Brinda each took one of Karrol's arms around their shoulders and helped her across the deck. The klarnmates followed the witch down three steps and through a door below the quarterdeck. Inside was a cramped corridor leading to the witch's cabin and one other, and a stairway spiraling down.

The witch closed the door behind them and proceeded down the stairway. The *Plover's* design was typical for small trading ships:

crew's quarters and galley forward, main cargo holds amidships. Aft, below the quarterdeck and main cabins, were compartments that could serve either for storage or as extra accommodations for passengers. Amlina took the Iruks through this part of the ship, past partitions and empty lockers, to a relatively spacious room at the very stern. Small windows of stained glass opened onto the ship's wake. There was a portable oil stove and some bedding—padded mats covered with canvas.

"You'll need more sleeping mats and blankets," the witch said. "And I'll see if the cook won't consent to brew you some tea."

Her display of hospitality only increased Lonn's suspicions. "We're glad to be out of the cold," he said. "But don't think to keep us locked in down here."

"You won't be locked in," Amlina said. "But I hope your own good sense will keep you here at least till tomorrow. My crewmen hate and fear you—and not without reason. Until I pledge to them that you can be trusted and order them to make peace with you, there isn't likely to be peace. So the less you are in their eyes the better."

"We don't fear your Larthangans," Lonn asserted.

"I don't want you slaughtering them any more than I want them slaughtering you," Amlina replied. "You Iruks have shown me daring and resourcefulness in action. More, you've shown that you can break the slave chains of the Archimage of the East. Perhaps this was accomplished by the energy of the meltwind, for the time of its passing is one of great potential. No matter, it was an impressive feat of will. But you must also show me that you can be patient and peaceable. If not, there can be no place for you on this voyage."

Saying no more the witch departed. She returned a while later with the cabin boy and two other crewmembers. They brought extra bedding, oil for the stove, and a tray with Karrol's rations and a pot of tea. The Larthangans put everything down and left in haste. The witch bid the Iruks a peaceful rest before going.

Karrol was unconscious and never woke as the mates undressed her. They hung her clothing on hooks behind the stove, where Lonn and Draven had already put theirs. They dried Karrol's hair and skin with towels, then covered her with blankets.

* * * * *

Karrol slept until evening when the cabin boy brought supper, leaving the tray outside and hurrying away before the Iruks had opened the door. The mates took their meal seated in a half-circle around the stove. As they ate they told Karrol how they had come on board the *Plover*, and what had passed between them and the witch. When the tale was done Karrol stared moodily at her empty bowl.

"So now we're waiting to find out if this witch is going to kill us or take us on as her toadies."

"As her partners," Draven amended. "And what other choice do we have?"

"I don't know," Karrol grumbled. "I'd like to take the ship by force and drop the witch into the sea."

"And sail the ship with a hostile crew?" Eben demanded. "Or do you mean to sail it with no crew at all?"

"I said I'd like to," Karrol murmured. "Not that it's practical."

"Obviously it's not," Lonn said. "Our best hope seems to be to make peace with the witch, convince her that she needs us as much as we need her."

"Agreed," Eben said. "I just hope the witch's magic can lead us to Glyssa."

Draven lay back and stretched, poking his feet under the stove. "We've reason to be cheered, mates. Yesterday we were all apart, out on the ice and destitute. Now we are fed—not well, I admit, but fed—and warm and dry. We have a ship and a witch to help us hunt for Glyssa."

"At least the five of us are together," Brinda agreed.

Karrol had checked for more tea but found the pot empty. She put it down with force. "We won't be a klarn again until we have Glyssa back. So don't be saying how well off we are. Not with Glyssa out there alone somewhere, and maybe dead."

The mates stared at her gravely.

Karrol sniffed, holding back tears."I'm sorry. I'm just so tired. And I'm frightened for Glyssa." She bowed her head and sobbed.

The Iruks gathered around her, patting her shoulders and murmuring comfort.

"Lonn," Karrol cried. "I'm sorry I blamed you. I know it wasn't your fault. I know I would have drowned in the sea if you hadn't risked yourself to save me."

"It's all right," Lonn said. "We are klarnmates—one soul."

Karrol nodded and wiped her eyes.

The Iruks sat down in a circle, leaving a space where Glyssa would be. They put their hands in a pile and pledged themselves to finding Glyssa and saving her, no matter what dangers stood in their way.

They sat in silence for a time, and then Eben began a chant. All of them joined in, the same chant they had sung in the ritual the night the klarn was joined.

Through wind and sharp wave
Through ice and blood
We hold to the klarn
We are fearless
Many hands, one heart
Many eyes, one soul
Many spears, one hunter
We hold to the klarn
We are fearless

Six

Next morning after breakfast, the Iruks pushed open the door of the witch's cabin without knocking and trooped inside.

The delicate glass lamps that Lonn remembered illumined the chamber, but the hanging prisms and desmets were nowhere in sight. The witch's narrow silk tapestries were hung all together, curtaining off the rear section of the cabin. Amlina looked up from the table where she was seated next to Kizier the windbringer.

"Come in," the witch said wryly. "You have my permission to enter."

Her sarcasm was not lost on Lonn. "The cabin boy said you sent for us. We assumed that meant you wanted us to enter."

"Pardon our not knocking," Draven said. "We don't always remember the customs that you civilized folk think so important."

"No matter," Amlina rose and gestured to cushions set around the table. "Sit down."

She wore a dark blue robe of heavy silk embroidered with gray and white designs. Hammered silver earrings hung from her ears, and a silver fillet set with moonstones bound her pale gold hair. She stepped to the rear of the chamber, past the tapestries.

"Greetings," Kizier whispered in his soft bostull voice when the Iruks were seated. "I would have liked to welcome you aboard sooner, but as you know I have limited mobility."

"We are grateful to you," Draven said, "for speaking to Amlina on our behalf."

"I advised her as best I could for her own good," the bostull replied. "I am only glad it coincided with your interests."

Amlina returned from behind the curtain carrying a light silvery thing that she set down in the middle of the table. It was a peculiar construction of glass, thin metal, and mirrors, with fan-like arms and tiny chimes, all rigged on a spindle attached to a base set with four candles. The thing looked like one of the desmets Lonn remembered from Amlina's treasure.

Amlina lit the four candles from a taper. The thing started twirling on the updraft of heated air, the chimes tinkling. The mirrors and glass caught and scattered the many lamp fires in the chamber so that light and shadow revolved on the cabin walls. Lonn stared at the spinner with a weird and deepening fascination. His breathing began to sound loud in his head.

"Let us talk honestly." Amlina was seated again. "If I decide to make a pact with you and take you on as my bodyguards, will you swear to heed my instructions and obey my commands without hesitation or argument?"

In a strange, unreal state of mind, Lonn saw his mates staring at him. They expected him, as klarn leader, to respond. He turned to Amlina. Impelled somehow by her admonishment to speak honestly, he replied without coloring the truth.

"We are not slaves to swear obedience. We will do whatever we must to save our mate. That is our concern."

"Yes." The others muttered in agreement. "Lonn is right."

Lonn caught Amlina's slight frown before his eyes were drawn back to the spinner—which continued to turn with inexplicable attractiveness.

"They are headstrong, Kizier, unruly" the witch was saying. "I'm afraid their wildness will prove more a danger to us than a help."

"They are fierce and proud," the windbringer said. "But not without self-control. Listen, Iruks: Amlina does not require that you place obedience to her above Glyssa's rescue. But she must be certain, first that you will not threaten the crewmen of this ship, and second that you will accept that she is wiser than you in the ways of deepshapers and the foes you are likely to meet on this voyage, and that you will accordingly obey her commands when the time comes."

"Understand," Amlina said, "this voyage will likely be long and dangerous. I have at least one powerful enemy, probably two. And should knowledge become general that the Cloak of the Two Winds is loose in the world, there might well be others. While you slept last night, I looked into your minds and weighed what I saw there against what Kizier has told me. You Iruks are violent and audacious. I know you would not fail me for lack of bravery. But I must also know you won't fail me for lack of restraint. That is why I need your oath of obedience."

Lonn forced his eyes from the spinner and scanned the faces of his mates, trying to frame a response for the whole klarn. "We will swear to obey you," he finally said. "Except when your orders plainly run counter to the good of the klarn, or our hope of saving Glyssa."

Unaccountably, he was trembling, his face flushed.

The witch shook her head, dissatisfied. "I don't like it, Kizier. These barbarians haggle over terms like the bankers of Kadavel."

"No doubt they've had experience with Tathian moncy-lenders," the bostull said with amusement.

The witch scrutinized Lonn, whose eyes were back on the spinner.

"Very well," she said abruptly. "I accept those terms. You will swear them to me formally. I, in turn, will swear to put aside my grievance against you and to help you find your lost mate. Now, as a token of our pact, I need each of you to give me a hair plucked from your head. You must each do it yourself, and willingly."

"No." Lonn glared at the witch. "We know that you've done this to the crew. We'll not give you the means to enslave us."

"We will swear on the life of our klarn," Draven suggested. "That is all the token you need."

"Impossible." The witch was on her feet, pacing. "I must have the tokens or I have no means of enforcing the pact."

"You won't need to enforce it," Lonn stood himself, though his knees felt weak. "If we swear on the klarn, we will keep our word."

"I feel they can be trusted," Kizier offered.

"I know you do." Amlina walked slowly back to her place. "But if not, they could bring me disaster. I just don't know if they are worth the risk, Kizier."

"They are involved in the pattern of events," the windbringer responded. "To extricate them now would take effort and be of dubious worth. Why then fight the Ogo in this? Better to accept the risk with good faith, to view the Iruks as a gift, an opportunity. That is my reading of the matter."

Amlina peered at the faces of each of the Iruks in turn, Lonn last of all.

Suddenly her mind was made up. "Swear the oath to me now," she said.

Lonn blinked, his attention removed from the spinner once more. After glancing about at his mates he placed his hand on the table palm down. Each of the Iruks put a hand on top of it.

"We swear, on the life of our klarn, a pact of truce and alliance with this witch," Lonn said. "We swear to keep peace with her crew and to obey her commands in all but what will plainly do harm to us or to Glyssa. This is the decision of the klarn."

"Agreed," the mates all muttered.

Amlina swore the oath she had promised to the Iruks, then leaned over and blew out the candles. With the touch of a finger, she stopped the spinner from turning.

Immediately Lonn felt that a constriction had been removed from his mind. Whereas a moment before his thoughts had all been concentrated on the witch and answering her truthfully, now they were free to follow their own course again. His mates seemed to share the same odd sensation. They were looking about with puzzled faces or regarding the spinner with suspicion.

Amlina had returned to the rear of the cabin and was pulling aside the silk tapestries. "Here are your weapons," she said.

Eagerly the mates went to pick out their blades and spears. They examined the knives and swords briefly, then slipped them into sheaths and scabbards.

"You said the voyage would likely be long," Karrol spoke to Amlina. "Does that mean you've found our boat with your witch-sight?"

"Only a glimpse, if I saw correctly," Amlina answered. "Only enough to know it is distant from us. It's to be expected the journey will be long. I doubt there is a deepshaper in this part of the world capable of weaving such designs as stole the Cloak from you. Probably the Cloak is headed back to Nyssan, or perhaps to the Tathian Islands."

"Glyssa is getting farther away from us all the time," Eben said. "And we're not even sure we're sailing in the right direction."

"We're following your boat's last known course," Amlina replied. "Until my deepseeing can pierce the veils of energy hiding the Cloak, we can do no better. This evening, I will enter the *dark immersion*, the same trance in which you found me on the day you plundered this vessel. With luck, I will return to the surface in a few days with a clear idea of where the Cloak is going. Now let us announce our pact to the crew." Amlina was pulling on her fur coat. "If two of you will take Kizier, we'll go up to the quarterdeck."

* * * * *

The wind had shifted toward the west, and the *Plover* was sailing on a wider tack, tall mainsail and mizzen curved out to starboard. The morning air was crisp and clear, and the sun's light glittered on the water—diamond flashes in the aquamarine glow of the sea.

The Iruks stood at the edge of the quarterdeck, unhooded, long hair moving in the breeze. In their fur capes and leather harnesses, they stood as warriors stand, feet wide apart, hands on belts and sword hilts, their spirit and pluck restored with their weapons. Amlina stood with them, and Captain Troneck beside her.

Below, at the base of the steps, the entire ship's company had assembled. The sailors seemed to Lonn much as they had on the day his klarn captured this ship—perhaps a bit more haggard and sea-weary. They glowered up at the Iruks with angry and sullen expressions.

Amlina and the Iruks repeated the oaths they had sworn to each other, speaking loudly so the whole company could witness. When they had finished the witch addressed the Larthangans.

"These Iruks are to serve as bodyguards to help protect us for the rest of this voyage. You have heard them swear to be at peace with you. Now all of you must likewise swear to put aside your enmity with them."

But the Larthangans only stared at the witch, frowning stubbornly. Amlina watched them a few moments then turned to Troneck, whose head was bowed.

"Why are your men silent, captain?"

"Lady, they ... We have a grudge against these Iruks that is hard to dismiss. They've attacked our ship, wounded two of our crew. It would dishonor us to make peace with them and take them on as shipmates."

"I am ordering you to make this pledge," Amlina replied. "If there is dishonor, it is mine alone."

"A few of our men have sailed these seas before," Troneck told her. "They say the Iruks are well known here as crafty and bloodthirsty rogues. We're not sure they can be trusted to keep their pledge of peace."

"We do not want them on our ship," shouted one of the men below. His fellows grumbled in surly agreement.

"It is true they are pirates," Amlina admitted. "But I have seen in the Deepmind that they will be of help to us on this hazardous voyage. And I have seen in their souls that they can be trusted. I insist that all of you pledge peace with them."

The Larthangans still refused, though fewer of them now dared return the witch's gaze.

"Your men are disagreeable, captain." A shade of threat had entered Amlina's voice.

Troneck cast his eyes at her feet. "Lady, understand us. My men are weary. We've been at sea over a month now, on barely half-rations. First across the ocean with gale winds driving us, then attacked by these barbarians, then into uncharted seas to chase them. Now we're heading back the way we came, with no idea of our destination, and you want us to take on these pirates as shipmates. We are not adventurers, lady, only simple traders."

"Have you forgotten your condition before this voyage began?" Amlina asked, eyes flashing. "How I found you chained to the masts of your own ship in the harbor of Tallyba, waiting to be flayed alive in the Temple of the Sun Goddess? Have you forgotten how I freed you from those chains, gave you back your ship and brought forth a wind to blow us out to sea? Have you forgotten that in exchange for your lives you each pledged yourselves my bondsmen, mine to command so long as I have need of you? If you have forgotten, then I have a token, a hair freely given from each man's head, to remind you of your oath. Will I need to use those tokens?"

Troneck had paled. "No, lady."

"Then down on one knee, all of you, and swear you will keep peace with these Iruks. I want to hear every man's voice."

Reluctantly, Troneck dropped to one knee. In twos and threes the men of the crew followed their captain. Aloud they swore, on pledge of their lives, peace and cooperation with the Iruks.

"Good," Amlina said. "Now back to your duties. And be of good heart. In due time we will return to the Golden Land, and all of you will be made wealthy and called heroes."

The Larthangans dispersed, silent or talking fretfully among themselves.

"Pledge or no pledge," Eben whispered to Lonn, "we'd better post a guard while we sleep."

Lonn nodded. "And keep our blades at hand while awake."

"Lady," Troneck spoke anxiously to the witch. "Do not think me rebellious, but I must talk with you about our course."

"What of it?"

"Please. Let me show you on the charts."

Troneck moved between the ornate hatches and past the windbringers to the helm, where the long tiller was locked in place. He opened a compartment set against the rail and pulled out a yellowed chart, which he unrolled on the deck. Amlina and the Iruks gathered about him.

Lonn was familiar with Tathian charts of the South Polar Sea. It took him only a glance to find the curved peninsula of Fleevan and the hooked cape where Fleevanport was marked.

"We are sailing this way," Troneck's gloved finger traced a northward course to the left of Fleevan. "Your islands," he said to Lonn, "are off the chart. They'd be down past this corner. I put our position roughly here, but perhaps you can correct me. Shortly before dawn we sighted some rocks, four rolling mounds in a line, and some smaller ones."

"The sea lion mating rocks," Eben said.

"That would put us closer to here," Lonn shifted Troneck's finger a bit to the north and east, closer to Fleevanport.

"So," the captain said. "We are sailing this way. Lady, as you can see this Fleevan is the last inhabited land we'll come near for hundreds of leagues. I think we have no choice but to make for it."

"Impossible," Amlina said. "The Cloak's distance from us may be increasing by the hour. We must follow without delay."

"But we are running out of provisions, and there won't be another chance to restock. Besides, we are on soft water now. Sooner or later the freezewind will blow. We could become icebound, far from any help."

"If the freezewind blows we will sail up onto the ice," Amlina replied. "If not, we will work ourselves free and go on."

Troneck was plainly distressed. "No civilized ships will be sailing in this season, but there may be pirates in these waters."

"We have these Iruks to protect us against pirates. That is one reason I've taken them on board."

"But the pirates we meet might be Iruks. Will these five choose to help us against their own people?"

"I've already told you, these Iruks can be trusted to keep their pledge."

"Well, if you say so," the captain grumbled. "One thing is certain: they are five more mouths to feed. You still haven't said what we're to do about provisions."

"What of this small island here," Amlina pointed to the map, "that the Tathian script names Windbock? It can't be many leagues distant, and it lies almost directly on our course."

"Windbock is desert," Troneck answered mournfully. "There are no supplies to be had there."

"You are mistaken, captain," Eben said. "There are provisions available on Windbock: edible berries and lichens, flizzards and shellfish. And there are springs of fresh water a short distance inland. We sometimes stop there in Third Winter, when we hunt that part of the sea."

"Can we gather enough to sustain our company for a lengthy voyage?" Amlina asked.

"With a little work," Lonn said.

"Good." Amlina turned to Troneck. "You will make for Windbock, captain, and lay in for provisioning. I will enter deep meditation this evening. By the time we're ready to depart from Windbock, I will inform you of our destination."

"I hope we make it as far as Windbock," Troneck muttered, rolling up the chart, "and don't get icebound or speared by brigands on the way."

"Do not go expecting disaster," Amlina answered, as though quoting a maxim.

She bid the captain and the Iruks good day and retired below.

* * * * *

Unable to beg a second breakfast from the ship's cook, the Iruks returned to their compartment in the stern. They fired up the oil stove, took off their harnesses and boots, and spread out their capes close to the fire. Karrol regretted aloud the loss of her cape in the sea.

"We may have a chance to get you a new cape," Draven remarked. "If the volrooms come out on Windbock."

Eben had a more troubling thought. "The captain is right about one thing: we may run into pirates between here and the island. And our neighbors could be among them."

"I know," Lonn said. "Let's hope the yulugg have led the fleet far enough east that we miss them."

Draven yawned. "As the witch told the captain, let's not go expecting disaster."

After devouring their noontime rations of tea and biscuits, the Iruks had nothing to occupy themselves until supper. Karrol found a cloth and began oiling the harnesses and iron weapons that had been drenched in the salt water. Draven and Brinda lay down to nap, though they'd had ample sleep from yesterday afternoon through the morning.

Too restless to sleep, Lonn and Eben wandered up on deck. They leaned out over the bowsprit for a time, discussing the klarn's prospects and eyeing the horizon for sails. Eventually, they walked back to the quarterdeck to hold conversation with Kizier.

The bostull, in his distinctive ornate pail, had been set down with the other windbringers and had attuned his mind once more with theirs. Bostulls were a gregarious species among themselves, though the content of their social interaction was generally outside of human ken. The only apparent sign of their sociability was that windbringers, when gathered in groups of two or more, often hummed together. For this reason, the Tathians called any assemblage of bostulls a chorus.

Having nodded to Troneck who stood by the tiller, Lonn and Eben sat down before the windbringers. They bid them good afternoon, and greeted Azzible and Kizier in particular.

Bostulls had human names for human convenience, to distinguish one from another. If the plant-creatures had individual names in their own language, they never mentioned them to humans. Thus Azzible had retained his typical Tathian name, though it might just as easily have been changed to something else. For two days Azzible had been part of this chorus and was already absorbed into its inner harmony. He returned the Iruks' greeting and replied to their questions about his well-being without particular interest. Typically for a bostull, he felt no special emotion or nostalgia about his time with the klarn.

That was what made Kizier so unusual, his human-like personality and keen interest in human affairs.

"Kizier," Eben said. "We've been talking things over and would like to ask you some questions. We're already a great distance behind our dojuk and heading for lands of which we know little, except that they are far-flung and crowded. What chance does Amlina really have of finding the Cloak and Glyssa?"

"Truly, it is impossible to predict," the bostull said. "Mainly it depends on how well Amlina can sense the emanations of the Cloak. It is a thing of great power, and will be hard to hide in the Deepmind. But the one who has it has already shown a high mastery of the shaping arts. Still, Amlina possessed the Cloak, however briefly, and knows the psychic feel of its emanations."

"How briefly did she possess it?" Lonn asked.

"For less than one of Grizna's cycles. She took it from the Bone Tower of the Archimage of the East, and was sailing with it back to Larthang when you Iruks intercepted our ship."

"So it is as we guessed," Lonn said. "Amlina herself stole the Cloak and feared pursuit by its true owner. That is why this coaster was sailing in First Winter and without escort."

"You surmise well," Kizier said. "Your one error lies in assuming the Archimage to be the Cloak's true owner. In fact, that witch stole it herself, more than a century ago. Amlina was returning the Cloak to its rightful owners, the witches of Larthang."

"We've heard this Archimage mentioned again and again," Eben said. "Always with a shifting of eyes and a tremble of the voice. But my impression is that you and Amlina don't think the Archimage is the one who has the Cloak now."

"You are correct again. The mind I sensed moving in your lodge house was unfamiliar to me, and it seemed a masculine mind. Besides, we don't believe the Archimage would cast such designs over a distance. Once she located the Cloak, she would likely come in person, to take it back and to revenge herself on whoever had it. For the first ten days of our voyage, Amlina wove designs to hide us and the Cloak from the seeking mind of the Archimage. Only then did she give in to exhaustion and enter deep trance to restore herself. It was in that state you found her when you took the Cloak. So far, Amlina's designs have held, and the Archimage has not found us—or, if she has, she has left us alone for the time being, to search for the Cloak instead. But sooner or later she will seek out Amlina, for she would never allow one who had stolen from her to go unpunished."

"Tell us more about her;" Lonn prompted. "Since we are Amlina's allies now, we should know about her enemies."

"Indeed you should," the windbringer said. "Well then, the history is that Beryl—for that is the Archimage's name—was at one time a witch of Larthang, of great accomplishment and renown. She advanced to the highest circle in the House of the Deepmind and was made the Keeper of the Cloak of the Two Winds. She would likely have one day become Archimage of the West, but her desires led her in another direction. As she grew older, she became obsessed with herself and could not bear the thought of aging and dying. She took up the studies of blood magic and sorcery, seeking to preserve the youth of her body and become immortal. But these arts are forbidden in Larthang, and when Beryl's peers learned of her unlawful studies, they threatened to break her mind unless she ceased. Instead, Beryl fled from Minhang, the Imperial City, taking the Cloak of the Two Winds with her. She journeyed across the seas and islands until she reached the continent of Nyssan, where sorcery and ancient rites of human sacrifice are still practiced. She came to Tallyba, called the Terrible, mightiest city of Far-Nyssan.

"With her knowledge of the Larthangan arts and the Cloak of the Two Winds in her possession, Beryl soon gained power and rank among the magician priests of Tallyba. She became High Priestess of the Temple of the Sun, which in the practices of Far-Nyssan means she is regarded as the incarnation of the Sun Deity. The victims sacrificed on the altars of that temple are in fact sacrificed to Beryl, their life-force flowing into her body and replenishing its vitality. So her thirst for immortality finds impermanent but effective satisfaction. In time, Beryl destroyed her rival priests one by one and demolished their temples, until she ruled Tallyba absolutely. Then she proclaimed herself Archimage of the East, the first to hold that title since the centuries of the Second Empire, when Larthang last reigned over the Three Nations. In the years since, Beryl has used the Cloak of the Two Winds to subjugate the cities and towns of Far Nyssan, laying waste to field and wood with the freezewind until the people submitted. Thus she is assured a constant stream of young captives for the altars of her temple."

"You speak of this witch with great passion," Eben observed. "More than I've ever heard in a windbringer's voice."

"Yes, with good reason," Kizier murmured. "I was not always a windbringer, you see. The Archimage of the East made me what I am."

Astonished, the two Iruks listened while Kizier related his own tale—how he had been human once, a wandering scholar born on the Tathian island of Glistre. In his 38th year, he had gone to Tallyba and become a resident of the Archimage's court.

"That was years ago," he said, "when Beryl's tyranny was not yet so monstrous and absolute. The city was still open to trade then, and not, as today, shunned by all free vessels, save those unlucky ones like this Larthangan that are blown there by ill weather."

Lonn glanced at Troneck and saw the evil memory reflected on the captain's stern face.

Kizier was still speaking, telling how his wealth of knowledge and tales had made him a favorite of Beryl's. Despite the wickedness and dark magic of Tallyba, Kizier had not feared for his own safety, since the position of wandering scholar, like that of bard, was considered a privileged and protected one by human custom.

"But Beryl finally proved herself beyond all human custom," Kizier continued bitterly. "When the day came that I wanted to leave she forbade me, and when I tried to escape she laid this ensorcellment on me, that I should be transformed into a windbringer, so I could continue to serve her with my knowledge and amuse her with my anecdotes, but would have no hope of ever escaping. I was a prisoner for twenty-six years in Beryl's palace, until Amlina, in making her own escape, managed to steal me away."

"Where does Amlina fit in all this?" Eben asked. "She is a Larthangan. How did she come to Beryl's city?"

"I believe I should let Amlina tell you that herself," the bostull said. "She can give you a better account than I."

Lonn and Eben exchanged frowning glances, wondering what the bostull meant to conceal.

"Then answer us this," Lonn said. "This question weighs on our hearts: Whoever has taken the Cloak, whoever is using Glyssa to bring it to them, what are they likely to do with her once they have it?"

"Again, it is impossible to predict," Kizier replied. "Perhaps she will be killed. But it is also possible she will be kept with her will enslaved, her life-force gradually changing its pattern, until she is no longer the woman you knew but a reflection of the deepshaper's will, a *thrall* as such mindless ones are called."

"You're saying there's no hope of getting her back?" Lonn's voice rose in anguish.

"There *is* still hope," Kizier answered softly. "The change, as I said, is gradual. Glyssa is tough-minded, and it would take a long time to destroy her will completely. If you find her in time you should be able to call her back to herself, with Amlina's help. I regret I cannot give you a more optimistic picture, but you must keep hoping. You must think and believe you will save Glyssa. All else being equal, the Deepmind tends to bring us what we expect."

Lonn and Eben looked at one another, their minds in ferment with all Kizier had said. They asked no more questions and presently Kizier shut his eye and joined the other bostulls in trance. As the Iruks left the rear deck, Kizier was humming with the rest of the chorus.

Seven

Schools of bluefish were sighted two days later, running east, some passing beneath the coaster's scudding hull. The Larthangan crewmen scrambled about on the main deck, unraveling nets and casting them over the side. In their minds the multitudes of fish meant a chance at extra rations.

In the storeroom below, Lonn and his mates were stirred to a different activity: strapping on harnesses and gathering their weapons. It was the first month of First Winter and the bluefish were migrating, escaping the Polar Sea for the warmer ocean. Inevitably, the runs of bluefish in this season were pursued by yulugg herds, also migrating. Often, the yulugg were chased by hunters.

"Less than three spears each," Karrol said, as Draven doled out the weapons. "We'll never hold off a hunting fleet with only these."

"Let's hope we won't have to," Eben said.

The Iruks hurried out on deck and climbed to the forecastle to keep lookout. The last of the bluefish schools swam past the coaster, and there was no sign of yulugg spouts, or sails. The Iruks breathed easier, though still they watched the hazy edges of the sea.

Behind them on the main deck, the Larthangans hauled in their nets, a meager catch of a few dozen fish flailing inside the meshes. Captain Troneck climbed the steps to the forecastle.

"What's the trouble?" he shouted. "Why are you dressed for battle?"

Lonn was starting to explain when the sailor atop the mainmast sang out the alarm. "Sails, Captain Troneck. Ahead to larboard. Lateens!"

"How many?" Troneck shouted.

"A dozen. More. "

"Hunting party," Eben said, squinting into the north.

"Pirates, you mean," Troneck said.

Now Lonn discerned the boats, taking shape in the bright zone where sea and sky blended—dojuks, running toward them.

"Hard to starboard!" Troneck yelled through cupped hands. "Stand by your sheets."

"No!" Lonn grabbed the captain's arm. "Belay that order. We can't outrun them. If we try, they'll attack for sure."

Troneck hesitated, then ordered his helmsman to resume the former course. "What else can we do?"

"Sail straight at them," Lonn answered grimly. "Make *them* turn aside."

"We can't fight twenty boats," Karrol said.

"I know," Lonn answered. "Maybe we can bluff them down. Spread out along the rails. If you have any ideas, let me know."

Moving at a run the Iruks arranged themselves about the three decks, Karrol in the bow, Brinda and Draven amidships, Lonn and Eben returning with Troneck aft. They climbed the steps to the quarterdeck and crouched down in front of Kizier. The windbringer's eye was open and alert.

"Kizier," Lonn said. "I know the witch doesn't want to be disturbed for any reason. But if we don't have her help now she might soon be disturbed by a hundred pirates."

"You must prevent that," the bostull stated firmly. "Her vulnerability in the dark immersion is a chief reason Amlina needs bodyguards. You must not try to wake her, Lonn. It could sever her ties to this world so that she'd never return."

"We'll do what we can," Lonn answered, standing. "But if it comes to a fight, don't expect us to win. Not against Iruks at odds of twenty to one."

"*You* must expect to win," Kizier said. "You must find a way."

Lonn glanced at Eben, who could only shrug, then out beyond the bow at the on-racing dojuks. They approached the coaster at a sharp angle to the wind, lateen sails billowing over the dark, knife-like hulls.

"You should be on the foredeck, Lonn," Eben said. "To speak for the klarn."

Lonn gripped his two spears tightly, "Keep hard to the wind, captain. And tell your men to stay out of sight, as many below decks as possible."

Troneck shouted that order through his megaphone, and the Larthangans aloft moved quickly to comply. A number of the crewmen were fleeing below as Lonn hurried across the main deck, passing near Draven.

"Tell them about the witch, and exaggerate her powers," Draven said. "Maybe we can frighten them off."

Lonn nodded. The truth, with a little embellishment, seemed the best choice to him also. He charged up the steps to the forecastle where Karrol was crouched, waiting.

The dojuks had sailed near enough that Lonn could make out the individual shapes of prows and outriggers. It was indeed the hunting fleet his klarn had quit ... only twelve days ago. It seemed like many more.

"There are boats of Ilga in that party," Karrol said. "Must we kill our own neighbors, Lonn?"

"I hope not. But they'll have to decide. Remember, we are sworn to protect this ship."

The fleet split into two packs as it neared the coaster's prow. The Iruks in the boats were beating their spears together, shouting for the ship to halt. Peering over the rail, Lonn recognized several klarns from Ilga in the forefront.

"Heave to!" the hunters called. "Surrender or we throw our spears."

Lonn jumped up on the rail. Gripping the forestay with one hand, he lifted his two spears high with the other. "Avast! Leave us unmolested. I, Lonn, son Orla, tell you this."

The first dojuks had sailed nearly even with the *Plover*, and from their hulls the Iruk pirates stared in surprise.

"Lonn, what do you here?" shouted a skipper named Bralluk. A respected warrior of Ilga, he commanded one of the lead boats. "What ship is that?"

"A witch's ship, and we are her allies. Steer away, I tell you."

"How came you there?" called a woman captain named Gertraun. Like Bralluk she was the generation older than Lonn and his mates.

The boats were gliding past him now, and Lonn moved aft on the forecastle to answer. "Our mate, Glyssa, was stolen from us by witchcraft. In our quest to find her, we were forced to make alliance with the witch who commands this ship."

"Lonn speaks true," Eben shouted from the quarterdeck. "Our klarn has sworn to protect this witch and her ship!"

"Turn upwind," Bralluk ordered. "We will talk more of this."

"We cannot," Lonn shouted back. "We sail in pursuit of our lost mate. Turn off and leave us in peace."

"Come about," other pirates yelled. "Come about or we fight!"

"We will not come about," Lonn called from the forecastle steps. "Turn and follow if you would speak more."

He watched as the dojuks moved past, swarming on both sides of the coaster. There was brief, loud discussion among the skippers of the boats and their mates. The few Larthangans who'd stayed on deck to man the sails muttered with nervous relief when the last dojuk slipped past the coaster's stern.

But Lonn knew it would not be so easy.

All at once the dojuks came about, sails sweeping, hulls bounding on the coaster's frothy wake. The boats turned smartly, all to leeward, and pursued the *Plover* on its starboard side.

Lonn directed his mates to the starboard rails and rushed himself to the rear deck. He took the megaphone from Troneck and raised it as soon as the boats were in earshot.

"Bralluk, Veela, Gertraun, Harful," he called the skippers he knew by name. "I warn you for your klarns' sake, keep away."

"Where is this witch?" Harful shouted. "We would see her."

Lonn's heart sank. Harful was a younger leader, tough and stubborn. Lonn had always considered him a bully. They had fought once when both were drunk.

"She is below decks," Draven called after Lonn hesitated. "Perhaps weaving magic to trap your souls, or a spell to drown you."

"Or perhaps there is no witch," Gertraun cried. "Perhaps your klarn has taken this ship and wants to keep all the loot for yourselves."

Angry grumbling passed among the close-packed boats. The hunters began shouting for surrender again and rapping their spears together. The dojuks had drawn nearly even with the coaster, close enough for the spears to be cast with deadly effect.

"Turn upwind or have our spears," Harful shouted.

"You will have ours in turn," Lonn answered. "We must protect this ship. Even against our own neighbors."

"We are many and you are few," Bralluk said.

"We have the high decks. Many of you will die before you take the ship. And those who live will still have the witch to deal with."

Lonn could sense their rage and suspicion warring against the uncertainty in their minds. The hunters had let out their sheets a bit and their boats were keeping pace with the coaster, bobbing over the wave made by the ship's prow.

"Show us the witch," Gertraun demanded.

"Let her come out on deck," Harful called. "Perhaps she'll pay us to leave her pretty ship alone."

"The hunting has not been good," Bralluk added. "Your klarn started this hunt with us. We have a right to a share of your booty. That's only fair, Lonn."

Many voices shouted their righteous agreement.

"I tell you there is no booty," Lonn shouted, brandishing his spears. "Leave us, and go back to your hunt."

"Show us the witch," Harful said, "Else I say you are lying."

Lonn jumped onto the rail. "Another day I would split your gut, Harful, for calling me a liar. But now I say just this: sail on and leave us in peace, or come and fight!"

There was a growing, confused uproar of voices as the pirates yelled back at Lonn and argued among themselves. A few of the dojuks veered in closer, but Lonn's mates lifted their spears and bluffed them back. Many of the pirates raised their spears in response, arms tensed to throw, awaiting the word from their skippers.

But the word did not come.

Finally, some of the boats parted from the outer edge of the pack and turned downwind, drifting south again to search for yulugg.

"Your fleet is dispersing," Lonn called to those who remained. "Go with them."

"We will leave," Gertraun answered. "But hear this: Since you refused us a fair share of your catch, we name your klarn outlaw. We claim the right to take what is yours, if not here, then on Ilga."

Along the *Plover's* rails Lonn's mates stared with grim resolve.

"Your naming us outlaws does not make it so," Eben replied. "We only do what we must to hold fast to our klarn, even as we were advised by Belach the shaman."

Eben was correct, under the law. Only tribal elders could declare the klarn outlawed and name what penalty they owed. Of course, that wouldn't save their lodge house on Ilga from being ransacked.

But this was not the day to worry over that.

The last of the dojuks swung away, yards creaking about their masts. The Iruks in those boats still eyed the ship with rancor as they rode away on the luminous sea.

"Beware of meeting me another time, Lonn," Harful shouted, his boat the last to depart. "When you do not have the high place to fight from!"

Lonn deemed it best to let that threat go unanswered.

When the hunting boats were out of earshot, a cheer was raised on the *Plover*—by Iruks and Larthangans alike. More crewmen had spilled from the forecastle onto the main deck. Draven and Brinda rushed up to the quarterdeck to join Eben and Lonn.

"We did it!" Draven danced about, waving his spears. "The five of us faced off twenty klarns."

"Lonn, you bluffed beautifully," Eben shouted.

Lonn only smiled with relief.

But then Karrol reached them from the foredeck, and there were tears of rage in her eyes. "Now every klarn on Ilga will hate us. We'll have no home to go back to, only an island full of enemies. And you're all laughing about it, you stupid men!"

"Brinda's laughing too," Draven answered lamely. "We did save the ship ..."

But Karrol wheeled and marched away. She went to sit alone at the coaster's bow and would speak to no one. Her reaction dampened all the exhilaration the mates had felt. One by one they wandered off, lost in their own thoughts.

All that day Lonn was haunted by the vision foretold by Belach the shaman—that this voyage with the witch of Larthang would take them far away from all that they knew.

He wondered now if they would ever return.

Eight

Windbock hovered white and ghostly over the blue waters of the sea. Ages of blasting ocean wind had sculpted the island's cliffs into fan-like ridges, lopsided domes, and elaborate twisted spires. In places the cliff walls had tumbled, spilling boulders over the beaches and leaving defiles and canyons that wove crookedly inland. Around the cliffs, through crevices, from the mouths of caves and tunnels, unending sea winds blew, singing in weird disharmony.

"Looks as desolate as I would have judged from the charts," Troneck complained. "Are you sure it will stock us for a long voyage, Iruk?"

"I have said so," Lonn answered.

Lonn stood with Troneck and Eben at the taffrail as the coaster skirted the island's southern shore. The warm northwesterly, which had blown reliably for five days and nights, put them in the lee of the island. Lonn pointed out some jagged boulders ahead.

"Keep well to seaward of those rocks," he warned the captain. "They're the peaks of a reef that runs all the way to shore. Beyond the reef is prime anchorage, shielded from heavy seas, and there's fresh water not far inland from the beach."

The coaster sailed well to leeward of the outermost visible boulder, then tacked in toward shore. A seaman on the forecastle yelled out soundings, and Troneck's megaphone was constantly at his mouth as he ordered the crew to man the booms, lower sails, and finally drop anchor. The *Plover* came to rest some eighty yards from shore, rocking gently in the tide.

"A fine mooring place," the captain allowed. "Though not a true harbor, it could easily be made one by the addition of a sea wall and pylons. I wonder that the Tathians never put a settlement on this island, lying as it does almost directly on route from Fleevan to the Isles of Tath."

"The story is told that they did once colonize Windbock," Eben replied. "In our grandparents' time, when the northerners first arrived in the Polar Sea. They established a small way station here for their trading ships. But the volrooms of the island considered this an invasion of their domain. One night they came out and ate all the colonists."

"Ha!" Troneck's laugh was uncertain. "This is a fable you are telling me."

Eben shrugged. "Perhaps it is true. Many believe that volrooms are ... wise, what the Tathians call *sentient*."

"You believe these tusk-bears may be sentient, capable of surprising a whole colony of men, and yet you're not afraid to hunt them?"

"We are Iruks," Eben answered, then turned to follow Lonn down the steps.

Having reefed all sails and secured their booms, the Larthangans were packing the boats and preparing to lower them over the sides. The Iruks had already placed their gear into one of the boats. Now they gathered together at the rail facing the island and put their hands in a pile.

Eben recited a chant for the safety of the klarn and the success of their hunt. Then Lonn addressed the volrooms:

"Tusked ones of Windbock, greetings. We are Iruks, a klarn from Ilga, many leagues to the south. We are coming to your island to seek water and edibles. We seek also your flesh to eat, if you will fight us for it. Come out and eat us, if you can. Otherwise, hide in your lairs as the rock squirrels hide from you in their burrows."

The boats were hoisted out over the waves and lowered on winches. The Larthangans who were going ashore, five men for each boat, climbed down the accommodation ladders. Before moving to follow each of the Iruks embraced Draven, who was staying on board. The klarn had decided that it was best for one of them to remain with the ship. Draven, more even-tempered and less restive than the others, had volunteered.

The Iruks clambered down the rope ladders and into the boats. While the Larthangans manned the oars Lonn and Karrol took charge of the tillers. The boats were skiffs, spacious craft well-designed for ferrying cargo from anchored ship to shore. The skiffs had wooden runners built into their hulls, but no masts or sails. On soft water they were rowed, over ice they were hauled like sleds.

The Larthangans rowed in measured strokes, oar blades circling through the cloudy blue sealight. As the boats pulled away from the ship the wind voices of the island became more prominent—at times a shrill wail, more often a cacophony of whispers.

"That noise will drive us mad," one of the sailors grunted.

"Soon you won't even notice it," Lonn laughed. He was in high spirits. It felt good to be at the helm of a boat again, and going ashore to hunt.

When the skiffs reached the lapping surf of the lagoon, all hands jumped overboard. They dragged the craft safely past the tide line, then talked briefly about how best to divide their labor. It was agreed to split into two groups, one to forage along the beach, the other to start inland in search of fresh water.

Karrol and Eben took the first group, five Larthangans with baskets and sacks, along the shore beneath the towering gray-white cliffs. They would gather edible plants and hunt for crabs, shellfish, and tortoise eggs. Lonn and Brinda led the remainder of the crewmen, who carried kegs and water skins, up a rocky slope and through a crevice.

Their path curved around a high outcropping of silver-flecked stone, then over and beneath a series of wind-carved natural bridges. Finally, they emerged in a gently declining ravine with steep walls on either side. Lonn and Brinda marched with spears in hand, their eyes constantly scanning the walls and ledges overhead. There were occasional cries of seabirds nesting on the cliffs above, and once a startled rodent scurried across their path. But Lonn saw no sign of volrooms.

They passed through an airy natural tunnel and out into a wider ravine. Here shrubs and graceful ferns grew in clusters, adding their verdure to the sandweeds and milk cactus the party had encountered up till now. It was in these small inland valleys that fresh water was most likely to be found. Lonn and Brinda started searching, putting their ears to the rock to listen for the murmur of underground springs, pushing fronds aside to look for open water holes. At last they discovered a trickle running clear and cold from a fissure in the canyon wall. They followed its meandering course along the base of the rock, pushed through a circle of dense shrubbery and came to the edge of a deep, still pool.

* * * * *

Flowing water, murky gray to silvery bright, swirling in rings and whirlpools. Floating bubbles of fiery color, images and scenes, flashes of insight and knowledge. Thus Amlina the witch perceived the Deepmind on her fifth night of trance.

The *dark immersion*: awareness turned absolutely inward, thereby fully outward. In the first hours and days, the individual's mind dissolved, a surrendering plunge, a dissemination through the whole of the Deepmind. Only gradually, in two or three or four days, did the mind begin to regather, energized now by the infinite creativity of the Ogo. A deepshaper needed this ritual trance or their powers began to weaken. How often depended on the strength of the shaper, but a witch of Larthang normally immersed herself in accord with the moon cycle of Grizna—at least once in 32 days.

So Amlina had drifted back to consciousness after two days in the luxurious bliss of unknowing. Lying down one moment, she had sat up on her bunk the next, legs folded beneath her, unaware that her body had moved or even yet that she had a body. From her first moment of returning awareness her mind had sought the Cloak of the Two Winds.

She had planned it this way, fixing the image of the Cloak in her mind as she performed the gestures and incantations prior to immersing. With a strong and disciplined will—and with the luck of the Ogo in favor—a deep-gazer could perceive objects and events they desired, however remote in time and space.

But so far Amlina had not seen the Cloak. Some other shaper was concealing it, and the concealment still held, as it had against her earlier, intuitive searching. This other shaper was strong, efficient in his designs. (It did seem to be a male. Amlina's sense of the mind thwarting her efforts agreed with Kizier's impression.)

But Amlina had known already that the shaper was strong. Doubtless this very knowledge had undermined her efforts to see the Cloak up till now.

This thought, examined as it occurred, bothered the witch. It showed by its reflective self-interest how close she was to the surface mind. And still no glimpse of the Cloak. Dolefully, Amlina released all will and let the stream of impressions take her.

She saw the moors of western Larthang, where she had passed her childhood—under the domination of an ill-tempered, tyrannical mother. To escape her mother's scoldings and harangues she had often run alone on the moors, spending every free moment away from the house. So Amlina perceived herself now, in this scene of the Deepmind. She appeared perhaps eleven, ambling over a slope covered with bluebells and orange fop-flowers. A lovely place, but the girl was vaguely frightened and chanted an old hymn to ward off evil. Perhaps a heath demon lurked nearby.

Amlina blinked with impatience.

The scene of the moor vanished, a scattered image in a liquid mirror. The scene had no counterpart in her memory. Perhaps it was a dream she'd once had, or a daydream—for all mental levels had their reflections in the Deepmind. Perhaps the scene held a symbolic key to the knowledge Amlina sought.

But this was frustrating. The knowledge she needed was direct and objective. She had no time for delving into symbolism.

Her body shifted on the bunk.

Already the troublesome concept of time had returned. She must be very near the surface level. Even now her eyes could dimly perceive the ship's cabin, with its desmets and hanging prisms, amidst the drifting waters of the Deepmind.

The dark wooden beams of the cabin recalled to her a city where she once had lived: Kadavel, with its wooden piers and miles of boarded streets. It was a crowded Tathian city, haughty and filthy, a trading center auspiciously located at the crossroads of the Three Nations.

Thoughts of Kadavel had recurred several times since Amlina first regained the spark of awareness. She wondered if this was the Deepmind's answer, that Kadavel was where she must search for the Cloak. But perhaps she was clutching at this for lack of any true revelation. This uncertainty prodded her mind as she stared at the cabin, now in clearer focus.

Uncertainty, and yet the need to believe with absolute certainty—such was the constant dilemma of the deepshaper. The Ogo did not always conform to the designs one cast upon it. Yet if one did not believe in those designs absolutely, they were that much less likely to succeed.

Amlina had all but returned to the surface mind and had not succeeded in finding the Cloak. Or had she? The witch reviewed the various ideas and images that lingered in her memory: ships and islands and moors, Larthang and Kadavel and Tallyba, the frightening face of Beryl the Archimage, who even now must be hunting Amlina and the Cloak—unless indeed it was she who had taken it. (This could not be ruled out.)

Amlina uncrossed her legs and stood, faltering a little as her ankles were numb. She brushed past the dangling trinkets, neglecting for now the precise rituals of taking them down and putting them away. She opened the door of her cabin and stepped outside. She needed to talk with Kizier.

Traversing the short passageway, she became aware of the hunger and thirst that inevitably followed several days of deep trance. Yet there was also a feeling of light-headed vitality, a lingering sparkle in her vision, a tingle to the air in her lungs.

She opened the door onto the main deck and discovered that it was nighttime. Four or five or six nights since she'd isolated herself in her cabin? She did not know. She breathed the cool, fresh air with pleasure. The ship was unrigged and riding at anchor. A glance over the rail disclosed the dark shore of the island, and campfires burning on the beach.

One of the Iruks approached Amlina from across the deck. She saw it was a male, the one called Draven.

"Have you found Glyssa?" he asked her.

"I don't know. I have impressions. I must talk them over with Kizier." She mounted the steps to the quarterdeck, Draven following directly behind.

Amlina touched the stalk of the windbringer and stroked him once, gently. Kizier's eye opened. With his windbringer's intuition, he could tell at once that she had reached no definite conclusion.

"What were your perceptions?" he asked.

Standing on the quiet quarterdeck, her voice a murmur, Amlina rehearsed the thoughts and images she recalled.

"And when you were in the outer stages and purposefully turned your mind to the Cloak?"

"I felt resistance, viewed empty skies and waters."

"And sensed some motive or nature concealing the Cloak?"

"Barely," Amlina said. "Only that the one hiding it seemed to be male and ... steeped in ancient knowledge. Otherwise, I could not assign personality or definite motive."

"You know nothing more than when you started?" Draven asked.

Amlina could not repress a sigh as she looked at him. But in his face she found not the reproachful glower she'd expected, only worry and sympathetic concern. Draven was more kindly disposed toward her than the other Iruks. Amlina had noticed this before.

"I am doing what I can," she told him softly.

"Now," Kizier said. "I ask you where the Cloak is. What picture comes to mind?"

"The walls of Kadavel," Amlina said, turning her gaze to an inward focus. "And above them in a dark sky, the shining face of Beryl."

Kizier watched her without response.

"The juxtaposition is improbable," Amlina complained. "If Beryl had the Cloak she would not take it to Kadavel."

"Is this something you know beyond all doubt?" the bostull asked.

"No. Admittedly not. But nor do I know that Kadavel is the answer I am seeking."

"Yet you must choose a direction," the windbringer said.

Amlina was quiet for a time. A cold breeze rippled over the deck. The sea lapped at the coaster's hull. The Iruk called Draven stared at the witch with patient intensity. Amlina shivered and pulled her silken robe tight at her neck.

"Your comrades are on the island?" she asked Draven.

"Yes. Gathering food." Then, anxiously: "Why do you ask?"

Keen of intuition, these Iruks. Amlina saw there was no use dissimulating with him. "As I felt that chill I saw them surrounded by violent radiances. They may be in danger."

* * * * *

Lonn tensed and held his spear ready to throw. He peered across the dim beach into the deeper gloom below the cliff. He might have seen a movement there, a flash of gray in the darkness.

Behind him the low surf tossed, and the Larthangans padded over the wet sand, digging and collecting. During daylight the party had made two trips back to the watering place and had filled the large casks they had brought ashore. The skiffs were more than half packed with this water and with eggs, drying herbs, and roots. Tomorrow they would ferry this first load of provisions back to the *Plover*. Since nightfall, when the tide went out, the Larthangans had ranged along the bright shoreline, foraging for clams, sandfish, and other comestibles. Lonn and Eben had accompanied them, leaving Brinda and Karrol to take turns napping and guarding the skiffs.

Noiselessly, Eben moved up beside Lonn. "Something?"

"I'm not sure," Lonn said. "Wait here."

Lonn stole up the gentle slope of the beach. The darkness thickened about him as he left the glowing lagoon behind. The breeze stirred and Lonn sniffed the air, all senses alert.

Nothing.

He crept forward to the place he thought he had seen the movement, where the shadow of the cliff began, and peered along the rugged wall.

Still nothing.

Lonn turned and headed back toward the shore, still listening intently as he moved. This vigilance saved his life.

The brush of sand under massive paws made him whirl as the volroom charged. The beast had been crouching by some boulders and Lonn had mistaken its gray-white bulk for one of the rocks. Now he glimpsed gleaming tusks and tiny eyes and just had time to level his spear before the brute collided with him.

"Volroom!" Lonn shouted, staggering backward.

A roaring answer came from the darkness along the cliffs. The volrooms had come out on Windbock.

Lonn lost his footing and crashed to his back in a patch of weeds. The volroom, stalled a moment by the spear stuck in its shoulder, now leapt at him. But Lonn rolled aside and scrambled to his feet.

Three more tusk-bears were loping toward him from beneath the cliff.

"Karrol, Brinda!" Eben's bellowing voice grew louder as he raced up from the shore. "Volrooms!"

Lonn apprehended all this in an instant, as he bent low to meet the first volroom's attack. The creature reared on hind legs, nearly as tall as Lonn and easily three times his bulk. But it could not match the Iruk's speed. Ducking beneath the swiping claws Lonn plucked his spear free. Head tucked low and shoulders hunched, he lunged, growling in reply to the volroom's roar. The spear pierced the animal's belly, puncturing the tough layer of muscle and sliding into the soft entrails. Hot blood spurted over Lonn's arms and harness.

Enraged, the volroom clutched at him with fore and hind paws, seeking to drag him down. Scratched through his leggings, Lonn managed to squirm free, stumbling, then righted himself. He drew his knife and sword in a swift-handed motion.

The wounded volroom staggered toward him, claws raised. The other three had drawn near and were circling in on all fours.

Then Eben arrived with a ferocious yell. He stopped next to Lonn and flung a spear. His yell was punctuated by a yip of pain as the spear struck a volroom in the side.

Drawing his steel Eben darted forward, wheeling and stabbing, occupying two more tusk-bears while staying clear of their claws and teeth. Meantime, Lonn sidestepped the feeble charge of the first bear and cut its snout with his sword. The blow brought a stream of blood that half-blinded the volroom, which turned and shook, unable to spot the Iruk. Lonn leaped behind the confused bear and finished it with a sweeping overhead sword blow that cut deep into the creature's neck. The bear collapsed on the sand and shuddered as it died.

Karrol and Brinda were racing across the beach with shouts of excitement. Eben was still nimbly fighting off two of the bears. The fourth volroom, wounded by Eben's spear, circled clumsily, uncertain whether to attack or retreat. Lonn jerked his sword free of the dead volroom's neck and charged to stand with Eben.

Seconds later the women arrived and helped end the fight.

Karrol's spear drove one bear to the ground where Lonn's thrusting sword found its heart. Brinda and Eben cornered another volroom against the piled boulders and stabbed it to death with their swords. The last volroom turned to flee and Karrol pursued it, spear held high. Lonn started to go after her, then realized she would need no help. Screaming with glee she caught the limping bear and fell upon it. Lonn saw her spear descend again and again until the volroom's roars had ceased.

Drenched in blood, Lonn checked himself for damage. He found only shallow scratches on his legs and a stiffening shoulder that had been wrenched in the shock of the first bear's charge.

"Foolish volroom," he muttered to the slain bear at his feet. "If you could not rouse your fellows you should never have tried to take us four against four. Did you think that because we are separated our spirit is broken? We are still a klarn. We will be together again."

* * * * *

For two more days the Iruks and Larthangans gathered provisions on Windbock and ferried them back to the ship. No more volrooms showed themselves. The Iruks skinned and butchered the four they had killed, scraped and stretched out the hides and set the meat in the sun to dry. The bones they buried in the sand, performing a rite designed to ensure the replenishment of the volroom race.

When the skiffs had returned four times to the coaster and the larders and water casks on board were nearly full, the klarnmates loaded the meat and furs onto the boats and prepared to take their leave. In the late afternoon, the sailors pushed the skiffs out into the gleaming water. The Iruks lingered on the beach, holding hands as they faced the tall cliffs. They gave thanks to the island for its hospitality and to the Volroom Spirit for providing them with meat and furs and the chance to test their hardihood.

When the skiffs had been hoisted back on board and the last of the provisions stowed below, Amlina assembled the whole ship's company on the main deck and addressed them.

"In accord with the guidance of the Deepmind, I have decided on our destination. We sail at once for the Tathian city of Kadavel on the island of Lustre, there to find and regain the Cloak of the Two Winds for Larthang. Captain Troneck estimates that with good weather we will reach the city in 20 to 25 days."

"With good weather and no freezewind snagging us," Troneck grumbled.

"We will anticipate only good fortune," the witch said.

But for all her brave words, Lonn detected a note of uncertainty in Amlina's voice. The Larthangans seemed relieved: at least the Islands of Tath were a civilized region. The crewmen dispersed at Troneck's orders, to hoist the anchor and unfurl the sails.

"What of Glyssa?" Karrol asked the witch. "Did you see her?"

Amlina frowned at her distantly before answering. "Her image was not disclosed to me. I am sorry." The witch took her leave then and retired to her cabin.

The Iruks went below decks to stow their harnesses and weapons. They searched out some pegs and leather thongs and used them to stretch the partially cured furs in an empty corner of the ship's hold. By the time they returned to the main deck, it was evening and the coaster was underway, leaving Windbock and the South Polar Sea astern.

Part Two

To Kadavel on Lustre

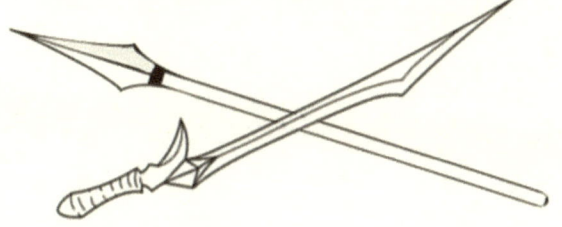

Nine

The *Plover* journeyed northward on the trackless ocean. No sail or island disturbed the small ship's perfect solitude, no rock or yulugg spout. There was only the huge sky and the wide, glimmering waters.

The Iruks were often at the rails those first days out, watching the far horizons with a kind of superstitious wariness. To them, the great ocean was the limit of the world. They never ventured far upon it, and then only with caution. Their ancestors had believed that the ocean turned to a lifeless realm of steam not many days north of Windbock. Iruks of the present day knew of other shores to the north, the Isles of Tath and distant Nyssan. As for the east, they were not so sure. Lonn's klarn had heard one travelling scholar claim that Glimnodd was a sphere, that the eastern ocean eventually joined the ocean in the west. But the Iruks were far from convinced.

They took the question to Kizier, who was amused by their skepticism. "Oh, yes. Glimnodd is round and circled by the Ocean. One Tathian poet refers to 'The world-girding Ocean,' and 'The belt-buckle Isles of Tath.' "

"What islands lie ahead on this part of the Ocean?" Lonn inquired. When his klarn had sailed the ocean in the past it was always to the south and east of Windbock, chasing yulugg herds.

"To the east," Kizier said, "there is no land save a small, half-legendary isle called Alone, very far and hard to find. To the west of us lie the Worm Isles, the dwelling place of furworms and other monsters spawned in the Age of the World's Madness. But you know the southernmost of those islands at least. It is Dekyll, where you first encountered this ship."

"We know Dekyll but never land there," Eben answered. "We know of the fire-breathing worms."

"Just so," the bostull said. "North of the Worm Isles lie the Shoals of Sarn, where once was a prosperous human realm. But that land sank during the centuries of disruption. Now it is a place of whirlpools and treacherous reefs shunned by seamen of all nations. Some mariners call the Shoals 'The Drain of the Sea,' claiming there is a hole there where the ocean falls into a lower world. But this is usually regarded as an ignorant and fatuous idea. North of the Shoals are the Tathian Isles, chief of which are Glistre, Borga, Xinner, and Lustre, where we are bound."

That afternoon the northwest wind, which had blown favorably since the last sea-change, began to slacken. The breeze puffed intermittently for a day and a night, then died altogether. The chorus of windbringers strove continually to bring forth gusts, but their particular deepshaping power was less effective in periods of full calm. Much of the time the *Plover's* sails hung lifeless in the still air.

Apparently, the witch had no designs or spells capable of aiding the windbringers—at least none that had much effect. Amlina stayed mostly in her cabin, but what she did there the Iruks could only guess. When she did come out, usually in the afternoons, it was for short periods only, to walk the decks and breathe the fresh air, to stare out to sea or talk a bit with Troneck or Kizier. Her replies to the Iruks' inquiries never varied much: she had not yet seen Glyssa nor the Cloak, but was searching for them still; she thought the weather would change soon, but could not say exactly when.

On the fourth day of calm, a misty gray wall rose in the south. In a few hours, the front overtook the *Plover*. A stiff wind filled the sails and the ship was able to run before it. But the new weather was not entirely heartening to the voyagers. Wind from the south meant a drop in temperatures and soon, likely, a freeze.

That evening no stars came out and Grizna's face did not break through the clouds. A chill rain began to fall, and past midnight it changed to sleet. A slick layer of ice soon covered all parts of the ship, and the sailors on the night watch slipped and cursed as they moved about the decks.

Below in their storeroom cabin, the Iruks slept close together under blankets and furs. Toward morning, Lonn was visited by a dream.

He saw himself on board the dojuk, but none of his mates were there. He manned the tiller, but otherwise the hunting boat somehow sailed itself, running fleetly over smooth ice. There was beauty in the swift glide of the dojuk, a beauty Lonn had lately missed. But something troubled him in the dream, something he could not name.

Soon the dojuk came upon a ship, a huge flat-bellied craft with three masts and three black sails. The wind that had driven the dojuk died, and the boat slid up near the three-master and stopped. Lonn watched as men climbed down from the ship and shuffled toward him across the ice. Then he saw with a shock they were not men, only empty white robes that moved like men.

Silently the white-clad ghosts climbed aboard the dojuk. One of them loosed the halyard and let the yard drop with a crash. Lonn wanted to stop them, to repel these eerie boarders. But he could not move—his limbs would not respond to his will. He could only stand helpless and watch as several of the robes lifted the mast from its step and let it topple forward, banging as it hit the prow. Lonn could not understand why they did this. Then one of the robes came and touched him on the hand and gestured that he must follow. He could not resist, though every particle of him wanted to. He found himself stepping across the ice toward the black ship and noticed with a surge of horror that now *he* was wearing a loose white robe.

Lonn stood with the line of ghosts along the ship's rail, looking down at the partly dismantled dojuk. There was a tall figure in black and silver at the stern of the ship, whose face was hidden by a cowl but whose hands showed, gray and scaly like fishes. The hands pointed down at the dojuk and a roar blew out of the sky.

A cloud of silvery light rippled into being. The ice about the dojuk shimmered and changed to water. A moan of awe sounded from the empty robes. The silver light was spinning, stirring the dojuk in a deepening whirlpool that spiraled down from sky to sea in an unbroken sweep of force. Lonn looked on in despair as the dojuk was pulled under. Then the wind shrieked to a higher pitch and bits of ice flew in the silvery whirlwind. The melted water heaved and shuddered, then solidified into gleaming ice. No trace of the dojuk remained.

Lonn moaned and turned in his sleep. The dream changed, a progression of images fading one to another: the black ship racing over shiny, frozen seas; groups of ghostly robes performing intricate rituals in the holds of the ship. Lonn saw himself taking part, still wearing the hooded robe, still unable to move except in unison with the others.

Then he dreamed the ship entered a harbor, a huge and crowded port. Above the harbor rose a gigantic city of wood and stone. A wooden wall ran along the waterfront, with massive gates, their arches carved into dragons. Staring at one of the dragons, Lonn felt a tingle of dread. He looked down at his hands and saw they were vague, fading. His body was disappearing, he was becoming another empty robe.

But it was not Lonn—He knew this with an icy, stabbing insight. In that moment all the pieces of the dream came together. It was not Lonn who was fading, *it was Glyssa.*

"No ... No! Glyssa!"

"Lonn. Wake up!"

"No!" He came awake, staring madly in the cold storeroom.

"What is it? What did you dream?" His mates clustered about him, sleepy-eyed except for Draven who had been keeping watch and was holding a spear.

"What of Glyssa?" Karrol demanded.

Staring at the floor Lonn told them of the dream. It was exceptionally vivid in his mind, as few dreams ever were, and he repeated every detail.

"The witch should hear this," Draven declared.

"No," Karrol said. "You know it's bad luck to tell a dream outside the klarn."

"Amlina is our partner now," Draven said. "The dream may help her find Glyssa."

But Karrol held out stubbornly. The klarn argued the matter for some time, Brinda and Eben insisting on considering every point of view. Lonn hardly listened. He sat hugging his knees, still plunged in the desolate emotion of the dream.

Finally, the klarn decided to bring the dream to Kizier. If he thought it important enough, they would share it with the witch. They considered it less unlucky to divulge private klarn matters to a nonhuman creature. The mates put on their clothes and tramped upstairs to the quarterdeck.

It was a dreary morning, the sky ominous. The sleeting had stopped but the decks were still slippery. The wind blew strong and bitter on the coaster's stern.

"Kizier," Draven squatted down to touch the windbringer. "You must hear what Lonn has dreamed."

Lonn repeated the dream in a mumbling voice, his mates filling in details here and there that he neglected. When he had finished, Kizier had him go over the description of the city and harbor once more.

"You were right to inform me," the bostull whispered excitedly. "Take me below to Amlina's cabin. We must tell her at once."

"Will the dream help her find Glyssa?" Karrol asked.

"Take me below," Kizier said. "All of you come."

Brinda and Draven lifted the windbringer's pail and toted him down the steps, Lonn and the others following.

"Knock on the door first," Kizier said as they approached Amlina's cabin.

Karrol leaned around them and rapped sharply on the door. The witch asked who it was, then told them to enter.

The Iruks pushed open the door and stopped, gaping in wonderment. Amlina sat on a cushion in the center of the room. Her eyes were open and alert, yet her body seemed in a state of utter repose. All about her was motion, shifting patterns of shadows and multicolored light. The flicker of tiny lamps was scattered and reflected by prisms and desmets, which spun on their silk threads as though moved by an impalpable breeze.

"Come in," Amlina repeated.

The revolving of the trinkets slowed as the Iruks carried Kizier inside and set him down by the witch. Amlina did not rise, and the klarnmates sat or knelt on the floor around her.

"Lonn has had a dream," the bostull said. "A visionary dream, I think, of true events."

Amlina listened while Kizier told the dream, using practically Lonn's exact words and missing not a single detail. The witch's placid expression never altered, though her eyes did widen once, when the bostull mentioned the carved dragons on the harbor gates.

"So you think he's seen Kadavel and the Cloak arriving there?"

"It seems likely, does it not?"

The witch sighed. "That the dream pictures Kadavel is obvious enough. But that doesn't necessarily mean the Cloak is there. Isn't it just as likely that Lonn picked up the image of Kadavel from me, since it's often been in my mind's eye these past days?"

"Perhaps," the bostull said. "On the other hand, it is now 24 days since Glyssa disappeared with the Cloak, her craft driven by its wind-making magic. If I estimate speed and distances correctly, we might expect her boat—or a ship she'd transferred to—to reach Kadavel at about this time."

"I will grant you that," Amlina said, stretching her arms. "I've calculated it about the same."

"What is more," Kizier said, "these Iruks have a strong mental bond among members of their group. Lonn, as leader, seems to be a focal point of that bond. The designs concealing the Cloak would not necessarily sever such a bond, especially if Glyssa's mind was reaching out to her friends."

The witch considered. "Perhaps you are right, Kizier. Perhaps it is a hopeful sign."

"Perhaps it is much more," the windbringer answered. "If Lonn truly made contact with Glyssa, across distance and whatever barriers exist in the Deepmind, then perhaps the contact can be re-established."

"Could be," Amlina allowed. "If his dreaming is lucky."

"You miss my point. Perhaps Lonn can be taught to make this mental contact while awake."

"How?" Lonn demanded.

"By training you to deepsee."

"Now wait, Kizier—" Amlina began.

"Don't you see?" the bostull interrupted. "This could be the reason the Iruks are here, the purpose they are meant to serve on this voyage."

"But you speak of a process of training that takes years," Amlina protested. "And there's no teacher available. Certainly, I'm not equipped to train him."

"You recall your own training, don't you? I know you have a copy of *The Canon of the Deepmind*, which contains the initiation ceremony. Besides, didn't you tell me once that in the arts of the *wei* the teacher is only a guide, that the student mostly teaches herself?"

"Yes. But the learning takes time, much time."

"But some visionary breakthroughs commonly occur all during the training, especially soon after initiation. Is this not so?"

"If this training may help us find Glyssa, then we must try it," Lonn told the witch.

"Do not be so quick to volunteer," Amlina said. "You have no idea what we're talking about. The training of a deepseer is difficult and painful. It requires the initiate to abandon normal patterns of thought and belief. It means opening yourself to the immeasurable power of the Deepmind. There are some who venture into those depths and never find their way out."

Lonn looked at Kizier.

"What Amlina says is true," the bostull admitted. "It would be unfair not to warn you of the perils. All I can promise is that she and I will do all we can to guide you if you wish to try."

The klarnmates stared solemnly at Lonn, but he had little sense of their opinions. It was solely his decision, and his heart told him there could be only one.

"I will undertake this training," he told the witch. "You will teach me."

"I will think about it," Amlina said.

"It might be better to start at once," Kizier suggested, "while the dream is still fresh in his mind."

Amlina frowned, pondering. Abruptly, she rose to her feet and went to open one of her trunks. She picked out a small gilt-covered book and thumbed through the pages, still frowning. She read for a few moments, looked over at Lonn, then finally walked back to where the Iruks were sitting.

"Very well," she said to Lonn. "Since you and Kizier both insist on this, we will try it. You must take off your boots and belt and sit cross-legged on the floor. The rest of you must leave."

"I don't like this," Karrol muttered in Iruk.

"Go," Lonn said.

The mates glanced at one another and grimly nodded their assent. They bid Lonn good luck, touched his shoulder, then filed from the cabin.

Amlina moved about the chamber blowing out the lamps, except for one which she placed on the floor in front of Lonn. She instructed him to breathe slowly and deeply, and to focus his eyes on the small flame inside the glass.

Lonn obeyed, but when the witch had kept him in that position for a very long time without further instruction, his thoughts grew restless and his eyes left the lamplight. He spotted Amlina sitting on her bunk, reading the small book in the blue light of the stained glass window.

"Keep watching the flame," Amlina said.

"For how long?"

"Until I tell you otherwise. Initiation is normally preceded by weeks of such exercises. Do you want to undertake this training or don't you?"

Scowling, Lonn gazed down at the lamp. He estimated that the morning had turned to afternoon by the time he heard the witch move from her spot. He steadfastly refused to look at her until she had sat down on her cushion and told him to do so.

Amlina wore the same silk gown as before but had removed her jewelry and slippers. She looked pale and girlishly pretty to Lonn, but her voice was stern and forceful.

"You seek to look into the One Mind, the Allmind. To do this you must surrender your body, surrender your thoughts, surrender all hopes and desires and fears, that you may look upon the Ogo with complete openness and detachment. Are you willing to surrender yourself completely?"

"Yes."

"Say it."

"I am willing to surrender myself completely."

"Relax."

The word had a surprising effect on Lonn who had thought himself fully relaxed already. But now he sensed release, tension flowing out from all his parts.

"I will touch you in the places where your nerves gather," Amlina said. "With each touch, the feeling in that place will disappear."

She placed her fingertips on the soles of his feet and murmured a short invocation. There was a burst of warmth in his feet, and when that faded all sensation was gone. Amlina repeated the touch at his knees, his groin, his lower back, his heart, the back of his neck. When it was done, Lonn no longer felt his body, only his face floating in the shadowy cabin.

"Close your eyes," Amlina said.

Eyes shut, Lonn felt her fingertips on his forehead and heard her whisper.

"Know that you are thought. This world called Glimnodd is but thought, one thought of an infinity. Infinite worlds and suns and seas, infinite bodies and minds, all are only thoughts of the One Mind, which comes to know itself by thinking. Know further this: that the One Mind is within you, with all its worlds and suns and creatures. Now let your inner eye be opened that you may see what the Ogo gives you to see."

Amlina chanted briskly, magic words Lonn did not know. A jolt of energy entered his forehead, bursting at the center of his skull. Instantly this energy radiated outward, surging through the cabin and echoing back to Lonn. Eyes still closed, it was as if he could suddenly see in all directions at once. His mind vibrated with perceptions of scintillating lights and spinning forms. The witch's hanging trinkets whirled and reflected his mind's energy, heightening, intensifying his consciousness.

Then, as Amlina's chant ended in a series of high notes, Lonn's awareness exploded from the cabin. In a glittering rush his mind soared upward, past the sky, beyond the spheres of the moons and sun, out to an unending chaos bright with the fires of innumerable stars.

For an unknown time, his mind floated in that outer chaos. He saw stars born from dust, collecting, spinning, flaring into brilliance, then bursting asunder, fading into darkness and dust again. He saw worlds, spherical worlds as the bostull had said, uncountable numbers of them swimming among the stars. The worlds were filled with life, creatures beyond number, spawning, devouring, being devoured ... Knowledge came to him, born of these visions yet known for truths: *These cycles were eternal.* Dust and light, creation and destruction, life and death—all were only thought, the will of the One to know itself: *Ogo.*

To Lonn, the visions were stupendous, stunning. And, upon reflection, appalling. All living things were only thoughts, flickering then dark forever. Terrible. *Unendurable.*

"Open your eyes."

He stared wildly: shadows and shapes he could not recognize. He was breathing hard, choking.

"Relax," Amlina said. "Be at peace."

Streams of sparks glittered before his eyes. The ideas of infinity and eternity loomed gigantic in his mind.

"Relax."

Amlina touched him and her touch made him obey. He breathed easier, and the flashes of light diminished. The flow of vision began to take on recognizable forms. He saw the gleam of three eyes watching him with intent concern. Around the eyes, half lit, half lost in darkness, the shapes of Amlina and Kizier.

Amlina and Kizier. Then he remembered that he was Lonn. Lonn the son of Orla, the leader of his klarn. He had undertaken this witch's rite in order to search for Glyssa.

Lonn rocked forward, grimacing. The thought of Glyssa pierced him with anguish. He recalled his dream, felt again the awful moment when he realized that Glyssa was fading. He was breathing heavily again, trembling.

"Relax," Amlina said.

Lonn shook his head. "Glyssa ..."

"Where is Glyssa?" Kizier asked.

"She is lost. She is vanishing!"

The shadows seemed solid, closing him in. He looked at the windows, and suddenly he had to get outside. He jumped up and bolted for the door.

"Stop!" Amlina cried.

Some quality in her voice made him freeze. He stood shaking, staring at the door, longing to escape, his panic as fierce as it was senseless.

Amlina moved to him. When she put a hand on his shoulder he crumpled to the floor and curled up, whimpering.

"Don't be afraid," Amlina said. "Your fear arises from lack of detachment."

Her words meant nothing to Lonn. He stared into the darkness that drifted and quivered about him. Glyssa was fading to nothingness, and he and his mates were helpless to save her. How could they go on without her? And it was his fault. Glyssa was lost because Lonn had dreamed of this ship and had greedily clung to the dream despite omens and warnings that were plain to others. Glyssa herself had tried to warn him.

"I wouldn't listen," Lonn whispered in abject despair. "I wouldn't listen."

Amlina's voice murmured wearily above him. "This was not well-decided, Kizier."

The witch let Lonn lie there for a long time, but finally she must have helped him up. Lonn remembered sitting on the floor before the lamp again, and Amlina and Kizier asking him about Glyssa. But their questions made him withdraw into silence. Thinking of her was too painful. After a while, the witch gave up trying. She took out the mirrored spinner she had used when she first spoke with the Iruks in this chamber, and set it going for Lonn to watch. The entrancing motion calmed him, and eventually he slept.

* * * * *

Lonn awoke alone, lying beneath a fur in the Iruks' cabin. The stove was warm to his touch and daylight shone behind the small windows.

The same day or the next? Lonn had no idea.

He pulled on his sea boots and found his way groggily to the steps. He was going to knock on Amlina's door but changed his mind and went out on deck instead.

A cold wind blew from the south, and the sky was overcast. The sea was leaden, glossed with a pearly aura. Lonn spotted his mates on the foredeck, practice-fencing with their swords and knives. They hailed him as he walked forward.

"Lonn," Draven said. "We thought you might sleep all day. Are you all right?"

"Is this the same day I started it, or the next?"

"The next day," Draven laughed. "Amlina brought you downstairs in the middle of the night. Your eyes were shut and she was guiding you. She said you were sleeping though you walked, and that we should let you sleep it off. We were worried. Karrol almost got into a fight with the witch, trying to make her explain what she'd done with you."

"I didn't like the way you looked," Karrol said. "And I still don't. What happened, Lonn?"

He leaned his back against the railing. "It's hard to explain. She used power from her hands to make me relax. Then I began to see visions. It was like dreaming, but I was awake."

"Did you see Glyssa?" Eben asked.

"No, I don't think so."

"Amlina said it was only an initiation," Brinda remarked. "And that she warned you it could be painful."

"She did warn me," Lonn grumbled, then changed the subject. "Somebody lend me their blades so I can practice."

He borrowed Draven's sword and dagger and fenced a while, matching feints and thrusts first with Karrol, then Eben. It was vital for fighters to keep in practice, and the slippery deck was excellent for honing agility and balance. But Lonn's thoughts were elsewhere, and he didn't provide his mates much of a challenge.

The Iruks stopped fencing when food was brought, their midday rations of hot soup, water and a half-cup of brandy for each. The brandy had lately been added to the daily fare due to the turn of cold weather and a shortage of tea. The diligent cabin boy served them, as he did the Larthangans on duty, from a covered pot and two full water skins. He also carried a sack with wooden cups and bowls inside.

Karrol tasted the soup and spat it out, cursing the cook's ineptness in the preparation of volroom meat and herbs. The soup was indeed a greasy mess, but Lonn had no appetite anyway. He gulped down his water, then savored the brandy, making it last four swallows.

After that he stood at the rail and stared out to sea, thinking again of his dream, of the horrible vision of Glyssa fading to nothing. With the best of winds, the *Plover* was still many days from Kadavel. Could they reach it in time and then find Glyssa in that massive, swarming city?

Or was it already too late?

As Lonn peered into the distance ahead of the ship, a *frizzier* approached, a mild variation of the freezewind. The air shimmered with streaks of white, and a crystal-thin ice layer formed on the water. The delicate ice ripped and rattled with the heaving of the waves beneath, and the coaster's running hull made a constant crackling sound.

Amlina came out from her cabin and joined the captain on the rear deck. Lonn made his way aft to speak with her, and the other Iruks tagged along. As they topped the stairs, Lonn heard the chorus of windbringers, which included Kizier, humming in light trance.

The Larthangans were bending on more sails for speed and maneuverability. A true freezewind was almost sure to follow the frizzier, it was only a question of when. The coaster would need all its speed and responsiveness to climb from the freezing sea onto the ice.

"I think we should turn now and start tacking, lady," Troneck said. "The Icemaker can blow up your back mighty quick sometimes."

"You have my vision to guide you," Amlina replied. "The Deepmind will tell me when it is best to turn and I will tell you."

Troneck shut his mouth tight and glared behind them at the dim horizon. Lonn could sympathize with the Larthangan's displeasure. He would not appreciate the witch telling him how to sail his dojuk.

"How do you feel today?" Amlina asked him.

"Terrible," Lonn answered, more frankly than he'd meant to. "Do you think any good came of it?"

"What do you think?"

Lonn remembered his panic and the insurmountable feeling of despair. "I didn't see Glyssa. Not that I recall."

Amlina gave a rare smile. "If the Deepmind had presented you with that vision on your first unpracticed attempt, I would have been very surprised. Glyssa is hidden by a strong design."

"But you think he may succeed in time?" Draven said.

Amlina shrugged. "In the Deepmind anything is possible, as Kizier is so fond of reminding us. Lonn may have a gift for deepseeing, but it takes time to develop such a gift. There's no telling if there's enough time for it to be of use in looking for Glyssa and the Cloak."

Her glance returned to Lonn. "And of course the training is hard. It won't often be as dramatic as the initiation, but it will sometimes be as painful. It has truly been said that gazing into the Ogo will unravel a mind that is not strong enough."

"Lonn's mind is plenty strong," Draven clapped his mate on the shoulder.

"Maybe you should let Lonn decide that for himself," the witch answered.

"What do you think?" Lonn turned the question on her. "You guided me in the initiation. Do you believe I should continue?"

The witch's sea-blue eyes peered at him, seeming to weigh his soul. "Last night I would have said no. But I've had a little time to reflect and remember that initiates often go to pieces, and I mean ones who've had long and expert preparation. As I've said, you may be gifted, and in time you might master the gift. But nothing is certain, except that it is risky. Think it over for a few days, let your mind rest and absorb what—"

The witch started and looked behind her at the sky. Lonn realized that the windbringer's had ceased humming.

"Turn to starboard, captain." Amlina pointed the exact course she wanted.

Troneck shifted his iron tiller and shouted to his men to haul in their sheets. The *Plover* veered in the water, the mizzen boom swinging over their heads. The tall sails bent out as the ship moved on its new tack.

A short time later Amlina had the captain edge closer to the wind.

They were racing southeast now, wind on the starboard bow. Sparks of change-light began bursting over the sea to windward. Then a wave of scintillating white appeared, looming in the gray distance.

"Stand by your lines," Troneck roared. "Stand by the runner chains. Windbringers, now's the time! Push us faster if you can."

Lonn glanced at the alert-eyed bostulls and sensed their mental efforts—sensed them with peculiar clarity, his mind somehow feeling their wills at work. The wind gusted over the decks, and the sails strained farther out. The two-master lunged forward as the glittering freezewind swept toward them.

It was quite possible for even a heavier, slower ship to run up on the forming ice of a freezewind and keep sailing. The magic change provided a buoyancy of its own, the glowing sea letting loose tremendous energy as it changed to ice. The problem was speed and angle, the deep-riding hull had to meet the materializing ice just so.

"Down ice runners," Troneck ordered.

Lonn heard the rattle of the chains and felt the rumbling through his feet as the runners locked into place.

"Prepare to turn," Amlina said, staring wide-eyed at the nearing wall of light.

"There's still time to gain speed," the captain protested.

"Turn when I tell you," Amlina answered. "Turn now!"

"Not yet," Troneck gripped the helm tightly but did not move it.

"Now!" Amlina cried.

"Turn!" Lonn yelled. For suddenly he trusted the witch's deepseeing, suddenly he knew she was right.

Troneck hesitated a moment more, a look of anguished indecision on his face. Then he swung the tiller hard, and the coaster's prow swerved into the wind.

The towering wave of light rippled over the foredeck a moment later, angled slightly to starboard. Lonn ducked and shielded his face like everyone else as the freezewind engulfed the vessel.

There was a moment of abysmal cold, and the wind's whir changed to a high shriek. Then the deck lurched underfoot and Lonn was flung sprawling. The *Plover* shook with a fierce groan of timbers, then grew still.

The freezewind blew away to the north, leaving the coaster stuck motionless in the new-made ice.

Ten

On the tilted decks of the *Plover* the Iruks and Larthangans picked themselves up in silence. The wind had died off to a whisper, the ship's canvas flapping drearily overhead.

"Lower those sails," Troneck yelled. "Jump now! We'll crack a mast if the wind picks up. Damn our luck. I knew this would happen. I knew it."

"Your thinking so made it happen." Amlina stepped toward him in a fury. "You waited too long to turn!"

The burly captain retreated a step, then dropped to his knees and grabbed the fur hem of Amlina's coat. "Forgive this worthless one, lady. I did what seemed best at the time. I thought it too soon to turn. I thought we would slow too much."

Lonn looked away, glowering at the man's cowardice. The crewmen on the rear deck stood frowning, eyes lowered.

"Enough," Amlina yanked her coat from Troneck's cringing grasp. "On your feet, captain. Let's go and see about cutting ourselves loose."

Leaning awkwardly, the witch clambered down the steps and across the main deck. Lonn and the others followed, their sea legs suddenly weak and rubbery on the stationary vessel. Rope ladders were hastily lowered from the port rail, the low side of the sloping deck. The Larthangans stepped back to let Amlina climb over first.

"Bring axes and hammers," Troneck ordered them, "and oil stoves to set on the ice. Rouse the night crew. Every man's to work."

Amlina and the Iruks were first down the ladders, Troneck and his men descending after. In the frosty blue sea light, they crouched and peered beneath the hull.

The whole length of the keel was embedded, two feet or more at the deepest parts. The two ice runners on the port side were deeply buried as well. Here and there a rib had caught an inch or so of ice, but otherwise the outer planking was free. Still, the crewmen shook their heads and muttered in fretful voices.

"It'll take us days to chop free with this crew," Karrol said, glaring at the slender Larthangans. "Or months."

"We'll be here months if we don't cut free," Brinda replied. "We can't count on another meltwind, not this late in the season."

"We're lucky it wasn't worse in this bucket," Eben said.

It wasn't luck, Lonn thought, it was Amlina's guidance. But he did not make this claim to his mates.

Ice axes, hammers, and stakes were lowered from the deck of the *Plover*. The Iruks gathered with the crewmen to receive the tools. Troneck and his lieutenants handed them out and assigned everyone places to dig. The Iruks were given heavy axes and asked to start at the rudder. This was the task Lonn would have chosen for his klarn, for there the ice was deepest and the Iruks had more muscle than the Larthangans.

After the tools were distributed Amlina spoke to the crew. "Work as hard and fast as you can. I shall likewise be working in my way. I believe we shall soon be free of this obstacle. You must believe it also." She ended with a pointed glance at Troneck, then moved to climb back on board.

Some of the crewmen started to chop above the ice runners while the rest crept beneath the hull to work. Lonn and his mates walked to the stern and arranged themselves around the buried rudder. Setting their ridged boots wide apart, they lifted their axes and brought them down, attacking the ice with vigorous, determined strokes. The ice near the surface, last to be formed, shattered easily when struck. Lower down the sea was frozen harder and soon their heaviest blows shocked back at them, rattling their bones. Still they continued battering away at a furious pace. The sea would only freeze harder in the night and, should a snowstorm blow in, it could bury the coaster twice as deep.

Only when the ache in their backs and arms became unbearable would the Iruks pause to warm themselves at one of the oil stoves. Three of the portable stoves had been lowered from the ship and fired up, not only to warm the crewmen but to heat the iron spikes their mallets drove into the ice.

As twilight dimmed the overcast sky, the Iruks were nearing the bottom of the rudder. The cook had boiled up a thin soup that he lowered over the side in covered pots. Of all the crew members only the elderly cook was exempted from the ice chopping, a mark of the Larthangans' characteristic veneration of the aged. The soup, along with a double ration of brandy, was drunk from cups while the work continued. The wind, which had lulled in the afternoon, stirred again in the gathering dark—a chill whisper around the coaster's ornate hull.

Finally, the Iruks finished with the rudder, chipping away the last of the ice with their knives. Lonn and Karrol swung the rudder back and forth on its pivot to be sure it would turn. Then the mates shouldered their axes and climbed from the hole they had dug.

By now the forward ice runner had been freed, and a low trench cut so it could ride up onto the ice. Work on the aft runner was well along. So, after warming themselves, the Iruks crawled beneath the hull to join the work on the keel.

This labor proved more tedious. The curve of the hull overhead forced them to kneel or crouch at a sidewise angle. The ice was difficult to reach, much less strike with an axe.

By midnight the crewmen were nearly spent, their efforts growing feeble. Although the keel was still embedded a foot deep, Troneck elected to try pulling free. Twin lengths of thick anchor chain were drawn from low portholes in the bow, their ends fastened to iron spikes. Two parties of Larthangans dragged the chains well ahead of the ship and hammered the spikes in deep.

Meantime the strongest of the Larthangans and the five Iruks climbed up the accommodation ladders and entered the forecastle. Down a spiral of steps, below the level of the galley and the seamen's quarters, Troneck and his men led the Iruks to a wide compartment dominated by a great capstan. The capstan was couched on a mechanism of gears and weights and attached to the two lengths of anchor chain. The device was fashioned to augment the strength of those turning the capstan drum. Normally used to raise the anchor, it had this second function, to help free the ship when icebound.

The Iruks placed themselves at the capstan bars with the Larthangans, so that every space was filled. They turned the wheel until the chains clinked taut, then waited. On a signal relayed from the foredeck, they began to push.

Tired as they were, the Iruks and Larthangans pushed with all their strength. The chains tightened about an inch, but no more.

"Push!" Troneck groaned, straining at the bar next to Lonn.

The drum moved a little, then slipped back. The ship creaked but did not budge. The relay man at the door kept waving them on, but they could not get the capstan to turn.

Three times the Iruks and Larthangans heaved in unison, hissing and grunting. Each time it seemed the ice must give and the ship lunge forward, if only they could push a bit harder. Each time they failed and collapsed on the bars in pain and exhaustion.

After the third attempt, Troneck gave up. He ordered his men upstairs for food and sleep and sent the same word to those still out on the ice. Lonn considered disputing this decision, but only for a moment. He and his mates were as weary as the Larthangans, and it seemed that a few hours work in the warmth of the day, with all hands rested, should be enough to free the ship.

* * * * *

When Lonn woke and looked out the window the next morning, he knew it had been a mistake to quit. Wet snow was falling, a steady shower plummeting down from a gloomy sky.

The Iruks fortified themselves with hot food and brandy in the galley, then took their axes and climbed down to the ice. The crewmen were already at work, shadowy figures in the falling snow, which shrouded the sealight and lent an eerie pall to the scene. The snow was shin-deep, and the men had to constantly shovel it aside to uncover the ice. Lonn estimated that two or three inches of the snowfall had already frozen, burying all parts of the ship that much deeper. The Iruks marched to the stern and began digging at the rudder.

The day passed cold and miserable, the workers struggling just to keep the ship from freezing in any farther. Stiff and sore, their muscles protested every exertion. Larthangans and Iruks alike suffered cramps and had to stand over the stoves until they passed. During one such period, Lonn observed the line of bent sailors working at the keel. They seemed to chip and hammer with listless indifference, as though they had already accepted defeat. Lonn cursed as he returned to work, his sense of desperation growing.

Nightfall brought a drop in temperature and an even lower sinking of morale. The snow kept blowing, piling up about the keel and runners, diminishing the seaglow until the work crews could no longer see where to strike. Lanterns were brought down from the ship, and in their weak light the labor continued. But it was soon apparent that in the dark the voyagers were losing their battle with the storm, falling behind the rising tide of freezing snow.

In those hours it was only the thought of Glyssa, her name spoken one to another, that kept the Iruks from giving up. The Larthangans had no such incentive. More and more they stood around the stoves, staring dumbly at the piling snow and the dark, unmoving hull. Troneck's threats and curses had no more effect than his shouts of encouragement and soon he abandoned both. When one of the sailors laid open his foot with an errant axe stroke, the captain called a halt.

"It's no use, men. Pack up and get on board. We'll have to wait till this weather breaks."

"Stop!" Lonn struggled through the snow to where the captain stood, the other Iruks tramping behind. "If we quit now we may never get out," Lonn shouted.

Troneck waved the objection aside. "It's no good. My people are exhausted. So are yours. We'll have to wait is all."

The Larthangans were trudging past, heading for the ladders. Lonn felt they must be stopped, but could think of no way short of force. He turned to his Iruks and saw dejection and utter weariness on their faces.

"What's the use?" Eben muttered. "We're not doing any good."

Even Karrol did not argue to stay.

Lonn shook his head in disgust and shouldered his axe. The Iruks lined up with the Larthangans to climb the ladders.

They ate a cheerless supper in the galley, then returned to their compartment in the stern. They barely had the energy to light the stove and pull off their wet clothes before crawling under the furs to sleep.

* * * * *

The klarnmates awoke early in the morning and pushed open the small windows. The storm was over but it was impossible to tell from their angle how much snow had piled about the ship. They put on their dry and stiff clothing and dragged themselves upstairs to the main deck.

The sky was white, covered by high, light clouds. The decks seemed deserted; no watch had been posted. Then Lonn spotted Amlina leaning over the railing amidships. She turned as the Iruks approached, looking as drained and tired as Lonn felt, yet she smiled.

"The ice is not too deep."

Lonn glanced over the side to check by the runners. It was not so bad as he had expected. The snow must have ended soon after they had gone to bed. Still, after two days of chopping, they were slightly worse off than when they started.

"I hope your efforts are nearer to success than ours," Eben told the witch. "Otherwise we may be stuck here half a year."

"Shun negative thinking," Amlina replied. "I have cast a design into the Deepmind whereby we shall soon be sailing free. Now we all must apply positive belief to that design."

"Does that mean we can stop digging?" Karrol asked.

Amlina ignored the sarcasm in her tone. "On the contrary, positive belief must be accompanied by positive action. We must do all we can to bring about the desired end. Chopping might still be the way. In fact, starting today I will be helping you with the work."

"I think you lack the brawn for such toil," Draven observed. "Couldn't you help us better by weaving more witchery?"

Amlina smiled faintly. "It's true I don't have the strength to swing a mallet or axe. But the broken fragments of ice must be cleared away, and that is work I can do. As for witchery, the design has already been cast. I shall continue to visualize our ship sailing free whenever the thought occurs to me. You should do this also, as it will reinforce the design."

"That's all your witchery can do?" Eben asked with rancor.

"That is the way of deepshaping. The more an image is seen and believed in the mind, the more likely it is to come forth into being."

"Suppose it doesn't?" Eben pressed her.

Amlina looked him calmly in the eye. "Shun negative thinking."

"Let's get to work," Lonn grunted. "I'm sure the cook hasn't fixed breakfast yet. We'll eat later."

"I'll see your food is brought down to you," Amlina said. "I'm going now to rouse the crewmen."

The Iruks lowered themselves down the creaking ladders and started to work at the rudder again. The orange sun was burning through the clouds in the east, brightening the sky.

"Let's hope we can dig the hull out soon," Eben said. "We can't rely on the witch's imagining things to get us free."

"She can do it," Draven answered. "Remember how easily she imagined us into those chains when we first came on board?"

"Forcing your will on exhausted stragglers is one thing," Eben argued. "Vying with the sea and air is another. She had no spell to bring the wind when we were becalmed."

"Eben's right," Karrol said. "If she were so mighty a witch, she could just melt the ice and we'd be on our way."

Lonn said nothing. He wanted to have faith in the witch's magic as Draven did, but the aching in his arms and the banks of ice about the ship seemed to argue for skepticism, at least.

Presently the Larthangans hauled themselves down from the ship and began to chop and hammer in their methodical manner. The Iruks paused to stand at one of the stoves and eat their breakfast. Lonn observed Amlina at work, crawling about in her coat and scarf, her gloved hands scooping chips of ice out of the way of the axes. She moved clumsily and slipped more than once while Lonn watched, yet she kept going. It was hard to tell if her presence inspired the Larthangans or not. Mostly they seemed uncomfortable, embarrassed to have the witch before them on her hands and knees.

The work that third day was a growing agony. The Iruks' vitality had been sapped by the two previous sessions, and their progress was slow and halting. Often their blows would miss or the axes slip in their sore hands, falling with a force that wrenched shoulders and backs. Cramps returned, sharper than yesterday, and the Iruks joined the haggard groups of Larthangans who spent more time around the stoves than at work on the keel and runners.

The weather turned harsh in the afternoon, cold wind gusting from the south. By evening flakes of snow were flying on that wind. Lonn sensed futility building in the hearts of his klarn.

"Another storm like yesterday and we're finished," Karrol declared.

Eben began a chant to the Spirit of Winds, begging that the storm blow away from the ship and leave them untouched. Soon all the Iruks were singing with him quietly, amid the wind and gathering dusk.

For a while, it seemed the Spirit of Winds had heard them and was kindly disposed. The wind slacked off to a light breeze, and the Iruks were able to finish cutting loose the aft runner.

Now only the keel remained to be freed, and most of the Larthangans had been working on it all day. Lonn began to hope that in a few more hours they could make another try at dragging the ship out.

But then the wind picked up, laced with sleet and snow. From a long way off Lonn could see the squall approaching, sweeping over the ocean in waves, blotting out the sealight. Soon the snow was swarming thick about the trapped coaster, piling over the diggers' feet and against the keel. The sealight was smothered and the oil lamps, hastily lit, glowed dimly in the blinding storm. Snow-ice clung to the Iruks' furs, melted on their eyebrows and the men's beards, then refroze. Raw wind stung their faces.

By the time the snow was ankle deep the Larthangans had had enough. A few of them strode to the captain and shouted at him, shaking their heads and gesturing with their tools. Troneck relayed their pleas to the witch who acquiesced somberly. She could not force them to work in this weather and did not try. The crewmembers gathered their equipment and hurried to the ladders.

"What are we waiting for?" Karrol started in a grumble but her voice cracked at the end. "This is hopeless."

Blizzard winds howled about the Iruks and Larthangans as they pulled themselves up the slippery ladders in the dark.

* * * * *

"We'll never chop free now," Karrol declared, leaning over the port rail.

It was mid-morning and the klarn had come out on the main deck to verify what they had guessed from their window in the stern. It could hardly have been worse: fully one-third of the hull had been buried by the blizzard.

"What do we do now?" Eben asked.

"I don't know," Lonn said. "What can we do?"

"Since there's no hope of digging free," Karrol answered, "I think we have no choice but to pack our furs and take to sea on our skates."

"We tried that once," Draven said. "Remember?"

"Wait," Eben held up his hands. "Maybe Karrol's right. If we stay, we'll probably be stuck here till we starve, and who knows what will happen to Glyssa? According to Troneck's charts, we're not that far from the southernmost Tathian island. We could probably skate it in three or four days and make our way to Kadavel from there."

"Even if we made it to Kadavel," Draven argued, "how would we find Glyssa and save her without Amlina's help?"

"We could try," Karrol replied. "It's better than staying here and rotting."

"I'm not counting on rotting," Draven said. "I'm counting on the witch to get us out."

"No doubt you'll still be counting on her when the thaw comes in First Summer," Eben told him angrily. "But we can't wait that long."

"It's not a decision to make in haste," Brinda said. "I suggest we get some breakfast, then go back to our room and have a meeting."

With shrugs and frowning nods the klarnmates expressed their agreement.

Descending the steps in the forecastle, they heard Amlina's voice coming from the galley below. They found her standing beside the great iron stove, speaking to the Larthangans. The whole crew was present, slumped on the narrow benches or leaning in the doorways that led off to pantries and sleeping quarters. Amlina looked over as the Iruks reached the bottom of the stairs.

"Good morning. I'm glad you're here. I was just telling the men that much of the snow is not yet frozen. A few hours of hard shoveling now will save us many hours of ice-chopping later."

Staring dumbly, the Larthangans obviously shared none of the witch's enthusiasm. The Iruks made no comment, only walked to the wide iron stove and picked up bowls.

"After we've cleared the snow we should rest for a full day," Amlina said. "And have extra rations."

A milky stew of mashed roots and varied fish ends bubbled over the fire. The ship's cook had stubbornly refused all the Iruks' suggestions on how to prepare the wild provisions gathered on Windbock. Instead, the surly old man had insisted on adapting Larthangan recipes, with increasingly awful results. The Iruks winced as they spooned the stuff into their bowls.

"Extra rations cooked this way would be no boon," Eben told the witch irately.

The Iruks chuckled grimly or else glowered at the cook who stood nearby, bony arms crossed over his chest, frowning with sour dignity. Draven reached past him for the wineskin while the others got cups. The klarnmates sat at the only empty table, the one where Amlina stood.

The Larthangans had all finished eating, yet they did not stir to get their tools. Utterly drained by the three days of chopping in the cold, stunned by the depth of snow that had buried the ship in the night, the crewmen simply could not motivate themselves to face the cold again. Lonn sensed all this in one of those instants of illumination that had come to him occasionally since being initiated by the witch. He knew that Amlina sensed it also.

"Captain Troneck," she said quietly. "It's time to work."

Troneck sat near the far end of the stove, disheveled in his shirt and trousers. He stared at Amlina through watery eyes.

"Lady, I know it's time. But ... the men are tired. The digging seems hopeless."

"It is not hopeless." Amlina raised her voice for emphasis. "No one must think it so. This design must be believed in: that we will soon be sailing free. Every one of you must envision this whenever the question comes to your mind."

"It is hard," Troneck muttered. "Lady, we must rest from the cold today."

A few of the crewmen summoned the energy to nod or voice their support of this idea.

Amlina shook her head. "It is imperative that we dig while the snow is still soft. Remember, you have all sworn your lives to my service. Do not force me to use threats."

"Listen to her," Karrol grumbled in Iruk. "I'm glad she never got a hair from our heads."

Amlina stared at her, seemed to read the tone if not the meaning of her comment. "I know you Iruks agree with me," the witch said, turning to Lonn, "that the snow must be cleared without delay."

Lonn stolidly returned her gaze.

"Of course we do," Draven declared. "We'll be down on the ice right after breakfast."

"No we won't," Karrol said in Iruk.

"We have to stick with the witch," Draven answered. "We need her help."

"We don't need her," Karrol said.

"We're undecided," Lonn admitted to Amlina's inquiring look. "There's been talk of our leaving the ship and trying to reach land on our skates."

"You'd be foolish to try that," Amlina responded. "This ship will reach Kadavel long before you could find your way there on your own. Even if you got there, you'd have little chance of finding your mate without my help."

Lonn stared into Amlina's eyes and knew that she was right. But could he trust this knowledge, or was the witch using some charm to persuade him? Anyway, he could not decide for the whole klarn.

"We'll have to meet and talk it over," he said.

"There's no time," Amlina replied angrily. "The snowfall is hardening while we stand here and debate."

"She's right," Draven tossed down his spoon and stood. "Let's break out the tools."

"No," Karrol said. "We're going to have a meeting."

"We can meet later," Draven said. "First the snow."

Lonn found himself standing. "Draven's right. If the meeting votes for skating, we will have wasted only a few hours by digging now. But if the vote goes for staying, we will have left ourselves much worse off than we need to be."

"I won't do it," Karrol said.

"Let me suggest a compromise," Eben offered. "We stay and work for three more days. If it doesn't look like the ship's going to get free by then, we go on skates."

"Fair enough," Lonn said. "Brinda?"

She lifted a shoulder. "I'm with Eben."

"That's three of us." Lonn looked at Karrol.

"I think it's a waste of three days," she said. "But all right."

Draven shrugged. "I don't like the idea of skating at all. But I'll go along."

Most of the klarn's discussion had been in Iruk. The witch had waited, watching intently.

"We're ready to work," Lonn told her. "What about these lazy sea rats?"

Amlina surveyed the roomful of Larthangans, most of whom refused to meet her gaze. "These Iruks and I are going to shovel the snow from about the ship. I will not force you to join us. But think on this: if we do not get free and sail on to Kadavel, there's no telling who may end up possessing the Cloak of the Two Winds or what damage they may inflict on the world with its power. If you give up now, you may be giving up not only your own lives but your loved ones, your country, the whole human world."

Saying no more, Amlina led the Iruks toward the galley door.

Grudgingly, Troneck pushed himself away from the stove and followed. "Come on, men."

In twos and threes the crewmen dragged themselves after their captain. Amlina smiled fiercely as the Larthangans gathered at the lockers where the axes, mallets, and shovels were stored.

"I thank you for your courage."

The *Plover's* company was crowding up the spiral steps when the hull gave a loud creaking and shifted its tilt. Lonn clutched the rail as the clamor of bewildered voices mingled with a second shuddering groan.

"Go up," Amlina waved him on excitedly. "Go!"

Lonn rushed up the steps and flung open the door to the main deck, his mates and the Larthangans behind him. The coaster gave a third heaving groan then settled, rocking gently as if in water.

Clouds of steamy vapor rose on all sides of the ship. Lonn stumbled to the nearest rail and peered through the mist. His senses had not been lying: the ice and snow entrapping the hull were gone. The ship was floating.

Below, dark bulky creatures swam amid slabs and blocks of ice.

"Fire turtles!" Eben spoke with awe at Lonn's shoulder.

"It is done," Amlina murmured. "The Deepmind is setting us free."

While they watched, one green reptile head surfaced, glittering with the dripping sealight. The turtle gulped air, then breathed a jet of yellow flame that licked and melted the ice still clinging to the aft runner. To left and right other heads appeared and other flames. More hissing vapor lifted about the ship.

The whole ship's company hung watching from port and starboard rails as the fire turtles dissolved the last of the nearby ice, leaving the *Plover* afloat in a pool of bright water hardly wider than the ship itself with runners down. Then the giant turtles took breaths of air, long breaths to fill the enormous lungs beneath their shells, and disappeared beneath the surface.

Lonn marveled at the strangeness of it. A score or more of the turtles had surfaced for air at just the right place and had lingered to free the icebound ship. Brute reptiles, they had acted as if with intelligent purpose; solitary beasts, they had come together to carry out that purpose— a miracle.

"Amlina did it!" Draven shook Lonn by the shoulder. "I told you not to give up on her!"

Lonn roared with glee, then hugged his mate, bending back and lifting Draven in the air until both fell still embracing into the snow. Across the main deck, Iruks and Larthangans alike reacted with the same unabashed elation. Some hugged, some leapt and capered, some sank to their knees in the snow and wept with joy and relief.

Amlina moved among them, gesturing for quiet. "Listen, my friends. The Deepmind has answered our need by sending forth its creatures to help us. Truly a celebration is in order. But we're not free yet. The ship must be dragged up onto the ice, and the sooner the better."

Troneck stepped up beside her and began issuing orders in a hoarse voice. First, all decks and spars had to be cleared of snow to lighten the ship. All hands went eagerly to work, their desperate tiredness now forgotten. Brooms, pails, and cooking vessels were pressed into service, along with the shovels carried up from below. The snow was gathered together and dumped over the sides. On the quarterdeck the bostulls were brushed off—some of the poor creatures had been buried past their eyes—and roused from their trance state. Their help might be needed later, to get the ship underway.

Sails were raised and trimmed to the breeze so that the prow drifted against the edge of the ice. The overflow of water from the melting had flooded across the ice in all directions, leveling the snowdrifts. The result was a glazed plain, quickly refrozen—ideal conditions for raising the ship.

The Iruks and a company of Larthangans went below to the capstan room. The anchor chains and spikes were still in place from their earlier attempt to free the vessel. Lonn and his mates stationed themselves at the capstan bars in tandem with the crewmen. On a signal relayed from the foredeck, they began to push.

The drum screeched and inched around. The *Plover* shivered with a dull scraping noise then tilted back. Lonn could feel the ship sliding upward as the capstan slowly cranked.

Then suddenly the hull tipped forward and the scraping noise changed to the smooth hiss of runners on ice. A jubilant cheer from the decks above confirmed that the ship was free. Lonn was amazed at how easily the capstan had turned. The Larthangans, he decided, were justly renowned for their ingenious mechanisms.

The spikes were retrieved and the heavy chains hoisted back on board. Then the stiff, battened ice-sails were lowered, the *Plover* forced to wait until last night's snowfall froze to a smooth, slick surface. But by noon the telltale witchlight was glinting over the frozen ocean, and with the help of the bostulls the ship got underway.

Eleven

That evening a bright fire blazed in the great stove of the ship's galley. Near the fire, basking in its warmth, stood the six windbringers, carried below for an overdue warming and washing of their roots. The tables were crowded with Larthangans and Iruks, feasting and drinking together in boisterous good cheer, their long-standing animosity put aside.

This new camaraderie had started in the afternoon when the Iruks and off-duty crewmen had shared the first cups of brandy. Before long the klarnmates found themselves getting drunk with the elderly cook, who decided the barbarians were not such bad types after all. He even poured them each a drop from a treasured private bottle of rice liqueur, which instantly raised the Iruks in the estimation of the other Larthangans present. The Iruks, in turn, lauded the cook's generosity and the courage and cleverness of Larthangans in general.

To express their thanks, Draven insisted they would help the cook prepare the night's feast. They started simmering the volroom meat early, skimming off the fat, adding herbs and roots at the proper time. They roasted clams seasoned with wild sage and made a separate soup of sandfish and ginger, instructing the cook and sipping brandy as they worked. The meal that resulted was more bountiful and appetizing than any served on the *Plover* in a long time.

Amlina broke with her custom and ate in the galley that night. She sat close to the stove, Troneck, Kizier, and the Iruks sharing her table. She had adorned herself with silver bangles and a bright scarlet and green silk gown. Her face was powdered, lips and eyelids glistening with paint. With makeup, she looked older, no longer girlish, but a dazzling lady.

And the witch was merry to a degree Lonn had not seen before. She included herself in the free drinking and encouraged the reluctant Troneck to open another keg of brandy long after the food had all been eaten.

"I drink to the providence of the Ogo," she said when her cup was refilled. "And to all of you, my companions, for your persistence and bravery, so sorely tested these past days."

When this toast had been drunk Draven raised his tumbler, sloshing some brandy over the rim. "And we drink to Amlina," he said. "It's her witchery that got us free. All our chopping in the end amounted to nothing."

"Not so," Amlina said. "All our efforts together manifested our freedom. That is the way it must be viewed."

"I don't understand," Eben said, chin resting languidly in his hand. "The fire turtles would have melted us free whether we had dug for three days or not, wouldn't they?"

"Impossible to know," Amlina said. "My design apparently brought the turtles. Whether they would have come if we were not also chopping at the ice is a meaningless question. All we can say for certain is that we did everything we could to free ourselves and now, with the help of the Deepmind, we are free. Is this not so, Kizier?"

"Just so," the windbringer answered. "Is that not enough to know?"

"I don't care how you explain it," Draven answered, laughing. "It's plain to me that you are a great and mighty witch. We are glad to be your allies."

He glanced around at his mates then drained his cup. All the Iruks drank with him, Karrol and Brinda a little grudgingly, Lonn and Eben with gusto.

"Thank you." Amlina lowered her eyes. "It pleases me to have your confidence. The truth is, I seldom consider myself either great or mighty. More often, I wonder if I'm even competent as a deepshaper."

"You've handled us Iruks and these Larthangans competently enough," Lonn observed, surprised by this confession of humility from the witch, not fully certain it was genuine.

"I'd have thought you considered yourself a superior witch," Eben agreed. "That is, to judge by your demeanor, and by your having stolen the Cloak of the Two Winds and made the great witch of the East your enemy."

Amlina smiled wryly. "There are moments when I am visited by a very lofty idea of my potential. But more often, I wonder at my temerity. The truth is, I stole the Cloak because I had no choice."

"Tell us the tale," Draven said. "Kizier has never told us how you came to have the Cloak."

"Very well." The witch's eyes were far away, her expression softened by the brandy. She took another swallow, then began.

"When I first left Larthang, I had not the slightest intention of seeking the Cloak of the Two Winds. I was a student at the Academy of the Deepmind until my twentieth year. But then I failed my requisite examinations and was denied the chance for further studies leading to the gray mantle of an adept. Having no better prospects, I bought passage to the Isles of Tath, determined to pursue my studies abroad. Trinketing was my passion, the making and wielding of magical devices. It's a shaping art not currently fashionable in Larthang, which is partly why I failed as a student there. But I soon realized the Tathians could teach me little of trinketing. Their magic lore is inferior to Larthang's in all save their alchemy. Eventually, I concluded there was only one witch in the world to teach me what I wanted to learn: Beryl, the Archimage of the East. She is known as the greatest trinketer of the age, and not only because of the Cloak of the Two Winds.

"One night, when possessed by exactly such a lofty idea of myself as I mentioned, I decided to sail for Tallyba." Amlina's expression grew solemn, her finger caressing the rim of her cup. "As soon as I arrived in Beryl's presence, I knew I had made a disastrous mistake. I had disregarded the tales of her evil sorceries, believing that the deepshapers of Larthang would spread such reports because Beryl was an enemy they had never managed to conquer. But the tales were true: Beryl is inhumanly terrible. She *does* drink the blood of human sacrifices and sustains her youth with their lives. She looked straight into my mind, declaimed my fears and weaknesses, terrified me with her acuity and the power of her will. I was lucky that it really was in my mind only to learn from her. She recognized that I had my own grudge against the witches of Larthang. Perhaps she saw in me a reflection of her younger self. She had me imprisoned for a time, then forced me to serve as a kitchen drudge to humiliate me. But, in the end, she did make me a kind of apprentice and taught me some of her trinketing art and of the Nyssanian sorceries she had acquired. I knew there was a constant danger that she might turn on me, drain away my will, but I always managed to keep a part of my mind to myself. That's what saved me in the end. After I'd been in Tallyba almost seven years, I realized that Beryl was tiring of me. I no longer amused her. Before long, she would either have made me into a thrall or else killed me. So I waited until she was in deep trance, then fled from the city. I knew where she kept the Cloak of the Two Winds and had heard the chants she used to unlock the compartment. I stole the Cloak because I knew I could use it to drive a ship quickly across the seas.

"So now you understand. I came to have the Cloak only because of circumstances. It was never a thing I set out to do."

"Then why did you chase the Cloak once you lost it?" Lonn demanded. "Why are you chasing it now? You could just sail on to Larthang."

"No. What I said this morning about the Cloak's potential for damaging the world is true, not something I made up to try to inspire the crewmen. It was bad enough when Beryl had the Cloak, but at least she was trained in Larthang and understands the need for restraint. If the Cloak should fall to someone else, as I believe it has, there's no telling how it may be abused or how that abuse might affect the Deepmind. I set the Cloak loose in the world. I feel obliged to get it back to Larthang if I can. Perhaps it is only my inflated idea of myself once more, but I do feel that way."

The galley was quiet, most of the Larthangans gone to bed or else passed out at the tables. The Iruks leaned over their empty cups.

"Now you know the truth of my story," Amlina said. "Do you still consider me so great a witch?"

"Absolutely," Draven replied. "That you survived at all proves you are formidable."

Eben nodded. "I've had my doubts about your witchery, I admit. But the way you freed us from the ice is proof enough for me that you are mighty."

"And you, Lonn. What do you think?" Amlina asked.

"I agree with Draven and Eben," he answered guardedly. "You are plainly a better witch than you give yourself credit for."

He glanced to see if Karrol or Brinda would comment, but found their faces sullen. The women were uneasy, he realized, with this bright, feminine version of Amlina, so captivating to the men of the klarn.

This thought disturbed Lonn, for he was not sure himself how far Amlina should be trusted. He recalled how Captain Troneck had cringed before the witch's anger when the ship was first icebound. If he and his mates stayed in Amlina's company long enough, might they also become her servants or, worse, her thralls?

Yet what other choice did they have, except to sail with her, and remain on their guard?

Then Lonn thought of something else—another choice, one he alone must make. And whether he could trust the witch or not, he saw clearly what the choice must be.

"Perhaps it's time to retire," Amlina remarked.

"Wait," Lonn laid a hand on her arm. "You told me to consider for a few days whether or not to continue the training. I've not been thinking about it much but ... I've had these glimpses, ideas bursting into my head that I know are true or right. I've just had one that tells me I *should* continue the training, that it is our best hope of finding Glyssa."

"Splendid," Amlina grinned. "Those flashes of insight you mention often occur after initiation. They are considered messages from the Deepmind."

"This is well," Kizier declared. "Just as every effort was made to get free of the ice, so every effort should be made to find the Cloak and Glyssa. And this path is one shown to us by the Deepmind."

Amlina touched her heart in a salute to Lonn. "I will do my best to train you, my friend. I will base your daily regimen on that of a student at the Academy of the Deepmind. And we shall see what the Ogo brings."

* * * * *

Lonn's training began the next morning. For the first half of the day, the witch made him sit on the quarterdeck with eyes shut and concentrate on watching the backs of his eyelids. This, Amlina said, was a simple form of meditation, designed to bring the mind to a state of clear and watchful detachment.

Lonn found the exercise futile, a deliberate inactivity that seemed to accomplish nothing. But each time his eyes came open Kizier would order him to shut them, and when Lonn protested the windbringer reminded him that the training's purpose was to search for Glyssa.

"'To learn to see with the mind you must first stop seeing with the eyes alone," the bostull said. "Last night you boasted you were sure this training was your path. This morning you bridle at taking the first step."

Lonn had already begun to reconsider last night's brandy-fueled optimism. But instead of pursuing that thought he shut his eyes and concentrated again on the lids.

Later Amlina came out on deck and taught Lonn a short chant, the words, in Old Larthangan, meaningless to him. He was required to repeat the chant while trotting in place—for more than an hour. After that, the witch had a keg of nails brought to him from below. She told him to pick out the nails one by one, place them on the deck, then put them back into the keg one by one.

"Normally small bamboo sticks are used," "she said. "But these nails will do as well."

"What should I be thinking about?" Lonn asked.

"Think about what you are doing."

When he had taken out the nails and put them back seven times Amlina told him to do more running in place and chanting. Then he meditated once more, this time staring at the empty sky. The witch came to him again near sundown, saying he was finished for the day and to go and have his supper.

"But I haven't done anything," he said. "I mean, I haven't tried to see Glyssa."

"The first stage of the training does not involve deliberate attempts to deepsee," Amlina explained. "Visions, if they come, must arise spontaneously. When you are not practicing, think of Glyssa from time to time, ask to see her. That may help."

"I think of her all the time," Lonn said.

"Then you can do no more."

"How long does this first stage last?"

"Normally three months or more. In your case, we shall see. The unfolding of power cannot be hurried, Lonn. Have patience."

Lonn followed the same routine the next day, and the next, and the next.

Soon the Iruks were remarking that Lonn was becoming withdrawn and moody. He spoke little at meals, took no part in the klarn's weapons practice. When his mates inquired if he had had any luck yet in seeing Glyssa, he only scowled and shook his head. He had not even dreamed of her, not since that one dream he had told to the witch.

Absorbed in the deepseer's training, Lonn hardly noticed the passage of time as the coaster voyaged north. Three days after escaping from the ice, the ship came in sight of land, towering black cliffs jutting straight up from the sea. This was the south coast of Xinner, southernmost of the Tathian Isles. The coast was bare and sparsely habited, with no apparent harbors or anchorages. The *Plover* skirted the eastern cape of Xinner and continued north. Two days later they raised the small island of Gline and stopped to trade at a village there.

Gline was bleak and rocky, gray cliffs rising over gray beaches. The village was humble, huts of mud and reeds clustered on the beach, a few fortified dwellings carved above in the cliffside. Fishing boats lined the shore, wooden craft somewhat like dojuks, but smaller and with only one outrigger.

As soon as the coaster's sails were stripped down, the crewmen loaded the skiffs with brandy, oil, and silks and lowered them to the ice. The Iruks, dressed in harness and armed with spears, accompanied the boats ashore—all except Lonn who was busy with his training.

When the trading party returned in the late afternoon, Lonn was perched in the rigging, meditating on the white sky. As Troneck came on board, he complained loudly about the stinginess of the Glinesmen. It was not a trading season, and the villagers had stores of oil and wine laid in. Realizing the Larthangans needed food, the islanders had held out for an extremely favorable rate of exchange. Suspended high over the deck as he heard the captain's lamentations, Lonn felt himself more akin to the world of the clouds than the mundane world below. It struck him then how much the witch's training was changing him.

* * * * *

On the evening that the *Plover* sailed from Gline, Amlina entered the dark immersion. By practicing shallower *wei* trances, the witch had pieced together a map, a guiding picture of the near future, of what obstacles she might encounter and how best to seek the Cloak in Kadavel. But there were blanks and obscure places in the picture. Amlina hoped to clarify these through the deep trance.

She lay in her bunk as the Iruks had first seen her, in silk robe, fur-trimmed coat, and moonstone fillet. The tiny lamps glowed about the cabin, their lights reflecting on the narrow strips of tapestry. The trinkets dangled, spinning at times or swaying with the heeling of the ship.

For the first two days, Amlina's mind was diffuse through time and space, and she had no awareness of herself or her purpose. On the third day purpose returned, a vaguely remembered thought: the object of great power, the Cloak of the Two Winds, she must see it, find it. Now her mental strivings elicited shapes and shadows. She glimpsed the outline of seawalls and towers ... Kadavel. Somewhere in Kadavel, she knew, the Cloak was hidden.

Time passed. Thoughts and emptiness by turns filled her mind. Often she pictured the Cloak, black and silver, vivid with power. But always it was wrapped by a shiny mist of darkness, so she could discover no clue of its location. She visualized Kadavel again and again but only perceived the places she knew from memory—and those in no specific detail or order. She envisioned the Iruks with their reckless ferocity and lingering distrust of her. Somehow it seemed their trust would be crucial to her in Kadavel, but she did not know how or why.

On the fourth or fifth day, a feeling of unease stirred in Amlina. She sensed someone searching for her, even as she was searching ... Beryl, it must be. The Archimage of the East was the most dangerous blank on Amlina's map. If Amlina could trace the Cloak to Kadavel, surely Beryl could do so as well. If Amlina's deepseeing had failed so far to perceive Beryl's appearance in the near future, it was probably because Beryl hid herself.

Of course, Amlina too had her concealments. The moonstone fillet she wore was a talisman. Each day she visualized an aura of white light emanating from the stones, surrounding and protecting her. Deepshapers commonly wrapped themselves in such defenses, but since leaving Tallyba Amlina had charged her barrier with the specific thought of hiding her from Beryl's mind. Still, the barrier had been weakened by the design she had cast and by her releasing her will now to the dark immersion. And of course Beryl was mighty. Amlina expected that sooner or later she would have to face the Archimage. She must prepare for that meeting.

Amlina took a deep breath, and the prisms and desmets spun around on their threads. In the depths of her trance she conjured Beryl's image. The face of the Archimage leapt into view, a face kept young in appearance by sorcery and human lives, yet old in experience and wickedness. Amlina knew Beryl's habits and practices as well as anyone. If Beryl had a weakness it lay not in her knowledge or skill, both unsurpassed, but in her character—perhaps in her pride, her contempt for inferiors, perhaps most of all in her dread of her own mortality.

Amlina studied Beryl's face for a while, her mind open to the surfacing of further intuitions. But no ideas arose. After a time, it seemed that the face was staring back. Amlina realized she had been thinking of Beryl too long.

She sought at once to turn her mind away, to dissolve the face and look instead into emptiness. But the face refused to vanish. It hung quivering amid the silvery waves Amlina threw against it. The eyes continued to stare at Amlina, more and more intently, bright and malign.

The trinkets swung and rattled as Amlina turned on her bed. Suddenly she sat up and opened her eyes. Beryl's face remained, floating in the lingering trance-light against the dim background of the cabin.

In terror, Amlina struggled to her feet, seized by the wild urge to flee, to escape Beryl's view. After two lurching steps, she caught herself and stood shuddering among the trinkets, fighting down her panic. In a moment, she shut her eyes and sank to the floor where she sat with feet tucked at her hips.

Ignoring Beryl's face as best she could, Amlina breathed deeply to calm herself. Her fingers found the moonstone fillet and she worked its charm—casting her awareness into the moonstones, seeing them change the thought to white light that poured out to engulf her. Amlina watched the light raining forth, growing deeper and brighter until Beryl's face was lost in its brilliance.

Amlina waited a long time in her barrier, until she was sure Beryl was no longer watching. Then, timidly, she opened her eyes. The cabin was empty and still. Amlina let go of the fillet and stood, her head reeling. She lurched to the bunk and sank down. She had been a fool to dwell so long on Beryl's image, more of a fool to try to run, as if Beryl's mind could be physically escaped. She had forgotten how easily the Archimage could terrify her, make her lose her wits.

It was difficult to assess how costly the blunder might prove. Amlina only knew that Beryl had seen her, not how clearly or what she might have learned from the vision. That Beryl had not spoken suggested that the contact had been tenuous—probably too tenuous to launch a mental attack, if indeed that had been Beryl's intent. Knowing Beryl, she would be willing to wait. Having found Amlina once, she would expect it to be that much easier to find her again.

Amlina fingered the moonstone band in her hair. She must keep the aura bright and strong. The thought of the Iruks recurred to her. They too would need protection. She had some extra moonstones in her jewel box, pieces of an unfinished necklace ...

* * * * *

From Gline the coaster traveled north, across open ice. The south wind had abated and now the breeze blew mostly from the west and northwest. The days were fair, and though the seas remained hard the weather was not bitter cold as it had been farther south. They had entered the warm latitudes, according to Kizier. The sun, which had risen higher as they journeyed north, now crossed the sky almost directly overhead.

Lonn continued to practice his exercises, day in and day out, with no variations. While Amlina was in the dark immersion Kizier served as trainer, though this duty only required that he enforce the routine against Lonn's occasional protests. Adhering to the strict mental disciplines was still not easy for the Iruk, whose active mind constantly strained against being still. But each time he maundered from the path, Kizier patiently brought him back.

"Stillness," the bostull said. "The mind is a pool whose bottom is infinite knowledge, so the sages of Larthang teach. To view the depths with clarity there must be stillness at the surface."

Maintaining contemplative stillness was especially hard for Lonn in the hours he spent with his mates. Except for Draven, the Iruks were growing more dubious about the training.

"I don't like what's happening to you, Lonn." Karrol said to him one night. "You're not the same. You're distant, out of yourself. How do we know the witch isn't turning you into one of those mindless ones?"

"Because we trust Amlina," Draven said.

"I don't trust her," Karrol answered. "I don't."

Twelve

Four days north of Gline the coaster raised the shore of another island, Borga. From viewing Troneck's charts the Iruks knew they were finally nearing their destination. North of Borga lay a narrow channel, gradually widening to the west. At the end of the channel, where the islands of Borga, Lustre, and Glistre came together, stood the city of Kadavel.

"With this wind, six or seven days yet," Troneck answered their query gruffly. "Barring some new disaster."

Lonn's mates paced the decks in growing anticipation. For hours they watched the passing shoreline, with its forests of slash pines and cedars and its lush blue-green shrubbery. Though it was now late in First Winter, only a dusting of snow had fallen on the island. Nor did they encounter large settlements such as the Iruks had expected. They sighted only fishing villages, such as they had passed farther south, along with an occasional castle or fortress built on a promontory. The great Tathian cities lay mostly to the west, Kizier explained, on the sheltered bays, and inland.

Gradually the coastline of Borga changed, growing flatter. Forests and meadows gave way to broad, monotonous marshlands. Then, at the northern tip of the island, a line of ships came into view.

Lonn was perched in the shrouds meditating when the lookout close to him on the mainmast shouted the warning. The ships were still a long way off but Lonn could tell at a glance they were drommons, sleek Tathian war galleys, guarding the entrance to the channel.

He leapt from his place and slid down a lanyard, not taking the time to descend the ratlines. Before reaching the deck he was shouting for his mates to fetch their weapons.

"Drommons!" he yelled. "More than you've ever seen."

The Iruks knew the swift Tathian warships well, having run from them more than once on pirating forays in the shipping lanes of the Polar Sea. The drommons had two masts with lateen sails, as well as oars for soft-water running. Each galley carried forty fighting men, marines armed with bows, lances and swords. The ships had high fighting decks and boarding bridges. Most were equipped with iron rams and long tubes in the prow that belched a fiery liquid. The Iruks went below and armed themselves, more by instinct than plan. There was plainly no chance of fighting through such a fleet.

The sails were being reefed and the coaster's speed was slackening as the klarn came back on deck. They found the captain at the quarterdeck rail, observing the fleet through a spyglass.

"They fly the banner of the Dragon Amid the Waves," he muttered, "The flag of Kadavel."

"What will you do?" Lonn asked.

"I don't know what! That's for the witch to decide. I hope she comes out here, and soon."

Banks of white cloud loomed over the drommon ships and the marshy shores they guarded. The *Plover* followed a long easterly tack that gave a panoramic view of the still-distant fleet. The drommons made no move from their orderly rows, though by now they must have spotted the coaster.

Amlina marched up the steps from below, leaning to one side to compensate for the tilt of the vessel. The witch had hardly ventured from her cabin in the days since rising from the deep trance. She looked frail and haggard to Lonn, yet she took the spyglass from Troneck's hand impatiently and used it to scan the lines of drommons.

"Come about and aim for the center of their formation," she said. "Bring us alongside their command vessel, which lies there."

Troneck shouted the proper orders. "I hope they don't decide to attack us before we can hail them," he said.

"They will talk," Amlina answered. "I have foreseen this obstacle."

The *Plover* came about and glided toward the upwind fleet. Two hundred yards from the front line of drommons Troneck gestured to the helmsman, who eased into the wind. The coaster's momentum slowed, prow aimed at the center of the line where a larger drommon stood, its extra-tall masts streaming with pennons of red and gold.

On the decks of the galleys, rows of lancers and bowmen stood tense and ready, as if expecting a fight from this one small trading ship. Amlina waved her arm in a wide, slow greeting.

Two crewmen crouched, ready at the ice-brakes, and dropped them at Troneck's signal. The *Plover* rumbled to a halt, balanced on keel and starboard runners, heeling to that side. The Tathian flagship lay some thirty yards off the starboard beam.

On the high forecastle of the flagship, a trumpeter blew an imposing set of notes. Then a herald called out through a megaphone. "You are detained by the war fleet of the Princely City of Kadavel. Reveal to us your nationality and reasons for sailing in this channel."

Amlina took the megaphone from a willing Troneck. "We are traders of Larthang," she answered. "We seek the port of Kadavel to ply our business."

The herald exchanged words with a tall man in gold armor and purple cloak, then shouted to the Larthangans again. "This is no trading season. Why do you sail this time of year?"

"We were trading off the coast of Near Nyssan," Amlina called back, "when a gale blew us out to sea. There we were caught by a freezewind and icebound many days. It's only now we've been able to fight our way back to land."

There was another pause, then the herald told them. "Hold your position. My lord Admiral Dantonius will board your vessel. If you tell the truth, you'll be allowed to sail on."

A dozen of the Tathian marines climbed down the side of the flagship, followed by the man in gold armor. They deployed themselves on his either side and accompanied him across the glowing ice toward the coaster. On the decks of the drommons, the rest of the marines still stood in battle readiness.

Amlina ordered that a rope ladder be lowered for the boarding party. She descended to the main deck to greet them, Lonn and his mates following. The Iruks kept glancing nervously at the nearby drommons, Karrol and Eben fingering the hilts of their swords.

"Do not draw your weapons," Amlina warned. "Leave everything to me."

They waited near the mainmast while six of the Tathians climbed over the bulwark and arranged themselves at attention. Then the man in gold and purple appeared, stepping onto the deck with a gloomy, suspicious expression on his red-bearded face.

"Lord Dantonius," one of the men announced as more of the marines climbed over the rail. "High Admiral of the Kadavellan fleet."

"My lord Dantonius," Amlina stepped forward and bowed. "You are most welcome. I am named Korre Kuan-Sen, daughter of Liffaniel, the owner of this ship. Our home port is Randoon of the Onyx Gates."

The admiral gestured abruptly to his men, all but two of whom marched off to search the holds and cabins. "You are in command?" he asked. "A woman?"

"My father sent me on this voyage for education," Amlina replied, her voice more soft and husky than Lonn was accustomed to hearing. "I am his lone heir, and one day will be mistress of his shipping concerns. But tell me, my lord, I thought Kadavel a prosperous and open market. Why should a war fleet block the way there?"

"Because the navy of a foreign power sits on the ice some thirty miles out from here," Dantonius said. "We fear an invasion may be imminent."

"What foreign nation do you mean?" Amlina asked, her voice losing some of its artificial sweetness to surprise.

Dantonius hesitated. "I am the one to ask the questions." He glanced about, eyes settling on the Iruks. "You and most of your crew are plainly Larthangans," he said to Amlina. "But these armed ones in leather and furs are barbarians—of South Polar stock unless my guess is wrong."

"They are Iruks from beyond Fleevan," Amlina admitted.

"Then why are they onboard your ship? You said you were blown here from Nyssan."

"Indeed. But we traveled there by way of the southern seas rather than the more usual routes. My father wanted me to be acquainted with a wide range of countries and markets. We took on these Iruks in Fleevanport. They've been good sailors, and they double as bodyguards. Don't mind their weapons. When they saw your sails they naturally jumped to arms."

Dantonius scanned the klarnmates again. "They've a reputation as brigands, these Iruks. But they're seldom seen outside the South Polar Sea. What made these five sign up with you?"

"Ask them yourself. They are versed in Low Tathian." Amlina's voice sounded coy, as though she mildly resented Dantonius' switching his attention from her.

The commander snorted and started to repeat his question to the Iruks, but Eben interrupted him. "We were curious to see more of the world."

"You are so suspicious, Admiral," Amlina touched his arm lightly. "I assure you, no one on my poor ship means to make war on Kadavel."

The admiral's frown relaxed into a brief smile. As the conversation continued Lonn realized that Amlina's mien, concocted of sweetness and femininity, was a mask meant to charm this Tathian. And it was working.

The marines returned two by two and reported on their search of the ship and the meager items they had found. Lonn wondered that they didn't mention Amlina's trinkets and magic devices, but surmised that the witch had had the foresight to put them away.

"Since you must now be convinced I have told you the truth," Amlina said, "may I ask you a question? How serious is this threat of invasion? Please be candid, my lord. If the danger is grave, it may be better for us to bypass Kadavel."

"The danger is impossible to reckon," Dantonius confessed. "It is not the fleet of ships we fear. We're a match for any war fleet in the world. But this is the navy of a great witch, she who is called the Archimage of the East. That is what worries us, for there is already ungoverned sorcery loose about the city."

"Sorcery? What do you mean?" Amlina asked.

"It started 14 days ago. First the sealight began to flicker on and off in the city harbor and canals. The glow has been erratic ever since, at times shining brilliantly, at others fading to nothing. Then one afternoon a freezewind blew across the channel, but a short time later a meltwind came from the opposite direction. Since then the Two Winds have clashed back and forth, melting and refreezing the harbor, at times roaring their conflict above the city itself. Scholars say it is worse than when the Witch King of Borga besieged Kadavel with an army of windbringers. The temples on the Long Acropolis are crowded with supplicants, some of them paid by the city fathers of course, but many there out of genuine fear."

"And you believe it is the Archimage preparing to invade Kadavel?"

"News of her fleet's presence beyond these straits reached the city six days ago. The connection is obvious since this witch of Tallyba possesses a great magic artifact called the Cloak of the Two Winds. We were dispatched at once to take up this position. We are ordered only to watch for the enemy and not to leave the vicinity of our own shores—where it is believed the charms of our State Sorcerers can more efficiently aid us if there is an attack."

"But it is tedious and worrisome to only wait," Amlina said softly. "I understand."

Dantonius regarded her appreciatively and nodded. "Young lady, you are free to sail on, whether to Kadavel or elsewhere, you must decide." He bowed to Amlina, then waved to his men to debark. He was about to follow the last of them over the rail when he turned back to Amlina.

"We will lend you the aid of our windbringers to get you underway,"

"My lord, I thank you," Amlina bowed, an innocent smile on her face.

"You handled him adeptly." Draven grinned as they watched the Tathians walk back across the ice. "Was it witchery that turned the admiral so pliantly in your hand?"

"In a sense," Amlina replied. "It is a minor art, part witchery, part acting, termed the passive persuasion. One shows to another the face they are most likely to accept and cooperate with. I was never especially good at it—too willful my teachers always said. But it wasn't difficult with this admiral. I sensed he would respond favorably to a charming but rather inept merchant woman. I've had dealings with Kadavellan men before."

The witch turned away, stalking toward the quarterdeck, and the Iruks followed.

Troneck's men were hastening about, unreefing sails and raising the ice-brakes. The bostulls of the *Plover*, aided perhaps by those from the Kadavellan fleet, brought a brisk counter wind to the coaster's sails. The ship lurched into motion, and gained speed as it passed through the ranks of the Tathian warships.

"How long now to the city?" Amlina inquired of Troneck, who had taken charge of the helm.

"Tacking against this west wind, three days or four."

"I don't believe the wind will change," Amlina said, staring absently down at the ice.

"What do you make of the admiral's news?" Lonn asked her. "About the winds and sealight in Kadavel?"

Before she could respond Kizier interrupted, asking that she repeat the tidings. Amlina crouched on the deck and informed the bostull of all they had heard.

"So apparently we have seen correctly," the witch added. "The Cloak is indeed in Kadavel. And it is being misused."

"Dangerously misused," the windbringer affirmed. "And the Kadavellans think it is Beryl's doing, a prelude to invasion."

"She will be in Kadavel," Amlina muttered. "If I had any doubts before, they are gone. I will meet her there. I know it."

Her eyes caught Lonn's. "I want you Iruks to bring all your weapons to my cabin this evening and leave them. I will weave designs on them to increase their usefulness."

Lonn nodded solemnly, but Karrol objected.

"Our weapons are fine as they are. We never let anyone outside the klarn handle them."

Amlina answered coldly. "In this case, you must make an exception. Your blades and points will not be lethal against creatures of magic unless they themselves are imbued with magic."

Karrol frowned and started to answer, but then pressed her lips together. Lonn read no disagreement on the faces of Brinda or Eben.

"We will bring you our weapons," he told the witch.

Thirteen

Fighting against the west wind the *Plover* sailed on toward Kadavel. As hours passed the channel widened, but the shores on either side remained swampy fields of reeds and sedge. No human habitations were sighted that day or the next, nor any habitable land.

But the following morning Eben called his mates to the prow. Lonn, who was running in place and chanting, went with them. Eben had sighted an enormous, distant structure towering over the ice. As the coaster veered to another tack other structures came into view, standing behind the first. It was some time before the shapes of the structures could be made out.

"The first one is a fish," Karrol declared. "With its tail in the air."

There were seven of the giant statues in all, the second also shaped like a fish. The forms of the others were harder to discern, though Lonn thought the last two seemed human. The statues were of black stone or metal, Lonn could not tell which, and colossal. The first fish on its pedestal loomed perhaps two hundred feet above the level of the ice.

As the ship drew closer the Iruks could see more details. The fish was like no fish ever carved by human hand. Its form was bizarre, disproportionate. The face had character, an intelligence in the bulging eyes, appetite in the gaping mouth.

"Ugly," Draven said.

And now they could tell what the other statues showed: a progression, through various stages, from fish to human form. Yet the last statue was not exactly human. The back was elongated, the shoulders slumping. The eyes still bulged and the lipless mouth still gaped. The overall effect was hideous.

Lonn shivered. "Let's go and hear what Kizier knows about these."

The *Plover* was gliding beneath the first huge statue when the Iruks reached the quarterdeck.

"They are called the Serd Monuments of Lustre," the windbringer said. "Gruesome, are they not?"

"Yes," all the Iruks agreed.

"Just so. Sculpted according to a completely nonhuman aesthetic. They represent the transformation of the serds from their fish form to their air-breathing land form. They are among the few artifacts remaining on Glimnodd from the time when the serds ruled."

"If these are examples of their art," Draven said. "I can understand why few others remain. What I don't understand is why these haven't been dismantled."

"Because no one knows how," the bostull answered. "The statues are neither metal nor stone but some unknown, impervious substance. They have survived numerous attempts to destroy them, both by magic and human engineering. They were built to stand till the end of the world, and perhaps they will."

The Iruks' eyes were raised, studying the gigantic monstrosities with morbid fascination. The things reminded Lonn of something from a nightmare, yet he could not pull his gaze away.

"One good thing about passing the monuments," Kizier remarked. "It means we are nearing Kadavel."

* * * * *

That afternoon Amlina sent the cabin boy to summon the Iruks to her quarters. The klarn arrived to find eight of the witch's dangling trinkets hung in a circle above the low table. The Iruks' weapons lay on the table, the knives and swords carefully arranged, the spears neatly packed in their quivers. Amlina, wearing a quilted robe embroidered with orange flowers, gestured at the table.

"You may take back your weapons. I have done all I can to fortify them,"

Each of the Iruks picked up a spear or blade, hefted it or tested the point. Lonn could discern no obvious change in the sword he held, yet he sensed a subtle difference. Perhaps the sword felt a bit lighter and easier to handle. It seemed charged with some indescribable energy.

"You can test the weapons outside," Amlina said. "I trust you'll find them undamaged. I have something else for you."

She opened her jewel box. Inside lay six small moonstones in settings of beaten silver, fastened on leather thongs.

"They are amulets," the witch said, "one for each of you and one for Glyssa when we find her. I want you to wear them around your necks for as long as we are allies."

Draven grinned as he took the first amulet from the box.

"Wait," Karrol said. "I'm not sure we should wear your necklaces. We'll have to talk it over."

The other Iruks said nothing. Draven frowned as he put the amulet back.

"The decision affects the klarn," Lonn explained to Amlina. "Karrol has the right to demand that we talk it over."

"Very well." Amlina laid the jewel box on the table. "But take them with you. And while you discuss whether to wear them, consider this: the amulets were made to protect you against evil. The stones are attuned to the stones in this fillet I wear. They will give you to share in the protective aura in which I enwrap myself. This is not a gift a deepshaper gives lightly, since to extend the barrier can diminish its power."

"We are honored and grateful," Draven told her, with deep feeling.

"Go and have your discussion," Amlina said. "Lonn, I want you to return at sunset and bring Kizier. If you've decided not to wear the amulets, you can return them to me then."

The Iruks gathered up their weapons, Lonn taking the six amulets in his hand, and left the witch's cabin.

"Why are you so contrary?" Draven said angrily to Karrol in the passageway. "You insulted Amlina with your suspicions."

"The witch makes me suspicious," Karrol replied. "Why are you so blindly trusting?"

"Easy," Brinda said. "Let's not fight each other just because we have our swords back. Let's go below and hold a proper meeting."

The klarnmates stashed the weapons in their room, then sat down around the stove. Lonn placed the six moonstones on the straw mat before them.

"I don't trust the witch, and I think I have good reasons," Karrol asserted to start the meeting. "She has Lonn's mind so emptied that he walks around looking half-dead. Draven's turned into her toady, saying yes to whatever she wants without thinking. And did you see how she simpered and slinked with that Tathian admiral?"

"It got us past the fleet, didn't it?" Draven said.

"Yes. But how do we know she hasn't been using that passive persuasion on us all along, showing us whatever face will make us most agreeable?"

"It hasn't made you agreeable," Draven scoffed.

"Stop interrupting. You should be glad one of us is keeping her head. Now these necklaces she wants us to wear. Suppose their real purpose is to sap our wills, make us her slaves? I say no, I won't wear it."

She sat down heavily and Draven jumped up.

"Amlina is our ally," he said. "From the start, she's done us nothing but good. She took us on her ship, fed us, made us her partners. All this after we robbed her of the Cloak and brought her this trouble in the first place. Not once has she given us reason to distrust her." He picked up one of the necklaces, showed it around. "Now she offers to share her own magic protection with us. I say we'd be fools to refuse."

No one else seemed ready to speak, so after a few moments Lonn took his turn, quietly and laconically stating that he agreed with Draven's view. After that Eben stood, remarking that Draven's assessment had convinced him also. The witch had not given the Iruks cause to distrust her. Until she did, Eben felt the amulets should be worn. When he was finished there was a short silence, and then Brinda rose and spread her hands.

"It seems the vote's already decided. And I don't disagree with it, mates. But I do think it's good that Karrol is suspicious of the witch. It will keep us on our guard. If it begins to seem these amulets are draining our wills, then we can take them off. Meantime let's wear them and see."

"Suppose we've lost our wills before we know it?" Karrol asked sullenly.

"I believe we would sense it happening in time to prevent it," Brinda answered.

"Then the klarn has decided," Lonn said, placing his hand in the center. "We will wear the witch's amulets."

The others put their hands on his, except for Karrol.

"No," she said. "I always give in to the rest of you, against my own judgment. But not this time."

"The klarn has decided," Lonn told her firmly.

"You can decide however you like," Karrol snapped. "But not for me. This is what I think of the witch and her tricks."

She snatched one of the amulets and jumped to her feet. Before anyone could stop her she had pulled open a window and flung the amulet away.

The mates stared at her, open-mouthed.

"You've wounded the klarn," Draven accused.

"Don't blame *me* for that," Karrol answered defiantly. "It was wounded when we lost Glyssa. It was wounded when you let me skate after her alone."

"But we followed you," Brinda said.

Karrol started to answer, then threw up her hands. A look of hopeless rage crossed her face. She turned away, marched from the storeroom and slammed the door.

Lonn looked around at the others, all of them stunned. To wound the klarn in an act of defiance diminished the group spirit, bled away its protection. But, on reflection, Lonn had to admit there was some truth in Karrol's words.

Normally, during a hunt, the klarn spirit was perceptible, a strength they could feel inside. Since they lost Glyssa it had been different. Lonn had sensed some of the spirit's power after they pulled Karrol out of the sea, and again in the fight with the tusk bears on Windbock. But this voyage on strange seas, the long days of inactivity, and most of all Lonn's training with the witch—all had weakened the klarn. The bond between them now seemed looser, less real.

Hold fast to the klarn, Belach the shaman had told them. But *could* they hold it together? And would *it* still protect them?

To Lonn only one thing seemed certain. They needed to find Glyssa and rescue her. And soon.

* * * * *

That evening, Lonn carried Kizier to Amlina's cabin. The witch told him to put the bostull's pail down on the floor and sit beside it. Lonn noted that the desmets and prisms had been rearranged, placed as they were on the night of his initiation. On Amlina's instructions, he removed his boots and belt. The witch set a glowing lamp on the floor before him.

"I see you are wearing the amulet." She sat down and crossed her legs. "I'm glad you decided to."

"All of us except Karrol," Lonn answered, and told her how the meeting had ended.

"I am sorry she bears me such ill will."

"She broke the unity of the klarn," Lonn muttered. "It's a bad thing to happen, for all of us. But Karrol is stubborn."

"I hope she won't suffer for her stubbornness," Amlina said. Then her tone lightened. "Kizier tells me you've been diligent in your exercises."

"He has indeed," the bostull affirmed, blinking.

"I don't know what good they've done," Lonn answered.

"Then be not hasty to judge," Amlina said.

"I haven't seen any images of Glyssa, or dreamed of her either."

"I have told you before," the windbringer said. "The Deepmind yields its gifts in its own time, in its own way."

"Relax," Amlina told Lonn. "Straighten your back. Close your eyes. Take deep breaths."

Lonn obeyed.

After a while Amlina's voice returned, quiet and soothing. "I am going to introduce you to the second stage of the training. At your initiation, I used my mind-force to open in you the portal of deepseeing. This time, you will open the portal yourself."

She instructed Lonn to visualize a globe of light, white and brilliant, like sunshine on snow. He was to imagine the globe at the base of his spine. Once he saw it there she told him to picture it rising slowly up his back. With her words to guide him, Lonn saw the globe more and more clearly, felt it warm and tingling, watched it ascend. When the globe reached his head it seemed to burst, filling his brain with dazzling radiance. Distantly, Lonn realized his limbs were trembling.

"Now the light settles and dims," Amlina pronounced. "Slowly it changes, white light to silver. And you are looking at the sea. Everywhere is silvery water, tossing and flowing before your mind's eye, gently tossing and shifting ..."

For a long time, Amlina kept him watching the sea image. Whenever his mind wandered she would sense it and describe again the waters he must keep seeing. Finally, the vision of gleaming water overwhelmed him, dissolving his sense of himself, till there was only the water and no longer Lonn watching it.

So that, when Amlina's voice told him to picture Draven's image in the water, Lonn was momentarily taken aback to be reminded of his own existence. But then Draven's image appeared, clear and solid, and Lonn, wondering at it, forgot himself again.

Amlina asked if he could see Draven and he nodded. She told him to describe the picture and Lonn did so, telling her of Draven's expression and what he wore.

Then Amlina told him to envision Karrol as she was in that instant. Immediately Lonn could see her, seated alone on the forecastle, frowning as she watched the passing shore. He described the picture, and Amlina said it was well-seen.

Next, the witch told him to picture his home island and the klarn's house there. Lonn saw the lodge house as it appeared from the shoreline, atop the sloping beach. But the house was partly dismantled and many of the klarn's possessions were strewn across the ground. Gertraun and those other hunters, Lonn knew at once. They had carried out their threat to plunder the klarn's house. A groan of anger rose in his throat. His head started swimming.

"Relax." Amlina touched his forehead with her finger, soothing the upsurge of feeling. "Describe what you see."

Abruptly, Lonn opened his eyes. Amid silvery glitter he saw Amlina's face.

"Close your eyes," she said calmly, and he obeyed.

"You must not turn over control to your emotions," the witch admonished. "Relax and keep your eyes shut. Breathe slowly and deeply. Concentrate again on seeing the bright water. Let there be no image but this in your mind, no thought but of this."

For perhaps an hour Amlina made him watch the waters of the Deepmind, gently bringing his attention back to that image whenever it strayed. At last his self-awareness vanished as before, leaving only the restless waves of gray and silver. Then Amlina told him to picture Glyssa.

At once Glyssa's image appeared before his mind's eye, her face gaunt and pale, her eyes stricken. She gazed at him with a desperate, pleading look, and Lonn shuddered with pain and remorse.

"Do you see her?" Amlina asked, her voice soft as before, but tense.

Her words made the image ripple like a reflection in a pool. Much of it scattered, but the pleading eyes remained.

"Do you see her?" Amlina insisted.

"Yes."

"Describe her surroundings."

But as Glyssa's image resettled Lonn could see only blackness about her, shiny and dense.

"It's dark."

"Keep looking," Amlina said. "Light will come."

But instead the vision wavered again, threatening to vanish.

"She's alone," Lonn said, the knowledge coming from nowhere. "Frightened."

"She can speak to you," Kizier's voice suggested. "Ask where she is."

Lonn trembled as he mouthed the question. Then his head shook. "She can't answer me. She can't move ... even her hand."

With a sob, Lonn slumped over sideways and curled up. He had glimpsed Glyssa's state of helplessness and isolation. He knew he had touched the truth, and it racked him with an unbearable grief. Glyssa's image had dissolved entirely now, and sparks of silver blew like snow through his mind.

Amlina laid a hand on his shoulder and told him to sit up. Abruptly he did, blinking and rubbing his eyes. At last they cleared, and he saw Amlina and Kizier watching him with sober concern. Lonn shook himself, then leaned his forehead on his fists, breathing heavily, trying not to weep.

"You are gifted with deep vision," Amlina said after a time. "But you have too much emotion. You saw Glyssa in truth, but your feelings of pain dispersed the image."

"What should I have done?" Lonn asked.

Amlina sighed. "You did all you could, which was to look and react. It's your reactions that need tempering. But that takes time. Of which we have little. At least you did see her, which indicates she is still alive."

"Let me try again," Lonn said.

"Not now. Your emotions are aroused. They need time to settle. Besides, Glyssa is hidden by strong designs, no doubt the same as hide the Cloak. That is the meaning of the shiny darkness you saw."

"Then how will we find her when we get to Kadavel?"

"By whatever means the Deepmind provides," the witch said. "We will take up lodgings, and I will search with the deepsight. The perspective will be different once we are inside the city. If, in a few days, I have not discovered the Cloak, I will guide you into another trance and we will look for Glyssa again."

Amlina extinguished the lamp on the floor and stood. "Meantime you should rest and meditate as much as time allows."

Numb and shaken, Lonn carried Kizier through the dim passage and up the steps to the quarterdeck.

"You should rejoice." the bostull said as Lonn put him down. "You were able to see Glyssa and know she is alive."

"I know," Lonn said. "But the pain I felt—her pain—was terrible."

He shivered at the recollection and looked off astern. Low in the east hung Rog, a blood-red sickle cutting the clouds.

* * * * *

All that night Amlina sat in wei trance, viewing the image of Glyssa that she had apprehended from Lonn's mind. But though Amlina moved in the Deepmind with practiced skill, she could see no more of the vision than Lonn had seen: a small and frightened woman surrounded by shiny blackness, the image constantly rippling, threatening to dissolve into the dark.

Fourteen

A turmoil of clouds, blue-gray and pink, hung over Kadavel in the dawn. Beneath the clouds, the city spread in an enormous confusion of gabled roofs and twisting streets, crawling gradually up to two stark outcroppings of black rock—the Long Acropolis and the High. Along the waterfront stood broad quays of wood and stone, and beyond them reared a wooden wall, broken every few hundred feet by tall gates with dragon arches. Lonn recognized the boldly carved dragons: This was indeed the harbor he had dreamed.

He and his mates stared in wonder as the city drew near. Kadavel was even larger than the Iruks had expected, perhaps ten times the size of Fleevanport, the largest town they knew. Lonn's elation at recognizing the city gates was dampened by a seed of despair. Glancing around, he saw similar awe and apprehension reflected on the faces of his mates.

How would they ever find Glyssa in such a place?

For the last day and night the wind had been slack, the *Plover* relying mostly on the bostulls. The channel had continued to widen until the shore of Borga dropped away entirely, leaving open ice to the south. To the north the coast had altered, rocky hills appearing some distance inland, columns of rising smoke there testifying to habitation. Then, in the night, the *Plover* had passed villages built on stilts along the marshy shore.

Finally, in the first morning light, the coaster entered the harbor of Kadavel, called the Shipway. It stretched a mile across and several miles long, enclosed by two curved sandbars. The *Plover's* whole company had assembled on the decks to watch the city draw near on the starboard side, or to scan the rows of anchored vessels to port. In this non-sailing season, the Shipway was crowded with barges and freighters from all corners of the Three Nations. Every shape of hull and type of rigging the Iruks had ever seen was here—and others they had never imagined.

Troneck had argued against sailing along the front row of ships, declaring that all the slips so near the city would obviously be filled. But Amlina had insisted, saying they would find a mooring at exactly the luckiest place.

The coaster's arrival was spotted from the city quays and a number of boats, their lateen sails hoisted, started out to intercept the newcomer. These were skimmers, small flat-bellied craft that ferried passengers and freight back and forth from the anchored ships to the city.

Five of the skimmers were racing toward the coaster when suddenly a meltwind blew. It seemed to ripple into existence just a few yards astern of the *Plover*. The Iruks hardly knew it was coming before the blinding witchlight and flash of heat was upon them. Lonn watched the scintillating curtain sweep on across the harbor, dropping the lines of moored ships down to toss on the newly soft water.

It was a moment before he realized the water was dark, absolutely dark, the seaglow gone from it. Lonn and his mates exchanged looks of unease. They had learned to expect this from the Kadavellan admiral. Yet being told of it had not prepared them for the weird, unnerving sight of a broad expanse of lightless seawater. The Larthangan crewmen were equally startled. Troneck had to bawl the command through his megaphone three times before men moved to haul in the ice runners.

Off to starboard, the skimmers had adjusted their sheets to the shifted breeze and were pulling near the coaster. Amlina took Troneck's megaphone and called to the Tathians.

"We seek a berth in the inmost row. Is there such a one toward the middle of the city?"

"By a twist of luck there is," shouted the helmsman of the foremost skimmer. "Just yesterday a Xinnerite freighter was divested of a prime slip for failing to meet its fees. Throw us your line and we'll show you the place."

The line was tossed and one of the three-man crew fastened it to the skimmer's bow. This action, Troneck explained, gave the lead boat first claim on the *Plover*, the right to collect its taxes and mooring fees. The men in the trailing boats shouted to inquire whether more than one skimmer would be needed. Amlina answered no, whereupon the skimmers turned through the wind and headed back to shore.

Meantime the lead boat had pulled alongside the coaster and the skimmer men were climbing up a ladder lowered to accommodate them. Dressed in wools and leathers, with sea boots that reached to their thighs, the three Tathians crossed the main deck with a crisp gait. They trotted up the steps to the quarterdeck, glanced curiously at the armed Iruks, then bowed to Amlina and Troneck.

The leader of the three held up a seal worn on a chain around his neck—his license from the city's harbor authorities. He told the helmsman to hold course, that the mooring place was not far off. Then he demanded to know what cargo the ship carried and from whence it had sailed in this off-season. Amlina repeated the story she had used on the admiral, of their being blown out to sea from the coast of Nyssan.

"We've almost no cargo left in our holds," she admitted. "We'll need to hire ourselves out to a shipper of your city."

"You may have a long wait for a contract," the harbor man replied indifferently. "There are many empty ships in port, and the winter season doesn't start till next month."

He dispatched his two crewmen to search below in order to verify Amlina's report, then took an abacus from inside his doublet and began to make calculations.

"I'll charge you for only two small-month's harbor fees today, though the odds are you'll end up staying longer. When the 22 days are over, I'll call on you again."

"Myself and these five bodyguards will be going ashore in your craft," Amlina told him. "You may add that charge to the others."

"Will you be needing supplies ferried out for the rest of your crew?"

"No. They will go ashore in our skiffs to purchase what they need."

The Tathian nodded, his fingers busy with the counters. Troneck interrupted him to ask about the darkening of the sealight.

"It's been going on and off for more than half a month now." The Tathian shrugged. "Sometimes the Aubergale blows out the sealight, sometimes the Glazer does. Sometimes the light goes on and off when no winds are about. If there's a pattern to it, no one's figured it out. If there's a cause, no one knows what it is."

"It makes me shiver to think of," Troneck complained. "Doesn't it worry you Kadavellans?"

"Some it does. Me, I'm a businessman, and so far my business has not been affected. If it keeps up into the sailing season, and traders began to shun Kadavel because of it, then that's another matter. Meantime I'll tend to my own business and not look for more to worry about than that. Your vacant slip lies ahead."

The coaster approached the empty berth, a single gap in the long line of close-anchored vessels. The dry dock consisted of a concrete ramp set with stone runners. As the ship's prow floated to the bottom of the ramp, Troneck barked orders for all sails to be lowered. When this was done, six of the sailors scrambled over the side and stepped onto the lower part of the dock. The rest of the crew were dispatched below to let out the anchor chains and stand by the capstan. The crewmen on the dock dragged the twin chains up to the top of the ramp and locked them onto stout bollards. Troneck shouted word to the men below to turn the capstan. The chains were pulled tight, the deck tilted, and with a thunderous roll the *Plover* was hauled up the ramp.

A dry dock allowed a ship's hull to be repaired, the ice runners scraped and sharpened. Crucially, it also kept a craft from becoming icebound if a freezewind blew. With the incline and rollers, a ship could easily be launched again onto either ice or soft water. Lonn had seen dry docks before: the more expensive berths in Fleevanport used the mechanism. Here in Kadavel there seemed to be hundreds.

While the ship was being secured, the two Tathians returned from below and reported to their skipper. He double-checked his figures and announced a sum to Amlina. The witch paid him in small silver coins, nearly emptying her purse. The skimmer man presented her with a set of documents from a sealed leather packet. He and his men then climbed over the side to prepare their skimmer for casting off.

Amlina handed Troneck the small number of coins she had left.

"At the prices they charge, this will buy us supplies for eight or ten days at the most," he said.

"After that, you can sell what's left of the cargo."

"As you say, Lady. But with the tariffs and hauling charges, there won't be much left to purchase supplies. And in 22 days there'll be the harbor fees to pay again."

Amlina sighed. "If you've not heard from us in that time you are free of me. You can sell my possessions in the Street of the Magic Vendors. The price they bring should see you back to Larthang, whether you find a cargo here or not."

"And you'll release us from your spell?"

"I promise it. On the condition that you swear to see Kizier safely back to Larthang, that he may give an account of the Cloak at the House of the Deepmind."

"Very well. I swear it."

JACK MASSA

Amlina looked him deeply in the eyes, then turned away. She knelt before Kizier and touched his upper leaves gently.

"I will miss your wise advice, my friend."

"I wish I could go with you," he said. "I will send you light in my thoughts, of course. I wish I could do more. You Iruks, take good care of her."

Surprised by the bostull's show of affection for the witch, Lonn merely grunted.

"We will guard her well," Draven promised.

The klarnmates followed Amlina to the main deck, where Karrol and Eben lifted two large bundles. One was Amlina's, carefully wrapped in canvas and tied with cord. The other belonged to the Iruks and consisted of their spears and skates rolled up with spare furs. They lowered the gear over the side, then clambered down the ladder. They marched down the edge of the ramp and boarded the skimmer, sitting three abreast in the center. The Tathians pushed off from the dock and hoisted the sail, which the boat's lone windbringer managed to fill at once with a favorable wind.

As the skimmer started across the harbor toward the immensity of the city, Lonn noticed that the seaglow had returned, sparkling in the flapping waves. In the sky the clouds still hovered, towering thunderheads sliding over lower white formations.

"We wish to land at the Luxury Market," Amlina told the skipper. "Is the Jeweler's Walk still located behind the Quay of the Silk Traders?"

"It was moved several years ago," the skimmer man answered. "It now occupies the rear quarter of what used to be the Bazaar of Exotic Wines. We will drop you at the nearest gate."

When the skimmer was halfway to the city docks a freezewind blew. The skipper told his mates to trim sail and his passengers to duck their heads. Lonn and the others did so, feeling the breeze pick up, then change to an icy gust. The boat leaned and bumped hard, jumping up, then burst ahead with hull-set runners rustling on the new ice. Lonn looked up, then immediately shaded his eyes. The witchlight had intensified to a blinding glare.

Running fleetly now, the skimmer pulled abreast of the marble quays. They sailed past two of the high dragon gates before the helmsman turned abruptly, swinging upwind with a hissing sound and a spray of ice flakes slashed up by the runners. The craft stopped neatly beside the steps of the pier.

Amlina got exact directions to the Jewelers' Walk before stepping ashore. The Iruks had already jumped from the boat and received their bundles, tossed to them by the skimmer men.

"Keep close together," Amlina said as they mounted the steps. "You could easily get lost."

Even in this off-season, the waterfront here at the center of the city was crowded. Skimmer men and stevedores carried bundles up and down the steps, warmly-dressed peddlers hawked their wares, city guardsmen patrolled on the backs of gangling six-limbed mounts called aklors.

Amlina and the Iruks crossed the wide pier and passed beneath the dragon arch. They found themselves at the entrance to a long enclosed avenue with cedar porticoes lifting up to a wooden roof. This was the start of the Luxury Market, and the Iruks had never dreamed anything like it. The avenue was thronged with vendors and shoppers, wool-clad Tathians mostly, but also Larthangans in heavy silks and furs, and people of Nyssan in their long coats and feathered bonnets. Most went afoot, but some rode aklors, and many of the well-to-do reclined in palanquins with stove pipes jutting through the roofs. In the swarm of people from so many far-flung realms, the Iruks elicited little notice. The place resounded with a babble of voices: dealers accosting passers-by, customers haggling over prices.

Amlina led the Iruks down the avenue, past stalls of imported rugs and fine tapestries, through the Bazaar of the Lamp Vendors with its booths of fire boxes, gilded braziers, scented oils, and wind-proof lanterns.

"Why did you bring us here?" Karrol demanded of the witch.

"Because I am out of money. I need to arrange for our finances. Afterward, we'll find an inn."

"We finally arrive in this city and all you think about is money and a roof," Karrol bickered. "We are here to find Glyssa. We ought to start looking at once."

"That is impractical," Amlina said. "To search in the Deepmind I must have solitude. And all of us must be fed and kept warm, so that we'll be in condition to act when the time comes."

"I had thought the time would have come by now," Karrol grumbled, this time in Iruk.

They marched on, passing the Bazaar of Fine Porcelain and the Gallery of Clocks, then turned down a side lane cluttered with stalls selling carved jade, glass cages with live butterflies, pots with singing flowers.

At last they reached the Jewelers' Walk, where the booths sparkled with silver, gold and gemstones arranged in locked cases. This section was heavily guarded and the patrolmen, with their truncheons and leather armor, kept a close watch on the barbarous, sword-bearing Iruks. Lonn and his mates did their best to appear innocent and nonchalant as they kept pace with the witch. Amlina walked with arms folded in sleeves, her visage alert as if listening for something. She passed numerous stalls before stopping at one presided over by a man whose enormous belly was covered with heavy gold chains and necklaces. Glancing about, Lonn noticed the booth was out of the direct sight of any guardsman, though a half-dozen could come at once if summoned.

Amlina smiled at the jewel merchant and introduced herself as Soo Ang-Zinn of Clom Fei in Larthang. She explained that she had some pieces to sell, not ordinary jewelry but the artifacts of a witch.

"Their witchery means nothing to me," the dealer said as Amlina handed him her moonstone fillet. "I pay only according to their value as jewelry. The Street of the Magic Vendors is five bazaars north of here."

"I see." Amlina sounded downcast as she lay four etched silver bangles on the counter. "How much will you buy them for as jewelry?"

The fat man half-smiled as he appraised the bangles, then the fillet again. "Silver's rather a glut on the market right now. Gold and electrum are the fashion. The headband is fairly made, though this bit of firescale lowers its worth. The bracelets are commonplace. I can offer you forty ellas for the lot."

"But they are worth much more than that," Amlina said. "These stones are from the Liihan Mountains in western Larthang. Their sheen is unlike any other in the world."

Here Lonn noticed that Amlina's hand was removing an emerald ring from a case beside the dealer's chair. Her hand had reached right past the fat man, and he ought to have noticed. But his eyes remained locked with Amlina's.

"The sheen of the moonstones is unremarkable," he said.

The conversation continued in the same tenor, Amlina extolling the pieces of jewelry as persistently as the dealer demeaned them. They bargained for a price, but the Tathian would not go above fifty-five ellas nor Amlina below ninety. In the meantime, her hand sneaked past his considerable girth and picked up three more rings with faceted stones. Lonn recalled that the dealer had been arranging merchandise in that particular case when Amlina approached the booth. He realized it was the witch's mental influence that had caused him to neglect shutting and locking the case.

"I believe I am wasting your time," Amlina said when she had pocketed the fourth ring. "Perhaps I will try the Street of the Magic Vendors after all."

"Sixty ellas," the dealer said with a yawn. "Final offer."

Amlina shook her head, took back her pieces and bid the man good day. The Iruks followed her to a booth on the other end of the bazaar, where she sold the four pilfered rings for one hundred ellas each.

"This sum should see us through our stay in Kadavel." She spoke quietly as they left the Jeweler's Walk. "I'd rather not have to commit larceny more than once."

"But it was larceny so deftly committed," Draven laughed.

"I didn't know you had it in you," Lonn agreed. "I was convinced you meant to sell your own jewelry."

"Never," Amlina said. "These pieces are invested with my heart and mind."

* * * * *

The travelers proceeded west, past the Bazaar of Exquisite Perfumes and the Lane of Gilded Mirrors. Beyond the heavily-guarded Tables of the Money Changers, they skirted the northern portion of the huge Mart of Exotic Wines. A number of wine shops and cafes bordered here, and Amlina and the Iruks stopped at one. They munched on cheese and fresh bread and washed it down with mead from the Isle of Glistre—except for Amlina who drank only water.

Following the meal they continued west, passing bakeries and candy shops and the Bazaar of Rare Spices, and coming at last to the end of the Luxury Market. After descending the steps of a long colonnade they paused, standing beneath the sky for the first time since entering the city gate. The day had turned unnaturally dark, black clouds filling the sky and flashing occasionally with high lightning. The wind gusted sharply, and the Iruks secured their capes in front and pulled on their hoods.

Amlina peered into the entrances of the several streets that opened before them. At last she made up her mind and started across the open square.

Trudging behind her, Lonn and his mates entered a narrow street. Wooden buildings rose on either side, their upper stories leaning over the street and nearly touching in the middle. The street itself was also of wood, built on posts above the extensive marsh that underlay much of Kadavel. Only farther inland, toward the two acropolises, was the city built on solid ground.

Though it was the middle of the day only a few people passed by, hurrying along through the cold and dark. Amlina and the Iruks traversed a chandlers' quarter, then another neighborhood occupied mostly by butchers. They saw numerous inns and hostelries along the way, but Amlina insisted that none of them would do. For one thing, she did not want to stay too near the Luxury Market, for fear the jewelry dealer might spot them again. More importantly, she had to find a favorable location for deepseeing. The place had to be relatively quiet and properly aligned with the patterns of force in the city.

"Each place has its qualities," the witch explained. "I must find one in harmony with our purpose."

She led them on, farther from the Luxury Market, around toward the waterfront again. Lonn caught glimpses of the city walls, and presently they turned into a wide street ending on one of the dragon gates. The chandlers' neighborhood had smelled of wax and perfumes, the butchers' of blood and offal. This street smelled of the sea and fish. Lonn's impression that they had come to a fishermen's quarter was confirmed by the shops, which specialized in nets and other gear, and by a sign on a building halfway down the block, which pictured a hook about to be swallowed by a moonfish.

"There." Amlina's voice had a note of certainty.

She led them to the door beneath the moonfish sign. Inside the vestibule, they were met by a sharp-featured woman who looked them over guardedly.

"We require two private rooms," Amlina said. "The length of our stay is indefinite. I will pay you for the first ten days in advance."

"Well, for the six of you, with meals, the charge would be ... say twenty ellas for ten days."

"You grossly overcharge." Amlina reached into her purse. "But my funds are ample, and I am not inclined to dicker."

She handed some silver coins to the old woman, who examined them dourly then placed them in her pocket.

"I have only one room upstairs at the moment," she said. "The others are off the common room."

"We'll take the one upstairs and one down," Amlina said. "Kindly show us the way."

"Very well." The landlady turned and led them down the short corridor. "I am Elzna, the owner here. Who are you, if I might ask? We don't see many of your sort in this district, that's for sure. Are you just in from the Shipway?"

"We arrived in the city this morning," Amlina answered. "My name is Olicia Wor-T'sing. I am a scholar from the Academy of Foreign Nations in Larthang. These are my porters and bodyguards."

"Bodyguards are they? And women too."

They were crossing the large common room, all of rough-hewn wood, with a round stone fireplace at the center. Couches and sleeping mats were spread near the fire, a few of them occupied with afternoon nappers. Off in the corner, a quiet game of bones and dice was in progress.

"What's your business here, if I may inquire?" Elzna said.

"I am here to study and write," Amlina explained. "Scholars are sent out by the Academy every 72 years to update our knowledge of the various civilized realms. That is my task in Kadavel. It requires that I have a quiet place to work and that my solitude be absolutely undisturbed."

"Solitude, is it? Well, it's mostly quiet here, but I can't promise anything absolutely. These are unsettled times, you know. What with the winds in the harbor and rumors of invasion. Now this darkness in the middle of the day. Who knows what's going to happen next? I don't, that's for sure."

"So long as none of your tenants or servants disturb me," Amlina said, "I won't hold you responsible for cataclysm or war."

Perhaps a dozen private chambers bordered on the common room. The landlady opened the door to one of these and showed them inside. The room was furnished with two cots, a small table, and an oil lamp. One shuttered window opened onto an alley outside, another opposite onto the common room. A wood stove in the corner provided heat. Amlina assigned this room to the Iruks. While they were settling in she asked Lonn to carry her bundle upstairs.

He and the witch followed the landlady back across the common room and up a flight of creaky steps to an upper gallery. Amlina's room was larger and better furnished than the one downstairs, with a big featherbed, a couch, and a writing table. There was also a chest for clothes, a woven rug on the floor and worn tapestries on the walls. The landlady opened the flue of the small fireplace and showed Amlina the cupboard where fuel and kindling were stored.

"I will hang my trinkets and began searching at once," Amlina said when Elzna had gone. "You and your companions rest tonight. And make sure that crone of a landlady feeds you well. I paid her far better than I had to."

"We know how to handle innkeepers," Lonn answered.

"Don't start any trouble," the witch warned. "We must remain inconspicuous. But be alert. Keep an eye on who comes and goes, especially anyone who comes upstairs."

"Do you expect trouble here?"

"I'm not sure what to expect."

Fifteen

When Lonn had departed, Amlina shut and bolted her door, then went to unwrap her bundle. Murmuring prescribed verses, she unfolded the carefully-wrapped trinkets one by one. She attached the trinkets to silk cords and the cords to tacks. Standing on a chair, she stuck the tacks into the ceiling. She hung the trinkets in a prescribed arrangement—choosing in this case the *Hexagram within a Decahedron* as most auspicious to her purpose. She lit five lamps and placed them on the floor, measuring their distance from each other by counting finger-widths.

When this was done, Amlina prepared to enter trance. She sat cross-legged on the floor amidst her trinkets and lamps. She breathed deeply, stilled her body and mind. Slowly, she brought the shimmering globe of energy up her spine, to burst silently inside her head.

The portal to the Deepmind opened, but for a long time Amlina did not try to see. Instead, she concentrated on surrounding herself with white light, the sparkling radiance of her protective aura. She watched the barrier growing brighter, until at last she believed it strong enough to protect her. Then she focused on extending the barrier to encompass the Iruks as well.

When at length Amlina was satisfied that her allies were as well protected as herself, she turned her attention outward, to seek the Cloak of the Two Winds. At once she was aware of the difference between this and the last time she gazed into the Deepmind. From onboard the *Plover* the space of the Ogo had seemed relatively uncluttered. Inside the walls of Kadavel the Ogo teemed, multitudes of minds reflecting. Amlina perceived them as waves emanating from innumerable sources, clashing and mixing, disrupting her vision. She had known to expect this obstacle, having practiced deepseeing here and in other cities in the past. No doubt this was part of the reason she had been able to trace the Cloak to Kadavel but no farther. The normal confusion of the Ogo here would help conceal it. The only way to deepsee clearly here was to relax the will, let the mind ride the weltering currents until it became attuned to the chaos. This was what Amlina set out to do.

She opened her consciousness and the streams of impressions took her. She perceived the city as a gleaming maze of walls and spaces, spreading out from her in all directions. Beyond the maze, on one side, she felt the harbor, cold and frozen, yet tingling with captured energy. To the other side, farther away, she sensed massive rocks, the two acropolises, charged with telluric and human power.

Everywhere were sentient beings, a vast number of them. For a long time Amlina could only sense the confused clamor of those many separate minds. But at last the noise grew quiet, and she conceived of the many as unified—the collective mind of the city.

She allowed the collective mind to vibrate over her, drawing to herself its thoughts. In a flash, she envisioned the common room downstairs, the tenants of the inn grouped around the fire, grateful for its warmth. She saw their empty dinner plates, felt the fullness in their stomachs. She experienced their cheerfulness as they drank and conversed, their curiosity over herself and the Iruks. Beneath lay dimmer emotions, mostly repressed: unease at the ominous weather, the strange portents in the harbor and sky. Amlina's awareness flowed outward then, tasting these same emotions across the city— the abiding fear that had come to dwell constantly in people's hearts.

Conceiving the expanse of that fear, Amlina shivered. Next instant, an image of Beryl flicked into her mind. She viewed the Archimage's familiar countenance for a moment, then instinctively sought to turn away. To that image, she knew, her mind must not be open.

But Beryl's face would not disappear. It hung before Amlina, growing more distinct. Sensing her danger, Amlina touched the moonstone fillet and pictured white radiance pouring out to envelop her.

Beryl's image faded behind the barrier of light, but did not dissolve. The green eyes glared, piercing the barrier, wilting Amlina's concentration.

Suddenly the face caught fire, bursting into a dazzling mask of orange flame. The flame burned through Amlina's aura, heated the skin of her eyelids. Then she heard Beryl's whisper.

"Little Larthang, I have found you."

Amlina opened her eyes, yanked from her trance by terror. The flaming mask hovered before her, as real in the room as the trinkets and lamps. Amlina glimpsed two disembodied hands, fiery orange like the mask, reaching for her.

She tried to jump up and flee but the hands seized her throat, forcing her to sit. The fire burned her neck, but not unbearably. The grip was tight, but not yet a choking grip.

"They are Gloves of Far Reaching," Beryl said, "devised by the priests of the Star Gods in Tallyba to strangle sacrificial victims. The mask is a complementary trinket of my own design. Did you think I had shown you all my secrets, little fool?"

Amlina sought to pry the gloves from her neck, but their fire intensified, scorching her flesh. She tried to strike Beryl's mask, but her hands only swiped weakly then dropped—Beryl's will numbing her will even as Beryl's eyes bored into her mind, searching, reading.

"You've lost the Cloak. I knew this already. Ignorant little Larthang, did you really think you could hold it? Reveal to me all you know of the Cloak. Do not try to conceal, it is useless."

Even as she heard those words Amlina felt the core of her mind break open to Beryl's probing.

"You know little more than I," Beryl said at length. "The Cloak is somewhere in Kadavel, probably close to this Iruk woman. I have sensed the hand of another wielding the Cloak's power, disrupting the Ogo about this city. He is stealthy in his designs, this one. I've glimpsed him only briefly. But I will discover him in the end ..."

Pursuing this chain of thought the Archimage had allowed her grip to loosen, all but forgetting her former apprentice. Desperately, Amlina seized the chance.

Her hands shot up, palms covering Beryl's eyes. By the power of *pure shaping*, Amlina sent bolts of pain through those eyes into Beryl's brain. The fiery gloves let go of her throat and moved to clutch her wrists. Amlina eluded them and flung herself aside.

Staggering to her feet, she fled across the chamber, screaming for the Iruks to help her.

Ghoulishly, the disembodied mask and gloves gave chase.

One burning hand gripped Amlina's sleeve and set it smoldering. But Amlina tore free and reached the door. She flung back the bolt and pulled the door open, shrieking again for the Iruks, just as Beryl caught her from behind.

* * * * *

Lying in bed but not yet asleep, Lonn and his mates heard Amlina scream. At once they jumped from under the covers. Wearing their deerskin garments they rushed from the chamber, each pausing only to grab a sword or spear.

With Draven in the lead, they ran across the fire-lit common room, where most of the patrons were up and looking about in confusion. Lonn heard Amlina scream again as they dashed up the steps, knocking aside the landlady who had started up with a lantern to investigate.

A couple of tenants from nearby rooms had reached Amlina's door already. They stood at the threshold, staring inside, dumbfounded. Lonn and Draven shoved them out of the way and started into the room.

But what they saw caused even the Iruks to pause—Amlina being strangled by a pair of flaming hands, a flaming face above, and nothing more.

Unnerved for a moment, Lonn and Draven gathered their wits and charged.

The mask looked up and saw them coming. The gloves whipped Amlina about like a doll and flung her against the legs of the onrushing Iruks.

Lonn and Draven stumbled over the witch and fell in a tangle. Behind them, Brinda and Karrol had to lurch aside. From the rear, Eben threw a spear.

One of the gloves swept out, leaving a trail of flame. Eben's spear followed the glove's gesture, changing its path in mid-flight to stick harmlessly into the wall.

The mask tilted back and laughed with mockery. "How puny and inept are your bodyguards. How well they suit you, little Larthang."

Amlina's robe smoldered, emitting black smoke. Draven beat on the silk with his palms to put out the fire. The other Iruks scrambled up and went after the flaming apparition.

But before they could reach it the gloves floated up, touched the mask and pulled it forward. Next instant the mask was gone.

"I will return for you, Amlina," the voice called from nowhere. "Know that and live in fear."

The Iruks hacked and thrust at the gloves, nearly striking each other in their fury. But the flaming hands floated high, avoiding their weapons. Then one glove gripped the fingers of the other, pulled them forward, and that glove disappeared.

"And if you chance to see the Cloak, little Larthang, think of me. You *will* think of me."

Mocking laughter answered the Iruks' grunts of frustration as the last glove was removed by an unseen hand. Then a strange wind filled the chamber, shaking the desmets and tapestries. Together the wind and laughter seemed to recede into distance, leaving a brittle stillness.

The Iruks looked at one another in bewilderment and unreleased rage. Amlina lay quivering on the floor, face hidden by her hands. Her sleeve was black and tattered and some of her hair had been singed. Lonn could see blisters rising on her neck.

Kneeling beside the witch, Draven put a hand on her shoulder. "Amlina, it's over now. The thing is gone."

"Who was it?" Eben demanded. "Or what?"

"It was Beryl," Amlina cried, then collapsed into pitiful weeping.

The Iruks could not quiet her. They had never expected to see the witch so completely unstrung. It disrupted their own confidence even more than had the fiery apparition.

"Leave me alone," Amlina cried. "Leave me."

Draven, anguished worry on his face, motioned his mates to join him at the door. A crowd of tenants had gathered outside, watching in mute amazement.

"I'll stay with her," Draven said. "The rest of you break up this crowd of gawkers, then get some sleep."

Lonn and the others nodded gravely. Karrol glanced disapprovingly at Amlina's shuddering form, then pushed out through the doorway. Lonn, Eben, and Brinda followed, shut the door, and dispersed the onlookers.

"What is it? What's happened?" Elzna the landlady strained to see at the rear of the crowd.

"It's all over," Lonn told her. "Everyone can go back to sleep."

* * * * *

Away from the mazy cluttered streets of the harbor district, beyond the dryland quarters where the wealthy dwelt in their mansions and villas, past the guild halls and government buildings, upon the very tip of the High Acropolis, stood the Palace of the

Prince-Ruler of Kadavel, currently occupied by one Hagen of the House of Hessilan.

On this night, near midnight or just after, Hagen sat in a brightly glowing hall high in an upper story of his palace. The Prince-Ruler was medium-sized, brown-haired and bearded, firmly muscled under the maroon and purple velvets he wore. His mouth was stern and his eyes brooding—although he was surrounded by a scene of riotous gaiety.

Princes and retainers in brocaded jerkins stood about or reclined on couches, laughed and wagered, drank sweet mead from enameled goblets, pawed lovely courtesans in low-cut gowns.

The central attraction in this hall full of merriment stood on an iron pedestal in front of Hagen's chair—a miniature arena six feet in diameter. Inside the arena, tiny chariots raced round and round, drawn by tiny wolf-steeds, and inch-high gladiators with pins for spears fought dragons the size of human fingers.

Not the dragons nor the wolves nor the gladiators were real. All were illusions generated by the witchery of the arena. This witchery operated with a kind of intelligence, so that the contests were never repeated or predictable. Hagen had captured this Arena of Illusions in a naval raid against the island of Gon Fu. It ranked among his chief amusements, but tonight it could not divert the Prince-Ruler from his glum preoccupations: the evil portents in the city, the Archimage's fleet at sea.

Abruptly the shouting and laughter grew quiet. Looking up, Hagen noticed a woman standing at the far entryway. She had made no sound, yet her very presence had drawn the attention of everyone in the hall. She stepped forward, and Hagen found himself transfixed by her shining eyes.

Could it be? he wondered.

The woman was tall and slender, beautiful with a strange, unmanning beauty. Her blue fur coat, open in front, revealed numerous necklaces, a golden girdle, a dagger in a ruby scabbard.

Her white and gold tunic and elaborate feathered headpiece were obviously Nyssanian. But her delicate features and pale skin spoke of noble Larthangan blood.

It must be, Hagen thought.

The intruder walked a straight path across the hushed and crowded hall, servants and aristocrats alike stepping back to give her way. As she came near, Hagen spied a movement about her bosom. A small monkey-like creature with a long tail and a hairless, human head crept out of the woman's collar to sit upon her shoulder. The courtesans let out fluttery sounds of surprise and disquiet. The retainers murmured nervously. The appearance of the treeman, as the half-legendary beast was called, quashed Hagen's last doubt of the woman's identity.

"I am Beryl Quan de Lang, Archimage of the East, Queen of Tallyba, Empress of Far Nyssan." She faced the Prince-Ruler above the Arena of Illusions. "Don't fault your sentries, my lord. Their vigilance is adequate. I simply darkened their minds as I passed. I have a matter of importance to discuss with you—if you will pardon my abrupt entrance."

Hagen had risen from his chair. "My lady, your noble personage and air of command convince me you are who you say. As lord of Kadavel, I am pleased to greet you, though surprised that you come unannounced and unattended."

Beryl smiled, her finger touching a necklace of large black beads. "I find it convenient to come and go unobtrusively. But do not imagine me unprotected."

"Indeed not," Hagen lifted a hand. "I never meant to imply you were incapable of protecting yourself. Chamberlain, a chair for the Archimage of the East."

Beryl waved the offer aside. "I will stand."

"As you wish." Hagen deliberately, cautiously resumed his own seat, while all others in the hall remained standing. "What matter do you wish to discuss with me?"

"A certain possession of mine was stolen recently," Beryl answered. "The Cloak of the Two Winds."

She judged Hagen's response, then glanced about, seeming in an instant to meet the eyes of all present. "It was taken from my Bone Tower by a former apprentice of mine, a foolish young witch. She tried to evade my pursuit by sailing back to Larthang via the South Polar Sea, but she lost the Cloak to Iruk pirates at the Cape of Dekyll. These brigands in turn were victimized by a deepshaper of this city, who ensorcelled one of the Iruk women to bring the Cloak here. I believe it arrived in Kadavel approximately 20 days ago."

"That was shortly before the Two Winds began blowing wildly over our harbor," Hagen said.

"No doubt the two facts are linked," Beryl affirmed.

Now Hagen scanned the faces of his courtiers, seeking to make certain they were as surprised by Beryl's tidings as himself.

"This is the first we've heard of the theft," he told Beryl with conviction. "When word reached us that your fleet was anchored off Lustre, we assumed you were the one making havoc of our winds and waters. Now it seems we owe you an apology."

"None is needed," Beryl said. "Your conclusion was reasonable."

"You are gracious," Hagen replied. "Of course we will do all in our power to see that the Cloak is returned to you. I must confess I am no expert in such matters. I have little to do with witchery, unless it be harnessed for simple amusements such as this toy of Gon Fu."

He gestured to the arena where the races and duels continued, oblivious to the great outer world. The treeman crawled about on Beryl's shoulder making sharp, twittering sounds.

"I realize you are no mage," Beryl said, "nor even a dabbler in the shaping arts. And yet I've seen in the Deepmind that your fate is somehow tied to the Cloak. Why should this be?"

"I cannot imagine," Hagen answered.

"Perhaps I can," Beryl mused. "You are the monarch of a powerful city-state. You have extensive overseas holdings, and no doubt covet more. Though no deepshaper yourself, you have deepshapers in your employ. And you've doubtless heard it said that the Cloak of the Two Winds won my empire almost by itself. Indeed, I can see how a ruler in your position might consider the Cloak a most enviable prize."

Hagen shrugged uncomfortably. "I have no wish to possess such a prize. Kadavel is strong and prosperous already. At least we have been up till now. I don't know how long even we may prosper under the conditions of these past days. Therefore, my only wish for the Cloak of the Two Winds is that it go back whence it came."

"Then be comforted," Beryl gazed into his eyes with cold fire. "For soon that wish will be granted."

"Well enough. How may I assist in bringing about this end we both desire?"

"Only leave it to me." Beryl raised her hand and an amber ring with the stone worn on the palm side glinted at Hagen. "But if by chance you should learn where the Cloak is, you *will* think of me, won't you?"

"Of course," Hagen said, then knitted his brows.

* * * * *

Beryl saw that the cantrip held in the amber ring had locked onto Prince Hagen's mind, fixed there by his own words of agreement. Should knowledge of the Cloak's location reach Hagen, his first thought would be of Beryl—and that thought would search her out through the shimmering, indefinite ways of the Deepmind.

"Good evening, my lord," Beryl nodded and turned to depart.

"Wait," Hagen called, "Allow me to offer you the hospitality of my palace."

"Thank you, but no," Beryl answered without pausing or turning her head. "I prefer less conspicuous lodgings."

As the Archimage moved toward the distant doorway the treeman looked back from inside her collar, chattering and jerking his head rapidly up and down.

Moments later, as Beryl was descending a grand staircase lit by candles in gilded holders, the treeman crept out to stand on her shoulder and chirp in her ear, making sounds only her mind could interpret as language.

"Mistress, Mistress. Why tell him so much? What reason in this?"

"The same reason I had for sparing the Larthangan pup when I could have burned her lodgings down around her. Either of them might lead me to the Cloak."

"But will he seek it?"

"Oh, yes. If his fate was not bound to the Cloak before it is now. He is ambitious, and even to one who only partly comprehends its power, the Cloak is a compelling temptation. This very night he will summon his spies and henchmen and set them on the trail."

"Oh, you are wondrously clever, mistress. How can any of them hope to defeat you?"

"They cannot," Beryl said.

But the very thought that she had spoken these words now gave her pause, raised a shade of fear. Amlina's theft of the Cloak had caught Beryl off-guard. For the first time in over half a century, she had been challenged and—however temporarily—bested. Rage and indignation at this betrayal now drove her actions. But more than that: a tiny seed of doubt had been planted, an excruciating sense of vulnerability. To quell those feelings, she must not only regain the Cloak, she must crush all who opposed her. Amlina, in particular, must be painfully destroyed.

Brooding on these things, Beryl moved on through Hagen's palace, past the rigid sentries whose minds she had earlier darkened—who now dared not even breathe until she had gone.

* * * * *

Amlina lay on her bed and stared torpidly into the fire that Draven was tending. The blisters had risen high and, on her instructions, Draven had pierced them with a scalding needle. Then he had applied a salve from the small store of medicines the witch had brought ashore. Now, stepping from the fireplace. Draven glanced down at her and smiled.

"Your neck looks better already."

Amlina responded vaguely. "Oh. The burns will heal in a day or two. The ointment will take care of that."

"Then you'll be all right," Draven said.

Her gaze returned to the fire. "Beryl broke down my barriers with such ease. I didn't even sense her near me until it was too late."

The Iruk stared at her grimly.

"You can leave me," Amlina said. "There's nothing more you can do."

"Someone should be with you."

"Beryl won't return tonight. She wants me to live in fear of her a while. Besides, her first interest is finding the Cloak. She knows she can come for me at any time."

"I will stay," he insisted.

Amlina felt his compassion, and it raised a response in her heart. It had been so long since she had felt close to anyone, been able to trust ... She hesitated, then moved over and asked him to sit beside her. Draven slid onto the bed, warming her with his nearness.

"Let me hold your hand," she murmured.

Squeezing his hand in her icy fingers, she could feel his strength flowing into her. She thought she might be draining his vitality, but perhaps it only seemed so. Draven did not flinch or try to pull away, or even seem to notice. It was one of the paradoxes of witchery that a deepshaper, who could wield enormous energies to shape events, might also be frail, deficient in the normal energies of the body. Amlina brought Draven's hand to her chest and let it rest wrapped in both her hands.

Draven gazed at her with heartfelt concern, and she sensed other, less conscious feelings in him. Apprehending the Iruk's passionate nature opened her heart, and she began to cry. Draven held her, and it was a long time before she calmed enough to talk.

"I'm so afraid, Draven. Beryl is famous for engendering fear, and rightly. I cannot defeat her. I was only deluding myself to believe it."

"We will find a way," Draven said. "You are a great witch, Amlina. You proved it when you called the fire turtles to free our ship."

Amlina shook her head, sniffling. "That was by far the greatest magic I ever worked, that and summoning the winds with the Cloak. But to Beryl such feats are commonplace. She is much stronger in the Deepmind than I'll ever be ... I didn't tell you the whole truth about myself, Draven. I said I failed at the Academy of the Deepmind, but I also failed here in Kadavel when I tried to make my living as a sorceress. My whole life is a story of running from one failure to the next. I was only sent to the Academy in the first place because I showed no signs of attracting a husband by age 16 and my mother didn't know what else to do with me."

Draven was frowning, trying to keep up with the rush of her words.

"I'm sorry for you and your friends, that you've gotten involved with me. I've forced honesty out of you, but I've not given it in return. The truth is there's not much chance you'll get Glyssa back. Her mind is probably destroyed by now."

Draven seized her shoulders and thrust her to arm's length.

"Stop talking that way! We will find Glyssa, and she'll be all right. You will help us find her."

His anger roared into her, making her tremble. She stared at him through glazed eyes.

"We will find her," he repeated calmly. "And we will kill Beryl, or else be killed ourselves if it can't be helped. But we will fight her, and you will fight her too. You must. There's no other choice. None."

Amlina shrank from his fierce gaze, ashamed to have come apart in front of him, more shamed by his courage in contrast. She nodded, and he let go of her, staring again with solicitude, his rage vanished.

"I'm sorry to have burdened you with my cowardice," she said.

"Oh, you are too hard on yourself," Draven answered. "You are no burden. Even we Iruks get afraid sometimes. But we have each other to hold on to. You have no one. It's no surprise if you lose heart."

Amlina's eyes were tearful again. She leaned against him, and Draven wrapped both strong arms around her.

A while later, the Iruk noticed that the fire was burning low. But he did not stir to add more fuel. Amlina was sleeping in his arms.

* * * * *

Asleep downstairs in the pile of furs and mattresses the Iruks had spread on the floor, Lonn dreamed of flaming gloves and masks swarming everywhere, and his klarn trying to fight them. But in the dream the Iruks' knives were useless and their swords melted in their hands. Soon their clothes and hair were on fire ...

Lonn woke stiff and frightened. He opened his eyes and saw Karrol and Eben huddled beside the stove.

"This is awful," Karrol whispered. "Lonn groaning with nightmares, Draven upstairs coddling the witch, you and I too spooked to sleep. I hate this inn. I always hated the inns in Fleevanport, and I hate this one."

"In Fleevanport we always got drunk," Eben said. "We need a good dunking in a barrel of mead to lift our spirits."

"What we need is to find Glyssa and go home," Karrol answered. "Now Amlina's lost her nerve. What if she doesn't get it back? What if she can't help us?"

"Then we'll find Glyssa ourselves," Eben asserted. "I hope."

Lonn rolled over and tried to sleep.

Sixteen

After breakfast the next morning, the Iruks trooped upstairs to Amlina's room. They rapped on the door then pushed it open — and were astonished to find Draven and the witch asleep together. The two opened their eyes and sat up as the klarnmates came to surround the bed.

Lonn tried not to show his surprise. "Are you feeling better, Amlina?"

She looked around at them, blinking. "Yes."

"We talked things over at breakfast," Lonn said. "We think we should start searching for Glyssa today."

Amlina looked confused but made no answer.

"Eben came up with a good plan," Lonn continued, "that we begin on the docks, question those whose business involves the comings and goings in the harbor. Someone may have seen Glyssa arrive, or something else that could help us."

"I don't know," Amlina said.

"We have to try," Karrol declared. "Even if you say there's no chance of our finding Glyssa, we have to try."

"It's not that." Amlina seemed to have trouble finding words. "I'm not sure you should go off alone."

"We can take care of ourselves," Lonn asserted.

"Come with us," Draven said to the witch.

"No, I can't. Not today."

"Well, we can't wait," Karrol said. "We've been helpless for too long."

"There's lots of waterfront to cover," Eben added. "The sooner we start, the better."

Lonn shared these sentiments with his mates. Eben's plan made sense to him, and this morning the witch seemed incapable of acting at all.

"Shouldn't we make every effort to help ourselves?" he asked her. "Just as we did when the ship was icebound?"

The witch let out a breath before answering. "Very well. My purse is on the writing table. Take some silver coins. And mark the streets carefully. I'll expect you back by nightfall."

"Will you be safe here alone?" Lonn said.

"I can stay with her," Draven replied.

"No," Amlina said. "I don't think Beryl will return soon. If she does, one of you or all of you together wouldn't have much chance of stopping her. Besides, it's better if I'm alone. After last night I need to cast off my fear and seek renewal and guidance in the Deepmind. For that, I must have solitude." She put out her hand to cover Draven's. "Don't worry about me, my friend. Your courage has restored my own."

Draven smiled and patted her gently on the shoulder before leaving the bed.

As the mates walked along the gallery to the stairs, Eben said, "You and the witch acted like lovers, Draven. Did you couple with her last night?"

"No," Draven laughed. "Only let her cry on my shoulder."

"And sleep pressed against you," Karrol grumbled. "Very sweet. I'm surprised you didn't kiss her goodbye."

"Maybe next time," Draven grinned heartily. "What is there for breakfast?"

The Iruks stopped at the hearth in the common room where Draven found porridge, muffins, and tea. He carried the food back to the Iruks' room and ate while he put on his clothes.

The mates helped each other get into harness, and donned their hooded capes. On Eben's suggestion, they tied skate-blades to their belts. After walking all day along the docks, they might have the opportunity to skate back, if the harbor was frozen. They took swords and knives, but left their spears behind, hidden under the bedding.

It was near mid-morning when they strode across the deserted common room.

"Wait! Wait there." Elzna the landlady hastened down the stairs to detain them.

The Iruks halted in the vestibule, and the landlady placed her wiry frame between them and the door.

"You had me so flustered last night I didn't demand a proper explanation. I want one now. What was that commotion about last night?"

Lonn jerked a thumb toward the upstairs. "Ask the Lady who employs us. She'll explain."

"No, no. I just came from her door. She wouldn't let me in, said she can't be disturbed. But I can't have my whole house disturbed either. And in the middle of the night. Tell me what it was."

"A burglar," Draven said. "She was attacked by a burglar. We drove him off."

"We've never had burglars in this neighborhood. The guests who saw it said there was fire, things floating in the air. I glimpsed one myself, and I smelled smoke."

"The burglar threw firebrands at us," Eben explained, "then escaped up the chimney."

Elzna frowned suspiciously. "I want to inspect the room for damages. I have a right to that, it's the law. If your mistress doesn't let me in this afternoon when the maid goes to change the linens, I'll have my two husky nephews break down the door, I promise you."

Lonn suppressed the temptation to pick up the scrawny crone and hang her from the nearest coat hook. Instead, he took four silver coins from inside his harness.

"Here is double the money that was advanced to you. There is no damage to the room, but you can have this to ease your mind about it. The lady is not to be disturbed, for changing linens or any other reason. Do you understand?"

Lonn had slapped the coins into her open palm. He held them there tightly, gripping her wrist with his other hand.

"I will see she's not disturbed." Elzna's voice quavered with a mixture of fear and greed. "It's very quiet here in the daytime, as you already know."

"Good." Lonn pulled the landlady out of their way before releasing her. Then he opened the door and led his klarn out into the street.

* * * * *

The sky was overcast but the dense, unnatural dark of the previous day had lifted. The air was chilly and wet, a suggestion of rain or sleet on the breeze. The Iruks marched down the wooden street and through the high-arched gate in the city wall. They stopped on the broad pier, where numerous fishing boats lay belly-up. Beyond their hulls stretched the Shipway, soft water this morning, tossing, glinting dully beneath the silver-gray sky. The rows of anchored ships rode small and vague in the distance.

"Which way?" Lonn asked his mates.

The Iruks looked in both directions, the enormity of the city bearing down on them. The piers ran off as far as they could see to east and west, and behind the wall stretched a jagged horizon of rooftops and gables.

"Let's try going west," Eben said. "We were east of here yesterday."

The mates started along the pier, past the rows of dry-docked craft. A few of the boats were being worked on, having their bottoms scraped or the planking repaired. But this was not a fishing season and most of the fishermen spent their days here, as they did in Fleevanport, warming themselves in their guild lodges, cozy buildings nestled against the city wall.

The Iruks entered the first lodge they came to and found the main room crowded. Some of the lodge members were having a late breakfast of barley cakes and tea; others sat playing games with dice and bone counters. A few had already started on a lazy day of mead drinking.

The mates waited in the doorway until they had attracted considerable attention.

"Do not be alarmed," Lonn said. "We are Iruks from the South Pole, and though we are excellent fighters we mean you no violence. We are searching for a friend of ours, a woman of our race. We believe she arrived in Kadavel about a month ago. We will pay well for information that helps us find her."

But the fishermen only shrugged or shook their heads. Eben questioned them further, describing the dojuk and asking if they had seen or heard of such a boat. Lonn in turn told them of the black ship that in his dream carried Glyssa to the city. But the fishermen had seen no craft like the dojuk, and they pointed out that the three-masted barge was a common vessel in Tathian seas, many of which might presently be found in the Shipway. The men drifted back to their previous occupations. A few lingered long enough to invite the Iruks to share their hearth and a mug of tea, but the mates declined the offer and went on their way.

Their reception at the next lodges and boathouses where they stopped was much the same, and their luck no better. While they were walking along the docks a sudden freezewind blew, rushing over the harbor. The sealight intensified to a sparkling glare on the new ice, and the air turned sharply colder.

The cloud cover had thinned and the sun appeared, dim and high, by the time the mates reached the end of the fishermen's quarter. Now the boats docked along the quays were skimmers like the one that had ferried them ashore. The fish-sellers' stalls gave way to porticoes and warehouses built behind the city wall. But this district was hardly busier than the last, since there was little work these days for skimmers and even less for the stevedores who lived in the neighborhood.

These men too had their lodges, bigger and dirtier, sour with the smell of spilled wine and unwashed bodies. The Iruks stopped at three such buildings and were greeted with less friendliness than by the fishermen. The stevedores had a lean, predatory look. Had the Iruks not been so well-armed and dour-looking themselves, Lonn suspected they might have been fallen upon and robbed.

By now the mates were footsore and cranky. Kadavel had begun to seem endless and they had covered only a small part of it.

"Glyssa may not even be in this city," Karrol muttered when they sat down to rest.

"Let's get some food and drink," Draven said. "We've been walking too long."

They stopped at the first tavern they came to, a grimy establishment a short distance inside the city wall. They lunched on baked fish and bread while keeping wary eyes on the tavern's customers—a mean-looking assortment of rogues who stared at the Iruks with unconcealed malice. When they had finished eating Lonn stood on the table and questioned all present about Glyssa and the dojuk. He was just as glad that no one offered information, since he would have doubted anything these men told him.

But as the mates departed from the tavern they were followed by a small man in a patched cloak. Brinda noticed him first, glancing over her shoulder, and told the others in a quiet voice.

"Should we jump him?" Karrol asked.

"No," Eben said. "Let's see what he does."

The Iruks passed through the harbor gate and started along the pier. They had not gone far when the Tathian hailed them in a croaky voice. As they turned he was running up to them furtively.

"That outrigger boat you described in the tavern? I've seen the very one. How much will you pay if I show you where it is?"

The man was middle-aged, short and bent, his bearded face scarred by the pox. Perhaps he was a porter or scullery man, perhaps a cutpurse. Lonn distrusted him.

"We have lots of silver," Draven said. "Show him, Lonn."

Lonn took out their money, six silver coins left and some coppers got as change at the tavern. "Show us the boat and you get half. If we find our woman there you get the rest."

The little man licked his lips. "Follow me then."

He led the Iruks west along the waterfront. Presently the lodges and warehouses gave way to rows of two-story buildings, all of dark wood, with upper porches and shutters on the windows. The pier broadened and there were boathouses along the water and long buildings with fenced-in yards—like the boatyards in Fleevanport but larger. Next they came to an area of stone quays where several drommons lay in dry dock for repairs. There were barracks here and fortifications patrolled by Tathian marines. The sentries stared warily as the Iruks passed.

"I don't like this," Karrol muttered.

"How much farther?" Lonn demanded of their guide.

"Beyond these naval precincts there are more civilian boatyards. I saw your outrigger boat being dragged into one of these. There were armed men about."

At the place where the stone pier ended the Tathian paused.

"I am troubled by a persistent question," he said. "Suppose I show you where your boat is. How do I know you will keep your part of the bargain? Before I take you to the place, I want part of the money."

Lonn hesitated, then took out his knife instead of his silver. The Tathian flinched but did not try to run.

"Take us to our boat," Lonn said. "If we find it you will be paid. Now move."

The man led them a short distance farther, into a sprawling area of warehouses and large boat works. He pointed to a shipyard made up of several buildings and surrounded by a staked fence.

"I saw the boat pulled on rollers into yonder gate. This happened two or three small-months ago. Now the silver."

"After we've seen the boat," Lonn said. "Lead on."

But the Tathian shook his head. "I'll stay here. I don't know exactly what you're planning, but you are carrying weapons. If there's to be violence, I want no part of it."

Lonn shrugged. "Stay here then. But if you've lied to us, don't be waiting."

"I only told you what I saw," the man protested. "The boat was pulled in there. I can't promise it is there still."

The Iruks left him and tramped across the open stretch of pier to the boatyard. The wide, stout gate was shut, and so they climbed a nearby ramp to a long porch sheltered by a roof. They opened the first door on the porch and stepped into a dusty chamber lit by oil lamps, with counting tables and shelves along the walls piled with scrolls. Several men in tunics and wool shawls were at work in this office. They stood at their benches and stared curiously at the Iruks.

"Do not be alarmed," Lonn told them. "We are here looking for a boat, a hide boat with a frame of bone and two outriggers."

An older man in embroidered jacket and the cylindrical hat of the merchant class appeared from behind a curtain opposite the door.

"We have no craft like that," he said. "Our boats are made of pinewood here in the Tathian Isles."

Lonn considered what to say next, but Draven spoke up.

"We are seeking to buy a boat," he said. "About a forty-footer. If it must be wood then it must, but a trim craft on the ice, and seagoing."

"We make boats to all specifications," the man replied guardedly. "We can build what you order, but of course we must have part of the money in advance."

"We need a boat at once," Lonn answered. "Let us look through your yards and see what you have."

"At the moment we have only a couple of skimmers finished. Nothing of seagoing capacity."

"Let us look through your yards anyway," Draven suggested. "Perhaps we'll find something that's nearly ready."

The man shook his head and took a step to block their way. "That is impossible. You must know that we men of Tath guard the secrets of our shipbuilding trade. We have no boat such as you need. I suggest you look elsewhere."

One of the clerks left the chamber hurriedly, no doubt to summon aid.

"We Iruks build our boats of yulugg bone and hide," Lonn said. "We have no interest in your trade secrets. We wish to search your yards to satisfy ourselves that our own stolen boat is not here."

"Ridiculous," the boat merchant said. "And not to be allowed."

"A man saw our boat brought in here," Lonn answered. "We will search whether you allow it or not."

"No!" The Tathian backed up and gripped both sides of the doorway. "Begone, I say."

"Move aside!" Lonn put a hand on the merchant's chest and shoved hard.

The man stumbled back into the corridor, and the Iruks stepped over and around him.

"Help!" he cried. "Spies! Ruffians!"

The mates marched angrily down the hallway, pushing past a timid clerk who stiffened and clutched the wall at their approach.

Through the door at the end of the corridor, they found themselves on a long porch overlooking a courtyard full of boats, frames, and scaffolding. A quick glance disclosed no sign of their dojuk, and a quick glance was all the mates had time for.

The clerk who had left the office earlier was hurrying up the stairs to the porch with a crowd of men at his back. There were seven brawny workmen with the clerk and more rushing forward across the yard. The men had armed themselves with knives, mallets, and iron bars. They looked able and ready for a brawl.

But the Iruks also were ready. With whooping cries they flung themselves down the steps, landing amid the startled Tathians with knives and swords drawn.

The Iruks struck with overwhelming speed and ferocity, but they did not strike to kill. One workman went down screaming, his forearm laid open. Another toppled sideways clutching a stabbed shoulder. Others tumbled down the steps, knocked off-balance by the Iruks or else tripping as they tried to retreat.

The men at the bottom of the steps turned and fled, dropping their makeshift weapons. The Iruks chased them briefly, stamping the ground and brandishing their blades. The fight was over in moments, the Tathians in full flight, the Iruks whooping in triumph.

Knowing it was necessary now to hurry, the mates divided up. Lonn and Draven went to search the far side of the yard and the buildings and enclosures there. Brinda, Eben, and Karrol took the near side and the rear. They tracked carefully over the main yard, searching the plank floor for pieces of bone or hide or anything to indicate a dojuk had been disassembled here.

Shouts of alarm still echoed through the compound. One group of workmen tried to block Lonn and Draven from entering the buildings on the far side. But the two Iruks drew their weapons and rushed, yelling so fiercely that the workmen lost heart and broke before more blood was spilled. For the rest, the Tathians fled on sight of the Iruks, who discovered many of them hiding under boats or in lockers as they searched.

Lonn and Draven kicked in the doors of woodworking rooms and tool lockers but found no trace of any Iruk boat piece. They checked a sail-making room and a wide stall where finished boats were being painted. But again they found no sign that the dojuk had ever been there.

They hurried back to the main yard, where their mates were waiting. Karrol reported that they too had discovered nothing.

"The boat could have been torn down and disposed of by now," Eben said. "Or our informer could have been lying."

Lonn noticed that the courtyard was empty. Even the wounded men had crawled or been carried away. A premonition of danger rose in him. "Let's get away from here," he said.

The Iruks had started back to the porch when the door through which they had entered the yard burst open. Armored men poured in, marines with lances and shields.

"Halt in the name of the Prince-Ruler," came the officer's command as more and more lancers charged through the door.

The Iruks backed away, eyes darting around the yard.

"This way!" Lonn yelled.

He made a dash for the front gate, ducking between two high-built hulls in case the marines cast their lances. He and his mates reached the gate well ahead of their pursuers. Karrol tore back the bolt and everyone pounced on the gate and shoved it open. The mates rushed outside—to confront ten more marines with lances lowered.

"Stand or be run through," one of them said.

The Iruks stiffened, looking at each other. The Tathians relaxed their guard just a fraction.

"Go!" Lonn yelled.

The mates leaped upon the surprised marines, dodging their late, feeble thrusts, grabbing the shafts of their lances. Lonn yanked on one spear, pulling his man off-balance and tripping him with an out-thrust leg. Karrol got control of another lance, turned the point around and lunged, driving its owner to his back. Draven ducked in, grabbed a third man's legs and flipped him over. The others kicked and pushed, struck swift blows with fists or forearms. The suddenness of the Iruks' attack caught the Tathians so off-guard that in seconds the mates had won free.

They were escaping across the pier as the main detachment of marines charged through the boatyard gate. The officer commanded the Iruks to halt once more, then ordered his men to cast lances. The Iruks heard the iron points strike the dock behind them as they fled, one lance just missing Draven's leg. But in pausing to throw, the marines gave the hard-running Iruks time to open more ground.

The mates sprinted to the place where they had left their informer, but as Lonn expected the man was gone. Then Lonn spotted a second detachment of marines running toward them from ahead on the pier.

"Now what?" Karrol demanded.

"Under the dock," Lonn said.

With no time to debate the Iruks followed his lead. They raced to the edge of the dock and dropped over the side, landing crouched on the ice. They crawled beneath the weathered breakwater and found themselves in a low sprawling forest of posts and beams, faintly lit from below by the icelight.

There was just enough room to stand, but instead the Iruks sat down, pulling out their skate blades and strapping them to their boots. Their fingers worked frantically as the rumble on the planks above grew louder, marines approaching from both directions. Some of the lancers were down on the ice and crawling under the dock by the time the mates were up and ready to skate.

They slid off beneath the pier, ducking every few yards to pass under the crossbeams. Advised they were escaping, the marines still on the pier ran to try and keep up. But soon their pounding footsteps faded behind the skaters.

When they neared the stone quay the Iruks turned and burst from under the dock, sprinting straight out from shore. The frozen harbor was rough and jagged, difficult to skate but not impossible for Iruks. Karrol even stopped to dance obscenely and taunt their land-bound pursuers—until her mates grabbed her and pulled her on. When the marines had shrunk to tiny figures on the distant docks, the Iruks wheeled and started skating parallel to shore.

"We're all right unless a meltwind blows," Eben said.

"Don't even think of that," Lonn yelled.

The Iruks kept their distance from the city piers until they had passed the naval base, then slanted in toward the civilian neighborhoods beyond. They had far outdistanced any pursuit by land, and Lonn saw no iceboats giving chase. The sun was sinking over the city to their backs as the mates skated on, toward the fishermen's district and the safety they imagined there.

Seventeen

Shadows filled the streets of Kadavel as the Iruks skated ashore and found their inn. When they walked in the door their spirits were lifted by the aroma of roasting meats and bubbling mead. The mates went to the kitchen and filled tankards from the caldron of mead to take back to their room.

They drank a second round over supper and were about to start on their third when a serving girl came up to them in the common room. She said Amlina wished to see them upstairs. The Iruks refilled their tankards and brought them along.

They found the witch seated by her fireplace in a quilted robe embroidered with tiny flowers. Her blond hair was combed and bound with the silver fillet. She smiled as the Iruks came in.

"I'm glad you're here. I have good news."

"What is it?" Lonn asked.

"There is a certain technique of deepseeing," Amlina explained, "designed as a last resort, when all other methods have proved useless and one is tempted to despair. This technique assures an answer from the Deepmind. It requires the seeker to relinquish all personal intents and desires and accept that answer, whatever it be. Thus the technique is called 'Bowing to the Sky.'"

The Iruks were leaning against the hearthstones or sitting on the floor, sipping their mead as they listened to the witch.

"I enacted the Bowing to the Sky this afternoon," Amlina continued, "asking how I ought to proceed in searching for the Cloak. Often it takes days for an answer to surface, but this time it came in a few hours: an image of the six of us seated in a wei circle, deepseeing together. As I looked on this vision I knew with certainty that our searching in that way would bring success. I see now why Kizier sensed you Iruks had an important part to play on this journey. Through you, I can find the Cloak again—not just through Lonn, but through all of you. Your closeness to each other and to Glyssa is the key."

"What must we do?" Draven asked.

"Each of you will need to undergo the initiation, as Lonn did," Amlina said. "I must warn you as I warned him, the ritual can be painful and so can the path it opens."

"Lonn survived it," Draven answered. "We will also."

"Every mind reacts differently," the witch said. "Some initiates experience only clarity and joy, with no distress whatever. Others are overwhelmed with confusion and anguish. Some few never fully regain their wits. There is definite risk to your minds, all of you must know this."

The mates looked at each other, clenched their lips, nodded in solemn agreement.

"The risks don't matter to us." Lonn spoke for them all. "We will face any danger to save Glyssa and reunite the klarn."

"All right," Amlina said. "But there is also something else. In group endeavors of this kind, a harmony of minds is essential. For this harmony to flourish, there must be honesty and openheartedness. I think you have something of this openness already, with one another. But it must be deepened among you, and it must be extended to include me. There can be no reservations or hidden animosities among us, no lingering distrust."

The witch was gazing now at Karrol, who frowned angrily and lowered her eyes.

"I don't know."

"What do you mean you don't know?" Draven demanded. "How can you stand in the way now? This is our chance to find Glyssa!"

"I don't know that for certain," Karrol said. "Neither do you."

"It's the only chance we've got to work with at the moment," Lonn pointed out. "We obviously can't go searching the docks again, not for a while at least."

"Why?" Amlina asked. "What happened?"

"We had a little trouble with some marines," Lonn said. "Nothing we couldn't handle. But we had better lie low for a while."

The witch insisted on hearing all of it, so Lonn and Draven told her of the adventure. Their narrative was casual and lighthearted enough, their spirits buoyed with drink. But by the time they finished, Amlina was up and pacing fretfully.

"How could you do this?" she cried. "I told you over and over we had to be inconspicuous. So our second day here you're on the city piers brawling with marines."

"No harm came of it." Lonn leaned back on his elbow. "We weren't caught."

"Not yet. But the Prince-Ruler has spies in every district. How long do you think it'll take them to track down five barbarians from the South Pole?"

The Iruks glanced at one another and shifted uncomfortably.

"No one followed us back here," Lonn said. "I thought we'd be safe. Should we go to another inn then?"

"No." Amlina wrung her hands. "Tramping about the streets now would only make you easier to find ... Tramping about the streets," she repeated, her eyes staring intently at nothing.

Amlina stalked to the window and opened the shutters a crack to peer outside. "By the Deepmind. They've found us already."

The Iruks jumped up and hastened to look over the witch's shoulders. The street below was thronged with city guardsmen. Mounted on their willowy aklors, they had ridden up silently in the darkness. Now the men were dismounting, armed with truncheons and swords, their steel armor glistening in the glow of lanterns hung from saddlebows.

A loud pounding sounded on the door of the inn. On reflex, the Iruks drew their swords.

"No!" Amlina said. "You can't fight the whole city."

"What choice is there?" Lonn demanded.

"Surrender. I'll go with you. I'll get you out of it somehow."

Again they heard the banging on the door downstairs, then the door opening and voices raised.

"Let's run for it," Karrol urged. "We can drop down to the alley, or go out the back way."

"The building is surrounded," Amlina said. "Please. If you kill any guards there'll be no chance of my getting you free."

Now the floor rumbled with the tramping of boots on the stairs. Lonn and his mates stood rigid, hesitant. Despite the odds, it seemed less fearful to the Iruks to fight than to let themselves be captured.

"You've all sworn an oath on the life of your klarn," Amlina said, "to follow my counsel in moments such as this. I'm calling on that oath now."

The door shook as the men outside pounded. "Open to the Prince-Ruler's guards."

Amlina crossed quickly to the door. "I'll find a way out." She stared at Lonn. "Please, trust me."

She pulled open the door and the guardsmen marched in.

"What is it?" Amlina demanded. "What do you want?"

"Take them," the captain pointed at the Iruks with his sword. "*Carefully.*"

The guards tossed away their truncheons and drew their steel. They advanced into the room. The Iruks crouched, ready to fight, eyeing Lonn to see what he would do.

"Do not resist," Amlina urged.

When the guards were almost on him, Lonn whispered a curse and threw down his sword and knife. He raised his empty hands. The blades of the other Iruks rang hollowly as they struck the floor.

"Bind them," the captain said.

The mates struggled only a little as their arms were pulled behind their backs and tied with leather thongs.

"What does this mean?" Amlina shouted. "Why do you seize my servants?"

"Bind her also," the captain said. "You are under arrest by order of the Prince-Ruler."

"But why?"

"The charges were not disclosed to me. I have orders to take you. That is all."

The Tathians allowed the witch to put on her cloak before they tied her hands. They used their truncheons to herd the prisoners out of the chamber.

The inn's tenants were all assembled in the common room, and they gaped as the witch and the Iruks were marched down the stairs.

"Where are you taking them, my lord?" Elzna cried. "What are they guilty of?"

"Silence. Would you question the Prince-Ruler's commands?"

"No. But their belongings. What shall I do with them?"

"Leave them," Amlina said. "I assure you this arrest is some witless blunder. We will be back in our rooms before morning."

Lonn thought he heard the confused landlady murmur her compliance as he and his companions were herded out through the vestibule.

About a dozen guards stood watch in the street, while others were coming around from the back of the inn. Perhaps forty riders in all had been deployed to capture the Iruks. With the prisoners under control, the guards hung their truncheons on their saddles and prepared to mount.

The prisoners were led before one group of aklors whose saddles had double seats. Eight or nine feet at the shoulders, the aklors had oblong bodies, flat feline faces, and six long spindly legs. The guardsmen rapped their mounts sharply on the necks and the beasts responded by kneeling. Hands still tied, Amlina and the Iruks were forced into the saddles and made to sit against the backrests.

"This rude treatment is uncalled for," Amlina complained as her ankles were bound to the rear stirrups. "Your superiors will hear of it."

"Quiet," the captain replied. "Or would you rather be dragged the whole way?"

When the prisoners were secured the guardsmen climbed on the front part of the saddles and tugged on the reins. The aklors snorted, braced their bony legs and rose. On the captain's shouted orders the riders formed into a column two abreast and started up the street.

The aklors moved with the silent, eerie ease of spiders. Lonn understood how they could have filled the street below Amlina's window without being heard. The riders traveled northward for many blocks, moving away from the harbor. Gables and upper stories leaned ponderously over the streets. Above them, the sky was black and starless.

After some time the planks below the aklors' feet gave way to worn cobblestones. The streets sloped upward, gradually ascending toward the massive bulk of the High Acropolis, now plainly visible above the roofs. The column turned right and circled around to the sloping eastern face of the acropolis. From there the aklors climbed a wide paved avenue, past open parks and walled manor houses.

Finally, the column reached the summit, where edifices of black marble and tall iron statues enclosed a gloomy square. The tireless aklors plodded across the square to a fortified keep. The riders passed through a raised portcullis and stopped in a high-walled courtyard.

The guards dismounted, freed the prisoners' ankles and pulled them from the saddles. Legs wobbly, Lonn and his companions were pushed up a flight of steps and through a huge portal. They marched down a long corridor and then down several flights of steps to a damp sprawling chamber—the entrance, so they learned, to the

Prince-Ruler's dungeons. Here they were transferred into the hands of the palace guard, men in gilded armor and purple capes. Hands still bound behind their backs, the prisoners were made to sit against the wall, watched over by ten of the guardsmen.

After a short wait, a messenger arrived and Amlina and the Iruks were made to stand and go upstairs again. Escorted by the ten guards, they climbed a long spiral of steps inside a round tower. They traversed an elegant hallway and came at last to a sumptuous throne room. Fires blazing in two wide hearths reflected on the polished floor. Splendid tapestries hung from galleries along three of the walls. Fronting the fourth wall was a dais set with a great dragon-carved throne. Twenty guards flanked the throne, but otherwise the chamber stood empty.

The Iruks and the witch were lined up at the foot of the dais. Lonn saw some drapes move at a portal off to the side, and could barely discern a mutter of conversation. Then the drapes parted and a sturdy velvet-clad man strode through, attended by two white-bearded men in silk robes and tall silk hats—Tathian sorcerers by the look of them.

"I am Hagen," the man in velvet said, "Prince-Ruler of Kadavel."

"My lord." Amlina bowed her head tersely. "I must ask why myself and my servants have been dragged—"

"Be silent!" Hagen commanded. "These servants, as you admit them to be, broke into a boatyard this afternoon and assaulted several workmen. Worse, they manhandled ten of my marines and made fools of another fifty who tried to prevent their escape."

"Are these charges proven?" Amlina asked.

"Your servants have just been identified by a witness to the event. If you hope for mercy, young woman, you had better remember where you are and hold your tongue."

"I'm sorry, my lord," Amlina said.

Lonn caught the tone of passive persuasion in her voice. Perhaps the sorcerers heard it also, for one of them whispered something in

Hagen's ear. The prince's gaze narrowed on Amlina, and he gestured abruptly at one of the guards.

"Take this one to the next chamber. We will interrogate her separately."

Amlina started to protest, then checked herself. Impassively she accompanied the guard. Hagen waited until the witch had exited through a doorway beneath one of the side galleries, then turned to scrutinize the Iruks.

"I know why you forced your way into that boatyard. The man who just identified you is the same one that led you there. He is an informer in my employ. He steered you to that boatyard so he could slip away and summon troops to capture you."

"Why?" Lonn demanded.

"Because you are Iruks, and I had ordered that any of your race found in Kadavel be brought to me. My informer told me the questions you asked in the tavern about the woman, the lost crew member you are searching for. Is she not the one who brought the Cloak of the Two Winds to Kadavel?"

Hagen scanned the Iruks' faces, smiled as they stared back stolidly.

"Yes, I know about the Cloak. I know it is somewhere in the city, and I intend to find it. Tell me what you know of it, and perhaps I'll be lenient with you."

The Iruks kept silent, leaving it to Lonn to speak for them.

"We came to this city seeking our mate," Lonn said. "We have no interest in the Cloak."

"But you did possess it for a time." Hagen walked before the line of prisoners. "After you stole it from the Archimage's apprentice ... Is that who the Larthangan woman is who claims you for servants? Yes, I can see it on your faces. Unlikely that she should join forces with you. But then the whole affair is unlikely enough."

Hagen stopped before Lonn, eyeing him pointedly. "You are barbarians with no legal status here. I could easily have you put to death for your crimes. Before I decide on such drastic punishment, are you sure there's nothing you want to tell me about the Cloak?"

Grimly Lonn weighed his choices. He knew precious little about the Cloak, not that he believed any amount of information would convince Hagen to let them go. The Iruks' only hope seemed to be that Amlina could somehow witch the Prince-Ruler.

"We know nothing about it," Lonn said. "You must speak with the Lady who employs us."

* * * * *

Amlina awaited the Prince-Ruler in a lavish antechamber with gilded woodwork and pearled wall hangings. She sat on a silken divan, hands still tied behind her, the guardsman close by. She rose when Hagen strode into the chamber followed by the two State Sorcerers.

"Be seated," Hagen told her. He sat beside her and with his own dagger cut her bonds. Amlina gratefully massaged her wrists.

Hagen began, "You, I understand, are the apprentice witch who stole the Cloak of the Two Winds from the Archimage of the East. No, the Iruks did not tell me the story. I have my information from Beryl herself. She paid me a visit last night."

Amlina stared, concentrating, reading him. "You want the Cloak for yourself, don't you, my lord?"

"It is a treasure most enviable," Hagen admitted. "And its presence has caused chaos in my city. It's practically my duty to seize it, so that order can be restored."

Amlina made no reply.

"But I need information," Hagen continued, "if I'm to find the Cloak before the Archimage does. Since you've admitted the Iruks are your servants, I could hold you responsible for their crimes and have you put to death with them. But if you help me find the Cloak, I will spare your life."

"I don't know where the Cloak is," Amlina said. "All my efforts to see its location in the Deepmind have failed."

"Tell me everything you know of it," Hagen answered. "Everything."

Amlina replied with a lengthy discourse. She gave information about the Cloak, its appearance, history, capacities, but this was only part of what she did. By the murmuring tones of her voice, the movements of her eyes and fingers, she was witching the Prince-Ruler, softening his will so she could mold it to her purpose. The enchantment was subtle enough that Hagen never noticed. The two sorcerers who stood by apparently sensed something amiss, but they only shifted uncomfortably from time to time and stared balefully at Amlina. She finished by telling of her own experience with the Cloak, of how she had used it to flee from Tallyba.

"But if you only wanted the Cloak to help get you free of the Archimage," Hagen said, "why did you pursue it when it was stolen from you?"

"Because only with the Cloak would I have a chance of defeating and killing Beryl. And I know I will never be truly free of her until she is dead. She would have followed me back to Larthang, to Minhang itself if need be. Do you see these burns healing on my neck? Beryl paid me a visit last night also. I'm only alive now because she wants me to live in fear of her a while longer."

Hagen nodded, satisfied. "Of course, if I'm to keep the Cloak I must find a way to kill her. You lived in her court several years. What method would you recommend?"

Amlina gave a helpless shrug. "If I knew a sure way I would have done it long ago. Do not try to beat her with witchery. Many have tried that and met with defeat."

"Then how?"

"If you're resolved to be her enemy, then your best chance would be to attack her by force of arms. Even great witches are vulnerable to such attacks, though less so than ordinary mortals. Set a trap for her, using weapons that can kill at a distance. Crossbows would be better than lances, since the bolts travel faster. Her mind may turn many bolts aside, but if enough are launched one may find her heart. Make sure the tips are well-poisoned. Her life will not be easily snuffed out."

Hagen pondered her words. "I will do as you suggest," he declared. "You have been most helpful. I am going to keep my word and let you live."

"And the Iruks?"

He seemed almost ready to agree, then abruptly shook his head. "They must be executed."

"If you set them free with me," Amlina said, "there is a chance we could lead you to the Cloak."

"How?"

"The Iruk woman, the one they are seeking. We have reason to believe she is still alive and close to the Cloak. The designs concealing the Cloak conceal her as well, but not so completely. The Iruks have a link, an emotional bond that embraces all the members of their group. With the proper techniques, I think this bond can be exploited as a force in the Deepmind."

Hagen looked at the two sorcerers, one of whom shrugged. "It is possible," the other conceded.

"Suppose I keep you all here," Hagen said, "and set you to work on this technique?"

"The Iruks must believe themselves free," Amlina answered. "If they think they are condemned prisoners they'll have no reason for finding their lost mate. In this sort of endeavor, a relaxed and hopeful outlook is essential."

Hagen frowned, glancing again at the State Sorcerers. First one, then the other shook his head. They knew she was manipulating, Amlina realized, if not exactly how.

"Suppose I released you and the Iruks and had you watched?" the Prince-Ruler said. "What guarantee would I have that you wouldn't try to evade my surveillance and hunt the Cloak for yourselves?"

The insight came to Amlina that here was the crucial moment of persuasion. If she could overcome this objection, Hagen would be won.

"My lord, I've told you I seek the Cloak only as a weapon to kill Beryl. If you should find it and kill her instead, it's all the same to me."

"I'd be a fool to trust you with only that assurance," Hagen said.

"True. In fact, you have no guarantee. You'd have to rely on the efficiency of your informers. The prize you stand to win is certainly worth the gamble—assuming you can defeat the Queen of Tallyba."

Amlina's use of that title for Beryl was deliberate. Tallyba held dominion over numerous coasts and islands. The death of the city's tyrant queen would plunge Tallyba into such political turmoil as to make those territories vulnerable. Ready in advance, a strong maritime state such as Kadavel could take quick advantage of that vulnerability. Amlina could almost hear these thoughts racing through Hagen's mind.

"I will take the gamble," he asserted without even consulting his sorcerers. "I have every faith in my informers. Witness how quickly they found you and the Iruks this evening. I will allow you eleven days, one small-month. If you cannot lead me to the Cloak in that time, the barbarians will be arrested and put to death."

"And if we do, will you let us leave the city in peace?"

"You have my promise," Hagen said.

But Amlina could hear, clear as his words, that he lied.

The Prince-Ruler led her back to the throne room where the Iruks waited.

"Cut them free," Hagen ordered. "See they are escorted back to their lodgings."

* * * * *

The captain of guards hammered long and noisily before the landlady finally opened the door. Dressed in wool robe and nightcap, Elzna had brought an oil lamp and her two burly nephews to the door with her.

"Why do you disturb my house in the middle of the night?" she yowled, peering to see who it was.

"We've orders to return these people here," the captain said.

"I told you we would be back before morning." Amlina walked past the old woman, the Iruks following her into the warmth of the inn.

"You again!" the landlady slammed the door. "I might have known it. You and these savages have caused nothing but trouble since you came here. Now waking us at this unholy hour. I'll have no more of it, that's for sure. You're leaving in the morning."

Amlina had started for the stairs. Now she turned wearily to confront the woman.

"The city guards were in error." She spoke in quiet, soothing tones. "They mistook my bodyguards for other barbarians who started a fight today on the docks. I apologize for waking you, but we could hardly spend the rest of the night in the street."

The landlady crossed her arms. "It's been one thing after another, that's all. My mind is made up. You must leave tomorrow."

Amlina stepped forward, laying a hand on Elzna's shoulder. "I promise there'll be no more trouble. Remember you've been paid for ten days lodging—well paid. If you force us to leave, you'll have to refund my money."

The landlady clenched her lips and considered. "Well, I suppose it's not your fault if the guards made a mistake. I'll overlook it this time. You can stay—providing there are no more disturbances."

"You have my promise," Amlina said.

Elzna turned and shuffled away, ordering her nephews back to bed.

"Come to my room," Amlina told the Iruks. "We must talk."

They climbed the steps quietly and entered her chamber, Amlina shutting the door and bolting it behind them. She fastened the window shutters also, then knelt at the hearth to light a fire. The Iruks slumped in chairs or stretched out on the floor near the fireplace.

"How did you get the Prince to release us?" Draven asked. "Was it the passive persuasion again?"

"In part," Amlina said. "But I also had to tell him part of the truth, that I needed you to help me find the Cloak. He's going to have us watched in hopes we can lead him to it. When the time comes, we'll have to evade his spies."

"How?" Eben said.

"I'll weave a design to accomplish it," the witch answered. "Hagen gave us only eleven days. If we haven't found the Cloak by then, he intends to arrest you and put you to death."

The Iruks winced or clutched their heads and swore.

"Don't worry." Amlina smiled. "I believe we'll have more than enough time—if you will work with me. Our conversation was interrupted earlier. I must know if you are willing to undertake the deep searching."

The witch's gaze settled on Karrol, and all her klarnmates looked at her as well.

Karrol sighed. "I said I didn't know, and I still don't. I mean, I don't know if I can open myself completely. But I'll try. Obviously, we can't find Glyssa in eleven days by trying to search the city. So it seems we don't have much choice. Amlina, I know you've just saved our lives a second time, when it would have been easier to let us die. I know I don't have any reason to distrust you anymore, and I don't. I'll do my best to find Glyssa. That's all I can promise."

"That's all I hoped to hear," Amlina said. "Do the rest of you also agree?"

"Of course," Draven laughed. "When did any of us ever disagree with Karrol?"

"Good," Amlina said. "I suggest you use the rest of the night for sleeping. We'll do the initiations in the morning."

The Iruks bid Amlina goodnight and walked downstairs to their room. Tired and sore, they pulled off their clothes and crawled into bed. But their minds were alive with the day's tumultuous events, and it was a long time before any of them could sleep.

Eighteen

"Messages from the Deepmind are abundant and clear," Amlina translated from the book she held. "All things may be viewed if intent is pure."

"But what does that mean, pure intent?" Eben demanded. "You must make your terms clear to us."

The Iruks sat on the rug in the center of the witch's room, surrounded by tapestries, prisms, and desmets. Amlina sat in the circle with them, dressed in bright silks and silver jewelry.

"Pure intent." Amlina seemed to grope for a definition they would comprehend. "It means that the energy of your whole being is concentrated on looking, so that there is no longer any awareness of yourself, only of that which is seen."

"Sounds simple enough to me," Karrol said.

"It sounds easy," Lonn allowed. "But wait till you've tried it for hours at a time."

"It is easy," Amlina said, "once the mind has learned to still the body and the emotions which constantly seek to distract it. To attain perfect purity of intent takes years, lifetimes according to some."

"Then what hope is there for us?" Eben said.

"There is hope," Amlina answered, "because perfect attainment is not necessary for one to deepsee. The senses may interrupt one's visions, emotions distort them, but truth in the Deepmind can still be glimpsed. And for our purpose, a glimpse of the truth will suffice. This is what I want you to understand as we begin the initiation. Messages of truth and wisdom are with us constantly. All we need do to receive them is to quiet ourselves, even if only a little."

The witch laid aside the gilt-covered book and stood. She walked to her writing table and returned in a moment with a lighted glass lamp and a folded thing with flat silvery arms. As she unfolded it, Lonn recognized the spinner she had used in the past. She placed the spinner above the lamp in the center of the circle. In a moment the arms began to turn on the rising current of heated air, casting a whirling pattern of light and shadow over the walls and the Iruks' bodies.

"I found the spinner useful in easing Lonn's mind during his initiation," Amlina explained. "This time Lonn will remain at the outer level of consciousness and help me guide the rest of you. I want you now to breathe slowly and evenly and to focus your eyes on the light of this lamp."

Lonn waited in sober quiet until the witch judged the Iruks minds were still enough to continue. She took them through the first stages of the rite, asking if they would surrender themselves completely, making them say they would, then relaxing them more and more thoroughly by vocal instruction and by touching their nerve centers. Lonn recalled the numb, floating sensation that had come over him at the witch's touch.

"Close your eyes," Amlina told the Iruks. "Know that you are thought, that this world called Glimnodd is but thought. There are infinite worlds and suns, infinite minds and souls. All are only thoughts of the Great Mind, the Allmind which comes to know itself through thinking. Know further that this Great Mind is within you, within you all its worlds and suns and souls. Now let your inner eye be opened, that you may see what the Allmind gives you to see."

Amlina whispered the last sentence to each of the initiates in turn, uttered a brief chant, and touched each on the forehead. Remembering the vast, shattering visions of his own initiation, Lonn half-expected immediate and violent responses. But his mates just sat still and erect, breathing slowly. The witch returned to her place and sat with feet tucked at her hips. The delicate spinner continued to revolve.

After a time Draven laughed softly and opened his eyes. "There is magic everywhere," he whispered.

Amlina's face brightened. "Very true."

Draven watched the spinner for a time, then stared at the trinkets overhead. The other Iruks still had their eyes shut. Then Lonn heard labored breathing and saw that Karrol was becoming agitated. Amlina moved to kneel before her and told her to open her eyes.

Karrol blinked furiously and glared about the chamber, the color gone from her face.

"Relax." Amlina touched her arm.

"No!" Karrol threw off the witch's hand and tried awkwardly to get up.

Amlina and Lonn restrained her gently, Lonn whispering in Iruk to calm her. Karrol trembled with distress.

"Easy," the witch said. "What did you see?"

"I saw myself ... dying. I saw everything dying."

"Everything dies and is reborn," the witch said. "To be free of death you need only let go of your fear of death."

Karrol pondered this, her breath coming in fitful gasps.

"Be still." Amlina stroked her head. "Observe the spinner."

Karrol obeyed and grew calmer. Lonn noticed that the other Iruks were looking about, eyes round and shiny.

"Everything is long," Eben muttered. "Huge. More than ... more than I can say."

"There is no need to explain," Amlina told him. "Only look and wonder."

"But how can—How will we find Glyssa?" Eben asked.

"Let the thoughts of the Deepmind flow in you," Amlina answered. "They will show the way."

The spinner continued twirling, its sparkling motion at once calming and vivifying to the Iruks' expanded minds. Draven watched the trinket constantly, deep in trance, smiling blithely. Eben watched it also, but his usual expression was a puzzled frown, at times stretching to a grimace of utter confusion, at other times dissolving into merry, inexplicable laughter. Eventually, Brinda grew bored with the spinner, stood up and ambled about the room, examining everything with a strange, vivid curiosity. Amlina kept an eye on her but did not discourage her wandering.

Of all the mates only Karrol seemed as unsettled by the initiation as Lonn had been. She wept inconsolably for much of the day. Lonn held her in his arms often, and the others came over to stroke and murmur to her. But all the klarn's support did not seem to bring her comfort. At one point she started wailing aloud, calling Glyssa's name.

"Where is Glyssa?" Amlina asked her.

"We have to find her," Karrol cried. "We have to find her."

By evening, all of the initiates were lying quietly on the floor, either sleeping or staring dreamily at the lamps and trinkets. Amlina went downstairs to order supper. She and Lonn ate beside the fireplace, though Lonn had little appetite. He stared moodily at the low flames and embers.

"What are you thinking?" the witch asked.

"That one of the eleven days is already gone," Lonn said.

"We are on the right path," Amlina answered. "Perseverance will bring success."

* * * * *

Lonn woke to find himself still in the witch's room. It was dark outside, but his mates were up and dressed. Amlina was putting wood on the fire.

"It is good that we are all awake," she said. "There is still an hour or so before dawn and most of the city is asleep. This is an excellent time to begin deepseeing."

Amlina lit all of the lamps she had brought ashore and placed them in a circle around the rug. She had the Iruks sit with her inside that circle, beneath the desmets and prisms. On her instruction, all six of them held hands and began to breathe in unison. When they were deeply relaxed, the witch told the mates to picture a current of light passing through each of them and flowing around the circle, a ring of silvery energy bonding them together.

Lonn perceived the current of light clearly and knew that the others could see it also. The light glimmered with a peculiar reality created by their six minds imagining it as one.

"Feel its warmth, like sunlight," Amlina said, "relaxing you ever more deeply. See the light filling our bodies, brighter and brighter. Now the portal of deepseeing that before was opened by my touch opens to the light."

Amlina spoke some words of Old Larthangan and the silver radiance in their minds blazed to a blinding white. The Iruks' arms shook, their hands gripping tightly. Slowly the blaze subsided to a sparkling undulation of silver and gray, like the surface of a metallic pool.

"Perceive the sea of the Deepmind," Amlina said, "flowing in waves and currents of unending variation. Always it surrounds us, *Ogo*: infinite in complexity, ceaseless in motion ..."

She kept them watching the heaving surface an indefinite time. When any of their minds wandered all six of them sensed the distraction, and Amlina would bring them back to the vision of the silvery pool.

"We are afloat in the Deepmind," she said at length. "Scenes may be viewed from this place, any scenes we wish."

She invoked the image of the *Plover* and Lonn saw it, standing with reefed sails in the long line of vessels on the glossy, unlit ice of the Shipway. Next, the witch told them to envision the castle of Hagen and they could see it, perched atop the crags of the High

Acropolis like some nocturnal bird of prey. Then Amlina told them to see Glyssa.

Lonn beheld her at once, frail and sad in a white robe, her figure half-lost in shiny blackness. Then the blackness rippled, distorting the image, partially dissolving it.

"See Glyssa," Amlina said. "Speak what you see."

"She is thin and weak," Lonn answered.

"She is alone," Karrol cried. "Afraid."

A throb of anguished feelings spun around the circle. There was a dizzying sense of being wrenched away from each other and thrown adrift. Lonn heard groans and felt his mates moving. He opened his eyes to glittering daggers of radiance.

"Relax," Amlina said. "Close your eyes. Think of stillness."

She attempted to bring their vision back to the shining pool. But the Iruks were left sickened by the rush of painful emotion, more devastating by far when shared in group trance. Noting their distress, Amlina told them to lie down and breathe slowly. She chanted a long verse to settle their nerves and clear their heads of dizziness. When she finished, the Iruks sat up, all of them looking dull and drained to Lonn.

"You did well," Amlina said. "Karrol especially envisioned Glyssa strongly."

"I'm surprised to hear that," Karrol answered. "I didn't know if I was really seeing Glyssa at all. It seemed more that I was making it up, pretending I could see her." She looked doubtfully at her mates.

"I felt the same," Eben muttered. "That I was making it up."

"Such feelings are common until one is practiced at deepseeing," Amlina said. "Just continue, whether you feel you're imagining it or not. What we saw was Glyssa in truth, believe me."

"How soon will we try again?" Draven asked.

"This evening, I think." The witch leaned back and stretched. "Right now your emotions are too stimulated. There are meditations and exercises I want you to practice to quiet them."

Most of that day the Iruks sat downstairs in their room staring at the backs of their eyelids. They interrupted this discipline only to trot in place and chant the unknown verses of Old Larthangan the witch prescribed, then to meditate on the flame of a small candle until the candle burned out. Then it was back to contemplating their eyelids again.

After supper, the mates climbed the stairs to Amlina's chamber and sat again knee to knee in the wei circle. They envisioned Glyssa and were able to hold her image somewhat longer than before. They still could see no details of her surroundings, yet Amlina did not seem discouraged.

When the Iruks' minds were rested the witch told them to join hands again. Guided by her words the klarnmates formed a mental picture of the whole klarn together, Glyssa included, safely onboard the *Plover* and away from Kadavel, the witch and the Cloak of the Two Winds with them. This was deepshaping in its most pure and elementary form, the casting of an image into the Deepmind with firm belief that it would surface as reality. The Iruks viewed the image with surprising clarity and sharpness. Amlina kept the picture in their minds several moments, then told them to release it and brought their awareness back to the room.

"Well done," she said. "We will reinforce that image each time we have finished searching. That is all for now. Return tomorrow before dawn, and we will look again."

The Iruks spent the days that followed immersed in this routine of wei circles morning and evening, the hours between passed in meditation. Amlina had decided that this regimen was most in harmony with their purpose. Pure intent, she said, demanded a single line of action.

Time moved slowly and yet, looking back over a day, Lonn had little sense of what had filled the time. Mealtimes made their mark on the days, but the Iruks felt little desire to eat. Nor did they drink much, for fear of befuddling their senses. So food and drink left little impression in their memories. Curiously, they needed more sleep than usual, so that rising in the cold hour before dawn required serious effort.

The continual practice of meditation left their spirits calm, their minds somewhat vague and self-absorbed. At the same time, the mates developed an almost telepathic sensitivity to one another's thoughts and feelings. An unexpected result of this was a certain tumultuous discord, the klarnmates becoming openly hostile about the traits they disliked in one another. Karrol's negativity and complaining drew criticism, as did Eben's irascibility. Brinda was accused of withholding herself from the rest of the klarn, Draven of masking his real feelings with an air of false optimism. Lonn was the most criticized of all, or perhaps it only seemed so to him. By turns he was rebuked for being irresponsible and reckless, for being unwilling to make decisions, for being unable to remember his dreams.

The Iruks argued violently and often. But just as quickly tempers would subside and they would apologize and forgive, anger and resentment changing to comradery and warmth. All of this was normal, Amlina insisted, the process of a wei circle drawing close. The witch herself stayed aloof from the turmoil, keeping to the role of guide and instructor, shielding her own emotions from the Iruks' awareness.

"This is the logical way to proceed," she explained when they questioned her about it. "Your emotions are part of what we seek. Mine are not. They would only confuse our vision."

Each day, in the hour after sunset and the hour before dawn, the Iruks sat amid the beaming lamps and shiny trinkets and searched for Glyssa. The rituals of the circle and the glimmering ring of thought that bound them together became familiar to their minds. The Iruks came to know the meaning of the chants Amlina used and the functions of her various devices: lamps to radiate, tapestries to border and contain, desmets to spin and reflect, prisms to bend and scatter. The klarnmates even got an inkling of the metaphysics of the Deepmind, how thought and light combined to create substance and motion.

The visions of Glyssa too became familiar. At first, the pain the Iruks felt at seeing her dispersed the image within moments. But as the steady meditation brought their emotions under control, they were able to hold Glyssa's image for longer. Sometimes they saw her sleeping, sometimes standing or walking. On occasion, she seemed to be working, scrubbing a floor or carrying some burden. More often her movements were inexplicable and strange, as if she performed some peculiar ritual. Whatever her posture, Glyssa was always surrounded by the shiny blackness of the spell of concealment, so that the Iruks could tell nothing of her location.

Then one evening unexpectedly the blackness quivered and gave way in places to flashes of light. Surprised, the Iruks grew excited and lost the image in a few moments. But Amlina insisted the change was crucial.

"The design that hides her is beginning to unravel," she said.

Lonn and his mates tried wholeheartedly to believe she was right. Of the eleven days Hagen had given them, five remained.

* * * * *

Other minds also were searching. All over Kadavel witches and seers, sorcerers and priests poured their thoughts into the Deepmind. Working alone or in circles, they delved to find the meaning of the portents visiting the city, which daily grew more ominous and strange.

The Two Winds continued to blow ever more frequently on the Shipway—five or six changes now in a single day. The weather was violent and freakish. Sudden storms of hale and sleet lashed the city. Dense fogs aglitter with bits of suspended sea-ice rose to enshroud the streets, then sank again through the planks just as quickly. Most unnerving of all, a vast spiral of clouds appeared in the sky and remained day and night. Dark and gray, but faintly luminous at times with unmistakable witchlight, the spiral loomed like some tremendous inverted whirlpool poised to suck Kadavel into the sky.

The end of the world was at hand—so proclaimed several wild-eyed seers who spoke from the free rostrums on the Long Acropolis. Others maintained that this age of human dominance was passing and some new sentient race was about to appear. The official position, that the Archimage of the East was to blame for the portents, had begun to lose credence when the expected invasion failed to come. One after another, the major temples abandoned this explanation. The richly-clad priests who addressed the crowds from the temple steps started to preach that the portents were a sign of the displeasure of the Elements, whose worship had slackened in recent years. But certain boisterous iconoclasts charged from the free rostrums that the priests themselves were at fault, for their grasping materialism and spiritual shortcomings.

Despite the ill weather, the speakers never lacked for an audience. Besides the usual crowds of worshippers, supplicants, and pilgrims, the Long Acropolis daily was thronged with out-of-work skimmer men, sailors, and stevedores. Some of these credited the fearful predictions of world catastrophe. Others worried that if the portents continued the harbor would be unable to open for the winter sailing season, and the city's economy would collapse.

But even the most pragmatic in the crowds could not help but be awed by the weird spiral in the sky, which seemed uncannily to center exactly over the Long Acropolis.

After days of hearing the priests decry the people's lack of piety, and the iconoclasts decry the priests' materialism, most of the crowd was siding with the iconoclasts. Priestly orators were driven from the steps of their temples by angry mobs. Then rioters nearly succeeded in looting one of the temples. Companies of marines were hastily called up from the waterfront to bolster the harried city guard. Still, the discontented mob atop the acropolis seemed to swell each day.

Concerned by the increasing civil disorder, Prince Hagen forced his State Sorcerers to search without rest for the Cloak. Using crystals and mirrored lamps and aided by a whole troop of assistants and apprentices, the two sorcerers delved constantly to see the Cloak and cast numerous spells to break down the forces hiding it—all without success. For the Tathians had only the written descriptions of the Cloak to go on, along with the information Amlina had provided—which, though mainly true, was designed to be subtly misleading.

In the meantime, in a rented villa in a wealthy district of the city, Beryl the Archimage also watched the flux of light and shade in the Deepmind. She watched as a thorncat watches from a thicket, intent and silent, confident that the thing she awaits must inevitably appear. Twice each day Beryl cast a design: the image of herself wearing the Cloak of the Two Winds. That was all the deepshaping she did, vitalizing the idea that whoever was first to discover the Cloak—herself, Hagen, Amlina, or some other—she, Beryl, would be the one to carry off the prize.

So the currents of thought in the Deepmind drifted and flowed, crashing and combining, generating substance, gesture, and sound, making and filling time and space. Creating those minds that peered within to fulfill their destinies as surely as it created all else.

* * * * *

On the far side of a barrier existing only in thought, one other mind was watching, one that knew these currents well. For many years this deepshaper had watched the Ogo tides from this place called Kadavel, and he had learned to predict and use their shaping force. That was how he concealed the Cloak of the Two Winds so effectively.

The Cloak had come to him more than thirty days ago, and his work upon it had begun at once. He had hoped this work would be accomplished long before anyone could discover his hiding place.

But the task was proving more difficult than anticipated. The Cloak, woven by the legendary witch Eglemarde, was amazingly resistant. The deepshaper had hidden the Cloak with a cunning and potent concealment, one designed to take full advantage of the currents of Ogo force in Kadavel and empowered by mind energies drawn from numerous thralls. Yet the concealment was beginning to dissolve.

So the shaper had suspended his awareness in the Deepmind to observe those seeking the Cloak. Most of the seekers, he found, could be discounted almost at once. They did not know what they were looking for or, if they did, lacked enough knowledge of the Cloak to form a clear conception. This was true of the temple priests and of the pre-eminent deepseers and witches of the city. It was even true of the State Sorcerers, though they knew more than most.

In fact, there remained only two deepseers who could not be disregarded: the two Larthangan-born witches, they who had most recently possessed the Cloak. At first, the deepshaper thought it must be the elder witch, the Archimage, who had penetrated his concealment. But on observing both witches from behind his barrier, he learned it was the younger, the one called Amlina, who posed the immediate threat. It was her mind, in unison with the minds of her Iruk henchmen, that had succeeded in parting the veil of dark energy that he had woven.

This, the shaper decided, was fortunate. Beryl was a famously redoubtable foe. Better to attack the lesser witch first and perhaps thereby to learn more of the Archimage and her weaknesses. For it seemed inevitable that the new master of the Cloak would have to destroy both witches in time.

The deepshaper rose from the shallow water in which he had been lying face down. His gullet made a hoarse, bubbling sound as it sucked in air. The blood-red gills along his bulging cheeks closed up as his features resumed their human guise.

For he was no human, this shaper, but a serd.

His name was Kosimo, and he belonged to that fish-engendered race that had flourished in the Age of the World's Madness. For centuries his kind had ruled the land, enslaving humans and other sentient races, until being driven back into the sea by Tuan Tuo and the shapers of Larthang.

Kosimo did not consider that historical defeat to be permanent.

He walked to the edge of the moat and climbed slippery steps, briny water dripping from his coarse black robe. The moat connected through subterranean caverns with the back harbor of Kadavel, behind the Long Acropolis, and hence with the sea. Kosimo had built his sorcerer's lair here to be close to his natural element.

Atop the steps, he crossed a narrow ledge and passed through a portal cut in the glistening black stone. Inside was a large, low-ceilinged chamber. A few dim-burning lamps and certain flaming instruments gave scant illumination, but more than enough for the eyes of a serd, bred to the murky depths of the ocean. Tables and racks stood crowded with vials, bottles, and arcane devices of metal and glass. Numerous books lay stacked or open on shelves, for Kosimo had studied human arts as well as the potent sorceries of his own race. In the middle of the chamber was an open space with a gray and black mosaic pattern on the floor—an extravagant and baffling maze. A number of Kosimo's thralls, in white hooded robes, stood at the edges of the maze, motionless as pieces on a game board—lifeless except when their master chose to fill their minds with his bidding.

Glancing at the thralls reminded Kosimo of the Iruk woman, the one who had served as instrument to bring the Cloak to Kadavel. It was through her that his possession of the Cloak now was endangered, through her link to the other Iruks. Too late to kill her however: the violence of her death would only send a vivid signal to her fellows, a shriek across the Deepmind. Besides, once her native stubbornness was suppressed, the woman had made an energetic and useful thrall.

Kosimo considered. Perhaps he should entrap the minds of the other Iruks also, then use them to strike at the young witch. His lips pulled back in an expression like a smile. It pleased the serd's highly developed sense of aesthetics to turn his adversaries against each other. But no, the plan was flawed. Too difficult to cage so many minds at once, too easy for the witch to detect and break the design. Better to simply strike down the Iruks quickly, after first examining their minds to learn what they knew of the witch. It occurred to Kosimo that *drogs*, creatures formed of thought-energy, would be useful for both these purposes—first to focus his probing mind on the Iruks, then to dispatch the barbarians with swift efficiency.

The serd crossed the moist chamber to the stacks of books that constituted his library. Scaly fingers moved over ancient leather bindings until stopping on the volume he sought, a collection of Nyssanian incantations for formulating drogs.

With three thoughts Kosimo animated three of his attendant thralls. One came forward, took the book from his hands and carried it to the center of the tile maze. The other thralls brought two shallow bowls of stone and placed them on either side of the book.

While the thralls resumed their former positions, Kosimo walked to the center of the maze and sat down. With a gesture he lit the two bowls, which contained fish oil exuded from his own body. Then he leafed through the book until finding the incantation he desired. He read the verses through several times, committing them to memory, then shut his eyes and began to recite.

As he whispered the spell, Kosimo envisioned the creatures he wished to form. Strong arms would be required, ending in thick hands with steely claws. Bodies were unnecessary, only floating husks of energy to give the arms a center. But eyes were needed, eyes for the serd to look through, burning eyes that hurt to look upon. The form and will of the drogs would come from Kosimo's thoughts, their vast elemental energy from another plane, a realm of potential in the Deepmind tapped by the incantation.

Saliva dribbled down his chin as Kosimo, in trance, continued to mouth the verses. The words were potent, for soon the drogs hovered plain and precise in his vision. Then Kosimo poured his will into the drogs, till their burning eyes gleamed with purpose.

* * * * *

Lonn shuddered in his sleep. An inexplicable clamminess had touched his flesh. Something nagging and insistent probed at his mind. He coughed and rolled over, but the probing continued.

Visions of Amlina filled his brain, crowded and feverish.

Lonn breathed deeply and began to awake, but some force restrained him. He fell back under and dreamed of Amlina. He dreamed of when he had first seen her, lying entranced in her cabin; and later on the main deck of the *Plover*, when she had disarmed the Iruks and chained them to the mast; then later still, when she first began to train Lonn in deepseeing.

Lonn realized with a part of his mind that he was being forced to recall these memories. He strained to understand why, and in the moment of strain his eyes opened.

Surrounded by glistening blackness, a pair of red eyes glared down at him.

Sleep.

The command intruded forcefully into his mind. For a moment Lonn obeyed. The pleasant oblivion of sleep opened beneath him and he wanted to slip down into its darkness. But some voice of his own urged warning. *Sleep was a trap, the glowing eyes an enemy.* The thought of those eyes, nearly forgotten, came back and startled him. With a sudden effort, Lonn sat up and looked.

Huge muscular arms filled the air, one pair hanging over each of the Iruks. Crimson eyes stared down from the black spaces between the arms. Lonn shuddered as all the eyes shifted to look at him, baleful and angry.

"Wake up!" His voice croaked from a strangely constricted throat. "Get up!"

Then cold hands clenched on his neck and throttled him. Choking, Lonn gripped the fingers and tried to pry them off. But all his strength could not bend them. In desperation, Lonn wrenched backward and swung his fist at the opaque blackness that held the eyes. His knuckles crunched as through hitting an anvil, but the hands released his throat as the arms floated back.

Lonn scrambled up, screaming to awaken his mates. His arms flailed out wildly, driving some of the things upward. His feet kicked frantically to rouse his ensorcelled mates.

Startled for just a moment the bodiless arms and eyes swooped down again, moving through the air as if by the power of thought alone. Lonn dodged beneath grasping claws and staggered to the corner, where the Iruks' weapons lay.

"Wake up!" he shouted.

Karrol and Eben had sat up and were grappling with arms that now sought to strangle them. Draven and Brinda struggled weakly, unable to rise, crushed down by the gruesome creatures.

Lonn grabbed a quiver of spears and tossed it, spilling the spears out toward his mates. Clawed hands closed on his shoulder and one wrist as his free hand reached the hilt of a sword.

Growling his defiance, Lonn turned and whipped the sword through the air. Charged with Amlina's witchery, the steel blade sheared through the monstrosity's black center with a fizzing sound and an explosion of light. Two arms spun down in separate paths, crashed to the floor and vanished in bursts of fire that left only black smudges behind.

Scraped and bleeding, Lonn's mates had seized the spears and were fighting back. But the number of creatures in the room had doubled. The things were sliding down from a disk of blackness that hung in the middle of the ceiling.

Lonn snatched a spear from the floor and cast it at the disk. The bewitched spear struck the magic portal with a searing burst of light and a thunderclap. The spear shattered to splinters, but the black disk disappeared.

Roaring in triumph, Lonn sprang to the aid of his beleaguered mates. He stabbed one creature through the back of its black center, causing the arms to writhe upward and freeing Draven to slide from beneath and gain his feet. Lonn wheeled and slashed at another of the things as it grabbed for Eben's head.

Standing together now, the Iruks fought with skill and controlled ferocity. They protected each other, dodged and parried the bear-like swipe of claws, stabbed hard when the creatures came within range. The floating arms attacked relentlessly, but despite their numbers the enchanted weapons gave the Iruks the advantage.

Soon all but a few of the things were slain, or else struggling helplessly on the floor with wounds that quivered and hissed. Eben's spear brought down one of those still in the air. Karrol chased another into a corner.

Lonn saw too late that Karrol had left her back unprotected. Just as her spear spitted the creature she had cornered, one of the others dropped down behind her, reached around and sank its claws into her face.

Karrol cried out in pain and fell to her knees, clutching at the thing's hands. Lonn reached her an instant later and sliced open one of the arms with his sword. The creature fell back, wounded arm dangling. Lonn charged after, caught it against the other wall and ran it through.

As the thing expired Lonn whirled and looked about. The battle was over, the room black with the creatures' remains. Here and there a few arms still moved with feeble life, claws scratching vainly on the floor. One of the things flared up and vanished as Lonn watched.

Karrol knelt in the corner, wailing in misery. Her hands covered her face and blood dripped from between the fingers. Eben and

Brinda leaned over her, but she would not let them uncover her wound.

The chamber door opened, and Lonn saw that a crowd was gathered outside. Amlina pushed her way into the room, took a quick look and shut the door—but not before the landlady squeezed inside.

"What are you doing?" she demanded, then gaped about the room, struck dumb by the bizarre scene of carnage.

Amlina hastened to the far wall where the last of the creatures still shuddered with life. She spoke a command in Old Larthangan and the thing grew still, eyes watching her with mute intensity.

"Tell me with thought who sent you," Amlina said.

But then the arms curled over the thing's black middle and all turned to blinding fire and vanished.

"What were they?" Draven asked. "What does it mean?"

"They were drogs," Amlina said. "Made-beings. It means we have an enemy with great shaping powers, but we knew that already. It also means, perhaps, that we are close to finding the Cloak, so close as to worry the one concealing it and push him to this desperate act."

"My eye," Karrol cried as her hands were finally pulled from her face. "My eye is lost to me."

* * * * *

In his cavern chamber far away Kosimo the serd opened his eyes. He stared down at the open book, and the broken tip from the Iruk spear which lay before it on the floor. His design, which had seemed foolproof, had gone awry—defeated by the unexpected acuity of the Iruks and the charm the witch had given to their weapons. Kosimo had learned practically nothing about the apprentice witch that he had not known already.

A most unsatisfactory outcome.

Another solution to this vexing problem would have to be found, and soon.

Nineteen

This is more than I will tolerate!" The landlady had at last found her voice. "This room is a shambles. You've wakened every one of my tenants, again! I tell you, I'll have no more!"

"Silence," Amlina turned on her with such an air of authority that the woman shut her mouth at once.

"I'll hear no more of your complaining," Amlina said. "You will forget this incident completely. You will not speak of it again. You will not think of it again. Now go and send your tenants back to bed."

Stiff and wide-eyed, Elzna started to comply then paused. "But—"

"Tell them my bodyguards were practicing with their swords, that the disturbance will not recur."

"Yes. Yes, milady." Frowning with puzzlement, Elzna departed from the chamber.

Amlina stepped to where Lonn and his mates were clustered around Karrol, who still knelt on the floor.

"Let me see."

The witch bent over and examined Karrol's face. Streaked claw marks bled on her cheek and forehead. The eyeball was scratched and it oozed a bloody fluid.

"You have not lost your eye," Amlina said. "In a month's time it will be perfectly healed. That is if you allow me to treat the wound."

"Yes," Karrol answered. "Whatever you say, only save my eye."

"Fine." Amlina straightened up. "You are most compliant when you are desperate. If you had trusted me enough before to wear the moonstone I gave you, this might not have happened."

Lonn had not thought of it, but he and the others were still wearing the moonstone talismans.

"I am sorry." Karrol gazed at the witch through one teary eye. "I should not have thrown your gift away."

"Come upstairs." Amlina extended her hands. "The sooner the wound is treated the better."

Wary of another attack, the Iruks took swords and spears up to the witch's chamber. Amlina directed Karrol to sit on the bed, then filled a washbasin with water. She added to the water a tincture of blue liquid from a small glass vial.

"The blue essence will clean and protect the damaged tissues," she said, soaking a cloth in the basin.

Karrol gritted her teeth and held the bedpost while Amlina bathed her cuts. When the eye was thoroughly cleansed Amlina covered it with a linen bandage. She rubbed her palms together vigorously, whispered a chant, then placed one hand atop the other over the bandaged eye.

"Visualize blue light," she told Karrol, "shining through the wounded parts, soothing and healing. Now visualize your eye whole again, whole and perfect as before."

On the witch's bidding, Eben had cut a patch from a strip of leather and fixed it to a thong. Amlina fitted on the patch and tied the thong around Karrol's head.

"You must keep the eye covered for several days at least. I will continue to send you the blue light for healing. Lie back now and rest."

Amlina built up the fire while Lonn and his mates washed their wounds. The treated water stung Lonn's neck where the claws had scratched. The hand that had punched the thrall's middle was bruised and swollen. The other Iruks had various bloody scrapes puffing out on arms, necks, and faces.

"Let us sit in the circle now," Amlina said when the Iruks were done washing. "We may be able to trace the origin of the drogs while their appearance is still fresh in your minds."

"I don't think I can concentrate," Karrol said. "My eye hurts and I feel dizzy."

"Sit with us anyway," Amlina replied. "It is important that the circle be complete."

The five Iruks and the witch sat down beneath the trinkets and performed the rituals of deep breathing and relaxing. From the start, Lonn sensed a lack of stillness and clarity in the circle—perhaps from Karrol's discomfort, perhaps from the excitement they all felt as a residue of the weird battle. When Amlina told them to envision the two-armed creatures, the pictures came jumbled and frightening. The klarnmates were sickened as they relived Karrol's pain and shock in the moment the claw scratched her eye.

"Be calm," Amlina said. "The one who sent the drogs is linked to them. His image too can be viewed. We are looking upon it now."

But the picture that appeared was obscured by clashing swells of light and blackness. All Lonn could be sure of seeing were the eyes, gleaming and baleful, like the red eyes of the drogs.

After several vain attempts Amlina changed tacks and told the Iruks to picture Glyssa. But her image appeared tenuous and more fully hidden by the veil than it had been the previous night. The vision went dark after a few moments, and Amlina did not try to summon it back.

"Your minds are too unsettled," she said after breaking the circle. "Hardly surprising under the circumstances. Rest now. We will delve again in the evening."

"We didn't focus well," Eben said. "Glyssa's image hardly seemed there at all."

"The concealment may have been reinforced," Amlina told him. "It felt so to me."

"That worries me," Eben said. "Counting today we have only five days left."

"We are on the path shown to us by the Deepmind." Amlina rose to her feet. "You must put aside your anxieties and trust in what will be."

"That's well enough to say," Brinda answered. "But Eben has a point. Suppose the five days run out and we still have not found Glyssa?"

"No." Amlina touched one of the prisms to stop its slow turning. "We must not consider the possibility of failure. To do so can engender failure."

"Now wait," Eben said, standing to challenge the witch. "If the five days pass and Hagen's men come for us, we must at least have a plan for how to evade them and what to do next."

But Amlina shook her head. "That is precisely what we must not think about. We must adhere to the design we are shaping—that we will find what we seek in time and get safely away from Kadavel. Let no other possibilities dwell in your minds. This is crucial."

The Iruks regarded one another grimly.

"You've been working very hard," Amlina said. "Even meditation can grow wearisome if unrelieved by change. I suggest you relax today and not practice the exercises."

"We've been shut up in this inn too long," Draven said. "It would help if we could walk, get out in the air."

Amlina considered. "You'll no doubt be followed if you leave the inn. Still, I don't see any harm in that. So long as you don't try to evade Hagen's spies, I don't imagine they'll call in the guard to arrest you."

* * * * *

The Iruks went downstairs and found breakfast being served at the common room hearth. They lined up with the other patrons of the inn, and Lonn was surprised that no one asked them about last night's disturbance. Perhaps the landlady's bewitched responses had discouraged further inquiry on the subject. Or maybe the tenants were simply growing accustomed to wild commotions in the night.

Opening the door to their room, the Iruks were starkly reminded of the attack. The floor and bed furs were blackened with grimy smears. The air reeked with an odor like burnt hair or feathers. Draven pushed open the outside window but the chill, clammy air from the street only dampened the chamber.

The mates sat down with their cups and bowls and ate breakfast in silence. After taking their fill of the porridge and tea, they rose and put on their outer garb and harnesses. Taking swords and daggers but no spears, they marched across the common room and out the front door of the inn.

Wisps of sea-fog drifted over the plank street, sparkling with needlepoints of witchlight. In the sky above the city, the awesome spiral of cloud hung dark and menacing.

"I can see why many believe it's the end of the world," Eben observed as they stood in the middle of the street staring up.

"Let's walk," Lonn said.

Restless and uneasy, the Iruks started down the street toward the waterfront. If Prince Hagen's spies were following, they did so furtively. Lonn looked back every so often, but caught no glimpse of anyone.

The Iruks passed through the city wall and strolled out onto the empty pier. The harbor was fogbound, so that the lines of ships riding at anchor could not be seen. The mates had to step to the edge of the pier before they could tell that the Shipway was unfrozen this morning.

They walked east along the docks, treading through banks of fog and sudden open spaces. At times they could just hear faint footsteps some distance behind them, footsteps that would halt whenever they paused—sure evidence, Lonn concluded, that the Prince-Ruler's informers were indeed on their trail.

The Iruks proceeded as far as the Luxury Market, the spot where they had first landed in Kadavel. The stone quays were nearly deserted. Perhaps it was still too early in the morning, or perhaps the recent storms and chilling fog had discouraged normal commerce.

The fog was growing thicker, creeping out of the water like some vast, luminous ghost. Lonn and his mates crossed the quay and entered one of the dragon gates. On an impulse, they climbed a stairway and sat down to rest on the parapet of the city wall. The fog stretched below them like a glimmering carpet. Gables, cupolas, and sloping roofs floated vague and dim above the mists. The fog played tricks with the eyes, so that the bulky fortifications atop the High Acropolis stood out plainly, and seemed to brood down on them from near at hand.

"I didn't hear anyone come through the gate," Draven said. "Maybe we've lost our trackers."

"Don't worry," Lonn answered. "Hagen's men won't be so easily lost."

"Not now or five days from now," Eben said in a low voice, "if it comes to that. I don't care what Amlina says, I think we need to consider what we'll do if our time runs out."

"What do you suggest?" Lonn asked. "What can we do?"

"Well," Eben said, "if Amlina can cast a design to evade Hagen's spies, she could use it on the eleventh day, and we could slip away from the inn."

"And go where?" Lonn demanded.

All attempts to plan broke down on this point. The mates could think of no place in the city where they could hide from Hagen's spies. They might try to reach the ship. But, anchored in the channel, the *Plover* was unlikely to offer refuge for more than a day or two at best. The only sure escape was to leave Kadavel entirely. But none of them would consider going without Glyssa.

"This is getting us nowhere," Draven declared. "There's no use in making plans anyway if Amlina won't have a part in them. She says we must see things through the way we've started, and I don't see what other choice we have."

"Even if it means waiting and doing nothing when the Tathians come for us?" Eben said.

"Let's hope it won't mean that," Draven muttered. "What do you think, Lonn?"

Lonn stared morosely at the fogbound city. "I don't know. Maybe Amlina has a point about not considering that we might fail. It's as though we were hunting yulugg, and we've picked one out and chased it away from the herd and the other boats. Now we've caught the beast and it turns on us. We either kill it or we die, but there's no turning back."

"It's exactly like that," Eben said. "That's exactly how we got here, leaving the other boats and seeking the treasure ship that Lonn dreamed about."

They were quiet a few moments, Lonn regretting yet again how his dreaming had brought them all this trouble. And yet that dream still lived vividly in his mind, with its rich wonder and its promise of a better life for all of them.

Then, to his surprise, Brinda spoke. "You know what, mates? Assuming we get Glyssa back and she's all right, I'll have no regrets. With all we've seen and done, it's been quite a hunt."

"Yes it has," Eben agreed. "Far more fun than chasing yulugg all season."

Karrol stared dully through her one good eye. "Well, I haven't always been glad of it, but it's been an adventure, for sure." Her tone was weary, but not angry or blaming.

Draven grinned. "Just think what tales we'll have to tell our grandchildren on those long nights in Second Winter."

"If we have grandchildren," Eben laughed. "If we ever make it back to Ilga."

"We'll get through this, *and with Glyssa,*" Lonn declared, feeling it fiercely in his heart. "The klarn will see us through. Remember what Belach said: Hold fast to the klarn."

They pondered this for a bit, then Eben said: "It seems to me the klarn is changing. With all this witch-work we've been doing ..."

"Yes, I've felt that too," Draven said. "The klarn spirit is still there, but it's different. Of course, Glyssa is missing. And Amlina feels part of it now, as if she's standing in for Glyssa."

"No one is taking Glyssa's place," Lonn said. "All of this, all we've gone through, has been for Glyssa."

"I know that," Draven assured him. "I'm just saying the klarn feels different now. And, like it or not, Amlina is part of that."

Lonn found these words troubling, but on reflection had to admit they matched his own perception. The wei circle had both strengthened and altered the klarn. And Amlina's energy had seeped into the group soul.

"Changed or not," he finally said. "We must hold fast to the klarn."

All of the mates agreed with that. Lonn extended his hand and they readily placed their hands on top to affirm their unity.

As they walked back through the dank and foggy streets, they chanted softly together:

Many hands, one heart
Many eyes, one soul
Many spears, one hunter
We hold to the klarn
We are fearless

* * * * *

In the circle that evening the Iruks were able to see more light and details around Glyssa's image. The weave could be discerned on the white robe she wore, and her black hair, cut short, was visible inside the hood. But the nervous energy that had disturbed the circle in the morning persisted. The mates could behold Glyssa's image for only a few instants, and after glimpsing it three times were not able to bring it back.

"We did not keep still enough this time," Amlina said when she had brought them out of trance. "The concealment is weaker, but so was our concentration. Perhaps I erred in telling you not to practice today."

"We are anxious," Eben said. "Time is running out."

"You must not think that way," the witch exclaimed. "At your initiation, each of you spoke your readiness to surrender hope and desire. This surrender is crucial if you are to deepsee."

"But to surrender that way," Lonn said, "we'd have to give up caring whether we find Glyssa or not."

"Precisely," Amlina replied. "If you care too much you cannot see."

"I don't understand," Lonn complained. "You tell us we must stop caring, but you also say that our feelings for Glyssa make the bond that allows us to see her."

"I know," Amlina said. "The arts of the Deepmind are fraught with contradictions. The more you study, the more you will find this is true. In the present instance, let me make this distinction: there is the love you feel for Glyssa, and there is your desire to find her. Love opens your spirits and attracts Glyssa to you in the Deepmind. But desire incites fear, and fear closes your spirits. Your desire to have Glyssa back, your fear that you won't find her in time—these forces act as barriers that prevent your seeing her."

Around the circle Lonn watched his mates frowning, struggling to grasp the witch's argument. Woefully, Karrol let her head sink down to rest in her hands.

"Concentrate on your love for Glyssa," Amlina said. "Let go of your desire to find her. Keep this in mind as you deepsee. If you can do this, we will succeed. As the glimpses we managed tonight showed, we are very close to breaking the concealment."

Twenty

Lonn remembered climbing steps so wide he could see no end to them in either direction. He never recalled coming to the top, but somehow he found himself striding beneath a huge doorway, into a dark vestibule fragrant with incense. Beyond the vestibule, he paused on the brink of a colossal chamber with a lofty ceiling and rows of tall pillars on each side. The floor was empty, and at the far end the vast chamber opened onto another, large hall, and beyond that another still.

The scale and strangeness of the place was appalling. Keeping to the shadows, Lonn moved along the back wall, toward the line of pillars on the right. Peeking around the backmost column he saw a procession of white-robed figures moving toward him in single file. He had an overpowering impulse to flee, but his feet seemed anchored to the spot. The hooded figures approached. Each one regarded Lonn gravely, then passed on through a shadowy doorway in the rear wall. Suddenly Lonn's insides jumped as one of the figures stepped from the line.

"Glyssa!"

She pulled back her hood, revealing her black hair clipped short. She gazed at him earnestly. "Lonn, I'm so glad you are near me. I've been alone so long. Please come for me soon."

"We'll come as soon as we can. But we don't know where you are. What is this place?"

The last of the procession was passing. Glyssa replaced her hood. "I must go."

"No," Lonn said.

But Glyssa took her place at the rear of the line, matching her steps with the others.

"Glyssa!"

She walked through the darkened doorway and vanished.

Lonn rushed after her. But as he crossed the threshold he was flung back, as though struck by a huge hand. Next instant he was sitting up, in the dim room at the inn, his mates sleeping peacefully around him.

The dream had been so vivid, *so real*. Lonn clutched his head, groping with his mind to bring the vision back.

He was thinking that he ought to wake his mates and tell them of it when a knocking rattled the door. Lonn got up and pulled the door open. Amlina hurried inside, wearing her quilted robe, holding a small lamp.

"I caught a glimpse of your dream in the Deepmind," she whispered. "Tell me everything you saw."

Lonn sat by the stove and related to the witch all he could remember—the wide steps, the huge vaulted chambers, the pillars, the line of figures in white, Glyssa speaking to him. By the time he finished his mates were hovering around, listening.

"Excellent," Amlina said. "When I saw the dream flicker out I had the definite impression it was a message from Glyssa, perhaps dreaming herself. I confess that at times I've had doubts that we could save her, that enough of her mind could remain unchanged after so many days. But I sensed a strong spirit reaching out to you in this dream. It bodes well."

"But I didn't learn where she is," Lonn said.

"We have the images from the dream," Amlina answered. "All we need do is to summon them, and we can put you back into the dream. Come upstairs with me now. All of you come."

The Iruks pulled on their garments and hurried after the witch.

In her chamber, Amlina directed them to sit in the circle and begin the deep breathing, while she moved about lighting the lamps.

Still and relaxed, Lonn heard the witch sit down next to him. Soon he was watching the radiance flow around the circle in its familiar course, relaxing his body more fully and finally opening his mind to the seething silver-gray of the Ogo.

"I am going to speak specifically to Lonn," Amlina said. "But all of us will see what he sees. If any of you can see more than he is able to, then speak. The dream visited Lonn, but further illumination might come to anyone in the circle."

The witch told Lonn to envision Glyssa, to see her exactly as she had appeared in the dream. Immersed in the shared mental current of the wei circle, Lonn easily brought the image to mind.

All of them looked upon the image, Glyssa's white hood thrown back, her hair clipped short, her face thin and ashen. A pang of remorse at their long separation shot round the circle and made the picture hazy. But presently the emotion passed and the image of Glyssa steadied again.

"She can't tell me where she is," Lonn said. "I asked her and—"

"She doesn't need to tell you," Amlina answered. "You can learn it from the dream. Look around you, Lonn. Describe all that you see."

As Lonn turned his head, it seemed as if he actually stood in the place he had dreamed. "There are white pillars flecked with bits of silver and gold, rows of pillars on either side of the hall. The floors are gray stone, wide and empty. The ceiling is high, higher than the mainmast of the *Plover*. Two or three ships that size could fit in this single hall."

"You are doing well," Amlina said. "Walk back the way you came, to the entrance."

"But Glyssa ..."

With a flash of panic Lonn noticed that she was gone. He started for the dark doorway where she had disappeared in the dream, but the vision around him wavered and crackled, disrupted by the strong surge of feeling.

"Breathe deeply," Amlina said. "Relax. You are still in the dream."

But Lonn's spirit heaved in turmoil as other visions burst before his mind's eye. He saw Glyssa as the klarn had envisioned her so often, sad and thin and enclosed by blackness. He saw his Iruks with their hands bound, lined up before Prince Hagen's throne, then chained to the mast of the witch's ship.

"You need to surrender yourself, Lonn," Amlina was saying. "Surrender and look."

"I see Glyssa," Karrol spoke abruptly.

Lonn sensed a whorl of power rush through the circle. Then he saw Glyssa too, standing beneath the pillar again, the image from the dream recaptured.

Feeling the dream around him once more, Lonn seized the chance. Without need of the witch's prompting, he turned and walked toward the entryway. He did not allow worry over losing sight of Glyssa to distract him again. The thought came that this was what Amlina meant by surrender—to tread the path one must, laying aside expectation and fear. With each step the dream grew more real. Lonn could feel the others in the circle walking with him.

He reached the entrance to the hall and paused.

"Keep going," Amlina said. "Go outside."

Lonn crossed the vestibule and strode beneath the high arch. It was night outside, the air cold and moist. Lonn stood at the top of the wide steps that he had climbed in the dream.

"Go down a little way," Amlina urged. "Then turn and say what you see."

The night seemed to thicken as Lonn descended. He could no longer see the steps and nearly stumbled. When he turned, all he could make out of the building were two bulky forms and the tall-arched doorway between. The rest was obscured by shiny blackness.

"The design of concealment," Amlina said. "It makes a final defense to prevent our seeing. But now we have the power to counter the design. This vision arises from a dream belonging to one of us.

Thus the image is ours to control. Let the vision be filled by the light we share in this circle."

The witch gripped Lonn's hand tighter. A silvery incandescence fell like rain on the scene in his mind. The light shimmered, dispelling the shiny blackness from the building's facade.

"There are columns on either side of the doorway," Lonn said. "Beyond them are ledges with carved figures, dozens of them."

"Good," Amlina said. "Describe the carvings."

"There are birds and flizzards," Lonn said, "and people with wings. All sorts of creatures with wings."

"I see them," Amlina's voice betrayed her excitement. "Well done, Lonn. We have seen what we needed to see. Iruks, when I tell you to open your eyes you will open them and be awake, here in my room. Now open your eyes."

Lonn blinked and looked about the circle.

"We have our answer." Amlina squeezed his hand with elation. "We almost lost the link for a moment. But Karrol was able to see Glyssa again, and after that Lonn held on to the dream. My friends, you are all to be congratulated."

"But what answer do we have?" Eben demanded.

"The Temple of the Air on the Long Acropolis. I thought from the size and design of the chambers Lonn described earlier that the dream took place in one of the great temples. But I could not be sure *which* temple until Lonn took us outside to view the facade. The winged creatures symbolize the Element of Air. It can be no other place."

"Hah!" Draven clapped Lonn on the back. "I always said your dreams should be trusted!"

Hopeful as it seemed, Lonn was afraid to believe. "Can we be sure the dream was truly from Glyssa?"

Amlina fixed him with a bright gaze. "What do you think? Look into the Deepmind for the answer—All of you."

Lonn focused on the inner vision that the witch had taught him to use. In a moment he sensed a presence—the klarn spirit. For a long time, it had been diminished. But now it rose in his soul stronger than ever, a being of power that he was part of. And in that rising presence he felt certainty.

"Yes," he said. "The dream came from Glyssa."

Around the circle the mates were nodding, murmuring their agreement.

"Yes," Amlina said. "I too felt Glyssa's presence. And I felt no other hand involved, no concealed mind. Glyssa sent you that dream from the Temple of the Air. I am certain."

"Then let's go," Eben jumped to his feet. "Let's go at once."

The other Iruks rose as well, the desmets shifting on the draft they made.

"I hope our enemies are numerous," Karrol declared. "I am hungry for a good fight."

"Wait," Amlina said. "We still have the Prince-Ruler's spies to dispose of. It will take time for me to prepare and cast a design. It will be hours, perhaps afternoon, before we can leave."

"Then get started ... Please," Karrol told her. "The sooner the better."

"Not necessarily," the witch replied. "We might be safer traveling at night so as not to be spotted on the streets. On the other hand, it might be easier to enter the Temple in daylight, when we can lose ourselves in the crowds."

"We must go as soon as possible," Lonn said. "Glyssa has already waited too long."

Amlina thought it over briefly. "Very well. Go downstairs and pack your belongings. Whatever happens, I don't expect we'll be coming back here, so have everything ready to carry. But leave the bundles in your room. One or two of Hagen's informers are doubtless staying at this inn, and we don't want to warn them."

* * * * *

The Iruks hurried downstairs and picked their way quietly past the sleepers in the common room. They donned their fur garments, boots, and harnesses, placed their blades in their belts. They rolled and tied the bed furs and packed the spears in their quivers. As the mates headed back upstairs they heard the clink of breakfast pots and dishes from the kitchen.

They found Amlina dressed in traveling garb, wearing the moonstone fillet, her silver rings and bracelets, and a dagger in her belt. She had taken down the hanging trinkets and packed them along with the lamps in a rolled bundle. Her fur coat lay with her luggage next to the bed.

Amlina was kneeling on the floor with a number of small white candles. She motioned for the Iruks to sit down, then resumed her perplexing task. She studied the six candles with an intent, round-eyed stare. She would move one candle a short distance, then move another, then perhaps move the first one again, then resume her intent looking.

Lonn sensed his mates' impatience as keen as his own. But the Iruks controlled themselves, gnawing their lips or fingering their sword-hilts, knowing that the witch must not be disturbed.

Amlina lit one of the candles and used the dripping wax to fuse its side to another. She blew the flame out and set the double candle down, then knelt and gazed again.

Finally, she seemed to have all the candles placed to her satisfaction, and she stood. From inside her robe, she took a gold needle and a spool of white silk thread.

"I am ready to begin the ensorcellment," she told the Iruks. "It is called the Man-Fishing Trick, and shortly you will see why. My purpose is to capture the minds of Hagen's informers and then to draw them to this room. There are six informers watching us at the moment, according to what I've seen in the Deepmind. Two work together, the others alone. Except for the two working together the informers will arrive here one at a time. As soon as they enter it's up to you to render them helpless. Here is cord I got downstairs for you to bind them. Tear up the bed sheet to make gags. Bind them well, so that they are helpless even to make noise. Do you understand?"

Lonn and the others nodded.

"Good. In a moment, I will begin. Once I close my eyes and start the incantations, I must not be disturbed until all the spies are here and the design is complete. Do you have any questions?"

The Iruks had none. They set to work tearing up the sheet.

Amlina lit a taper and moved about touching the flame to the wicks of the six candles. When all were burning she sat down in their midst, some of them close to her, some several feet away. Carefully she threaded the needle and tied a triple knot in the thread. She drew in a deep breath, let it out slowly, and began to chant.

The Iruks listened in silence as the witch's voice, soft and high, recited the singsong Larthangan verses. Amlina held first the needle, then the spool up to touch her forehead. Next, with eyes still shut, she rotated until she faced the nearest candle. She placed the spool sidewise on the floor and pointed the needle at the candle, just inches away.

Her voice rose with the conclusion of the chant. She opened her fingers, and the gold needle hovered in the air.

The needle hung still for a moment, then began to move, flowing away from the witch's extended fingers, toward the lit candle. Resting on the floor, the spool revolved, giving out the silk thread. The needle's point touched the waxen surface, quivered and penetrated.

Amlina spoke a word of command and reversed her fingers, pointing now back at herself. The spool began to wind in the opposite direction. The thread strained taut, and then the candle was sliding toward the witch.

The Iruks stood before the fireplace and watched solemnly. They had known Amlina to perform more difficult feats, to be sure. But there was something inexpressibly eerie about this simple witchery of candles and thread. Lonn shifted, an uneasy squirming at the base of his spine.

Slowly, the lit candle drew near the witch's groping fingers. It was within a finger's length when Lonn heard a creaking on the stairs outside.

The Iruks looked at each other, then strode quickly to the door. Absorbed in the spectacle of Amlina's witchery, they had all but forgotten its purpose. Now they surrounded the doorway, cords and gag held ready. As the footsteps came close, Lonn grasped the handle and pulled the door open.

The candle touched Amlina's fingertips.

A portly man in flannel and leathers stepped over the threshold, his eyes half-shut. Lonn recognized him as a tenant who had appeared at the inn a few days ago. A muffled grunt was his only resistance as the Iruks grabbed him. Karrol caught him in a bear hug, pinning his arms to his sides. Eben thrust the gag into his mouth and tied it around his head. The others lashed his ankles together, then bound his wrists behind his back. Draven searched the man and removed two hidden daggers. The mates carried the spy to the corner and dumped him there.

Amlina had blown out the candle and withdrawn the golden needle.

She shifted her position a little, so she faced the next nearest candle, then began to chant once more.

Soon the needle was slipping through the air again and thrusting into wax again. Soon the second candle was inching toward Amlina's fingertips. Soon the second of Hagen's spies was entering the witch's room. The Iruks tied him securely and tossed him next to his fellow.

The last of the six candles was burning low by the time Amlina held it in her hands. She blew out its flame and chanted a verse of closure to the spell. Finally, she opened her eyes, looked up, and smiled at the Iruks.

The mates stood in the corner above a pile of five men and one woman, who even now seemed barely conscious. Amlina inspected the knots and gags and nodded her approval. She told the Iruks to place her mattress on the floor and tie the prisoners together on it, so they could not alert the people downstairs by pounding or kicking on the floor. While the mates saw to this, Amlina stowed the candles, needle, and thread with the rest of her baggage and put on her coat.

"Now we are ready," she said.

But as she was binding her coat's silver clasps, Amlina shuddered and gripped her forehead. Her teeth showed in a grimace and she uttered an exclamation of dismay.

"What is it?" Draven asked.

"Beryl," Amlina said. "I thought of her just now, as she laid the design upon me that I must if I learned where the Cloak is. I had set a counter-charm in my mind to prevent it, but such self-deceiving cantrips are flimsy at best, and Beryl's designs are strong. She will be at the Temple of the Air. I suppose it was to be expected."

Amlina finished fastening her coat. "Let us go quickly."

Lonn hoisted the witch's bundle onto his shoulder and followed his mates from the room. Amlina carefully shut the door, then led the others downstairs. Eben, Karrol, and Brinda strode across the common room to fetch the Iruks' gear, while Lonn and the others waited.

Elzna the landlady spotted them from the kitchen hallway and ambled over. "Are you leaving us?"

"Only for a day or two," Amlina answered. "We will certainly be back to finish our stay."

"But I just saw some people going up to your room. I believe they came in off the street."

"They are associates of mine," Amlina said. "They are going to stay in my room while I'm gone." She handed the old woman a silver coin. "Be sure they are not disturbed. *For any reason.*"

"Of course, milady." Elzna smiled. "No one will bother them, I promise you."

JACK MASSA

Part Three

In the
Temple of the Air

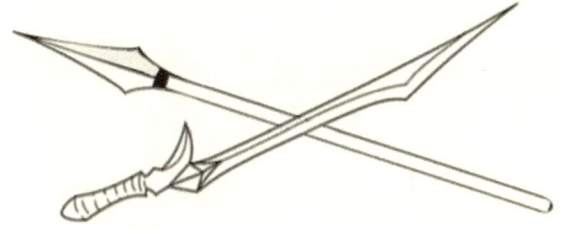

Twenty-One

The grand plaza at the summit of the Long Acropolis was designed as a hexagon with a great temple at every point. Each temple symbolized one of the Six Elements of the Tathian cosmology: Ice, Water, Stone, Fire, Wood, and Air. Other deities and doctrines were permitted their temples and shrines on the lower streets of the acropolis, but the summit was reserved for the official Tathian cult of Elementalism. Ever pragmatic, the Tathians had long held that direct worship of the elements constituting the physical world was the most logical and effective form of religion.

This day the grand plaza was crowded, as it had been almost every day for the past month. A colorful array of worshippers, supplicants, and pilgrims milled beneath the overhanging spiral of dark cloud. Solemn priests and temple acolytes hurried back and forth in pairs or larger contingents. Beggars and hawkers accosted passers-by. Mobs of loiterers stood listening before the free rostrums or the temple steps, to speakers who denounced everything from the maritime policies of the Prince-Ruler to the hairstyles of fashionable ladies. The mood of the people had not improved in the three days since the rioting here. Prince Hagen's marines still patrolled the Long Acropolis and stood in ranks on the steps of the major temples.

It was late afternoon as Lonn and his companions hurried along through the crowds. The day was cold enough that they were able to wear their hoods well up, partly masking their faces. They had managed to cross the city without incident, following a devious route from the harbor district to the zigzagging streets of the acropolis.

Now they had entered the grand plaza, passing before the Temple of Stone whose massy granite facade was decorated with panels of lapis lazuli and rhodochrosite. To their left stood the Temple of Water, with splendid fountains and cascading waterfalls, and next to it the Temple of Ice with its multiple spires of polished glass. On their right shone the Temple of Fire, of burnished copper and gold, and beyond that the Temple of Wood, whose stupendous exterior columns were fashioned from giant trees grown in the Age of the World's Madness.

But Lonn and his mates took in all these marvels with mere distracted glances. Their objective stood directly ahead, the Temple of the Air.

It loomed over the northwest corner of the plaza, an imposing edifice of glossy white marble. Two broad pillars dominated the facade, with a high-arched portal between. As Lonn drew closer the carvings came into view—winged creatures of every sort blossoming in sculptural profusion on arches, capitals, and ledges. There were men, women, and children with wings, hornets and butterflies, birds, bats, and dragons, winged turtles, flizzards and fishes, even a yulugg with wings.

"That's the place I dreamed of for certain," Lonn affirmed.

"I know." Amlina stared straight ahead as they walked. The witch was daunted, Lonn realized, by the prospect of facing the Archimage again. But he also knew more than that troubled her. Amlina was reluctant to go into the temple unprepared. She had not been able to cast designs or even to feel with her mind for what obstacles they might meet.

With Beryl alerted, there had been no time to plan. Amlina had agreed on that as readily as the Iruks. They had discussed the matter tersely as they trekked across the city, deciding their best course was to enter the temple as worshippers, then to slip away from the crowds and hunt for Glyssa—hoping that she, once found, could lead them to the Cloak.

"Just let us find Glyssa alive and herself," Lonn had said. "We'll take our chances after that."

But even on speaking those words, he knew they were a boast to cover his fears. Prince Hagen and his troops, Beryl the Archimage, whatever sorcerer or witch now possessed the Cloak—all these enemies arrayed against his klarn. Even with Amlina's magic, what chance did they really have against such powers?

They neared the temple steps, where lines of marines stood watch with lances and shields.

"Those men were transferred up from the waterfront," Eben said. "I hope none of them recognize us."

"Just take your time," Amlina answered. "And think of yourselves as worshippers."

Without pause but without hurry, Amlina led the way up the wide marble steps, past a throng of beggars and shouting peddlers who sold candles, incense, and cups of scented oil to burn as offerings to the Air. Nearing the top, the witch and the Iruks moved past the armored marines, drawing only casual looks despite their luggage and foreign dress—one more group of pilgrims from distant parts.

Lonn glanced uneasily at the overhanging figures as he and his mates walked beneath the arch. They crossed the vestibule, past a line of temple guards armed with halberds and broadswords and wearing gilded plate armor. A small group of acolytes in white hooded robes stood holding collection baskets. Amlina dropped a coin in one of the baskets as she passed.

The interior of the temple was even more enormous than it had appeared in Lonn's dream. Three naves, each slightly larger than the one before, led the spectator's eye forward a vast distance to a rounded apse. Numerous skylights and clerestory windows filled the upper vaults of the naves with shafts of daylight, adding to the overwhelming impression of airy space. Rows of flecked columns formed aisles to either side of the naves, and above the aisles hung upper galleries honeycombed with alcoves, niches, and light wells. The interior had no carvings, no art at all save the extravagant and yet austere architecture. The floor was of gray marble, empty except for occasional low platforms where worshipers sat to burn their offerings or contemplate the Air. Lonn guessed that between two and three-hundred people occupied the naves at present, yet the temple seemed almost empty.

"Where do we start?" he asked the witch, awed despite himself by the grandeur of the place.

"I think it wisest to begin with your dream," Amlina said. "We'll go to the place you saw Glyssa. This way, is it not?"

She gestured toward the right aisle, and Lonn nodded. Glancing about, the Iruks followed the witch along the rear wall of the nave. They stopped in the corner beside the rearmost pillar. The spot looked exactly as in Lonn's dream. Before them was the doorway through which Glyssa had disappeared. Inside it, a shadowy staircase could barely be discerned.

"We're being watched," Karrol whispered. "I can feel it."

Lonn glared down the aisle and across the nave but spotted no observers.

"I have the same intuition," Amlina whispered. "The master of this place knows we are here."

They had spoken of this possibility earlier. Indeed the witch had considered it more likely than not that their adversary would expect and be prepared for their coming.

"Let him watch," Lonn growled. "Let him try to stop us from taking Glyssa back."

His mates nodded with dour approval.

"Glyssa went through that door in the dream," Lonn told the witch. "I suppose we do the same."

"Yes. Did you have any sense of whether she went up or down the steps?"

"There were no steps in the dream."

"Then down, I think," Amlina said. "The quarters of temple acolytes and servants figure to be below."

Lonn's instinct concurred with the witch's reasoning. With wary glances over their shoulders, the companions stole to the open doorway and slipped inside.

Treading quietly, they descended the marble steps. Amlina walked with hands folded in her sleeves. The Iruks carried their bundles and quivers one-handed, their free hands clutching the hilts of swords concealed under their capes.

Soon, the weak illumination from the doorway above faded, and they were feeling their way through the dark. But when they reached a landing three flights down a dim, ruddy light appeared from below.

Down one more flight, the stairway ended. The companions passed under a pointed arch and found themselves on the edge of a wide, murky chamber, an undercroft to the nave above. Ranks of pillars supported the groin-vaulted ceiling. Red lamps scattered among the pillars provided scant, flickering light. The undercroft stood deserted and perfectly quiet, but now it was Lonn who had the gnawing impression of being watched.

The witch gestured toward the forward part of the chamber and a distant doorway there. They started through the shadows, keeping close to the right-hand wall, eyes and ears straining for any movement. They had traversed perhaps two-thirds of the chamber when Amlina stiffened, then waved the Iruks back.

Lonn and Brinda darted behind a pillar. The others leaned against the wall in the deepest part of the shadow. A door creaked open somewhere ahead.

The witch and the Iruks stood still and listened as the sound of slow, measured footsteps approached. Peering around the pillar, Lonn spied a procession of white-clad acolytes marching single-file through the center of the undercroft. The procession was exactly like the one in his dream.

The acolytes filed past, never glancing in the Iruks' direction. But then one of them stepped from the line, as Glyssa had in the dream.

Lonn suppressed a tremor of excitement. The stray figure was Glyssa's size and seemed to move like Glyssa as it bent and gazed across the shadowy hall toward his position. Oblivious to the danger, Lonn kept his head in view and stared back.

When the last of the procession had passed on, the solitary figure reached up and pulled off her hood.

"Glyssa," Brinda whispered at Lonn's back. "It is she."

Glyssa stood erect in the dull lamplight, thin and changed as Lonn had seen her so often in visions.

"Wait," Amlina warned. "See what she does first—"

But the Iruks had already cast down their burdens. Crouched low, they scurried across the undercroft through the pools of shadow and lurid red.

Glyssa remained still as her mates came near. Her eyes regarded them with a bright, fevered look. Lonn knew with a sudden, blood-chilling apprehension that some other mind watched through those eyes.

His mates must have sensed it also. When they came to within a few yards of Glyssa they did not rush to embrace her but hung back, hesitant.

"Glyssa—?" Karrol said.

Glyssa screamed, a harsh rending cry. Something purple and fiery flashed in her hand.

"Get back!" Lonn heard Amlina's warning shout from behind.

Glyssa flung the purple thing to the floor and it shattered in a blast of smoke and sparks. Lonn felt the shattering reverberate inside him, continuing after the noise faded, rattling until his bones seemed to splinter and he was crumpling to the floor.

* * * * *

Sensations came in fragments. Lonn felt himself being lifted up and carried. He blinked frantically, and at last his eyes could see shapes amid the purple glare that still dazzled them. A troop of acolytes were swarming through the undercroft, the helpless Iruks on their shoulders. Some of the thralls wore golden armor, but most were clad in white robes. They carried halberds, swords, or lengths of rope.

With a painful effort, Lonn twisted so he could look back.

Glyssa, her face vacant of emotion, had fallen into step with the rest of the temple servants. Lonn could not see if Amlina too had been captured.

Gradually the effects of the magic wore off. As feeling seeped back to his muscles, Lonn realized that his arms had been pulled to the small of his back and tied. By now they had left the undercroft. The ceiling passed close to him, an unending series of dark vaults and low arches. The procession traversed one dim corridor after another, then abruptly entered a well-lit chamber and descended a flight of steps.

Arching his back, Lonn saw they had come into a broad hall of white and gray marble, bordered by porticoes on three sides and a high, gleaming dais on the fourth. The chamber was already occupied by a crowd of unmoving acolytes. Squads of men in plate armor stood guard along the porticoes.

The Iruks were carried to the front of this audience hall and dropped on their feet. Lonn's knees gave way but hands from behind gripped his bound arms and held him upright. His head swam with dizziness. He shook it hard and squinted about.

Perhaps a hundred of the temple minions were assembled in the hall. The Iruks were lined up with swords or knife-points at their backs, facing the high dais. Lonn noticed with a sinking feeling that Amlina stood with them, her hands also bound.

"Keep your thoughts to yourselves," she whispered urgently. "Remember who you are."

Glyssa was standing behind the witch. Next to her lay the bundles and quivers of spears carried here from the undercroft.

From a curtained doorway at the rear of the dais a tall, slender man appeared. He wore a black gown embroidered with peculiar gold designs. He had a long thin face with well-trimmed hair and beard and large bulging eyes. He gazed down at the prisoners and his small mouth curled in a narrow smile.

"Welcome to the Temple of Air," he said. "I am Kosimo, Hierophant of the Temple. I have awaited your arrival all day."

He walked down the steps with a bizarre, sinuous grace that caused Lonn to shiver with instinctual loathing. Kosimo paused on the bottom step, regarding the Iruks. He held up his palms and spoke in a soft, bewitching voice.

"You no longer have wills of your own. You are servants to me, fingers of my hand, limbs of my body. You move only as my brain wills you to move. You are now one with the host of my slaves."

His voice made the space around the Iruks ripple with power. The power was echoed and enhanced by the attending crowd and by the very stones of this place. Lonn felt an irresistible calm creep over him, stilling his mind and nerves.

"Hold yourselves apart from him." Amlina's voice came from far away. "Remember who you are!"

"Stand there," Kosimo ordered sternly. "Do not move. You are my obedient servants now."

The deepshaper's will stole over Lonn, expunging all thoughts of resistance. Lonn existed only to do the master's bidding. The Iruks stood with faces dull and blank, eyes gazing straight ahead. Kosimo nodded his approval and ordered that their bonds be cut. Distantly, Lonn felt the pull of the blade, then his arms slipping to his sides. In desperation, he strained to hold on to Amlina's words: *Remember who you are.*

Kosimo had stepped over to the witch. "The barbarians cannot resist my control. Oh, I know that you have trained them. That is why I have assembled so many of my servants, to amplify my power in draining off their wills. I have found that these Iruks make excellent thralls once their wild temperaments are tamed. Your use of their minds to locate their lost female was an inspired bit of witchery, excellently done."

"You flatter me," Amlina replied. "You who enthralled this woman across the bounds of space and manipulated her into bringing you the Cloak."

Kosimo smiled with pleasure. "I seized her will across the veil of distance by an ancient technique. The difficult part was forcing her to use her own knowledge to rig and sail the Iruk craft. Eleven days and nights I sat working that ensorcellment. A worthy accomplishment of mine, I do agree."

"Exceedingly worthy," Amlina responded, "even for a serd."

"Yes. I did not expect my disguise to fool a witch of Larthang."

Doggedly struggling to assert his will, Lonn had finally managed to shift his eyes enough to watch the Hierophant. Now he saw the air waver around Kosimo's face. The eyes grew even larger and the lids disappeared. Hair and beard vanished, and the skin took on a hideous, glistening appearance.

"But tell me," the serd coaxed Amlina. "How precisely did you see through my disguise?"

"Intuition." Amlina shrugged. "The sense of humanity was lacking. I did not know any of your race still walked the dry land."

"No." A note of hostility pierced the serd's urbane manner. "My people were driven from the land long ago by your Larthangan ancestors. The agony and terror of that time still lives in our memories. So most serds cower beneath the waves, fearful of human deepshapers. But I was never so timid. I knew my race to be superior to yours. Witness how easily I have passed for human all these years while mastering the occult wisdom of humans, how easily I surpassed all rivals to gain this position of priestly power."

"And now you have the Cloak of the Two Winds," Amlina said.

"Yes. Long ago it came to me as I swam in the Deepmind that one day the Cloak would be stolen from the East. I began to plan my ensorcellments at once. I waited forty years for you to go to Tallyba and accomplish the thievery I had foreseen, half a lifetime to the pitiful spawn of your race, but not so long for a serd to wait."

"You mean to destroy the Cloak, don't you?"

"Indeed. Did you surmise this from the nature of the weather disturbances, or did you apprehend it just now from my thoughts? No matter. Soon it will be done. The Cloak will be unmade and with it the ensorcellments of Eglemarde. Then the stagnant balance that keeps your puny race supreme will topple and fruitful chaos overwhelm the world. Your race will be driven from power and mine, or some other more worthy, will take its place."

Lonn shuddered inside, but whether his body actually moved he could not tell.

"But you have possessed the Cloak for many days," Amlina said. "And still have not succeeded in destroying it."

"I will," Kosimo answered. "It hangs constantly in a blasting fire fueled by oil, sulfur, and coal. And each third hour I cast a design wherein the fabric of the Cloak is utterly consumed in flame. The disturbances of air and sea about this city daily grow more violent. And they are but a shadow of the disruptions that will follow. This second age of humans is drawing to an end."

The serd paused, letting his aroused passions grow calm. "Soon you will be dead," he told the witch. "And there is only one other who may have a chance of stopping me: the Archimage of the East. You were her apprentice, one of the few to ever best her. Yes, I know you stole the Cloak while she lay in deep trance, and that you've been fleeing from her ever since. Yet you know her traits and skills better than I. Help me to defeat her, and I will make your death easy."

"I know a great deal that might aid you," Amlina said. "But I will tell you nothing unless you promise to spare our lives."

Kosimo glared, considering how to answer.

"She cannot help you, spawn of fishes," a woman's voice rang from the rear of the hall. "Nothing can help you now."

Kosimo stiffened and gaped at the speaker.

Lonn could not swing his head enough to look, but it did not matter. He already knew whose voice it was.

Twenty-Two

L onn wished desperately that he could move, that he and his mates could grab Glyssa, draw their blades and fight their way free. His will battled to break the serd's spell, so that his arms shook with the effort. He could sense the same striving in the minds of his mates. But all the Iruks remained standing in their places.

Kosimo straightened to his full height. "So, witch of the east, you also have obligingly walked into my trap."

"Where is my Cloak?" Beryl said.

Kosimo did not wait longer. "Kill her," he commanded every thrall in the chamber.

Irresistibly, Lonn turned, as the sea of gaunt faces turned toward the rear of the hall. Those thralls with weapons leveled them and started forward. Lonn watched his sword and dagger being drawn by his hands.

"Wait," Amlina shouted. "Iruks, stay with me."

All the klarnmates except Glyssa paused for an instant. In that instant, Kosimo's power over them snapped, and they owned themselves again.

"Get Glyssa," Amlina said. "Draven, cut me free."

Silent and single-minded, the mob of temple servants advanced toward the portico where the tall witch stood.

"Get back!" Beryl ordered, holding up her hands.

So great was the power of her voice and gesture that all of Kosimo's mindless ones halted or fell back a step. Quickly Beryl unclasped a necklace of black beads and dashed it on the floor. Whirling funnels of smoke spouted from the broken beads, rising and solidifying into seven immense man-shaped things—drogs with tiny domed heads, bulky shoulders, and long arms that ended in sword-blades.

Kosimo had run up the steps of his dais so that he stood level with Beryl's position on the far portico. "Destroy those creatures," he commanded.

Obediently his thralls charged forward, whether armed or not. The seven-foot monstrosities lifted their arms and started down the steps, moving with weird mechanical precision.

Lonn and Karrol had darted to the backmost ranks of the temple host and grabbed hold of Glyssa. Fighting to obey her master's will Glyssa shrieked, kicked at Lonn and scratched Karrol's face, nearly tearing off her eye patch. But then Eben and Brinda reached her and each of the four Iruks took one of her limbs. Glyssa writhed and spat in hysteria as her mates carried her off.

"This way," Amlina gestured them to a curtained doorway on the left portico. Draven stood with the witch, holding the quivers of spears, which he had had the presence of mind to snatch off the floor.

The Iruks hauled Glyssa across the chamber and up the steps. As they reached the portico Lonn glanced back at the rear of the chamber—a wild confusion of twisting bodies and slashing blades, the blood-splashed drogs looming over all.

Glyssa screamed, trying to tear free. Grimacing, the four Iruks bore her across the portico and out of the hall.

* * * * *

Watching from his dais, Kosimo did nothing to prevent the Iruks' departure. The apprentice witch and her primitives could be dealt with later. The Archimage of the East was the real danger.

Kosimo's thralls battled with unwavering ferocity and absolutely no concern for their lives, yet they were proving no match for Beryl's giant sword-men. Except for the forty-odd temple guards in their plate armor, the Hierophant's minions were hardly equipped for combat. Two of the towering drogs had been borne down by sheer weight of numbers, their domed heads pierced so that now they writhed uselessly on the portico steps. But the other five were cutting through the massed temple forces, smashing halberd shafts and beating down swords, lopping off arms and splitting skulls. Blood spouted in arcs and collected in puddles on the floor. Kosimo felt the death agonies of his servants as dull pricklings of pain.

Another of the drogs was toppled and slain as the serd watched, but the current of the battle was against him. Then he spotted Beryl, walking along the side portico, coming toward him. She had managed to circle around the host of his thralls, who now fought and died near the center of the hall.

Beryl's eyes stared at him and Kosimo hissed with a tremor of fright. The Hierophant of the Air hesitated an instant longer, then abandoned his audience hall, retreating across the dais and through the curtained portal.

The Archimage of the East smiled to herself and followed at a measured walk.

* * * * *

Glyssa continued to thrash and kick as the Iruks carried her down a red-lit corridor away from the audience chamber. The noise of the fighting had dwindled in their ears when Amlina parted the velvet curtains of a doorway and gestured them inside.

They entered a lavish sitting room, perhaps part of Kosimo's own apartments, for the friezes on the walls and the ponderous gold statues reminded Lonn of the serd monuments the *Plover* had passed on the way to Kadavel. The Iruks stretched Glyssa out on a rug, holding down her arms and legs while Amlina straddled her.

"You must break the spell and bring her back to us," Lonn told the witch.

"I will do what I can." Amlina's fingers probed on Glyssa's forehead, then along the scalp beneath the short black hair.

Glyssa screamed horribly and tried to pull her head away.

"Silence," Amlina's voice had the tone of magical command. "Close your eyes and be still."

Glyssa whimpered, still straining to move. But finally, she succumbed to Amlina's will. The look of hysteria drained from her face and her eyelids drooped. She no longer struggled to get away, only shivered in irregular weak spasms.

"Good." Amlina moved so that she knelt beside Glyssa. "Her spirit still has some strength. It's been caged, you see, its vitality siphoned off by the serd. If we had come much later it would have been starved completely. As it is, we have a chance to bring her back. I can break the mind-cage, but once that is done her mind must be reached and brought back to the surface. Otherwise, it will sink into the depths and be lost. When I finish the chant call her name, speak to remind her of herself and her former life."

The witch shut her eyes and began to sing. Glyssa moved fretfully but did not resume her struggles. As Amlina's high, sweet voice recited the verses of Old Larthangan, Glyssa's expression grew calmer, until she seemed in deep repose. Lonn watched her intently, glancing away every few moments to check the door for intruders.

As Amlina's chant reached its climax Glyssa's eyes and mouth burst open as though she was trying to scream. A series of shocks convulsed her body, the Iruks gripping her limbs. Then Glyssa was still again, eyes shut, complexion pale and glistening with sweat.

"Now call her," Amlina whispered. "Speak to her for her very life."

The Iruks leaned over Glyssa and called her name in hushed, urgent whispers.

"Glyssa," Lonn said. "We are here. We have come for you at last."

"Dear Glyssa," Karrol called. "Come back to us."

"Come back to yourself," Amlina said. "The tyranny is ended. You are Glyssa again."

Presently Glyssa's eyes opened, dull and clouded. But as they glanced over the Iruks' faces they flickered with recognition.

"My klarn," she murmured. "Are you really here?"

Lonn and his mates cried out with joy. They pounded each other on the arms and embraced. They touched Glyssa's face and hair, seized her hands and kissed them fervently.

"Yes," Amlina said. "Give her your strength."

"It's been so hard to remember," Glyssa's eyes shone. "I tried to keep all of you in my mind but ... I thought I'd never see you again."

"It took us many days to track you down," Lonn answered, nearly weeping with relief. "But now it's done, and we have you back."

"I am Amlina," the witch said. "I helped your mates find you, and I rejoice that we came in time. But now all of us need your help."

"She is our ally," Draven told Glyssa.

"Do you remember coming here?" Amlina asked. "And bringing the Cloak?"

"Yes. I came on a ship. There was a storm or ... The dojuk was sunk. I remember it was the Cloak that drew the winds down from the sky and opened the ice. It was the master." A shudder of revulsion passed through her. "I hate him. I want to kill him, Lonn."

"Kosimo is fighting a great witch," Amlina said. "We would be most fortunate if they slew each other, but I don't expect that outcome. More likely, the witch will kill him and then come after us. We must find the Cloak before she does. Do you know where it is, Glyssa?"

Glyssa winced, groping for memory. "I came here through a secret way, steps and tunnels that lead down to the water. The Cloak was left down there, in the place where the master casts his magic."

"Can you lead us there?"

"I think so." She tried to get up. "I feel so weak."

"Rest a moment more," Amlina said, laying her palms on Glyssa's forehead. "Let this energy flow from my hands and restore you." She moved her lips silently for a few moments, uttering another charm. "Now when I tell you, your eyes will open, and you will feel strong and able to walk. Now your eyes are open."

The witch removed her hands and Glyssa blinked. She looked more herself, more vital and alert. Lonn and Karrol helped her to stand. Glyssa looked down at herself and immediately pulled the white temple robe over her head and threw it from her. She wore only a linen tunic beneath, but Lonn gave her his cape for warmth. Glyssa smiled weakly as she wrapped herself in the cape. Draven grinned and handed her a spear.

* * * * *

Behind the dais of the audience hall, Beryl crossed a dark alcove and entered an oily-scented chamber hung with gold tapestries. Firelight writhed across the room from two braziers burning at the far end. Kosimo stood between the fires.

"You were a fool to follow me to this room. Here my enchantments are invincible."

But Beryl sensed uncertainty in his mind. "Then the advantage is yours," she said, standing motionless, mentally probing for spells and traps. "But before one of us kills the other, we might as well exchange privities. How were you able to find the Cloak and bring it here, when I could not see it?"

"I waited and prepared for a long time," the serd answered. "For almost two centuries I have watched the ebb and flow of power among the great of humankind. I remember well the day you first stole the Cloak from the West. I saw by precognition that one day it would be stolen from you in turn. I waited many years for the young witch to go to Tallyba and fulfill that vision. She has great potential, that young one."

"She will not survive long enough for it to manifest." Beryl still had not moved.

"No," Kosimo granted. "As for bringing the Cloak here, it was not terribly difficult, not for a master of serdic arts. My race perfected ensorcellments that you humans have yet to conceive."

"And yet you were defeated by humans." Beryl stepped forward.

"That defeat is about to be reversed."

Kosimo jumped aside, revealing a long oval mirror that Beryl found herself looking into. Instantly the mirror began to draw her in, sucking at her spirit with tremendous hunger. Beryl's probing had not discovered the mirror—the serd had hidden it well.

The Archimage planted her feet and resisted. A sound like a fearsome wind howled through the chamber. For an unknown length of time, Beryl stood her ground, eyes fixed on the mirror, her mind struggling, partly within its illusory depths, partly still free. Kosimo stood rigid, eyes closed, augmenting the mirror's power with his will.

Then the front of Beryl's fur robe opened and a bone-hilted dagger floated out. The dagger hovered and turned, till the tip pointed away from Beryl. Then the weapon flowed across the room and crashed into the mirror, which shattered in a burst of fire and jagged pieces.

The dagger dropped to the floor. Kosimo hastily set his foot on it lest it rise up and strike him.

Beryl grinned mockingly. "Did you think to turn me into a thrall?" She moved something under her sleeve. "You've seen the quality of my black beads. Allow me to show you more of my jewelry."

She removed two of her bracelets and tossed them on the floor. Two coils of orange smoke reared up, then changed into orange serpents, their heads as high as the witch's shoulder, their fangs dribbling venom.

Kosimo tensed, fingers outstretched. Each of his hands followed the movements of one of the drog-serpents as they slithered toward him. His glance darting back and forth between the snakes, the serd did not notice Beryl's hand moving about her wrist—as if taking off a third bracelet and tossing it to the floor.

The serpents glided, closing in on their prey. Kosimo's body stood frozen, his head swinging back and forth.

One of the serpents sprang, jaws gaping.

Just as quickly, Kosimo reacted, a bolt of flame leaping from his fingertips and shearing off the serpent's head. Immediately the serd leaped back, showing an unguessed agility in his spindly form. The second serpent snapped its fangs where Kosimo's face had been. The serd responded with a second bolt of flame, slicing the serpent in two. Both pieces withered and vanished as the first decapitated snake had already done.

Kosimo released a pent breath and stared at the Archimage. "Did you think to best me with mere trinkets?"

But then the serd grimaced and clutched his wrist. Twin puncture marks had opened on his hand. Kosimo looked on in horror as a third, smaller serpent became visible, fangs embedded in his palm. The drog-serpent clung a moment longer, then dropped and vanished, its purpose done.

Kosimo gazed wildly at Beryl who was walking toward him.

"A trick," he whispered. "You've slain me with a trick."

"Obviously," Beryl said. "Your error lay in forgetting the lesson of history. My race is superior to yours. For all your supposed aestheticism, you lack our sensitivity. A human shaper would have felt the unseen serpent."

The treeman had poked his grotesque head from Beryl's collar. Seeing Kosimo drop to his knees, the treeman chattered excitedly and crawled out on his mistress' shoulder. He jumped to the floor and scampered off to investigate the chamber.

Beryl bent over Kosimo, clutching the front of his gown to hold him up. "Where is the Cloak? Show it to me."

"I am perishing," he gasped. "But you can save me. You are conversant with the sorceries of old Nyssan, the spells to seize a dying mind and encase it in a gem or bit of glass."

"But I have no interest in preserving you," Beryl answered.

"But you must not let me die. I can serve you, teach you."

"I have no time." Beryl shook him violently. "Show me the Cloak."

Kosimo's weakening will succumbed. The image of the Cloak's location and of the passages leading to it appeared in his consciousness for Beryl to read.

By the time the Archimage had the way fixed in her mind, the serd was beginning to gag on the venom. Beryl let him slump to the floor. She stooped and picked up her dagger from amid the fragments of broken mirror. She stood up, glancing coolly around the chamber as Kosimo writhed away his ancient life at her feet.

Satisfied that the serd was dead, Beryl turned and strode from the chamber, the excited treeman racing on her heels.

* * * * *

Amlina and the Iruks descended a dark and narrow stairway cut in the rock of the Long Acropolis. Lonn went first, sword drawn, his other hand holding a red lamp pilfered from an upper hall. Glyssa followed at his shoulder, wrapped in his fur cape, holding the spear Draven had given her.

Far underground the stairway ended in a black, musty vault. The lamp's red glow illuminated winged carvings on the doorjambs, their faces strangely long and emaciated. Lonn held the lamp high and could vaguely discern full-sized statues of hooded men looming in the darkness of the wide chamber.

"Burial chambers," Glyssa muttered. "We have to pass through here."

"Is there another way?" Karrol asked.

Lonn shared her misgivings. Iruks never liked trespassing in the domains of ghosts.

But Glyssa shook her head. "This is the only way I know."

She started along the wall to their left. Lonn and the others followed, passing dim alcoves full of statues and sarcophagi, all heavily draped in cobwebs. Except for their padding footsteps the vault was quiet. The air, thick and clammy to the skin, smelled of dust and burial perfumes.

Interspersed among the alcoves stood tall, unlighted portals. Glyssa entered one such doorway and led her mates down a curving passage. The crypt was even larger than had at first appeared. Numerous generations of the temple's servants lay entombed here, their graves ranging from elaborate monuments cluttered with sculptures to narrow shelves just long enough to hold a wrapped corpse. Lonn ground his teeth and hoped the multitudes of ghosts would not be stirred to angry life by this intrusion.

When they had passed several intersecting corridors, Glyssa halted and looked back with a pained expression. "We may have come too far. I'm not sure where we're supposed to turn."

"You must be sure," Amlina said. "We could be lost down here for hours."

Glyssa shrank from the witch. "It's hard to remember."

"You must," Amlina replied.

"Don't bully her," Lonn intervened. "Remember what she has gone through."

Karrol put her arm protectively around Glyssa and glared at the witch.

"I'm not bullying her," Amlina said. "But the way lies in her memory, and it can be reached. Glyssa, will you let me help you remember?"

"What do I have to do?"

"Just close your eyes." Amlina laid her fingertips on Glyssa's forehead. "Relax and let your mind be at peace."

The witch spoke some words of Old Larthangan, then told Glyssa to envision herself passing here before and to see the path she had taken. Soon Glyssa indicated that she was recalling the scene. Amlina told her that when she opened her eyes she would remember the way.

Glyssa's eyes had a soft, dreamy look when they opened.

"You can lead us to the steps now," Amlina said.

Glyssa nodded. She looked down the murky passage, then turned and led them back the way they had come. At the first intersection, Glyssa chose a different passage. She led the way down other twisting corridors, until Lonn's sense of direction was utterly baffled.

Their path ended in a cul-de-sac, an alcove thronged with foot-high statues. Lonn thought Glyssa's memory had failed them. But she grabbed one of the statues and pulled it forward. There came a rumble and a sharp grating sound.

Lonn thrust his lamp forward and saw the stone wall at the back of the cul-de-sac sliding open. The statue, he realized, was a lever controlling the secret door.

"Well done, Glyssa." Amlina put a hand on her shoulder.

Beyond the opening, a narrow stair curved downward. The Iruks and the witch had to bend to enter the passage, but soon it grew high enough for them to walk upright. They descended in single-file, Lonn first, then Glyssa and the others. The rough-hewn steps curled back and forth seemingly with no logic or plan. The companions had gone some distance when a growling noise erupted in the air.

Lonn pointed his blade, but no lurking enemy appeared from the dark. Instead, the steps and walls began to tremble. Lonn dropped his sword and clutched the shaking wall to keep from falling. He heard the confused exclamations of his mates as the lamp swayed in his grip, almost smashing against the rock.

The tremor subsided as suddenly as it had begun. The Iruks stood tense, holding the walls and each other.

"What does it mean?" Eben demanded of the witch.

Amlina's ear was pressed to the stone. "I think it means the serd has perished. The stone shuddered as it gave up his power. Hurry. We must find the Cloak before Beryl does."

The party continued downward until the steps ended in a wide, gloomy tunnel. The air was chill and damp with a strong briny smell. After thirty paces they stopped before a broad gap in the tunnel wall. A single carving leaned over the opening, a gargoyle-like fish with massive teeth. Below it stretched a lamp-lit corridor of polished green marble. A great slab of black stone lay broken on the tunnel floor.

"This is the entrance to his chambers," Glyssa said. "When last I was here this stone covered the opening. It only moved at his command."

"Now it is broken like all his designs," Amlina said. "Come."

The witch and the Iruks stepped over the broken chunks of stone and entered the high-ceilinged corridor. Doorways opened to the right and left, and the mates paused at one after another of these with increasing excitement. The rooms were filled with treasure: silks and furs and woven rugs, weapons and armor, expensive plates and serving vessels, carvings and jewelry, mounds of silver and gold coins.

"Look at this hoard," Lonn exclaimed. Suddenly he remembered his dream, of a ship laden with such treasure as this, rounding the Cape of Dekyll.

"Later," Amlina called from down the corridor. "First the Cloak. Hurry!"

Reluctantly, the Iruks tore themselves away and ran after the witch. They caught up with her at the far doorway, which opened onto a ledge overlooking a moat that glinted faintly with sealight. Across the moat, a flight of steps climbed up to a similar ledge and another doorway.

"The serd's casting place," Amlina surmised. "It's logical he would surround himself with water."

As she spoke, the witch was already moving down the steps. At the bottom, she waded into the moat without hesitation. Lonn could not tell how she knew the moat was shallow enough for wading, but he and his mates hurried after, slogging through waist-deep, slimy water. In moments they were climbing the steps on the far side, their dripping legs aglitter with witchlight.

Amlina hastened across the ledge and through the doorway, Lonn but a step behind. Inside he started and pointed his sword, ready to lunge. Two of Kosimo's white-robed thralls sat slouched against the doorjambs, mouths lolling open, dazed looks on their faces.

"They are harmless," Amlina called over her shoulder. "They can't even move without the serd's will to drive them."

In the red lamplight, Lonn saw Glyssa turn her head from the thralls and shiver.

"Come on," he said. "You're with your mates now."

The Iruks crossed the wide, low-ceilinged chamber, past tables and cabinets and several more inert servants littering the floor. They walked around a gray-black maze in the middle of the room—shunning it by instinct as Amlina had also done.

The witch had gone at once to the farthest alcove of the chamber, where a wide-mouthed fireplace burned with blue and yellow flames. Fires were also lit beneath cauldrons and barrel-shaped vessels spouting pipes. Amlina opened each of these in turn.

The Iruks reached her just as she flung open the door of an iron furnace and recoiled at the roaring burst of flame. Amlina looked about hurriedly, then held out her hand to Draven.

"Give me your sword."

She took the proffered blade, pulled up her sleeve, and leaned over toward the fiery opening. Shielding her face with one arm, she pushed the blade into the furnace and fished out a burning cloth of black and silver. She tossed it on the floor, and in a moment the flames vanished and the Cloak of the Two Winds lay whole and unburned on the tiles.

"Praised be the skills of Eglemarde," Amlina said with reverence. "Her Great Ensorcellment abides."

The witch touched the Cloak and found it had already cooled. She picked it up and slipped it on over her coat.

"Let us be gone from this place," she said.

The Iruks heartily agreed, thoughts of Kosimo's treasure filling their heads. When they reached the ledge overlooking the moat Amlina paused.

"Wait. I must be sure the Cloak has suffered no damage."

Deliberately, she pointed her left hand down at the water. In a moment a charge of light ran down the silver pattern on the Cloak's sleeve. A sphere of silver burst from the cuff and expanded as it flowed through the air. The scintillating veil of a freezewind danced over the moat, its whooshing voice reverberating against the stone walls. When the light and sound faded, the moat was glimmering ice.

"Thank you for demonstrating that its power is intact."

Beryl stood on the ledge across the moat, four of her sword giants lurking behind her. Their appearance had been masked by the passing curtain of the freezewind.

"Now, little apprentice," she said, "you may return the Cloak to its rightful owner."

"Exactly what I intend," Amlina called defiantly. "It belongs to the House of the Deepmind in Minhang."

"Ha! You are loyal to Larthang now?" Beryl scoffed. "Come, I know you better."

"You only think you know me. That was your mistake before." Amlina raised both hands and pointed them at Beryl, "The Two Winds together—lethal even to you."

"No!" Beryl thrust out her hand, fingers outstretched. "You cannot use it against me."

Amlina's arms trembled, but no power erupted from the Cloak.

"What's wrong?" Draven asked.

Amlina's eyes never strayed from Beryl. "She's interfering. She possessed the Cloak for over a hundred years, and it still responds to her will. *But I am wearing it now.*"

"Ignorant little Larthang," Beryl taunted her. "You cannot fight me, just as your puny henchmen cannot hope to defeat these sword-arms of mine."

The Archimage gestured sharply with her free hand, and the drogs tottered forward. The blood-splashed giants had slain nearly a hundred of Kosimo's servants, losing only three of their own number in the fray.

The Iruks threw off their capes and made ready for battle. Karrol and Draven had already passed out the spears—two or three to each of the mates. Now Draven hefted one over his shoulder.

"If we can harpoon the witch, I'll wager her monsters will curl up and vanish."

"Try," Amlina answered through clenched teeth. "Your spears might at least distract her."

Draven growled and flung a spear. In a moment, Lonn and the others did the same. One of their casts sailed high and struck the wall over Beryl's head. Others struck the black, steely arms and shoulders of the drogs and fell harmlessly to the floor. One spear Beryl swept aside with a wild gesture of her left hand, her right hand still pointed firmly at Amlina.

Then Beryl gestured again and the drogs lurched forward. They marched off the ledge and fell to the ice below. They braced themselves with their sword-points, climbed unhurt to their feet, and started across the frozen moat.

"You must hold them off," Amlina said. "Aim at their heads."

The Iruks cast their second spears. Barbed points struck arms and chests but did no damage. Only one spear found its way through the defense of hunched shoulders and waving swords. That drog's head popped in a hideous shower of fiery ichor and unliving flesh. The giant swung its arms in frantic gyrations. Its feet slipped and it fell, wriggling gruesomely.

The three remaining drogs advanced, shuffling awkwardly on the ice. Lonn realized that the slippery surface would favor the Iruks. He yelled this to his mates as they drew their steel. They leapt from the ledge, landed crouched on the bright ice, sprang up and charged. They skidded and slid as they crossed the moat, but their ridged boots and skaters' sense of balance kept them upright. The drogs bent and pointed their blades as the Iruks rushed them.

Karrol and Draven paired off to take one of the drogs, Eben and Brinda another. Lonn darted in against the middle brute, backed by Glyssa who still carried a spear. Away to the right, Lonn glimpsed Beryl descending the steps from the ledge. But then his whole attention was seized by two sword arms sweeping down at him from different angles.

Lonn tried to dance back, but lost his footing and had to scramble back on all fours. He might have died there had not the drog also slipped, thrown off-balance by the ferocity of its attack. Lonn clambered to his feet, knife and sword raised high. The drog righted itself with one sword, swinging the other to keep the Iruk at bay. Lonn deflected the blow with his dagger and jabbed with his sword, just missing the head. He ducked to avoid a swooping backward cut, while Glyssa thrust with her spear to occupy the drog's other arm.

* * * * *

Beryl was walking across the moat, untouched by the fighting around her, protected by the force of her deepshaper's mind. From atop the steps, Amlina watched her, their eyes locked, their wills battling.

When Amlina felt the Cloak once more in her power she lifted both hands and aimed them at Beryl. But Beryl's eyes grew huge in her vision and Beryl's thoughts came like a whispering in her ear.

You cannot use it against me.

"I can." Amlina steadied her arms and willed the power to flow.

You will take it off and hand it to me, Beryl's mind said.

Fiercely, Amlina rejected the idea. But then her sight rippled with sparkling waves, dizzying her. Next thing she knew she had taken off the Cloak, and Beryl was climbing the steps, hands outstretched to receive it.

With a cry of fright and rage, Amlina pivoted and fled back into Kosimo's chamber.

* * * * *

Down on the ice, Draven and Karrol had driven their opponent back to the wall of the moat. But there the tireless sword-arms were able to hold the Iruks off. The mates scored numerous cuts on the monster's legs and long arms, but though their blades were imbued with Amlina's witchery, they seemed to do no harm.

Over by the steps, Eben and Brinda were also holding their own, each guarding the other's flank and dueling one black blade. But neither could get close enough to deliver a blow to the head.

Meantime Lonn's plight was growing desperate. The drog assailed him relentlessly while Glyssa, unsure of herself and poorly armed, hung back. Only when Lonn slipped and the giant loomed above him would Glyssa charge in, poking with her spear and yelling to distract the brute until Lonn could regain his feet. Once she tried throwing her spear at the drog's head. But a swift blade knocked it aside, and Glyssa had to rush to the far wall to pick up another spear.

Lonn's harness and sleeve were sliced by the long, terrible swords. He fought back, wheeling and stabbing. But his arms were growing heavy, his breath coming in gasps.

From the corner of his eye, Lonn saw one of the monster's being slain. Draven had kept the drog backed to the wall while Karrol grabbed up a spear from the ice and flung it into the creature's puckered face.

The glimpse held Lonn's attention an instant too long. He tried to dodge a down-rushing sword, slipped instead, and fell on his side. Glyssa started forward, shouting and thrusting her spear as Lonn regained his feet. But this time the drog turned both swords on Glyssa and smashed her spear shaft in two when she tried to parry.

Weaponless, Glyssa flinched as the sword arm rose over her.

Lonn sprang, heedless of his own safety, and hooked the drog's elbow with his arm. Lifted in the air by the brute's enormous strength, Lonn twisted and lunged with his sword—just as the giant's free blade stabbed toward him.

The two sword-points struck simultaneously—Lonn's piercing the pulpy head, the drog's penetrating Lonn's harness and sliding between his ribs.

Lonn groaned as the drog's death spasm jerked the point deeper into his flesh. Then the giant's arm dropped, spilling Lonn free on the ice. Lonn slithered out of the way as the towering drog collapsed, gushing foul ichor. Lonn got to his knees, clutching his side to staunch the trickle of blood. Glyssa rushed to his side.

"It's not bad," he told her, though the wound hurt as if the point were still twisting inside.

In front of them, the drog continued to writhe, swords scratching the ice in feeble attempts to rise. But then Karrol ended its movements for good, driving her sword down through the bleeding head.

Draven had gone to help Eben and Brinda finish the last of the creatures. While they kept the two swords busy, Draven circled behind the giant. He brought his sword back over his head and swung it down in a murderous two-handed blow, splitting the head down the center. The drog's arms shot upward in agony. The monster spun, staggering several paces into the wall of the moat. Its legs continued to move mechanically as its body slouched against the rock, until finally growing still.

For a few heartbeats, the Iruks looked at each other, gasping air as the fever of battle drained. The four sword-arms lay slain, and except for Lonn's wound and a gash on Brinda's arm, no Iruk blood had been drawn.

Then Draven cast a glance at the far side of the moat, and started across at a sliding run. His mates hurried after, Karrol and Eben pausing to pick up two spears that lay near at hand.

* * * * *

Holding the Cloak, Amlina had stopped several paces inside the chamber and whirled to face Beryl again. When the Archimage appeared at the door, Amlina's jeweled dagger was flying at her face.

"Away!" With a finger Beryl swept the knife aside. Poking from her collar, the treeman's head dropped hastily from view as Beryl's own dagger leapt from her coat.

With mind-force, Amlina brought her knife swooping down again at Beryl's head. But Beryl alertly waved it off and sent it careering to the far end of the chamber. Amlina shifted the focus of her will to defense and parried as Beryl's bone-hilted knife arrowed toward her.

"Your strength of will surprises me," Beryl remarked, stepping closer. "Indeed, you've surprised me more than once of late."

Straining to ignore the distraction of Beryl's voice, Amlina called her knife back to her.

"But now the game is over," Beryl said, her own dagger hanging suddenly close to Amlina's nose.

Amlina had to throw all her will into pushing the point away. As she did so, Beryl seized Amlina's knife, pulling it close with her mind and then plucking it from the air with her hand.

"Now the game is over," Beryl repeated, one knife in her fist, the other floating as she willed.

Amlina squeezed the Cloak tight against her and cast out her will in a frenzy. From all over the chamber bottles, vials, and instruments leapt from shelves and tables and flew at Beryl. An aura of force sprang out to protect the Archimage. But a glass beaker found its way past Beryl's shield and smashed her forehead, dazing her, drawing a trickle of blood.

Seizing the chance, Amlina darted forward, calling Beryl's dagger to her hand. But Beryl recovered her senses in time and swept the knife away, just before Amlina could touch it.

The two witches stood close now and Beryl got hold of Amlina's coat sleeve and flung her to the floor. Amlina tried to roll free but

Beryl dropped on top of her. The knife in Beryl's hand moved toward Amlina's throat. Amlina gripped Beryl's wrist with both her hands to hold the point away.

"Now, little Larthang," Beryl purred. "You have often seen me drink the blood of sacrifices. You know how I savor the first drops, when the rush of terror is strong."

Amlina's arms quivered with strain as the dagger descended.

"I've waited a long time," Beryl said, "to taste your blood and your terror."

Amlina strove to clear her mind of panic so she could augment her failing strength with shaping force. But Beryl's green eyes seared her will, and the panic grew. The dagger's point touched her neck below the jaw, stinging as it pierced the skin. From within Beryl's collar, the treeman watched, slavering.

Then Beryl hissed and jumped up, whirling.

Draven and his mates were pouring through the chamber door.

"Stay back!" Beryl screamed.

As the Iruks staggered, fighting her command, Beryl snatched up the Cloak and retreated. Amlina lunged to grasp at her ankle, but Beryl sprang free.

The Iruks were coming on again as the Archimage stopped, a few paces past where Amlina lay. With the Cloak tossed over her shoulder, Beryl loosed one of the necklaces she still wore—two lengths of twisted gold wire joined to a large purple gem.

"Throw your weapons," Amlina shouted, searching frantically for Beryl's discarded dagger.

But before a spear could be launched Beryl touched the two ends of gold wire in front of her forehead. The purple stone flashed, emitting a violet aura that instantly enveloped Beryl and the Cloak.

Two hastily cast spears struck the sheath of light and disappeared.

"Keep back." On her knees, Amlina thrust out her arms to restrain the charging Iruks.

"No, come and take me," Beryl taunted from inside the luminous sheath. "Charge into the wall of severing light and annihilate yourselves. Why do you hesitate? Your caution only postpones your demise. For I will hunt you down, each of you that raised weapons against me. And I'll not give you so quick and merciful a death as this, I promise you. Remember that and ponder it often. All of Glimnodd cannot hide you from me."

While she spoke the light intensified, becoming so brilliant that Amlina and the Iruks had to shade their eyes. Then, with a last silent flare, the aura vanished, leaving only a dull gleam on the floor and the scent of something burned by fire.

"Where did she go?" Draven asked.

"Through a Gate of Spaceless Passage," Amlina answered wearily. "It will take her wherever she wills. Possibly back to her fleet at sea—or even to Tallyba itself. She would choose a place safe from pursuit. Such travel is hard, and she will need days to recover."

"Then we've lost the Cloak," Lonn muttered.

"Yes." Amlina touched the small puncture on her neck and looked dully at the smear of blood that reddened her fingertips.

"You are hurt." Draven peered at the wound with concern. "But not badly."

Amlina looked at Brinda's cut and the blood that stained Lonn's harness. "You'll both need tending and soon," she said. "Let us leave this place."

"Yes," Draven said. "But on the way we will stop in those treasure rooms."

"Very well," Amlina said. "But hurry. I will meet you there. I will choose my spoils from among the serd's books and devices."

* * * * *

The Iruks left the chamber, picked up their discarded capes and quivers, and tramped down the steps to the icebound moat. The destroyed drogs were decaying quickly, black forms shriveling, ichor bubbling as it evaporated in noisome trails of steam. The Iruks collected the few unbroken spears, then proceeded to the treasure rooms.

Lonn all but forgot the pain in his ribs as he and his mates rummaged through the temple's abundant wealth. The Iruks crowded their fingers with rings and their arms with gold bracelets. They stuffed their harnesses with jewels, found sacks and filled them with coins.

The mates were bundling together all they could carry when Amlina arrived with a large iron-bound book in her arms. The witch set the book down long enough to fill her purse and pockets with gold, saying she would make Captain Troneck and his crew a generous return for all their trouble.

"A pity we can't fill the holds of the *Plover* with this loot," Draven laughed. "Not that it matters. We'll carry away enough to last all our lives."

"Your joy should be tempered by this," Amlina said. "Beryl was not threatening idly. She does mean to hunt you now as well as me. Her pride will not permit any enemies to go unpunished."

"We're not afraid of her," Lonn answered. "She's the one who fled."

"Her head was injured," Amlina replied. "She was outnumbered, and her shaping powers had been strained by much use. Next time she will not retreat."

"Neither will we," Lonn boasted. "We are Iruks, fearless. And now our klarn is whole again."

His sentiments were echoed with enthusiasm by his mates. Even Glyssa smiled.

The Iruks hoisted the treasure sacks on their shoulders and followed the witch from the serd's lair. As they stepped over the broken fragments of the stone door, Amlina halted, peering up the tunnel in the direction they had come.

"I have a strong impression," she said, "that the Prince-Ruler Hagen is at this moment above us, searching through the temple with several score of his troops."

"I would not be surprised," Eben said. "We might easily have been spotted coming into the temple."

"Or Beryl might," Amlina agreed. "My bundled trinkets are still in the audience hall. I do not like to leave them, but I don't think it's worth the risk of going back. You did say, Glyssa, that this tunnel leads down to another exit, on the water?"

"Yes," Glyssa answered. "It's not far."

Ahead of them, the passage narrowed for a distance, then curled to the left. Amlina and the Iruks climbed a set of steps carved in the rock, then crossed a wide, rugged cavern. Down a second flight of steps, they passed through a thin cleft and emerged in the open air.

Epilogue

In the
Countless Arms
of the Sea

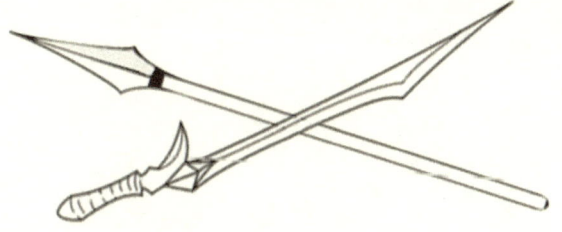

The fiery stars of Glimnodd winked and glittered through the arms of the cloud spiral—which had begun to fray, dispersing with the wind. The Iruks and the witch Amlina stood on a narrow strip of beach, black gravel laced by rime. At their backs, the sheer promontory of the Long Acropolis sprang up a hundred feet or more to the grand plaza and its ring of temples. Before them, the ice of Kadavel's back harbor glistened with witchlight.

They stole along the deserted shoreline until coming to a small inlet, where a row of fishing skimmers lay dragged up on the shingle. A few huts and shacks stood nestled on an overhanging crag, one of several small fishing settlements that hugged the cliffs of the back harbor. But no one was up at this hour to spot the intruders as they loaded their treasure into one of the boats. The prows were all chained together, but it took Eben only a few seconds to open the padlock with the point of his dagger. At Amlina's insistence, he locked the remaining boats back together and left a garnet necklace in place of the craft they were taking.

The Iruks dragged the boat over the gravel and pushed it out onto the ice. The fishing skimmer, smaller than the cargo boats of that name that plied the Shipway, was just large enough to hold them and all their loot. Draven and Karrol unreefed the sail and hoisted it on the short mast, while Eben took charge of the tiller.

Lonn's side was throbbing now, and he was content to let the others sail the boat. When he started to shiver in the frosty air,

Amlina made him put on Draven's fur cape in place of his own, which Glyssa still wore.

Eben steered directly out from shore, until the bulk of the Long Acropolis and the lighted domes and steeples atop it were veiled by glimmering mists. Then he pointed the skimmer southwest, heading around the western tip of the city.

By the time the boat entered the Shipway south of Kadavel, Lonn was shivering constantly. The ache in his side had sharpened and swelled to fill his chest and belly. Brinda was leaning on Karrol's shoulder, holding her arm and wincing. Near fainting with the pain, Lonn thought he heard the word "poison" murmured in connection with Beryl's sword-drogs.

The skimmer sailed behind the first row of anchored ships, keeping for the most part out of sight of the city docks. At last, the Iruks raised the *Plover*, resting quietly on the dry dock. Even as their boat pulled alongside the concrete ramp, Amlina was shouting for all hands to awaken and get the ship underway.

The mates had to help Lonn and Brinda scale the accommodation ladders. Several crewmen of the night watch assisted in hoisting the baggage on board. As the witch and the Iruks reached the main deck, Captain Troneck was stepping from the forecastle, buttoning on his coat.

"Get your men moving, captain," Amlina told him. "We must be away from Kadavel by daybreak."

"As you say, Lady," Troneck answered. "What's our course?"

Amlina glanced at the flags blowing overhead. The wind was fresh from the South.

"West," she answered. "Into the Arms of the Sea. Hurry, now. We might be pursued."

The witch led the Iruks to her cabin where they put down their weapons and sacks of treasure. She told Draven to light a fire in the stove, while she went to get medicines from her sea chest.

The cabin lurched and shuddered as the ship rolled down the ramp and slid onto the ice. Lonn lost his balance and dropped to his knees. Lightheaded, he clutched Karrol's arm as she helped him to a bench.

While Eben cut open Brinda's sleeve, Karrol unstrapped Lonn's harness. When she pulled the leather from his side the wound tore, spurting blood. Lonn gasped as a wave of pain and sickness welled darkly into his brain. Distantly, he heard Karrol calling for help as he slumped over, all perception fading.

* * * * *

Of the next several days Lonn remembered little. He was racked by nightmares in which his klarn was burned alive before the palace of Prince Hagen, or chased by Beryl's drogs through unending tunnels full of corpses. He would waken drenched in sweat, gagging with thirst but unable to swallow more than a sip of water down his swollen throat.

At least one of the klarn was with him each time he woke. Lonn vaguely recalled Amlina sitting beside him at times, laying cool, healing hands on his chest and forehead.

In the latter part of his illness the nightmares became fixed on Glyssa. By turns, he was convinced that she was dead, or that the klarn had given up the search for her, or that the search was doomed to continue forever. Finally, in a lucid moment, Lonn became aware of someone seated beside him, stroking his head. He opened his eyes and saw that it was Glyssa. After that, he knew she was alive and with them, and he rested easier. That night the fever broke.

The following afternoon Lonn awoke. He was lying under furs, on a bunk in a ship's cabin. Draven was leaning over him, feeling the back of his neck for fever.

"Hello." Draven smiled. "How do you feel?"

"Where am I?"

"Oh, the cabin across from Amlina's. She wanted you near, so she could visit every few hours and place hands on you for healing."

"How long was I unconscious?"

"Four full days plus a half. You had us worried, mate." Draven stepped over to the oil stove and returned with a steaming mug. He helped Lonn sit up and sip the broth.

"Amlina said you would probably come out of it before evening," Draven said. "She went into deep trance today, after your fever broke. It seems the swords of those monsters we fought were poisoned. Luckily, most of it had rubbed off by the time we took them on. Still, Amlina was impressed that you and Brinda managed to stay conscious so long after being wounded. Brinda had a touch of fever also, but she's fine now."

"And the rest of you?"

"Splendid." Draven grinned. "Feasting, drinking, counting our riches over and over. Karrol's eye is much better. Amlina said the patch can come off in a few days."

"What about Glyssa?"

Draven's exuberance flagged. "She's been ... distant, almost dazed. She spends a lot of time staring at the wake of the ship."

"Have you talked with her?" Lonn demanded.

"Of course. She seems frightened, Lonn, but more of the past than the future. Amlina says it's natural for her to be this way, that her spirit was starved of life and that it'll take time for the life to return. She said not to worry, but to keep an eye on Glyssa, and we are of course."

Lonn settled back on the pillow. From the tilt of the cabin and the smooth glide of the ship, he could tell they were still sailing on ice.

"I take it we got free of Kadavel," he said. "Was there pursuit?"

Draven lifted a shoulder. "None that's caught us. The wind's been steady, and Amlina wove some magic. With that, and the maze of channels we're sailing through, she's confident the Prince-Ruler's lads won't catch us."

"Maze of channels?"

Draven grinned, spreading his hands. "The Countless Arms of the Sea. That's what this web of waterways is called. And such a place you've never seen, Lonn—one winding passage after another, all bordered by cliffs of white and silver stone. And there are grand towns everywhere. The port where we stopped for provisions yesterday was on a small isle, but the town was as big as Fleevanport. Kizier says these channels are the main sea route between Larthang and Nyssan. Oh yes, Kizier sends his regards. The little one-eye was as happy to see us all safe as if he were a klarnmate."

Lonn finished the broth, and Draven set the mug aside.

"Where are we bound?" Lonn asked.

"That's undecided. In five or six days we'll reach the open sea, then we'll have to chose. When Amlina comes out of her trance, she wants to meet with us and talk it over. That book she stole from the serd's lair is a magic book, a *talking* book. It's given her some ideas. She has it in mind to go after Beryl, rather than wait for Beryl to come after her. She wants us to decide if we're willing to sail with her."

"Perhaps we should, " Lonn muttered. "Better to hunt than be hunted."

"Exactly." Draven smiled as he clasped Lonn's wrist. "But we'll meet with the klarn when you are stronger—the whole klarn, Lonn. Isn't that wonderful? We are together again."

* * * * *

After supper, Lonn felt strong enough to rise from his bed. All of the mates came to his cabin, and they performed the ceremony to put the klarn to rest. They set their spears against the bulkhead, poured libations, and declared the hunt to be over. They sent the klarn spirit into the timbers of the ship, to guard the whole company until they called it again.

As the group spirit passed from his body, Lonn slipped to his knees. He had overestimated his strength, and the mates had to help him back to the bunk. They left him to rest, and he slept deeply.

When he woke it was night, a small lamp burning in the cabin. Glyssa sat on the edge of the bunk, staring down at him.

"How do you feel?" she whispered.

Lonn grinned. "Better, now that you are here."

"Oh, I am glad. I've been frightened for you."

"No, Glyssa. I will be well, I promise."

Tears welled in her eyes. "You nearly died, because you protected me, because I was weak in the fight ..."

"No." Lonn reached for her hands, found them icy cold. "You were brave to stand with us at all, after everything you suffered."

She bowed her head. "I was afraid for so long. I had given up hope of seeing you again ..."

"It's all right, my Glyssa," Lonn stroked her hair. "The klarn is whole again."

"Yes, I know. And yet ... everyone seems so different to me. Brinda is solemn and withdrawn. And Karrol's the same, not her old self at all. Draven and Eben are elated, full of boasts about the treasure and the witch. They all seem like strangers to me ... But then I realize, I am the stranger. Oh, Lonn, you can't imagine what I've been through. We tell ourselves we are Iruks, strong and fearless. But we're really so small, so easily broken and lost ... No, you can't know what I mean ..."

"I do know," Lonn answered, recalling the terrifying visions he had seen when the witch first initiated him. "The world is vast and fearful, more than we can imagine, even now, and we are small and weak. And yet we are here and must live. I tell you this, Glyssa: Right now I don't care about any of that. I don't care about the treasure, or the witch, or what the next voyage might bring. I don't even care very much about the klarn. I only care that you are safe and here with me. That is enough."

Glyssa stared into his eyes, her face wet with tears. After a moment, she lifted his hands to her lips and kissed them. Then she pulled aside the cover and lay down beside him.

A deep peace and contentment entered Lonn's heart. He slept that night in Glyssa's arms, in the Countless Arms of the Sea.

JACK MASSA

Glimnodd Calendar, Map, and Glossary

Glimnodd has two moons. Grizna, the larger, has a period of 32 days. The small moon, Rog, has a cycle of 11 days. A *month* always refers to the 32-day Grizna cycle. The cycle of Rog is called a *small-month* or simply a *rog*.

A year has six seasons, each two months or 64 days long:

>First Winter
>Second or Mid-Winter
>Third or Late Winter
>First Summer
>Second or High Summer
>Third or Late Summer

A map of Glimnodd is available online at tinyurl.com/MapofGlimnodd.

Glossary

aklor - a tall, six-legged animal used as a mount in the Three Nations

Archimage - official title for the chief witch or mage of a nation

bostull - see *windbringer*

cantrip - a minor spell or 'mind trick'

Deepmind - the formative realm of which reality is a reflection

deepseer - one skilled in seeing outside the boundaries of time and space

deepshaper - one skilled in the arts of shaping reality through magic design - any magical working

desmet - a hanging trinket used to enhance mental power

dojuk - Iruk hunting boat, agile on sea or ice

drells - a delicate winged people whose land lies to the south of Larthang

drog - literally 'shell', a creature formed of magic, animated by the will of a deepshaper, guided by a single purpose

drommon - a Tathian warship, propelled by sail and oars

ensorcellment - a great act of magic

fire turtles - sea turtles that breathe fire. Normally considered non-sentient.

Fleevan - Tathian colony in the South Polar region. The capital is Fleevanport.

flizzard - a small winged reptile

Iruk (Iruks) - hunting people of the South Polar region

kiia - edible fern of the tundra; leaves are used to wrap dried fish

klarn - Iruk sacred hunting group, consisting of five to eight warriors. Members of a klarn share a group-soul that gives them strength and protection.

lamnocc - large deer of the Polar region

Larthang - Westernmost of the Three Nations. Home to a race of powerful witches.

mage - any skilled practitioner of magic. When capitalized: the top-ranking Larthangan witch of a city or province.

myro - sentient sea-creatures spawned from dolphins

Nyssan - Easternmost of the Three Nations. Home to several races. Normally spoken of as Near Nyssan and Far Nyssan.

Ogo - Larthangan name for the Deepmind. Literally, 'drift.'

serds - a sentient race evolved from deep-sea fishes; powerful sorcerers who ruled Glimnodd during the Age of the World's Madness

skimmer - small boat for ferrying cargo

Tath - Middle realm of the Three Nations. A group of islands, home to a race of seafarers and traders.

thrall - a sentient being whose mind and will have been subjugated by sorcery

torms - winged people spawned from birds

trinket - any object fashioned to contain or enhance magic power

trinketing - the art of constructing trinkets

Tuan - the ruler of Larthang, a sacred king or queen

volrooms - tusked, white-furred bears

wei-shen - Larthangan art of deepseeing

wei-xing - Larthangan art of deepshaping

windbringer - a sentient fern-like plant; skilled at attracting winds and therefore prized by mariners of all nations

witch - broadly any female mage; strictly, a woman trained in the Larthangan arts of the Deepmind

yulugg - giant sea mammals, similar to whales

Author's Note

My thanks to my stalwart Beta Readers, Marilyn Massa and John Kelly, whose suggestions and encouragement are deeply appreciated. Also to my editor, Jaime Henriquez, and cover artists, Daniel Kamarudin and Shaun Stevens, whose talent and professionalism added greatly to the final product.

The Glimnodd Cycle includes these books:

Cloak of the Two Winds

A Mirror Against All Mishap

Tournament of Witches

If you enjoyed this story, please consider leaving a rating and review on Amazon, as well as other sites. The algorithms of the publishing business make this extremely important to a book's success.

I love hearing from readers. You can connect with me at:

Web: triskelionbooks.com or jackmassa.com
Facebook: www.facebook.com/AuthorJackMassa/
X/Twitter: @JackMassa2

Also, check out my Substack at speclectic.substack.com.

www.ingramcontent.com/pod-product-compliance
Lightning Source LLC
Chambersburg PA
CBHW021306250626
47155CB00002B/401